FALSE
WITNESS

LARRY
BUTTRAM

Larry Buttram

10-1-05

Published in the United States by:
New Virginia Publications
9185 Matthew Dr.
Manassas Park, Va. 20111

SAN 256-0453

First Printing—2004

ISBN 0-9755030-0-6
LCCN 2004106188

PROLOGUE

FALL, 1956

The only thing good about the jeep was that it still ran. Rust had eaten through much of the body. The seats were threadbare exposing the springs. The windshield was cracked and the tires had little tread remaining. However, it still started—at least more often than not. It even had a new muffler—if only because the old one had fallen off making so much noise the owner feared being ticketed. But with all its problems it was the perfect vehicle for taking into the woods.

The fall air was crisp and fresh—a beautiful Tennessee afternoon. Just the perfect day for deer hunting. The young man walked quietly through the woods. He was unfamiliar with this part of the county but had heard the area was rarely hunted. He spotted a deer perch left by another hunter. With his gun strapped over one shoulder and his backpack on the other, he climbed the steps that had been nailed to the tree. He reached the platform about fifteen feet off the ground and tested it for sturdiness, then climbed aboard and seated himself against the tree trunk. While deer had excellent vision, they never looked up into the trees. They had no reason to—they had no natural enemies there.

He reached into his backpack and removed a sandwich and a Dr. Pepper. He ate his sandwich, occasionally tilting his head back to let the sun hit his face as it broke through the clouds. He sipped his Dr. Pepper as he waited patiently for his prey. The wait was not long. Soon, as he had hoped, he saw movement in the nearby thicket. He saw the outline of the deer through the brush. He saw the brown fur and the antlers. He took aim and fired. He heard a muffled sound, the shuffling of leaves, and then a thump.

Quickly the young man climbed down from his perch and ran to the spot where his prey had fallen. Once there, his excitement turned to horror. It was not a deer he had shot, but another hunter. His brown jacket was quickly becoming stained with blood. Lying next to him was a bow. A quiver of arrows was still attached to his back. Now that he was closer he wondered how he could have ever mistaken them for antlers. The young man began to tremble as he leaned forward looking for signs of life.

"Oh, get up, get up," he pleaded, although he knew it would never happen. His aim had been true. "Mister, what'cha doin' out here with a brown coat. Ain't you never been huntin' afore?"

He paced around in a circle, then bent down to check him once more. There was no movement—no breathing. He stood for some time, wringing his hands, trying to determine what to do. Finally, he again spoke to the fallen hunter. "Mister, I'm sorry but ain't nothin else I can do. I got ta be goin. Nobody'll ever believe this were an accident."

He turned and moved away, walking quickly. He then remembered his backpack up on the perch. He hurriedly retrieved it and headed back down the trail. It only took a few minutes before he found the beat-up jeep. He threw his gun and backpack into the back seat, and fumbled with the keys before getting them into the ignition.

"I know ya in bad shape, Bessie, but please just start for me one more time. I got ta get out of this place."

He turned the key as he prayed. The engine turned slowly but then came to life. He didn't look back as he drove out of the woods. He was back on the gravel road before he lost control. He took his handkerchief from his pocket and rubbed his eyes.

"I'm so sorry mister. I'm so sorry."

PART
ONE

ONE

JUNE, 1963

The small whirlwind headed directly towards the young boy, gathering dust as it moved along. The dust was the thing that Ethan Ward hated the most. He could feel the hot summer sun on his neck and shoulders. The stench from the nearby farm penetrated his nostrils. And the humid air made his clothes cling to his skin. But it was the dust that bothered him the most. It got in his hair, his eyes, and his clothes. And his white tennis shoes, which his mother had bought for him upon finishing seventh grade, were now almost brown. He held his breath and closed his eyes as he waited for the whirlwind to pass.

It would only be another fifteen minutes or so before he got to Billy Caldwell's house. There he could get a drink of water or, if lucky, maybe a Nugrape soda, and get rid of some of the dust. Afterward they could play a game of checkers, or go into the woods behind Billy's house and shoot his new B.B. gun. Maybe Mrs. Caldwell would ask him to stay for supper. By then his father should be off work and could pick him up on his way home.

He thought of cutting across Mr. Taylor's farm, but that had not turned out so well last time. The gullies and rolling, tree covered hills offered many places for a creature to hide. He had made it under the fence just ahead of Mr. Taylor's prize bull, and he did not want to take such a chance again. The extra few minutes he would save would not be worth it. He was glad he had not told his parents about it or he probably wouldn't be allowed to walk to his friend's house.

He was scanning the woods for the bull and did not notice the truck coming toward him until it was less than 100 feet away. It was moving slowly, so he had plenty of time to move to the side of the road to let it pass. It was unusual to see a vehicle this time of day. There were only a few houses on the dead-end road which ended at his parents' driveway, and except for Mrs. Thompson and his mother, all the others worked. The truck was old and dirty and unfamiliar. He watched curiously as it drew nearer. As it went by he saw two young black men inside. The driver had a serious look but nodded to him politely as they drove past. The passenger, who appeared a little older, smiled and waved. He nodded back and continued toward his friend's house.

He picked up pebbles and began throwing them at the fence posts. *It was the bottom of the ninth in the final game of the World Series. Jim Maloney, the ace pitcher of the world famous Cincinnati Reds was down to his last batter with a one run lead. He wound up and delivered the 3-2 pitch. The batter swung and missed. The crowd went wild.*

A noise from behind brought him back to reality. He looked back to see the truck had turned and was coming up behind him. He moved to the side of the road and kept walking.

The truck pulled up along side of him and slowed down. The passenger stuck his head out the window and called to him.

"Young man, can you tell us how to get back to highway 11? I think we missed our turn."

Ethan eyed the two men suspiciously. His mother had always taught him that he should treat everyone equally regardless of their color, but these were two strangers. The passenger seemed to sense his concern.

"Look, son, we're not looking for trouble. We just need to get back on the highway."

"O.K.," said Ethan, "but it's a purty good piece from here. You got to go back down this road for about five minutes and turn left at the white church. Then you go along for a little piece and turn left at Mr. Dawkins place—there's a big red mailbox out front. That's route

34. You got to follow it for a while afore it runs into highway 11."

"That's pretty good directions, son. We appreciate it. You need a lift somewhere?"

"No thankee'," he replied. "I'm just goin down to my friend's house. It ain't too far."

"Well, we'd be glad to give you a lift for your help. It's right on our way."

"It ain't far."

"It's awful hot out today. We got some soda pop if you'd like one. We promise we won't hurt you."

He held up a bottle of orange soda and took a drink. It was not Nugrape, but it looked awfully inviting.

"Well, O.K." said Ethan. He moved toward the truck. The passenger opened the door and jumped to the ground. He held the door open for him to climb inside. Ethan hesitated for a second, then climbed into the truck, the man climbing in after him. Once inside, the passenger reached into a cooler and handed him the drink. Ethan thanked him and turned to look at the driver who had yet to say anything.

"How ya doin?" the driver finally asked.

"Fine."

The sound of the door slamming made Ethan jump. The man laughed and patted him on his leg.

"It's just this old rusty door, son," said the passenger. "You have to give it a good jolt or it won't close."

Ethan just nodded. The driver put the truck in gear and started to pull away.

"So, you live around here?" asked the passenger.

"Yep," he said, "just down the road a mile or two."

"You walk down this road a lot?"

"Couple of times a week, I reckon."

"You're pretty much covered in dust, son," he said laughing as he brushed the boy's shirt.

"Yeah, Daddy says this road is either a dust pit or a mud pit. Reckon he'd druther have the dust, but not me."

"I understand, son," said the man with another laugh.

Ethan liked the passenger but felt uncomfortable with the other man who had hardly said anything. He thought he might get him to talk if he asked a question. He turned to him and said, "You'all live around here?"

The question was not answered. He appeared to be responding when he looked in the rear view mirror and blurted out, "Oh hell, we got a problem!"

"What?" asked the other man.

"Look behind ya."

The passenger turned to see a Greene County Sheriff's car moving up behind them.

"Where did he come from?" he asked. "Maybe he'll go on by."

"Right," said the driver sarcastically. Just as he did, the car turned on the flashing light. The two men shot each other a concerned look. Finally, the driver nodded to his friend and pulled the truck to the side of the road. They sat waiting, looking straight ahead. Ethan looked back and forth at the two men, then back at the Sheriff's car.

"What does he want?" he asked. No one answered. He waited for something to happen, but both men, as well as the officer, sat without moving. While it was only for a few seconds, it seemed like eternity before the officer got out of his car and walked toward the truck. He walked slowly and boldly to the driver's side, stopping just a few feet from the rear of the truck.

"What'cha boys doing out here today?" he demanded.

"We ain't bothering nobody, Deputy," yelled the driver out the window. "We just mindin' our own business."

"Mindin' ya own business," he repeated. "Then what'cha doing with that white boy?" he said.

"He jus' gave us some directions, so we wuz givin him a ride to his friend's house. That's all."

"Well," continued the Deputy, "Why don't you boys just get out of the car and we'll see 'bout things."

Ethan turned to the driver and spoke. "It'll be all right. That's Deputy Pratt. My daddy knows him. I'll talk to him. It'll be fine."

"You reckon?" he said sarcastically.

The men did not move fast enough for the Deputy. He removed

the gun from the holster and pointed it toward the truck.

"I told ya boys to get out of the truck, now! I already called in for back up and they'll be along any minute, so you just better do as I say."

The passenger's door opened and Ethan and the passenger walked slowly to the end of the truck. The boy stood shaking as the man stood with his hands raised.

"Deputy," he said, "you can ask the boy—we didn't do nothing to him. Like my friend said, we were just giving him a ride for helping us out."

The Deputy moved back from the truck a few feet so he could keep everyone in view.

"Yeah, well maybe ya just didn't have time to do nothin' yet," he shot back as he waved his gun in their direction. "You and the boy move on back away from the truck where I can see ya." Then turning back to the driver he yelled, "Now boy—I'll tell you for the last time to get out of the truck!"

What happened next would be frozen in Ethan's mind forever. The driver got out of the truck, but as he did so he pulled a handgun from behind his back. The Deputy, who had been distracted by the other man, saw it too late. He pointed the gun toward the driver just as the first bullet hit his chest. A second later another shot hit him in the stomach. Ethan watched in horror as the Deputy collapsed to the ground. He stood unable to move as the man walked toward the Deputy, staring down at him. Suddenly Ethan darted away and dove under the fence.

"Stop," shouted the driver as he ran toward him. The other man caught his arm and pulled him to a halt.

"What are you going to do—shoot him?" he asked sternly. "Let him go."

"I just....," said the driver, and shook his head as he walked back toward the truck. "We better get out'a here."

The two jumped back into the truck and started down the road, leaving the Deputy lying in the dust.

Ethan remembered Mr. Taylor's bull half way through the pasture. As fast as he was running he figured it would never catch him. He didn't know where he was going—just that he had to get as far away as possible. He ran to the edge of Mr. Taylor's property, crawled under the fence again, and headed into the woods. He could make it home in another ten to fifteen minutes, but that meant he would have to cross the side road that went down to the old abandoned Davis house. He pictured the two men along the road waiting for him. And he could not remember if he had told him where he lived. Maybe they were there waiting at his house. He worried about his poor mother who was home alone. No, the Deputy had said that he had already called for backup, so the men would probably be afraid to stick around. But, just in case, he would wait until he heard the sirens and then come out of the woods. To be safe he would find a place to hide. And he knew just the place. His older brother, Horace, had shown him a thicket in the woods where he went to smoke cigarettes. The bushes surrounding him were so thick it would be impossible for anyone to see him unless they were only a few feet away. He lay quietly in his hiding place, looking through the brush for the two strangers.

Mrs. Thompson's dentist appointment was at three o'clock. She decided she would leave early and stop at the Piggly Wiggly and the post office. It was a couple of minutes after two when she left her house. She pulled her Chevy into the road and headed toward town. As she came around the bend she was shocked by what she saw. There, beside the road, was a county Sheriff's patrol car with the red light flashing. At the rear of the car lay a deputy's body, his gun at his side. She quickly pulled to the side of the road, got out of her car and ran to the patrol car. As she drew nearer she recognized Andrew Pratt. Although she had never seen a dead person before, she was certain there was no life left in his body

"My God, my God!" she exclaimed as she stood trembling, wondering what to do. She soon heard a voice coming from the radio.

"Deputy Pratt, Deputy Pratt, please report your location. Are you there? We have been trying to raise you for almost an hour. Please report in!"

Although she knew nothing about police radios, she ran to the car and picked up the handset. She saw the button on the side and pushed it as she talked.

"Can you hear me?"

"Who is this?" came the reply.

"This is Jean Thompson. I'm just down the road from my house near Taylor's farm. Something terrible has happened to Deputy Pratt. It looks like he has been shot. I think he is dead. You better get here in a hurry."

Ethan waited for what seemed like hours before he heard the sirens. His body ached and he was more tired than he could ever remember. Instead of going back through Mr. Taylor's property, he followed the fence until he came to the road. He stopped in the bushes near the edge of the road to make sure it was safe to go on. What he saw was shocking. Besides Mrs. Thompson's car there were three sheriff's cars, a Tennessee State Police car, and one police car from nearby Greenville. Deputy Pratt's body was being loaded into an ambulance. There was also a fire truck on the scene—for what reason he was unsure. He estimated that there were at least twenty people scattered up and down the road. He watched the activity for a few seconds before stepping into the road.

As he drew nearer someone called, "There he is." A number of people came running toward him. He didn't know if anyone realized he had seen the shooting. He was soon surrounded by a half dozen policemen and rescue workers. From out of nowhere his mother appeared, wrapping him in her arms as she sobbed.

"My baby, my baby. Are you O.K.?"

He could only manage to nod his head.

"Where have you been? Did you see what happened here? Are you O.K.? Are you hurt?" she continued. Before he could answer Sheriff Benlow was at his side.

"Son, are you sure you are O.K.?" he asked.

"Yes, I reckon," Ethan said.

"Then did you see what happened here?"

"Yes, sir."

"Then I know you have had an awful experience, but I'm afraid I have to ask you some questions, and I don't have any time to waste. Can you help me out?"

"O.K."

The Sheriff bent down to talk to the youngster.

"Tell me what happened here, son."

Ethan recanted his experience, trying to remember anything he thought might be important. He told him about the truck driving by and the two men asking him for directions, then offering him a ride. He told him about the Deputy stopping them and pulling his gun. Finally, he told him about the driver shooting the Deputy, and him running into the woods.

"And you never seen these two colored boys before?"

"No, sir."

"How old would you say they were?" he asked.

"I ain't rightly sure."

"Well, were they more like high school boys, or more my age?" asked the Sheriff who was over forty.

"I'd reckon somewhere in between. Maybe around twenty-five or thirty. The passenger looked older."

"And they never did anything to you?"

"No, sir. We had just started to take off when Deputy Pratt pulled up behind us. But they was very nice to me. They even gave me a bottle of orange soda pop."

"Do you still have the bottle?" he asked excitedly.

"I don't remember. Maybe I dropped it somewhere. I reckon I was purty scared when the Deputy yelled and told us to get out of the truck."

The Sheriff turned and yelled at his men, "Look for a bottle of orange soda. It might have fingerprints."

One of his deputies soon found a partially full bottle lying in the dirt. He removed a pen from his pocket and used it to pick up the bottle.

"Is that it, son?" asked the Sheriff.

"It looks like it Sheriff," said Ethan.

The Sheriff stopped for a moment to ponder his next question.

"So they asked you for directions. Where did they want to go?"

"Back to highway 11."

"Great," said the Sheriff to no one particular. "So they are probably not from around here." Then, turning back to Ethan he continued. "Now, son, I want you to think hard and try to describe them to me. How tall were they? How big were they? What were they wearing? What was their hair like? Anything special you remember about them?"

Ethan described how the two men looked just average to him except that the driver was a little bigger. Both men were wearing coveralls but he could not remember anything else about their dress.

"Did either one of them have a beard...a hat...glasses?"

"Oh yeah," he remembered, "the driver had a beard and was wearin' sunglasses."

"But not the other one?"

"No, sir, but his hair was pretty long...a lot longer than the other and it kind of stuck up—like a bee hive."

Ethan's mother moved closer to him and put her arm around her son's neck.

"Sheriff, my boy's had a really bad day. Aren't you about through with these questions?"

"Just a couple more, Mrs. Ward. This is really important if we want to catch these boys. Your son is the only witness we got."

He turned back to Ethan. "Now, son, did you notice the license plate on the truck?"

"No, sir."

"Don't remember any of the numbers or if it was from Tennessee or not?"

Ethan thought for a moment, trying to recall the license plate.

"I don't remember any of the numbers, but I'm a mite sure it was from Tennessee. At least it was black and white."

"That helps a lot, son. Now, anything about the truck you can remember other than it was old. Do you remember what color it was? Do you remember the make, like Ford or Chevy?"

"I think it was dark blue, cept' it was purty dirty. It might have even been black."

"O.K., now, finally, do you know about what time this

happened? How long have you been hiding in the woods?"

Ethan looked around sheepishly. "I don't rightly know. I was afraid to come out."

"That's fine, son," said the Sheriff with a slight laugh, "but do you know about what time this happened?"

"I can answer that," said his mother. "He left for his friend's house right around twelve-thirty. I know because we just finished lunch and I looked at the clock. He left just a couple minutes after that. And it would probably only take him about ten to fifteen minutes to walk down here. I should have never let him go by himself."

"Does that sound about right, Ethan?" asked the Sheriff. "Did you stop or take a detour along the way?"

"No, sir. I was goin directly to my friend Billy's house. So I reckon the time was about right."

"Damn," he said as he turned to the other deputies, "that means these guys already got over an hour head start. How can it be possible that no one came by here in the past hour?"

"They ain't many people on this road, Chief," stated one of his deputies. "Only four or five families live down this way, and except for Mrs. Ward and Mrs. Thompson they all work."

"Fine," he continued. "And how come we didn't know where Pratt was? And what was he doing out here anyway?"

"Sorry Chief, I don't know," said his Deputy. I already talked to Becky and she said the last time he called in was almost two hours ago, and that was all the way up at Baileytown."

"O.K., " he continued, "we need to get to work. We're going to catch these boys. Put out an APB for any old pick up-any dark color. And I want every colored male in the county between the ages of eighteen and forty questioned." He turned to the Tennessee Highway Patrolman nearby. "Get this information to your dispatch as soon as possible" The patrolman nodded and walked away. "I want the Coroner's report by tomorrow. Any questions?"

Everyone nodded their understanding and hurried away. The Sheriff turned back to Ethan.

"Son, I want to thank you for your help. I'm sorry you had to go through this. Kids shouldn't have to see things like this. But we are going to catch them. If you can think of anything else, you be sure to let me know. O.K.?"

"Yes, sir," he replied.

With a pat on the head, the Sheriff left Ethan with his mother. She put her arm around him and led him to Mrs. Thompson's car to take him home. Just as they started to get into her car, his father's truck pulled up. His father jumped from the truck and ran through the crowd to hug his son. With a simple, "He's fine—we can talk later," his mother led them back to the truck. As they wove their way through the vehicles Ethan looked back to see the ambulance pulling away.

TWO

Ethan's seventeen-year old brother, Horace, was waiting on the porch when they got home. He had been fishing that afternoon and was not aware of the recent events. The four went inside and sat in the living room while Ethan explained again what he had seen. After a while his mother stated that he had talked enough. Ethan went into his room and resumed working on a model airplane he had bought a few days earlier. His brother and father went into the front yard to pitch baseball, while his mother began preparing supper. That night the family sat around the TV, saying little more about what had transpired that day.

At bedtime Ethan's mother moved the mattress from his bed onto the floor in their room. His father objected, but his mother stated that it was just temporary. While his father said that it would only feed his fear, once his son was asleep he loaded his shotgun and placed it beside the bed.

Ethan slept well for the first few hours, then the nightmare began. He was running through a cornfield when the cornstalks developed arms and tried to grab him. He pushed away from them and ran to the edge of the field. He crawled under the fence but the fence post turned into a monster and held him. The cornstalks started walking toward him. He was awakened by his mother's voice. "It's alright baby, you just had a bad dream." She lay with him until he fell back asleep.

The next morning, after breakfast, Ethan was in his room when his father came in.

"I'd like to talk to you, son," he said. Ethan nodded.

"Ethan, I wish I could take away everything that happened to you yesterday, but I can't. It was an awful thing for a young boy to see—for anyone to see I reckon. And I am a mite concerned what effect this could have on ya."

"I'll be alright, Daddy," he said.

"We'll I reckon you will be in time. But right now I know you're scared and confused, and probably a little angry. I ain't too good at words but I'd like ta try and help. Anything I can say ta help make it better?"

Ethan hesitated before asking his question.

"Have you ever seen a man killed Daddy?"

His father sat down on the bed next to him. "Well Ethan, you know I ain't never talked much about the time I spent in the war. Course you boys know the story 'bout how your mother and I met in Berlin, but I never liked ta talk about the war itself. It's something I don't like thinking 'bout, and I figured y'all didn't need ta know. But I guess now is a good time. Yes, son, I saw a lot of men killed. But I reckon that was a lot different from this"

"Why?"

"Well, first of all, I was twenty and not thirteen. There ain't never a good time for killin', but it's a mite easier to deal with when you're grown. And it was war, which is different from murdering someone like you saw."

"It turned out the same."

"Well, I reckon it did, son, but it's still not the same. You know when you go ta war what might happen. And there's a reason for it. We were trying ta protect people and save lives—the greater good they call it. Here was just two boys killin' who ever got in their way—for what reason we don't know. I know it might not sound like much difference, but when you get older you will understand."

"I understand," he said.

"Good, but I don't think that helps much. Is there something I can do to help you with this?"

"Well," said Ethan, thinking for a minute, "do you think they'll be back lookin' for me?"

His father gave him a knowing look.

"Son, I can't guarantee nothin', but I don't think we'll ever see them boys around here again."

"Why?"

"I don't think them boys is from around here, and I don't think they'll ever be coming back. Why, there ain't but a few hundred colored folk in the whole county, and everybody and their brother will be lookin for em' and their truck. So, I figure if they ain't caught they won't never be coming back here."

He didn't know if anything he had said had made things better. He was relieved to see his wife standing in the doorway.

"Can I talk to Ethan for a minute?" she asked.

"Sure," he said. "I need ta go chop some firewood anyway."

Ethan's mother came and sat down next to him on the bed. She was a large but attractive woman of German descent. Her voice was a combination of German dialect and Tennessee slang. While she loved her husband and her children, after eighteen years she still sometimes longed for her home in Berlin.

"So how are you doing, Ethan?" she said.

"I'm O.K. Mama," he said, meekly.

"So did your daddy help any?"

"I reckon. He said he don't think those men would ever be coming back."

"Not unless they are caught, which I think they will be. No matter what happens it will take time for you to get over this."

He just nodded.

"But there is something else I want to talk to you about, son."

"What is that, Mama?"

"I think it is time you know some things about me—about my family. I grew up in wartime Germany, you know."

"Yeah I know."

"But there's things you don't know. It was not a very pleasant time."

"Yeah, we been studyin' it in school."

"I'm sure you have," she said absent-mindedly. She hesitated for a moment then continued.

"Son, what I am about to tell you I hope you always keep to yourself, O.K.?"

"Yes, ma'am."

"I was born in 1921. We were not rich but we got by. My father was a shoemaker. It was at the beginning of the Depression in Germany but my brother and sister and I had a pretty normal happy life. My mother was always cooking and baking. My father was not as involved as I would like, but he was there if we needed him. Then, as I started to get older, the Depression began to get worse. In 1926 it got really bad. It was awful. People were starving—people were out of work—and people were angry. They wanted someone to blame. The Nazi Party came along, and they had the answer—it was the Jews' fault. They had the money, they owned the banks, they owned the stores, and they caused the Depression. So the only solution was to get rid of the Jews. And that is what Hitler did— millions of them. I had Jewish friends that I played with that I could no longer talk to. And, the worse thing for me was what happened to my father. He went from being a good, caring family man to a bitter, angry Nazi. He pretty much abandoned us and went to work for the Nazi Party as a guard at a camp. At the end of the war, when he knew all was lost, he killed himself."

"Oh, wow!" he said.

"Yeah, I know, son. You boys knew he died in the war, but it's time you knew the truth. And the reason I am telling you this now is this; people always have somebody to blame—somebody that's different from them—a different color, a different religion, a different accent—whatever. You saw something terrible yesterday, and the only thing you can do now is decide how it's going to affect you. I saw hate change my father into an angry, vengeful man, and eventually kill him. I don't want that to happen to you. It was awful what those two colored men did—and yes, they are mean and sinful. But it wasn't because they were colored. God made all men equal and gave us the ability to decide between good and evil. And that's what happened yesterday—they chose evil. But, remember, there's good and evil in all of us—you understand that?"

"Yes, ma'am," he said, still trying to cope with what she had told him.

"Alright, you think about what I have said. But then you figure out what you want to do today. I don't want you sitting around thinking all day."

She patted him on he head as she left his room. Ethan removed his baseball cards from a box on the dresser and began sorting them. He was lost in thought about everything that had happened and what his mother and father had said, when he heard a knock at the door. His mother went to answer it.

"Good morning, Sheriff," she said. "How are you today?"

"Fine, Mrs. Ward. How is Ethan?"

"As well as can be expected, I reckon."

"You reckon," he repeated with a laugh. "What is the German translation for 'reckon'?"

"There is no word for 'reckon' in any other known language except hillbilly," she said. "Is there anything new today?"

"No, not really. I just wanted to see how Ethan was doing and see if he remembered anything else. Can I talk to him?"

"Sure," she replied, turning to her son's room, "Ethan, you have company."

Soon Ethan appeared, holding his baseball cards.

"Good morning, son," said the Sheriff.

"Good, morning, sir."

"You doin O.K. today? You sleep O.K.?"

"For the most part, I reckon."

"Can we sit down and talk?"

Ethan and his mother sat on the couch, the Sheriff in a nearby chair.

"So, you remember anything else from yesterday we haven't talked about?"

"No, sir, I don't think so."

"Well, if something else comes to mind let me know. But there's one other thing I want to talk about. I'm sure you are pretty worried that these boys might come back looking for you, right?"

"Well, I thought about it."

"Well, son let me tell you—I can't guarantee it but, based on almost twenty years experience in law enforcement, I would almost guarantee you will never see them again except at their trial. And I'm gonna tell you why. But I'm gonna have to be very blunt."

"O.K."

"First, they were not from around here. This is a small county and nobody knows them or their truck. And I believe they were really just asking you for directions. If they wanted to hurt you they would have just pulled up and grabbed you. There wasn't nobody else around, and it would have been faster just to pull you into the truck. And I don't think they would have hurt you or they wouldn't have been so nice by offering you a soda pop. They were just lost— I don't know what they were lookin for—and they wanted help getting back on the highway."

"O.K.," said Ethan, "but that don't mean they wouldn't want to hurt me now since I seen what they done."

"That's a good point, son—but if that were the case they would have done it at the time."

"But I ran away."

"Son, how old are you?"

"Thirteen."

"And how tall are you?"

"Five foot six"

"And how much do you weigh?"

"About 130."

"And I know you're pretty fast, but, from what you told me both of these boys were about six feet tall, in pretty good shape and not too heavy, right"

"Yes, sir."

"Well, trust me, son, if they wanted to catch you they would have. Again, this is a really deserted road here, and it would have only taken a few seconds to run you down."

"But I went under the fence."

"That fence was meant to keep the bull in, not people out. They could have gone under those slats just as easy as you. And, son—I'm sorry, but I'm going to be very blunt here—but from what you told me, he could have shot you before you got to the fence if he wanted. He didn't because they were not set out on hurting anybody. I don't know why they turned on my Deputy, but they were not going to hurt a kid. Does this make you feel any better?"

Ethan thought for a minute about what he had said.

"Yes, sir, I guess so. But they still might change their mind since I can identify them."

"Well, yes, I guess anything in the world is possible. But for them to do that they would have to come back here. And I don't think there is a chance in the world of them risking that. They would almost certainly be seen. I reckon those boys will be keeping a low profile over in Knoxville or Nashville, or Memphis, or maybe even left the state. No, I don't reckon they'll ever be coming back here again—least not on their own accord."

Ethan nodded his head as his mother gave him a hug. The Sheriff rose to leave as Mr. Ward walked in the front door.

"Morning, Sheriff," he stated.

"Morning, Buster. You off today?"

"Yep, the power company said I could take a couple days off if need be."

"That was good of them. Well I was just leaving. Just stopped by to check on your boy."

"We appreciate that. I'll walk you out."

As they walked to the car, Mr. Ward asked, "So, anything new on the case?"

"No, not really, the next twenty-four hours will be the most critical."

"It's hard to believe that two colored boys could just disappear when everybody in the whole state is looking for them."

"Well, the big problem we had was they got a head start of over an hour."

"But it seems like someone ought to notice that truck."

"If I had to guess, I'd say that truck was at the bottom of a lake or river by now."

"Then they would have to be traveling by foot."

"Possibly, or they had someone pick them up."

"You think they had help?"

"No, not in plannin' the shootin' — that was a spur of the

moment thing. But you know how colored folk keep together. They probably got plenty folk that would cover for them."

"So, it's possible they may never get caught?"

"Anything's possible," said the Sheriff as he opened the door to get into his car, "but I think we'll get'em sooner or later. People love to talk and that's what usually trips people up. They can't keep their mouth shut."

"So why you reckon they shot him anyway?" asked Mr. Ward.

"Well, it could be any number of reasons. They were wanted for something; they didn't trust the law; they were afraid of being caught with your boy. Or, as we both know, Deputy Pratt was not exactly the nicest person in he world—some would even call him a bully, so who knows what he said to those boys.

"Ethan said not much happened."

"Yeah, I know, but something could have happened he didn't hear or didn't notice. He's a smart kid, but he is still a kid. He just might not have picked up on something. The thing I can't understand was why Pratt was there. He radioed just a few minutes earlier that he was on the other side of the county, and that was impossible. So what in the world he was doin there I don't know. It's possible he got a tip about these boys and wanted to be the hero by taking them by himself. He would do that you know. Anyway, if your boy thinks of something else let me know. But try not to worry—as I told your boy, I don't think they'll be coming back here any time soon."

"So what's the talk around town? You reckon we're gonna have any backlash against the coloreds cause of this?"

"I don't think so. You know as well as me that we don't have problems like a lot of other places. Why we even integrated our schools last year without being told. And folks know it wasn't any local boys that did the shooting. No, I don't think we'll have any problem."

"How is the Deputys' parents doin?"

"Not too good. Reckon they have had a run of bad luck in their lifes'. At least Andy didn't have a wife or kids. I guess that speaks for something."

"Thanks Sheriff," he said as he watched him get into his car. The Sheriff nodded and drove away.

THREE

FALL, 1963

Ethan was a different young boy when he returned to junior high school that fall. His innocence as well as his sense of security had been shattered. While everyone had expected the men who shot Deputy Pratt would be quickly caught, that had not happened. And, as the weeks went by, everyone knew that there was less likelihood of them being apprehended. The community was furious that not only could such a thing happen, but that the killers could get away. And even though his parents told him otherwise, Ethan felt as if it were his fault that they were not caught. The worst part for him was riding by the place where it happened every day. Before school began, to make things a little better, his parents bought a used car so his mother could drive him to and from school. While they explained she needed a car to run errands during the day, he knew it was for his protection. For as much as they said otherwise, he knew the possibility existed that the men could come back some day.

To keep his mind off the shooting Ethan kept himself as busy as possible. He joined the school's debating team. After a few weeks his mother said that she could even see a difference in the way he talked—he was losing his "hillbilly" dialect. He also began taking woodworking. While he doubted that carpentry would be a career choice, he found it interesting and soothing to create something from nothing. He created a coffee table for his mother, and was currently working on a toolbox for his father which he would give him for Christmas. He also had just begun practicing for the junior high basketball squad. To his surprise he quickly discovered that he was a very good athlete. He couldn't wait for the season to begin.

The weather was pleasant as his mother dropped him off at school. The temperature was in the forties but was expected to hit sixty by the end of the day. After shop class Ethan had lunch and chatted with friends. They talked about the things all eighth grade boys talked about—sports, girls, and music. After lunch he left the cafeteria and went to his gym class. He enjoyed the class since they usually got the chance to play "battleball", a game in which the boys divided between two teams and tried to eliminate the other team by hitting them with a volleyball. Each team could not cross into the other's "home territory" but would stand at a line and throw at members of the opposing team. If the ball was caught, the thrower was eliminated. Since Ethan was bigger and stronger than many of the other players, his team usually won.

After gym class the boys showered and headed for their next class. For Ethan, it was math—a subject with which he always had trouble. He was almost to the main building when he saw a commotion ahead. Kids were running, kids were shouting, and two girls were sitting on a bench crying.

"What's going on?" he asked as a boy ran by.

"They shot JFK!" he said as he passed. "It was just on the radio."

"You're kidding," Ethan said, then realizing he did not know who he was referring to. Seeing his puzzled look, a girl nearby turned to him and said, "JFK—President Kennedy."

"Wow," he stated, as the revelation struck him. He walked in shock toward his class. When he arrived his teacher was in the front of the room in conversation with two other teachers. His classmates huddled in groups discussing the news. Ethan found his seat and sat quietly, not knowing what to do or say. Soon, with tears in her eyes, the teacher turned to the class.

"Kids, I'm sorry to have to tell you this, but we just heard that President Kennedy has died."

She could hardly get the words out without crying. The other teachers hugged her as they sobbed together. The students sat mostly in silence, some crying quietly. A blond girl sitting next to him, Rachel, turned to him and said, "That's awful. Do y'all think they are going to let school out early?"

A black boy named Tommy overheard her remarks and turned to her with a look of shock. "President Kennedy has just been killed and *that's* what'cha worried about—Getting out of school!"

He turned and ran out of the classroom. Rachel turned to Ethan and said, "Jees, what's his problem? I just asked a simple question."

It was too late for the teacher to stop him as he ran by so she turned to Ethan and said, "Son, go find him and get him calmed down. Then both of you come back until we find out what the school is doing."

"Yes, Ma'am," he said as he got up and followed the boy out the door.

As he went into the hallway he saw Tommy running out the exit. He ran after him wondering where he was going. He reached the door in time to see him heading towards the football field. Ethan followed him as he ran to the bleachers and sat with his head between his legs. He quietly walked over and sat next to him.

"Are ya O.K.?" he asked.

"Why do you care?" he said.

"It wasn't me that said that," he said. "I'm just as upset as you."

"I doubt that."

"Why do you say that?"

Tommy looked up at him with tears in his eyes. "You don't understand, do you? He was the first one who treated us the same—like real people. He was our leader and now they done killed him."

Ethan did not know what to say. "He could only manage, "I'm sorry."

He sat quietly next to him for a while. Soon Tommy continued, "And that girl Rachel, she don't care 'bout nothing but herself. 'Will school get out early?' he mocked.

"I don't think she meant it like that," he said, "she just didn't know what was goin' to happen next."

"Right," he said sarcastically. "Wait until you get to know her."

They sat silently for a few minutes. Finally, Ethan said, "Mrs.

Gault said I should bring you back to class."

The two got up and walked slowly towards the building. Tommy spoke softly now, more calmly. "I bet you think I'm a big baby, don't cha?"

"Well, Mrs. Gualt and the other teachers was cryin' too. And I feel like it, so I reckon we're all just a bunch of big babies."

Even in all his pain, Tommy could not help but laugh. "I think you're alright, Ace," he said. Ethan put his hand on his new friend's shoulder as they walked back to the room.

School was dismissed early for any students who either walked or were driven to school. With such little notice they could not coordinate getting all the school buses there at the same time, so those students would have to wait for the normal dismissal time. Tommy was one of those kids. When finding out that his mother would be picking him up soon, Ethan offered his friend a ride home. Tommy eagerly accepted. He informed him that his father was the minister at a local church, Ebenezer Baptist. They dropped him off at his house which was adjacent to the church, then returned home to watch the news on TV.

The family watched in shock as the news unfurled. Soon they discovered that a man by the name of Lee Harvey Oswald was arrested for the assassination of President Kennedy. They were even more stunned as they watched two days later to see Oswald shot and killed by Jack Ruby. And, finally, they were deeply saddened to watch the funeral procession taking President Kennedy's body to its final resting place at Arlington Cemetery.

Ethan tried to make sense of it all. Only a few months earlier he had seen two colored men gun down a white Deputy in cold blood, but let him escape unharmed. Now he watched as a white man assassinated the President of the United States, and, as upset as he was, a colored kid was even more devastated. He remembered his mother's words about what prejudice and hatred would do to an individual. It became clearer what she meant, but he had yet to understand why it had to be that way, or more importantly, how to stop it. Maybe the answers would come in time.

It was only a week before the start of basketball season and both Tommy and Ethan were excited to find out they would be starters on the Junior Varsity team. Ethan would be one of the starting forwards and Tommy would be the point guard. The week was grueling with two-hour practices every day after school. Today's practice had been particularly exhausting. In order to make sure the boys were in their best condition for the season, the coach had them run up and down the gym steps for fifteen minutes. It was a weary and thankful team that hit the showers. Ethan showered and dressed first, harassing his friend for being so slow. Tommy informed him that perfection always took a little longer. Since it was Ethan's mother's turn to pick up the boys, he told Tommy he would wait for him in front of the building.

Most of the boys had already left so the parking lot was deserted as Ethan stood waiting for his mother. As much as she worried about him it was unusual for her not to be there when he left the building. It was an unusually warm evening for December, so he waited outside for her to show up. After a moment he heard the sound of two boys talking as they came around the building. He turned to see Ed Russell, who had been cut from the team the week before, and his older brother Ted. The brothers were known troublemakers. Once they saw Ethan they stopped and stared. Ted spoke first.

"Well, what do we have here, Ed?" he began. "Looks like a white boy who thinks he can play basketball."

"Looks like the purty white boy who took my place on the team," said his brother.

Ethan said nothing but returned their stare.

"Don't you have nothing to say now that tha' coach ain't backing you up?" asked Ted.

"I didn't do nothing to you boys," said Ethan. Ted walked closer to Ethan and got in his face. He was about three inches taller and ten to fifteen pounds heavier.

"You didn't do nothing?" he mimicked. "Nothing cept' take my brother's place on the team. And all because you're white. You reckon that's fair?"

"Leave him alone," came a voice from behind them. They turned to see Tommy coming out of the door.

"Well, if it ain't the cracker's little friend, Tommy. Our local Oreo. You know what an Oreo is, little brother?" asked Ted.

"No, what?"

"It's a boy who's black on the outside but white on the inside. Us colored boys not good enough for you, Tommy?"

Tommy walked closer and got in Ted's face.

"I don't care if you are older and bigger than me, Ted—I ain't scared of you. So you either put up or shut up. And if you start something I hope you brought your supper cause you're gonna be here a long time."

Ethan and Ed watched as the two stared at each other. Finally Ted turned to the side, brushed past him and walked away.

"You two ain't worth it. Reckon we know who'd get suspended if anything happened."

The two turned and walked away.

"Hey, Ted," called Tommy, "he didn't do nothing to you so don't be botherin' him again."

He did not respond.

Tommy turned to his friend. "You O.K.?"

"Sure," he said, then added indignantly, "I could have handled them."

"Well, 'thanks for helping me, Tommy'," said Tommy sarcastically.

"You know what I mean. I do appreciate it."

"Yeah, I know what you mean."

Ethan watched as the two went around the corner.

"Why do you think colored people and white people have such a hard time getting along?" he asked his friend.

"That's easy. People don't like anybody that's different from them."

"You reckon that will ever change?"

"It changed with us didn't it?"

Soon a car pulled up in front of the boys. It was not his mother's, but their neighbor, Mrs. Thompson.

"Is everything O.K.?" asked Ethan.

"Sure," said Mrs. Thompson. "Your mother's car wouldn't start and your dad wasn't home she called me. You boys ready to go?"

Ethan and Tommy climbed into the back seat. As they rode home Ethan thought of how lucky he was to have such a good friend.

FOUR

FALL, 1967

Fall was football time in Tennessee. The excitement began with the University of Tennessee Volunteers and continued into the high school teams. Now, even many junior high schools had football teams. The kids began to get their indoctrination into football in elementary school, and it soon developed into a life long passion. Tonight's game at Greenville High was no different. Even though the team had been struggling and was an underdog to favored Morristown, emotions were running high.

Ethan Ward felt the excitement in the air as he walked home after school. Car horns echoed throughout the neighborhood as did the chants of, "Go Big Green." He waved as a carload of classmates shouted as they drove by. He soon made it to his house which was only a few blocks from the high school. He noticed his mother's car in the driveway. He hoped there was no problem since her job as a nurse's aid at the hospital did not end until four-thirty.

"Mom," he called as he walked in the door, throwing his books on the table. "You here?"

"Here," she said as she walked from the kitchen.

"You're home early. Everything all right?"

"Sure. I had to refill your father's medication so I left a little early."

"Is he doing O.K.?"

"He seems fine—still as weak as ever. He only has another two weeks of treatment left, you know. Then, if everything goes as expected, he should start to get his strength back."

"I hope so," he said, as he walked to the refrigerator and removed a bottle of Nugrape soda. "You know, Mom, I was reading in the library today that more and more they think cancer is tied to smoking. I sure hope Dad decides to give those things up when he gets over this."

"Well I think cigarettes are only associated with lung cancer, which would have nothing to do with your dad. Anyway, as sick as these treatments have made him, he hasn't had a desire for a smoke in the past couple of months."

"Well I hope it lasts, because I think in time they will find out tobacco is the cause for a lot of other problems besides lung cancer."

"It's nice you've been doing so much reading on this Ethan. I'm sure your father appreciates your concern. His next treatment is at UT on Wednesday. Will you be able to go with me to Knoxville?"

"Sure. My teachers said I can take off whenever I need. I just have to tell them."

His mother opened the refrigerator door and removed a package of pork chops and began unwrapping them.

"But let's change the subject. You ready for the game tonight?"

"I am, but I don't know if the team is. I think it's going to be another one in the loss column."

"Now, son, you just have to be more positive. They might have a chance."

"Yeah, they could have a chance, if they let Tommy start at quarterback. Too bad he's not the right color."

"You don't know that's' the reason."

"Well he's the best player on the team."

"And the fact that he's your best friend has nothing to do with it?"

He just ignored her remark and opened the cupboard door searching for a snack.

"Don't do that," she ordered, "You'll spoil your supper."

"Mom," he said, "don't you know by now a teenager never spoils his appetite."

"O.K.," she said laughing. "So, you picking up Rachel and taking her to the game?"

"I reckon so," he said.

"You don't seem very excited."

"Yeah, I am. It's just that sometimes she can be....well, very self-centered."

"What teenager isn't?"

"That's not fair."

"I know, son, you're right. Anyway, I hope you two have a good time, but, remember, you have to be in by midnight. And remember to put gas in the car. And be careful. You know there are a lot of crazy people out tonight."

"Yes, Ma'am," he said as he turned to leave the kitchen. "Is Dad awake?"

"I think so. Ask him if he can eat a few bites."

Ethan walked quietly toward his parents' room. While the doctors had told them they had caught the cancer early and they expected him to make a full recovery, it was very difficult to see what the disease—and the chemo treatments—had done to him. His weight had dropped from 200 to just over 160 in the past few months. And he was so weak that at times he could hardly make it from the bedroom to the bathroom by himself. As Ethan looked into the room he saw his dad lying on the bed watching the Mike Douglas show.

"Hey, son," he said weakly, "come on in."

"How you doin', Dad?"

"Fine, fine. Just a mite tired. I'll be good as new in a few weeks."

"I'm sure you will. Anything I can do for you?"

"Nope. Just sit and talk ta me for a spell. How's it goin' at school? How's the team look? We gonna whup them tonight?"

Ethan sat and talked to his father until he became tired, then left so he could sleep. He went to his room and studied until his mother called him for supper. At six-thirty he left to pick up his girlfriend, Rachel, who was a cheerleader at Greenville High. Her house was on the same road where his family had lived previously. While it was still a couple of miles from his old house, just being in the area always brought back memories of that terrible day four years earlier. That was the main reason his parents had sold the house and moved into town—so that he would not have to re-live those moments every time he went by. He felt it rather ironic that his first girlfriend lived nearby. God certainly had a strange sense of humor.

He was five minutes late in picking up Rachel, which she eagerly pointed out to him. He ignored her complaints as much as possible as he drove her back to the school. He dropped her off in front of the school, then parked the car and walked to the concession stand where he talked to friends while waiting for the festivities to begin. Soon the crowd began arriving so he joined his classmates to watch the game. Unfortunately his predictions regarding the game were accurate. The home team did not score, losing to Morristown 0-13. It was not a happy crowd that left the stadium. Unfortunately the game left Rachel in a worse mood than before.

"This is a stupid team," she stated as they left the parking lot for the local hamburger joint. "They can't win anything."

"Actually, they are only one game below 500," he said.

"Only one game below 500," she repeated. "The purpose of playing a sport is to win. We haven't had a winning season in....forever."

"1964," he said.

"1964," she repeated angrily. "Why are you giving me such a hard time?"

"What are you so mad about," he said. "Football is not easy. The other teams are trying just as hard to win. Nobody likes to lose."

"Which you know a lot about, huh?" she shot back.

"Oh, so that's what this is about," he replied. "It's my fault for not playing."

"Well, everyone knows you would have been one of the best athletes the school has ever had. The coach still can't figure out why you sat out your senior year. Your father wanted you to play. You would have made a big difference in the team."

"And the fact that I didn't want to play football should have nothing to do with it, huh?"

"Well, it would be a big opportunity to make something out of yourself."

"It would be a big opportunity for you to be seen with a football star. Is that what you mean?" Ethan snapped.

"That's ridiculous," she shot back. "I don't need somebody else to make me feel important. I can get what I want on my own."

"Well that we can agree on," he conceded. "Can we not argue about this and just go get something to eat?"

"Fine," she said, as she stared out her window.

They soon arrived at Henry's Hamburger Hamlet, the local drive-in and teen hangout. A number of classmates came by the car to talk as they waited for their food. Shortly the players began to arrive, most looking rejected and tired. Some waved, others sat in their cars together or with their girlfriends. After a while Ethan's best friend, Tommy Bell pulled up with two other players. After parking the car he walked to Ethan's window to say hello. He had only begun to speak when Rachel announced she had to go to the ladies room.

"Sorry about that," said Ethan after she had left.

"It's O.K., Ace," he said. "I think she's made it clear she's not too partial to those of us of the darker persuasion."

"Oh, I'm not sure about that. She seems to dislike everything tonight."

"Then why do you put up with her, man? A young, handsome white boy like yourself can have any babe you want."

Tommy was correct. At six foot two inches and 190 pounds, in the past couple of years he had changed from a gangly kid to a handsome young man. And his wavy brown hair and quick smile made him very popular with the girls.

"Lately I been askin' myself the same question. I guess it takes time to get to know somebody. Can we change the subject?"

"Sure. How'd you like the game?"

"Well, if they had started you instead of waiting until the game was almost over we might have had a chance."

"I doubt it. Maybe next year."

"Yeah, maybe next year. Course we won't be around to see it. With my scholarship I'll probably be in law school over at U.T."

"Right. You might be smart, but I think they only give those out to boys with an A average. You think you qualify? The only thing that Rachel and I agree on is that you should have been out there on the field tonight."

"Let's not start again."

"But it's O.K. for you to talk about me, huh?"

"Of course."

"O.K. What'cha doin tomorrow. You working? Want to go fishing?"

"I got to work until one. I'm free after that. What about you?"

"I'll be at my dad's church until around then. Want to meet around two?"

"Sounds good. You want to pick me up?"

"Got it," he replied as he made a fist and banged knuckles with his friend. He turned and walked back to his car as Rachel left the restaurant.

The drive back to Rachel's house was silent and awkward. Finally, Ethan could contain his emotions no longer.

"That was very rude what you did to Tommy," he said bluntly.

"What?" she shot back.

"You know what. Leaving just as he came up to the car."

"He's your friend, not mine. If you want to be friends with a colored boy that's up to you, but I'm really shocked, especially after what you went through."

"They like to be called, 'black' now. And it's because of what I went through that I decided how people should be treated."

"Yeah, yeah, I know. 'We don't want to let prejudice destroy us'. I heard your story before. Well call them black or colored or whatever you want, they are still...."

She didn't finish, but both knew what she meant. Ethan decided it was useless to continue that discussion. He had tried before.

"Rachel," he began, "why did you ever go out with me?"

"That's easy. Despite being so naive and having no competitiveness, you are cute and big and strong, and sometimes have a good sense of humor. Why?"

"And how long have we been dating?"

"Four or five months. What are you getting at?"

"Cause I think the only reason you wanted to go out with me is because you thought you could convince me to not quit football. Then I would be the big football hero and you would be the head cheerleader and we would be the most popular couple around. I think every thing you do is about you."

"That's ridiculous," she said, flatly "I care about other people."

"Yeah, as far as how they can help you."

"Is that right! Or maybe I just intimidate you. Just because you want to stay here and be a hillbilly the rest of your life doesn't mean I should. I'll admit I want something better than what this town has to offer, but that doesn't mean I am heartless. You, on the other hand, will probably be here in twenty-five years still working at Western Auto."

It was then that Ethan decided there was no reason in continuing their relationship. He decided he would wait until they got to her house before he told her. Although he was certain, based upon the evening's events, that she would not object, he wanted to make his exit as quick and painless as possible.

They were just past the white church a half mile from her house when they saw the taillights beside the road. They immediately knew something was wrong because the lights were at a steep angle. As they drew closer they could see why—the car had left the road and ran into a tree. It appeared the accident had just happened. Smoke was coming from the engine. As their headlights shone on the vehicle, they saw two people in the front seat. The person in the passenger's seat appeared to be a child. The front of the car was badly damaged, however the rest of the vehicle seemed intact. Ethan pulled the car to a stop, opened the door and ran toward the vehicle. Rachel slowly opened her door and walked cautiously toward the wrecked car. As she did so she detected the smell of gasoline.

"Ethan," she called, "I smell gas, and I hear a hissing sound. You hear it? This is very dangerous."

"That's why we have to get these people out of here. It might catch fire at any second," he called as he tried in vain to open the passenger door. Rachel moved backward, hiding behind their car.

"It's too dangerous," she insisted. "It might explode. Come back."

He ignored her as he continued to pull on the door. Suddenly he turned and ran back to his car.

"Oh, good," exclaimed Rachel, "let's go for help."

But he ran past her to the trunk of his mother's car. He quickly opened it and removed the tire iron and ran back to the wrecked vehicle. He jammed the iron into the door seam and pushed. The passenger's door flew open. Inside he could now clearly see a young girl who appeared to be about ten years old. He tried to pull her out but discovered she was wearing a seat belt. Quickly loosening her belt he pulled her from the car. He carried her a safe distance, lay her on the ground, and ran back to the car. Again he had to pry open the door which had slammed shut. He climbed back into the car to free the woman. As he did so his extra weight caused the car to jerk and level off. He quickly grabbed the woman, who was covered in blood, pulled her from the wreck and carried her back to the area where he had placed the girl. As he did so he noticed another car had parked behind his and a man and woman were running toward them.

"Anybody else in there?" the man called.

"I didn't see anybody. You might check," he said.

The man quickly ran to the car and looked in the back window, then ran back to the others. It was as Rachel had predicted. There was no huge explosion, but within seconds the entire car was engulfed in flames.

"Man, it was good you came along when you did," said the stranger, "or both of these people would be dead. You're a hero, son." He patted him on the back. "My wife went to get help."

Within minutes he heard the sound of sirens. It was the second time in his life he had heard the sounds of sirens on this road. Hopefully this time no one would die.

It was almost one in the morning when Ethan got home. His mother was seated at the dining room table. He was not sure how to read the look on her face.

"You won't believe what happened, Mom," he began.

"Yes, I know. I was worried so I called the police. I know all about it. I think I will call you my little Moses."

"Little Moses?" he repeated looking confused.

"Yes, because I think you have been called by God. I can't wait to see what He has in store for you next."

"I hope just a long, unexciting life. If this is His idea of fun, I've had enough."

She smiled and walked across the room and gave him a kiss. Then, without another word, she turned and went to bed.

———————

As late as he got in, Ethan still arose by eight the next morning. His father was awake and sitting at the table. He told him that the affects of the chemo were wearing off, and, at least for the moment, he had more energy. He listened intently while his son recanted the previous evening's events. They just finished breakfast when the phone rang. Mrs. Ward answered it. The conversation was mostly one way, with her only occasionally acknowledging what the caller was saying. She hung up the phone and turned to her son.

"Well things just keep getting stranger and stranger," she said.

"What do you mean?" asked Ethan.

"That was Sheriff Benlow. First of all he said the people you rescued would be fine. They just had some cuts and bruises. And next, guess who it was? Senator Coleman's wife and daughter from over Knoxville way. They were here visiting a sick relative. They swerved to miss a deer and—well, you know the rest. The Senator said he would call you later."

"Wow," said his father, "our son is not only a hero, but could be a celebrity. I'm mighty proud'a you boy."

"Well, right now your celebrity son has to get ready to go to work at the local Western Auto. And Tommy and I are going fishing this afternoon. I hope no one falls in the river and has to be saved. If so I'll let him take care of it."

———————

Tommy picked up Ethan at his house just a little after two o'clock. He had been working at his father's church from early morning and had only heard the news on the radio as he drove to pick him up. He was as stunned as was everyone else in town to have a real live local hero—and his best friend no less. He could not wait until he got in the car to begin the questioning.

"What we got here, folks is a real, live hero," he cracked.

"Don't start."

"Don't start!" he said, "I ain't never known nobody that saved someone's life. You'll be the talk of the town, Ace."

"I was just in the right place at the right time. You would have done the same thing."

"And a State Senator's family no less," he continued, ignoring his remark. "I swear, Ethan, you shore have an interesting life."

"Well right now the most interesting thing I want to do is lay beside the river and drown some worms. Are you going to drive or not?"

Tommy shook his head, put the car in gear and pulled away. As they drove to the river he became more serious and asked his friend about the night's events. Ethan reluctantly related the story. They arrived at the river and drove for a short while until they found an isolated area away from other fishermen. They removed an old blanket from the trunk, threw it on the side of the riverbank while they readied the fishing equipment. Soon they were lying on their backs, having a soda, as they waited for the fish to strike.

"You know, Ethan," said, Tommy again, "seriously, I am proud of you. It must feel great to do something like that. Were you scared?"

"I reckon afterward. I didn't even have time to think about it when it was happening. I just saw those people in the car and knew if I didn't get them out they probably wouldn't make it."

"And the radio wasn't clear. Rachel helped you?"

"Hah," he snorted, "she was in the neighborhood."

"Just as I thought. By tomorrow we'll find out that she did the whole thing."

"Yeah, unfortunately I think you are right. I guess I never realized how self-centered she is. I was about to break up with her when we saw the wreck. Guess I'll have to start all over again now."

"Well, I think the timing would be good right now. You could have any babe you want. Even though you still ain't no football hero."

"You're not going to start that again are you?"

"Well, duh, yeah. We could of won the game last night if you had started at end. Those catches you made last year—wow."

"Or if you had played the whole game at quarterback."

"Well that's your opinion—not the coach's. For the life of me I can't figure out why you skipped your senior year."

"We been through this before."

"Yeah, and you ain't never gave me an answer. Least not the real answer."

"O.K., you're gonna harass me forever unless I talk about this I guess," he said after a moment's thought, "but I would appreciate it if you keep it between you and me."

"Don't I always, Ace?"

"All right, the truth is I would have loved to play my last year but I just couldn't do it with everything that was going on."

"Everything?"

"O.K., my father's cancer. There was no way, with my brother gone away to college that my mother could take care of him by herself. And there is the money thing."

"I thought your dad was getting paid while he's out."

"Yeah, fifty percent. And the insurance don't pay all the bills. That's why my mother had to take a job. If I wasn't there to help out it would kill her."

"Wow man, you never told me any of this. But I'm still surprised your mom would let you quit. She knows how much you loved to play football."

"I think I convinced her it would effect my grades and keep me from getting a scholarship, since we both know I would never get a football scholarship. At least she went along with it. Of course, as bad as my grades are I won't ever be going to college."

"Sure you will, man. You're plenty smart."

"We both know better than that man. Despite your ghetto slang, we both know which one of us has the brains. If it weren't for you I wouldn't even be passing Algebra."

"We'll, glad I'm better than you at somethin'. But what about Cumberland College? Horace likes it."

"It's a good college and more reasonable, but it still costs money, and right now we ain't got any. Like Rachel says, I guess I'll be working at Western Auto the rest of my life."

"Well, Ace, you can always come and help out my dad and me at the church. Good white help is hard to find."

"Right," he said laughing, then turned more serious. "Your father is a minister, so you should have the answer to all life's questions, right?"

"Course, Ace. And If I don't I make 'em' up."

"Then why do you think so many bad things happen in the world? I mean, it looks like those two people in the wreck are going to be O.K., but what if we hadn't come along? What if we were five minutes later? They would probably be dead. And why did President Kennedy have to be killed. What about Martin Luther King? And what about those guys that killed the Deputy—why have they not been caught?"

"You sure coverin' a lot of territory there, Ace."

"But it's all the same. I don't understand why God lets all these things happen."

"I have had this same conversation with my father. It's cause we live in a fallen world."

"A fallen world? What are you talkin about?"

"O.K., let's go back to the beginning. Why were we created? Why are we here?"

"I don't know, but I'm sure your gonna tell me."

"For fellowship with God. There's only one God, but He wanted fellowship so He created mankind—actually He created angels first, but that's another story."

"O.K., so He created us. That doesn't explain...."

"Slow down, Ace, I'm getting to that. So He created mankind and put us in paradise. I bet you didn't know that originally we were supposed to live forever—no death or disease?"

"How do you know that?"

"It's in the bible. Check it out. Anyway, we were supposed to live forever, except Adam and Eve disobeyed God and sin and death entered the world. That's what's known as 'original sin'. That's why people had to start offering animal sacrifices since they had no soul and could not sin. Their blood was pure. People had to provide sacrifices to ask God for forgiveness for sin."

"I never heard that. I mean I always heard about sacrifices, but I never understood why they had to do it. If God told people to provide sacrifices, then why is it considered evil to do it today?"

"Because when Jesus came He became the sacrifice for the whole world. He was without sin and His blood was pure, and He gave himself for all other sinners—like you and me—well, more for you. So anybody that's sacrificing animals today is saying that Jesus died in vain—or else they are making an offering to Satan."

"Wow," said Ethan, "that's pretty heavy. But I still don't understand why things have to be the way they are. If God is so powerful that He can do anything, why couldn't He create a world without pain and death?"

"O.K., let me tell you how my father told it. You and I don't have any kids yet—at least I don't, I don't know about you."

"Funny."

"Anyway, let's say in a few years you have a child. You want the best for that child, right?"

"Of course."

"You want the child to be safe, to not get hurt, to always do what's right, right?"

"Yeah."

"We'll how you gonna to do that? You could keep them in a padded room all their life. You could control everything they do. You could protect them every minute of their life and make every decision for them. Or you could bring them up the best way you know how and let them make their own decisions. If you don't, they are nothin more than a robot or a puppet."

"Yeah, but I'm not God."

"Glad you realized that, Ace, but it's the same. God had to give us our free will, and when He did He had to let us make all our decisions, good or bad. He couldn't say I'm gonna let you make what ever decision you want as long as it's what I tell you to do. Does that make sense?"

Much of it did make sense, however, it was too much to take in at one time. He would have to think about what his friend had said. He was sure they would have other conversations in the future.

"I have one other question for you," said Ethan.

"What's that?"

"Why do you call me Ace?"

"What?" he laughed. "After all these years you now want to know why I call you Ace?"

"I figured if I ignored you long enough you would stop but it hasn't worked. So?"

"O.K.," he continued, "it's because you always talked about Jim Maloney—you remember—the Ace pitcher of the Reds. Always complaining how he was underrated. I figure you're underrated so your name should be Ace."

"Oh well," said Ethan, "I had to ask."

FIVE

The next afternoon Ethan was in the living room watching the rerun of the Tennessee-Alabama game when the phone rang. His mother spoke a few words then called him to the kitchen.

"Ethan, someone wants to talk to you," she called.

"Who is it?"

"Just come get the phone."

He walked to the kitchen and took the phone from his mother.

"Hello."

"Hello," came the stranger's voice. "Is this young Mr. Ward?"

"Yes, sir," he answered curiously.

"Ethan, this is Senator Coleman calling from Nashville. I'm just calling to thank you for saving my wife and daughter's life's. I can never tell you how grateful I am—we all are, son."

"Oh, thank you," he replied, somewhat embarrassed. "I really didn't do much."

"It sounds like it's true what I've heard about you. You sound like a fine young man. I'm coming over there this evening and I'd like to meet you and show my appreciation for what you've done. Can we get together tomorrow?"

"Well, you really don't have to do anything, sir. I just happened to be in the right place at the right time. Besides, I have school tomorrow."

"Of course you do," he said with a laugh, "So why don't I come by after school and I can take you to a nice place for dinner. We can talk about your future plans and maybe see how I can help. Afterward, if my wife and daughter are feeling up to it, maybe we can go by the hospital and you can meet them. At least let me do that."

"Oh, O.K." Ethan said.

"Then I'll see you tomorrow around four."

"That's fine," he said.

"And if you want, son, you can bring your girlfriend."

"Thank you, sir," he said, "Good bye."

"See you tomorrow, son."

Ethan was still in shock as he hung up the phone. Because of the statement he had made about Rachel—leaving it up to him—he figured he already knew her involvement—or lack thereof—in the incident, or else he would have called her himself. Ethan also knew that if she heard about it and was not invited, she would be furious. But at the same time he could not bring himself to recognize someone who would have stood by while others died. He would not tell her.

––––––––––––

Ethan's meeting with the Senator was quite enjoyable. The Senator was discreet enough to take him to a nice restaurant in nearby Johnson City—somewhere Ethan would not be recognized by the townspeople—and they could talk uninterrupted. They talked of many things—the accident, Ethan's plans for the future, his father's cancer. He did not mention his experience with the Deputy when he was younger. He saw no need, and wished to put the incident behind him forever. He wondered if the Senator was aware of what had happened and was too polite to discuss it.

Even though it was well after visiting hours, the Senator had no problem in getting them in to see his family. They were even more excited to see their rescuer than the Senator had been. His daughter, Tina, reached out and give him a hug.

"It's my guardian angel," she said.

"No, just someone who happened to be in the right place at the right time," he responded.

Mrs. Campbell, who had been sitting in the chair near the wall, arose and also hugged her rescuer.

"Words can never tell how thankful we are, Ethan," she said. "We are eternally grateful."

The four sat and talked like old friends. At ten thirty the nurse insisted they leave. As the men started to leave Tina called to Ethan,

"You know, now that you saved me you are responsible for protecting me the rest of my life."

"Then I guess you better move to Greenville," he returned.

Before dropping him off at home, the Senator made him promise to call if he ever needed help. All in all, Ethan decided, it was a remarkable day.

Things had calmed down considerably since the car accident which was fine with Ethan. He was able to concentrate on his studies and help his mother more with his father. While his father seemed to be getting better, he was still weak. He had finished the last of the chemotherapy treatments a few weeks earlier, but Ethan could not understand why it was taking so long to recover. He was just now beginning to get his appetite back. His hope was to have all his strength back by Thanksgiving, a goal which his wife thought very ambitious. Even so, Ethan was happy to see his father recovering. He even felt well enough to attend a football game with him, although they had to leave early.

It had been very uncomfortable attending the football games lately since he had broken up with Rachel. She had not taken the breakup well, which Ethan did not understand since she had little feelings for anyone but herself. He figured that most of her anger was from the fact that someone had the nerve to break up with her. He tried to avoid her as much as possible and spent most of his time with Tommy and his other friends.

It was two weeks before Christmas and Ethan was busy with many things. Because of the holiday rush he was working more hours at Western Auto. He had yet to finish his Christmas shopping so planned to do that when he got off work that Saturday afternoon.

And he still had his homework for the weekend which he had not started. He quickly came in the door and headed toward his bedroom to change into blue jeans when his father called to him from his room.

"Ethan," he said, "you got a strange lookin letter there on the table. You might want ta check it out."

Ethan went to the dining room and picked up the envelope. It was a simple brown envelope with his name written in block letters but it had no return address. He noticed that it was post marked from Murfreesboro, Tennessee. He had heard of it but wasn't even sure where it was. He removed a road map from a kitchen drawer and saw that it was just south of Nashville. He opened the envelope and removed the contents. Inside was a handwritten note, again in block letters which said,"

> "Mr. Ward:
>   Young man, I was traveling through your county a few weeks ago and read about your actions saving those people in the accident. I think this country does not have enough heroes. Please accept this small token of my gratitude for your actions. I know you will use it wisely.
>   A Friend.
>   P.S. Now you are obligated to help a stranger sometime in your life.

Attached to the letter was a money order for $5,000. He could not believe his eyes. He ran to show his father and showed him the letter and check.

"Ain't that somethin'," his father kept repeating, "ain't that somethin'."

"Who do you think it's from?" asked Ethan.

"You know who it's from. Your new friend the Senator. Can't be nobody else."

"I was so excited I didn't even think of him," he returned. "I can't keep this. I need to call him."

"Now hold on, son," he said as he put his hand on his arm. "First of all, if he wanted you ta call him he would have signed his name. Second, you should just keep the money. If it is the Senator he's got more money than he knows what ta do with, with all those car dealerships he owns over in Knoxville. This money will let you go ta college and then, like the letter says, someday you can help somebody else out."

"Well, I don't know. I guess I'll wait until Mom gets home and see what she thinks. Of course it sure would be nice to be able to go to college. Dad, whatever I decide, let's not tell anyone else about this, O.K?"

"Whatever you say, son. It's your money."

His mother soon returned home from shopping and was greeted by her excited son. He could not wait to show her the letter and check. She was as shocked as they had been.

"Honey, this is unbelievable," she stated. "Who do you think it's from?"

"Daddy says the Senator. What do you think?"

"I don't know. Even though he seems like a real nice man, he's still a politician. Politicians almost always want publicity. Of course he could have done it this way since he knows how much you hate publicity. Can you think of any one else?"

"Right, Mom. I got plenty of people I know who have an extra $5,000 to give away. I have no idea who it is."

"Well, the question is what are you going to do? You can't send it back because you don't know who it came from. So you can either cash it or burn it."

"What do you think?"

"I think that is your decision, but I don't see any problem taking it. Who ever sent it obviously can afford it, and they wanted to do something good for somebody. You should consider using it for your college fund. And you know, son, with the war on now, it could keep you from being drafted."

"O.K.," he said, "I guess I'll have to think about it, but please don't tell anybody."

Both his parents nodded. Ethan put the letter back in the envelope and took it to his room where he put it on the dresser. He sat staring at it, wondering what unexpected turn his life would take next.

SIX

AUGUST 1968

Middle Tennessee State University is located thirty miles south-east of Nashville in the town of Murfreesboro. Students there boast that it is the geographical center of Tennessee, and likely the known universe. Murfreesboro, a town of over 20,000, had the feel of small town America, but still offered most of the amenities of a major city. The things that it lacked could be found in nearby Nashville. There was currently discussion among the town leaders of restoring a section of the town to its original early American condition. The community, known as Cannonsburgh Village, currently had a number of older buildings dating back to the turn of the century. The discussion centered around turning the area into a walking museum.

Middle Tennessee State University (MTSU) began in 1909 as a teacher's school. In 1925 it evolved into a four-year college. In 1965 the college was granted University status. Currently, while it offered a wide curriculum, its main emphasis was still in the education field.

Ethan considered many alternatives before deciding to attend MTSU. He visited the University of Tennessee in Knoxville but decided against it. Although he loved their sports teams, and found the campus to be very beautiful, he also found it to be big and impersonal. And its location—only one hour from home was another factor in eliminating it. Although he was very close to his parents, he decided it was time he became more independent. An hour's drive from his parents did not lend itself to independence.

At his brother's insistence, he also looked at Cumberland College in Williamsburg, Kentucky. While it was a much smaller college—and he did love its quaintness—he rejected it for much the same reason—too close to home. However its location was not the primary or only reason for selecting MTSU. It was also the right size—not so big that he felt he would be lost in the crowd—but large enough to offer things a smaller college did not. Those included a full sports program—football, basketball, baseball—even track and volleyball. And while he wasn't sure he would play a sport, he at least wanted that option.

However, the main reason for choosing the school was the curriculum. In his last year in high school he had decided he wanted to go into education or journalism, both fields in which MTSU had an excellent reputation. Whether he decided to be a teacher or a writer, he felt the school could provide him with the skills he would need. And he had until next year before he had to declare his major.

The fact that he had made the right decision regarding what school to attend did little to ease the apprehension as he arrived on campus that Wednesday afternoon with his parents. He was also somewhat embarrassed by his father's old beat up truck, but it was needed in order to carry all of his supplies. At least he didn't yet know anyone on campus. They found his dorm building and parked near the entrance. Luckily it was the first day for move-in so there were few other students in the building. He and his father began moving in his personal affects as his mother examined and organized his room. As they carried items up the steps he thought of how lucky they were that his father had beaten the cancer. He was again his old self with none of the lingering effects of the illness. An added bonus was that, at his son's insistence, he had quit smoking.

They finished the move and drove to a nearby restaurant for lunch. It was a little after three when they returned to the dorm. Ethan's mother stated, for the third time, that she did not understand why he needed to be there so soon when classes would not start for almost a week. Ethan explained once again that he needed time to register, buy books, and get accustomed to the campus. He also planned on looking for a part time job if he could find one to suit his schedule. In reality he knew that his mother's real issue was that she did not want to leave her son—whether it was this week or next. He wasn't sure if it was simply a mother's sadness over her son leaving home, or that she was still concerned for his safety. It had been over five years since he had witnessed the murder, and no arrest had ever been made. While he knew that after all that time there was virtually no possibility anyone would be looking for him, he also knew that a mother's concern is not always rational.

By four o'clock his parents had left, leaving him alone for the first time in his life. He felt a sense of independence, although, it was also a little frightening. Rather than dwell on it, he busied himself readying his new room. He worked for a couple of hours then took a walk to get acquainted with the layout of the campus. He stopped for pizza at a nearby restaurant and returned to his room by eight o'clock. He continued working in his room until eleven and fell asleep.

The next afternoon more students arrived at the campus. He was going over the college's rules and regulations when the door opened and a young man walked in. He was skinny—almost frail looking—with long hair and glasses. He stopped and looked at the number on the door.

"If you're looking for room 2b this is it," said Ethan. "You must be Rudy."

"Yes, Rudolph Reynolds from Louisville," he answered nervously.

Ethan reached out and shook his hand which was cold and clammy. The kid was obviously more nervous than he had been.

"Ethan Ward from Greenville, Tennessee," he said. "Welcome."

"Thanks," said his new roommate. "Which bed is mine?"

"Well, I took the one to the right, but I really don't care if you want to change."

"O.K." he said as he walked past him into the room. He said nothing more as he went about unpacking his two suitcases and putting his clothes away. Ethan turned to him.

"Is that all the stuff you have?" he asked.

"Oh, no. My parents came with me. They went to get sand-

wiches. They will be back in a few minutes with my other things."
He turned back to unpacking, saying nothing more.

Ethan could not figure out if he was extremely shy or just nervous. Whatever the reason, he decided to leave him alone for now. Soon Rudolph's parents appeared at the door. Ethan decided they were just as weird as their son so, after introducing himself, he made up an excuse to leave the dorm. He returned a while later after they had left. He decided it was better to have a strange and quiet roommate than a loud and obnoxious one.

The following afternoon Ethan found a part time job at the campus bookstore. It was only twelve hours a week, and only paid $1.10 an hour, but it fit in with his schedule and would provide more than enough money to meet his needs.

It was Friday afternoon and the beginning of his first weekend on campus. And, with classes beginning Monday morning, it would be the last carefree weekend for some time. While he wanted to enjoy the next couple of days he had decided that would not be possible in the company of his new roommate. His idea of a good time was watching re-runs of Bonanza on the dorm TV. Ethan had made a few other acquaintances though. Friday night he had pizza with his new friends. Saturday morning a number of guys got together for a game of touch football. That evening he and two other young men took a bus into town to see "Butch Cassidy and the Sundance Kid," a movie which they all enjoyed." They later stopped into a small Irish pub to listen to music. Since all of the boys were under twenty they could not order alcoholic beverages. Although it did not bother Ethan since he did not drink, he thought it unfair that someone his age could be called on to defend his country and possibly even die, but could not drink alcohol nor vote. It did not take long before the boys struck up a conversation with three coeds. Unfortunately the ladies, who were juniors, quickly discovered their ages and lost interest. Ethan was in his room and in bed by midnight, thinking how proud his mother would be.

He spent an uneventful day Sunday, readying himself for his classes the following day. Monday was a big day, with three of his classes beginning. It was a significant change from his high school days. While he didn't feel that the teachers were heartless, he did believe that they would have little concern should any student fail. Tuesday he only had one class, but worked from noon until four at the campus bookstore.

The next few weeks saw him fall into a routine—classes, work, and study during the week, and study, football, and partying with his friends on the weekend. In the next few weeks he met a couple of girls whom he dated, although nothing serious became of either relationship.

The first week of October was parents weekend and Ethan was visited by his mother and father as well as his brother. Horace informed him that he had just accepted a job as Assistant HR Manager at a bank in Kingsport. While he was excited, now that his draft status was again 1A he was concerned that he may be getting a "Greetings" letter from the Selective Service board. Since he had no control over it, he had to continue with his life. Ethan enjoyed a quiet day with his family, watching the Tennessee Football game in the afternoon, before they returned home. He saw them again at Thanksgiving before returning to school for the last two weeks of the semester. After two more weeks of class and one week of testing, he was on his way home with his first semester of college behind him.

Christmas was always an enjoyable time at the Ward household, and this year was especially so. Buster Ward had been cancer free for almost a year. Their oldest son had just graduated from college in the spring and was now working at a bank. And their youngest son was now a freshman at MTSU and doing well. A surprise was added this holiday season when Horace called to tell his parents his girlfriend and he had just become engaged and she would be joining them for the holiday.

To save his parents a trip, Ethan got a ride home from a classmate who was traveling to Bristol. He arrived at home on the fourteenth. The time at home he spent relaxing, visiting old friends, playing basketball at the high school gym, and shooting pool at the recreation hall at Tommy's church. Before he knew it, it was

Christmas Eve. As always, his mother had the house decorated beautifully. Wreaths were hung on the doors; garlands adorned the railings; and Christmas lights were strung along the edge of the house as well as in the bushes. Inside the house the aroma of cinnamon and apple cider permeated every room. The Christmas tree, placed strategically in the center of the living room, was adorned with ornaments and memorabilia from Christmases past as well as freshly made popcorn balls and peppermint candy canes. Candles were scattered throughout, casting magical shadows on the wall.

It was a little after nine when the Ward family returned from candle light service. They gathered around the living room while Mrs. Ward poured eggnog and placed cookies on a platter. Horace turned the radio to a station playing Christmas music. They made a toast and wished each other a Merry Christmas. Following tradition, each member was allowed to open one present. Ethan chose one from his brother. It was a Tennessee Volunteer sweatshirt.

"About time," said Ethan with a laugh, "My old one is ready to be used as a polishing cloth."

"Well," said his brother, "you better not be wearing that around campus. Someone just might take offense."

"Oh, it looks like your little brother is pretty capable of taking care of himself," said his new fiancée, Emily.

The family continued to open presents and joke with one another until after ten o'clock. At that time, Horace announced that he and Emily had to leave. It was about an hour's drive to her parents' house in Johnson City, and they had promised to spend Christmas morning with them. They said good-bye and Ethan and his parents sat at the kitchen table enjoying another cup of eggnog. It was not long before his father turned in for the night leaving Ethan and his mother alone.

"Well, son," she began, "I can't believe how much you have changed. You are a young man—no longer my little boy," she added with a smile but a tear in her eye.

"I'll always be your little boy, Mom," he said. "Just a big, little boy."

She smiled and patted his hand.

"Well, I ran into an old friend of yours today," she continued, changing the subject.

"Oh yeah," said Ethan, expecting what she was about to say.

"Yes, Rachel. She asked about you."

"That's nice."

"She's taking music lessons now, you know. She wants to be a singer."

"That doesn't surprise me. They can get a lot of attention."

"I still don't understand why you two broke up," said his mother. "She seems like a nice girl."

"Mom," said Ethan with a sigh of exasperation, "trust me. You don't know her. She has never done anything for anyone but herself. And she is also a racist. I can't believe you haven't noticed that."

"Well I have never had any deep conversations with her, son, so I will have to take your word. But people do change you know. And your father isn't exactly the most open minded person when it comes to that."

"Well, at least he tolerates people different from him. And believe me, Rachel hasn't changed. And if you got to know her, I think you would agree with me. Can we drop the subject?"

"Sure, Ethan. It's just a shame—you two make the most adorable couple."

They talked of other things—of Ethan's still undecided future plans; of the war; of his brother's new job and future wife. Finally, when his mother got up from the table, he noticed she was moving stiffly.

"Are you O.K.?" he asked.

"Oh yeah, she returned with a wave of her hand. "It's just a little stiff back."

"How long have you had it?"

"A few weeks now."

"You been to the doctor?"

"Yes, he didn't see anything serious. Said it was probably muscular and should go away in time. He gave me pain pills and muscle relaxants I can take when I want but they make me drowsy. It's fine, son. It'll go away in time."

He watched with concern as his mother shuffled down the hall. How old was she now? Only forty-eight. Not that old—and hopefully too young to start having health problems.

SEVEN

WINTER, 1969

A new year had begun. The holiday break was over and Ethan was back at school, still trying to recover from his beloved Tennessee Volunteer's loss to Texas in the Cotton Bowl. But within a few days his hectic schedule had driven all thoughts of the game from his mind. The manager at the campus bookstore was quick to appreciate his work ethic and integrity, and had increased his hours to fifteen per week. He had also raised his salary to $1.30 per hour, which was considerable for a part time employee.

Ethan was alone in the store at closing time when two young ladies approached him. One was Asian and the other was black, and he could not help but notice how beautiful they both were. The Asian girl was taller and more statuesque with long black hair, high cheekbones, and dark brooding eyes. The black girl was shorter—he estimated about five feet two—and one of the most beautiful girls he had ever seen. She had the face of a cherub—full cheeks and round, innocent eyes. He wondered if they might be models. The two glanced around the store, then walked toward him. The Asian girl smiled as she approached.

"I didn't know we had movie stars working here?" she began. Ethan's face quickly turned red—a response she was obviously hoping for. A quick glance at her friend told him she shared his embarrassment.

"Can I help you?" he asked, ignoring her remark.

"I'm sure you could," she said with a shake of her head, "but right now we just need a book."

"Sure," he said. "Which one?"

She became serious enough to give him the name of the book they were looking for. She stated that they were taking the same English Literature class and the teacher had added a book at the last minute. Ethan directed the girls to the books, which they took and placed on the counter.

"So, do you know anything about English Literature?" the Asian girl asked as she tilted her head and smiled.

"Uh, yeah, Shakespeare, Chaucer, Dunn. That's about it."

"That's more than me. Maybe I can come see you when I need some help."

Ethan looked at her then quickly at her friend who simply smiled and rolled her eyes. Not knowing how to respond he simply said, "Well, we're open every day from ten to three."

She watched him with a smile as he nervously rang up their purchases. The black girl paid first and politely said, "Thank you." The Asian girl removed a ten dollar bill from her purse, wrote her dorm and room number on it and handed it to him.

"In case there is a recall on this book I thought you might like to have a way to get in touch with me," she said with a smile.

"Thank you," said Ethan, his smile tepid. The girls put their books in the bag, turned and walked away. Ethan shook his head and began preparations to close the store. Before leaving he returned to the cash register and removed the ten-dollar bill and replaced it with one from his wallet. He wondered how angry the girl would be if he contacted her and asked for her friend's name.

For the next few days he carried the bill with him trying to decide what to do. The girl had obviously been attracted to him—or perhaps she flirted with all the guys like that. And while she was quite beautiful, he had never been attracted to women that aggressive. Her friend he found even more beautiful. And she appeared to be more sensitive and understanding. But he had never dated a black girl before—or Asian either for that matter. What would she do if he should ask her out? Would she reject him? Had the look in her eyes only been one of compassion for his embarrassment? And what if she did go out with him? Times were changing but there still was little interracial dating on campus. He had not even spoken to the girl and had already complicated the situation. He carried the bill in his wallet for a few days and finally spent it at the campus pool hall.

The next couple of weeks were routine. Ethan attended class, worked at the bookstore, and studied. He began playing volleyball and basketball whenever he had a spare evening. He went out with friends to the local pub or to a movie on weekends, but never ran in to either of the girls from the bookstore. Most weeknights he studied, sometimes in his room and sometimes at the library, if for no other reason than to get away from Rudy. While he had not had a conflict with his roommate, he found him very uncomfortable to be around. He never smiled or laughed or said anything even remotely humorous. And he worried continually—whether it was about school, or money, or what his parents might think. As he had said to Tommy in a letter, 'he was born without a personality'. Tonight he was in the dorm lounge watching TV. While Ethan was grateful for the solitude, he realized, like every other night, he would be returning to the room at nine sharp. He decided to go to the library to complete his studies.

It was a bitter cold night with temperatures expected to reach ten degrees by morning. He put on his Tennessee Volunteer sweatshirt and threw a jacket over it. The walk to the library was only five minutes, but still enough time to feel the effects of the cold. There were only a half dozen or so other students there. He found a table by himself and began studying his "History of Western Civilization" textbook. He found it quite interesting—to read the details of people and events from another time. After a half hour of reading he closed his book and left to find something to drink. He walked into the nearby snack room, put a quarter in the Pepsi machine, and watched as the can lodged in the bottom of the machine. He put his hand in the slot but could not reach it. He gently shook the machine trying to jar it loose. When that did not work he shook it harder. Finally, out of desperation, he hit the machine on the side, still to no avail.

"Here, try this," came a voice from behind. He turned to see the black girl from the bookstore holding out a quarter to him. "Put this in and it should jar the other one out."

"O.K.," he agreed as he took the coin from her and slid it into the machine. They watched together as the second can became lodged behind the other. They looked at each other and began to laugh.

"That went well," she said "Maybe we should give up and just have hot chocolate."

"That sounds good," said Ethan as they moved to the coffee machine. "It's probably better for you on a night like this anyway."

"My name is Sally," she offered as she held out her hand.

"Ethan—Ethan Ward," he said. "You're alone tonight?"

"Yes, Kim had other plans. Were you looking for her?"

"Oh, no," he stammered, "I mean she seemed like a nice girl. It's not that I didn't want to see her....but I didn't mean I was looking for her."

She just smiled and watched as the machine poured out the hot chocolate.

"Are you studying in here?" she asked.

"Yes, well just reading. What about you?"

"I just came in to copy information from some magazines for a report I'm doing."

"Oh," he said as he took his cup from the machine and walked back toward the library. "Well I'm sitting right over there if you would like to join me."

"Thank you," she said, "that would be nice. Let me get the magazines I'm looking for and I will be right back."

He watched her as she walked away, thinking how beautiful she was. She also had an air of innocence about her, yet did not appear naïve. He returned to his table and attempted to concentrate on his book. She returned with a handful of magazines and sat across from him.

"What are you working on?" he asked.

"It's a report for my business ethics class—how can we justify the cost of the space program when there are so many social and economic problems in our country?"

"And your position?"

"I think you have to. We will always have problems, but the only way mankind can advance is through knowledge. And your opinion?"

"What you just said sounded good to me."

The two made small talk for a while. He told her where he was from and discovered that she was actually from Murfreesboro. Her father was an English Professor on campus, although Ethan had never heard of him. With a smile, she asked, "So, did Kim embarrass you when we were in the store?"

"Oh no," he shot back, then after a few seconds added, "well, maybe just a little. You didn't help much."

"I didn't say anything."

"That's just it. Anyway, is she always like that?"

"Pretty much. We have only been hanging out for a month or so. I like her but sometimes she goes too far."

"Are you two roommates?"

"Oh no. My roommate would be embarrassed to be in the same room with her."

"I'm surprised you live in a dorm with your father being a teacher here."

"Professor—and I wanted to be on my own."

"What does your mother do?"

She lowered her head for a second, then turned back to him before answering.

"Unfortunately she was killed a few years ago in a car accident—a drunk driver. It's still kind of hard for me to talk about."

"I'm sorry," said Ethan. "So do you have any brothers or sisters?"

"Just one sister, Merita. She's the black sheep of the family."

He laughed at her comment. "Black sheep—that's good."

"Unfortunately it's true."

"Why do you say that?"

"Oh, maybe its because she started smoking when she was twelve. Maybe it's because she started drinking at sixteen. And now she lives with about a dozen other people in Haight-Ashbury—smoking pot during the nights and protesting the war during the day."

"Sorry," said Ethan, feeling he had nothing to contribute to the subject.

They continued talking for some time. He told her about his family and his hometown. They discussed their decisions about college and careers. They began discussing their classes. She informed him she had a learning disability.

"What is it?" he asked.

"Dyslexia."

"I've heard the word, but I don't know what it means."

"Well, it's when you read something backwards. Sometimes I get letters or numbers backwards. Like I might read "God" to be "dog.""

"Oh, that could be a real problem if you are praying for something important," he joked.

"Yeah, I know," she said laughing. "Did you hear about the dyslexic, agnostic, insomniac?"

"Dyslexic, agnostic, insomniac?" he repeated, "No, I don't think so."

"He stayed awake all night wondering if there really was a dog?"

Ethan burst out laughing. Other students nearby stared. It took him a moment to recover.

"That's one of the best jokes I have heard."

"Feel free to borrow it. Just remember where you got it."

"O.K.," he agreed, then, attempting to regain some seriousness he asked, "so, is school a lot more difficult for you?"

"It's different. You have to make adjustments."

"Like how?"

"I take a tape recorder to all my classes so I can replay what the instructor said. I also take very good notes on everything. And I try to make friends with the smartest kids so I can ask questions. But one of the best things I learned is using association."

"What do you mean?"

"Well, what are you studying now?"

"About when the Romans went into England and Scotland. They tried to conquer Scotland but found the natives to be too barbarian so they built a wall across the country to keep them at bay."

"I never heard of that. So what kind of things do you need to remember about it?"

"Well, the Roman Emperor's name was Hadrian. It became known as Hadrian's Wall. The wall was about seventy miles long and eight feet high."

"O.K.," she said as she thought aloud. "Hadrian and a wall—seventy miles long and eight feet high. How about this—a man eight feet tall and weighing seventy pounds comes into a room and hangs his hat on a wall. Hat....wall....seventy pounds....eight feet high. Does that make sense?"

"Yeah, more than the guy wondering if there really was a dog. That's pretty smart."

"Well, I'll be glad to help you with your studies if you help me with mine."

"Sure," he readily agreed. "Just say when."

"How about Thursday night here at the same time?"

"Sounds good," Ethan said. She held her hand to shake. Her hand was warm and soft.

"I guess it is about closing time," she said, then added with a laugh, " I guess we got a lot of work done. Oh well, I got two weeks before my report is due. How about you?"

"I still have to read this chapter, but I can finish it in the morning before class."

"Sorry."

"Don't be. I enjoyed it," he said, then, after thinking for a second added, "do you want me to walk you to your dorm?"

"Sure," she replied. "Better pull that Volunteer sweatshirt tight. It's cold out there."

Her dorm was only a short walk from his. They chatted about the campus, the teachers, and the war in Vietnam. She told him that she had not formed an opinion on the war. He told her that he thought it was something that the country had to do, and that each day he had guilt feelings about being safe at home when so many of his friends were fighting. They were soon at her door. There was an awkward hesitation before she turned to him and thanked him for walking her home. She reached out her hand to his. He clumsily shook her hand and backed away.

"See you Thursday night," she called.

He walked back to his dorm, not really feeling the cold. Many thoughts ran through his head. He felt she was one of the most beautiful girls he had seen, with her rosy cheeks, her dark and mysterious yet innocent eyes, her black hair with just a touch of auburn. But was part of the attraction the fact that she was black? He had heard that anything forbidden was always more enticing. And although he had seen a few other interracial couples on campus, it was still quite uncommon. How would people react if they began dating? And what was her interest in him? She seemed like she was attracted to him yet she might just be looking for a friend— someone to study with. The only thing that he was certain about at the present was that he would be at the library Thursday evening.

EIGHT

The next morning Ethan thought about calling the campus operator and getting Sally's phone number, but remembered that she had not given him her last name. This became another thing for him to worry about—did she do it intentionally because she did not want him to call her? If so, why did she let him walk her to her room? Maybe she didn't want to give him her last name when they first met and just forgot to later. And even if he could call her what would he say? Would he ask her out for the weekend? After a few minutes he attempted to put it out of his mind. He would see her in a couple of days to study again anyway.

It was a little after five on Thursday when the phone in Ethan's room rang. He turned down his radio to answer it.

"Hello," he said.

"Hi. Is this Ethan?" came the female's voice.

"Yes."

"Hi Ethan. It's Sally—you know—is there really a dog?"

"Yes," he said with a laugh.

"I'm sorry to bother you but—well I just went to the gym and came back to my room to take a shower and our whole building is without hot water. I hate to ask but would I be able to come there to take a shower? I don't want to go all the way back over to the gym."

"Of course," he replied quickly.

"Are you sure? I don't want to cause any trouble for you. I know the rule about women being in the men's dorm but I'll be out long before curfew. Do you think your roommate would mind?"

"Well, he's not here right now. He actually went out to get something to eat with a friend. So no, it's no problem. Are we still going to go study?"

"Sure, if that is O.K."

"Great, then come on over."

"Thanks. I'll be there in a few minutes."

Ethan began to look around their dorm room at the clutter. It was not too bad. He picked up the magazines and newspapers from the floor then quickly swept. He made his bed then turned on the stereo and sat nervously browsing through a magazine waiting for her to arrive.

Soon there came a knock at the door. Sally stood at the entrance wearing a sweatsuit and carrying a bag. She wore no make-up and her hair was matted from her workout, but she was as beautiful as ever.

"Hi," she said, "I really appreciate you doing this."

"No problem," he said.

"I hated to ask, but there is no hot water for our whole building, and the only other people I could ask were on the other side of the campus.

"It's no problem," he repeated as he stood aside to let her in. "Do you want something to drink first?"

"No thanks. If you want we could go get a sandwich before we go to the library though. I'm buying."

"You don't have to do that—buy I mean. But that would be fine."

She removed her jacket as he directed her to the bathroom, the one area that he had forgotten to clean. Sheepishly he said, "I'm sorry, the bathroom is probably pretty dirty. I can clean it for you."

"It's fine," she said, as she looked in. "It's actually cleaner than ours. I'll only be a few minutes."

After hearing the sound of running water he seated himself in the chair and returned to his magazine. Soon the sound of the running water was replaced by that of her hair dryer. She soon emerged looking as beautiful as she had the first day they met.

"That was quick," he said.

"I had to learn to be quick when I was young or my sister would make me pay."

"She sounds like an interesting person."

"Well, if you are really unlucky maybe you will meet her someday."
Ethan tried to not read too much into her comment.

"So, where do you want to go eat?" he asked.

"I don't care. Someplace where we can get a burger or sandwich. Is that O.K.? "

"Sounds good to me," he said as he picked up her jacket and handed it to her. As he put on his coat he added, "How about Lenny's? It's only a ten-minute walk from here. And since my room is on the way back we can leave our stuff here and get it on the way to the library. Is that O.K.?"

"Sounds like a plan," she said. He helped her with her jacket as they left the room.

The weather had warmed up considerably in the last couple of days, but the temperature was still in the thirties. The air was crisp and fresh with no clouds to block the view of the stars. They arrived at Lenny's, a small cafe on the edge of the campus which drew customers from the college as well as the local community. The restaurant was less than half full as they entered. While Ethan expected people to stare at them, that was not the case—or at least if it were, they were very discreet. The waiter seated them near a window. They examined the menu, decided to share a pizza and made small talk as they waited for their order.

"So," said Sally, "don't you think it's a little dangerous to be wearing a Volunteer sweatshirt while you're here?"

"No, not really," he said. "You'd be surprised at the number of people here who love the Vols. We're not rivals you know."

"Yeah, neither us nor Vandy really has much of a football program. Did you hear the one about us playing the Commodores?"

"No, I don't think so," he said cautiously, remembering her last joke.

"Yeah, the score was tied zero to zero in the fourth quarter. A train went by and blew the whistle. The Commodores thought it was the end of the game and walked off the field. We scored four plays later."

"Right," he said, laughing. "You like a good joke don't you?"

"Sure, people are too serious. But if you love Tennessee so much why didn't you go there?"

He explained his reasons for selecting MTSU, then asked her about her decision."

"To be honest," she said, "because of my father I never really considered anywhere else."

"Oh, you mean because he's a Professor here?"

"No, not really. It's more because of what happened to my mother. He has never really recovered. And then my sister left for the West coast. I really couldn't leave him. I thought of going to Vanderbilt, but this is just as good and less expensive."

"So, you didn't get a scholarship?"

"Are you kidding? You must be forgetting about my little handicap. I was lucky to get in college at all."

"Oh, sorry," he said. "Anyway, what is your major?"

"Education. I thought everyone here was planning on being a teacher," she said. "Aren't you?"

"Well, I still haven't decided but teaching is one possibility. I'm also considering journalism."

They continued talking until their pizza came. There was one question Ethan wanted answered. He asked, "If you told me I apologize, but I don't remember your last name."

"I don't think I told you, but it's Robertson. And yours is Ward—right?"

"Right."

It was almost seven by the time they had finished their meal and left the restaurant. Ethan attempted to pay the bill but Sally insisted on doing so in return for using his shower. She compromised by allowing him to leave the tip.

Once back at his room she stated she needed to use the restroom before they left for the library. He was waiting for her to return when he heard the knock at the door. He figured it was Rudy, since he had forgotten his keys on two other occasions. He absent-mindedly opened the door only to be stunned at the person waiting.

"Rachel!" he exclaimed.

"Hi, Ethan," she said calmly. "It's good to see you."

"What....what are you doing here?" he stammered.

"Well thanks for making me feel so welcome, but I'm living here now. Actually up in Smyrna which is almost in Nashville."

"Yeah I know where it is, but what....what are you doing there?'

"I got a job. Didn't your mother tell you I have been taking music and singing lessons. I plan on being a recording star. Are you going to ask me in or not?"

He looked around the room, trying to think of an easy way out of the predicament. There did not seem to be one. She solved the problem by walking past him into the room. As he tried to determine how to handle the situation Sally walked out of the bathroom. He worried about what Rachel's reaction might be, but she acted calmly and politely. Before he could respond she put out her hand and introduced herself.

"Hi, I'm Rachel Mills—Ethan's old girlfriend from back home."

"Oh... uh, hi," said, Sally.

"Yes, this is Sally Robertson," injected Ethan. "We were just going to the library to study. We help each other."

"Oh, I'll bet you do," said Rachel smugly.

"Rachel!" Ethan said sharply. Sally ignored her remark but picked up her jacket and bag.

"Well I'm sure you two have a lot of catching up to do so I will be going," said Sally

"That's not necessary," said Ethan.

"It's fine," she said as she walked toward the door. "We can study another time."

"It was good meeting you," said Rachel smugly as she walked out the door. Sally did not respond.

After she left Ethan stood staring at his old girlfriend

"Why did you do that?" he demanded.

"Do what?"

"You know exactly what. What right do you have to come in here like that—make a comment like that!"

"Ethan," she said calmly as she sat down, "you are right. That comment was un-called for and I apologize. Maybe I was a little jealous."

"Jealous! We haven't been together for over a year. How can you say that you are jealous?"

"Unfortunately it's true, Ethan," she said solemnly. "I'm sure your mother told you I was asking about you. I kept hoping you would call but you never did. So I just thought if I came by we could get together and work things out."

"I thought you said you came here to be a singing star?"

"I want that also, Ethan, but I thought....well I just thought that if I came by while I was living here that maybe things would be different and we could get back together. I didn't mean to cause any problem for you. I know you think I am a monster but I am not. I will be glad to apologize to your friend for my comment. Are you two dating?"

"We are just friends," he said. "We just met and decided to go study together. She just had to go to use my bathroom."

"She sure is cute."

"I guess," he murmured.

She sat with her hands crossed looking at the floor. There was an uncomfortable silence as each waited for the other to speak. Finally she said, "Look Ethan, it's true that I am sometimes self centered and thoughtless—I guess even a little narrow minded at times. But I'm not such a terrible person. And we had some good times together. I thought, since we've both grown up, maybe we could start over. I'm only living about a half-hour away and....well, anyway, I guess this was not such a good idea."

She got up and walked toward the door. Before leaving she turned back to him.

"I'm really sorry for any problem I caused. Please tell your friend."

She turned to walk out. He tried to deal with his feelings. Had he always been too critical of her? Was it possible that she had matured in the past year? This was the first time he had ever seen her so vulnerable....so apologetic. The least he could do would be to talk to her for a while.

"Look, Rachel," he said, "why don't you sit down and we can talk. I mean, you drove all this way so you should at least sit and rest for a few minutes. Can I get you something to drink? We have a little ice box with sodas."

"That would be nice."

They sat and talked for a while. Despite his caution Ethan discovered he was enjoying himself. She seemed although not exactly a new person, at least a much nicer version of the old. They talked about the people back home, about what she had been doing since high school, and her decision to become a country and western star.

"That really surprises me. You never told me you had any desire to do something like that."

"I didn't know," she said. "Terry and Renee and I went into Knoxville one weekend to do some shopping and spent the night at a hotel. They had a bar there and it was amateur's night and, after a couple of beers, the girls dared me to go up and sing. So I did and the crowd really liked me. Everybody said I had real talent. I mean, I always sang in the shower and in church, but I never thought I had any talent. Anyway, the best part, Ethan, was that I loved it. It really made me feel great. So I took some singing lessons and I started performing with a group out of Kingsport. We have been playing at local nightclubs on weekends, but you don't get much publicity around there. So my cousin told me about this place in Nashville where a lot of people have been discovered, so here I am."

"So where are you staying?"

"My cousin knew somebody in Smyrna who had an apartment for rent so I am staying there. I work at a restaurant during the day, practice my music during the evening, and sing when I can on talent nights."

"When did you get here?"

"A couple of weeks ago. I already had one group ask if I would like to try out for their band. I'm supposed to audition soon."

"Country and Western, I assume?"

"Yeah, I sort of model myself after Lynda Ronstadt—a crossover country,"

While Ethan was still irritated with her, he could not deny that he was still attracted to her. He felt sorry that Sally had been embarrassed and still did not know what he should do about it. Still he found himself at least entertaining the idea of getting back together with her.

They talked for a few more minutes before she abruptly got up. "Well, I guess I really should go. I've caused enough problems around here. If you decide you want to get together you can call me."

She handed him a piece of paper with her number on it. "And please tell Sally that I apologize for being so catty. She seems like a nice girl."

He stared at the number as he thought of his response.

"Well, maybe I will come by and watch you perform," he said.

"That will be great. I was planning on going to "Arnell's" Saturday. Amateur's can go up on stage during the band's break. You want to go?"

"Sure," he said, "if I can get there."

"That's right—you don't have a car. That's O.K. I can come and get you. How about around seven?"

"That sounds O.K."

She started to walk away then turned and kissed him on the cheek. Without thinking he returned the kiss. She smiled and walked away.

"See you Saturday," she said as she closed the door.

After she left, Ethan sat pondering what had just happened. He would have never expected Rachel to show up here, let alone him agreeing to see her again. Was he a fool? But she had seemed very sincere. It was the first time he could ever remember her apologizing. Maybe she had matured. And she certainly was as beautiful as ever. He could not deny how attracted he was to her.

But what about Sally? He didn't know yet if she had considered him more than a friend—just someone to talk to and study with. Even if she were attracted to him, what was the chance of their relationship lasting? Regardless, she was such a nice girl he would have to go by and apologize and see if she still wanted to study together.

The following afternoon he stopped at her dorm room on the way back from class. Her roommate called her to the door. He apologized for Rachel's behavior and asked if she would like to go study another night. While she was polite, she told him that perhaps they could get together sometime but she was going to be tied up for the next week. Ethan did not know how to respond so simply said he would talk to her soon. She watched from behind the blinds as he walked away.

NINE

As she had promised, Rachel was at Ethan's dorm room promptly at seven Saturday. Rudy answered the door and was stunned by how beautiful his roommate's friend looked. She was wearing a tight plaid skirt with a low-cut blue silk blouse. Her long flowing blond hair accented her black leather jacket. It made Ethan feel good to see Rudy's reaction. They sat and talked for a while, then Ethan showed her around the campus. They climbed into her car—a new Ford Torino which her father had recently bought for her.

They stopped at the local Shoney's restaurant before going to the nightclub. Ethan began to notice how much she had changed—how pleasant she had become. Unlike in high school when he worried constantly over who she might slander or attack next, he became at ease talking to her. And, rather than focus the conversation on herself, she asked him about his classes and plans for the future. The time passed quickly. At eight thirty they left for Nashville.

There was congestion going into Nashville because of an accident. By the time they got to the nightclub it was almost ten o'clock—still early in the evening. They took a seat as close to the band as possible. Soon the waitress came and took their order. Ethan ordered a Coke, and was surprised when Rachel ordered a beer. At the waitress's request she took out a driver's license which showed her age to be twenty-one. After the waitress left he asked, "Where did you get that?"

"Oh, didn't you know I was twenty-one?" she said with a laugh.

"Only if you aged three years since I saw you last."

"My cousin got it for me in Knoxville. It's no big deal."

"O.K.," he said cautiously, "but if you get caught I had nothing to do with it."

"Ethan, you are such a sweetheart," she said laughing "but you sure are innocent. I think that's what I like most about you. Besides, I can't get up there and sing without getting a little loosened up. I would be a nervous wreck. I promise I will stop drinking long before we have to leave."

Even though he was irritated with her, he decided not to let it ruin their evening. She was probably right—he was too straight. He would try and relax and enjoy the music.

The band was very good. They performed a mixture of country classics as well as modern songs. They received their greatest response after doing "The Tennessee Waltz". During their next set Ethan told Rachel he would request, "Rocky Top," a song that had been written a few years earlier and was quickly becoming associated with the University of Tennessee sports teams. Rachel begged him not to, saying it would show what hillbillies they were. He finally gave in.

At ten o'clock the band took their first intermission. The announcer came to the microphone to invite any members of the audience who wished to come up and sing. While Ethan expected Rachel to jump up, she just sat silently.

"Aren't you going up?" he asked.

"I have to get my nerve up," she said as she gulped the rest of her beer. "Next set, O.K.?"

"Oh, O.K." he replied as he sat back in his chair and waited. By the time the band had taken their next break Rachel had finished her third beer. Ethan started to comment but decided against it. The announcer again invited guests to come up and perform. Rachel took one last sip of beer and walked to the stage. She chose "You Don't Have to Say You Love Me," by Dusty Springfield. Ethan was nervous as he waited for her to begin.

While her nervousness could be heard in her voice, it quickly went away. Ethan was amazed at how good she sounded. He was surprised not only at the range in her voice but also her stage presence. She finished the song and took a bow to the applause of everyone in the room.

"That was great," said Ethan. "I mean you were really good—even professional."

"Thank you," she said. "So do you think I have a chance of making it?"

"Well I don't know much about the music industry, Rachel, but you sounded great to me."

"But would you support me?" she asked.

He unconsciously raised a brow. Was she saying that she expected their relationship to be permanent, or exactly what kind of support did she mean? He thought it best to not go into it now.

"Well, yeah, of course—however I can I will help you."

At the insistence of others in the audience she performed another song. This time she sang, "Ode to Billie Joe," a hit a few years earlier by Bobbie Gentry. At its completion she got an even bigger applause. She was ecstatic when she returned to the table.

"Wow, that is so exciting," she exclaimed. Then, leaning closer, she whispered, "it's almost as good as sex."

While he was embarrassed by her remark, he also found it stimulating. During their dating days in high school she had always made sure their romance did not go too far. Was she telling him now that she was ready for more? He would probably find out soon enough. By midnight it was obvious that Rachel was drunk. Ethan tried to get her to stop but she insisted she was fine. Finally, he told her firmly that it was time to leave. She looked angrily at him but quickly stopped and leaned in closer saying, "You're the boss."

He paid the bill and helped her to her feet. People applauded as they walked out together, her leaning on his shoulder. As drunk as she was, she had the presence to wave to her new fans as she left. Once they got to the car Ethan removed the keys from her purse, opened the passenger door and helped her in. Once inside she made a comment about being able to drive, but, as soon as the car began to move, she fell asleep. Traffic was light so the trip to her apartment took only thirty minutes. Once they arrived he helped her out of

the car and into the apartment. Once inside he sat her on the couch and helped her remove her coat. She was half asleep but conscious enough to put her arms around his neck and kiss him.

"You're drunk," he said.

"I may be drunk," she repeated, "but I know what I want. We're not kids any more Ethan Ward. You gonna stay here tonight?"

"I think maybe I better sleep on the couch," he returned. "That way you won't hate me in the morning."

"Quit bein' such a Boy Scout," she said. "Com'on." With that she took his hand and staggered to the bedroom. He put up only token resistance.

———————————

The next morning Ethan awoke at eight and went into the kitchen and poured himself a glass of orange juice. He sat on the couch and glanced through her back issues of TV Guide. He walked back into the bedroom to check on Rachel. She was still asleep, and not a pretty sight. Her head was back almost off the bed and her mouth was open. The most humorous thing was the snoring. He wondered what her new fans from the night before would think if they saw her now.

She awoke soon although she hardly spoke. Ethan brought her a glass of juice and two aspirins. She informed him her plans for the morning were to lie on the couch and watch TV. Unfortunately she had forgotten that he had no way back to his dorm room. Although he had sympathy for her, he was hurt when she asked if he could find a ride home. When he stated that he would hitchhike she apologized and got dressed. They arrived back at the campus by eleven. Having driven so she could rest, Ethan got out of the car and walked around to the passenger's side and opened Rachel's door. She gave him a quick kiss and walked to the driver's side and got in.

"I'll talk to you soon," he said as she closed the door and drove away. He thought of the change in her from the previous night, but dismissed it as a hangover. He hoped it was not a sign of the old Rachel's return.

They saw each other a number of times during the next few weeks, almost always on Saturday evening. And while she was pleasant enough, Ethan felt as if something were not quite right—as if she were trying too hard. He decided that he was examining the situation too much and dismissed his concerns.

During the next couple of weeks he contacted Sally twice—both with the same results. Although she was always polite, when he mentioned studying together she always had other plans. He again apologized for Rachel's comments but she dismissed it saying she had thought nothing of it. After the second trip he stopped going.

Valentine's day came on a Saturday—exactly three weeks from Ethan and Rachel's new "first date". To celebrate the holiday Rachel wanted to go back to the bar where she sang the first night, but Ethan wanted something more intimate. He finally convinced her to dine at a restaurant overlooking the Cumberland River. His compelling argument was that many Grand Ole Opry performers frequented the restaurant. The dinner was pleasant enough except for her continually looking to see what celebrity she might spot. After some debate he convinced her not to use her fake ID in such a spot since it was more likely to be challenged.

They got back to her apartment around eleven. As had been the custom for the past few weeks, Ethan stayed over. Feeling amorous he climbed into bed and pulled close to her. She pulled away, explaining that she was tired and did not feel well. He fell asleep wondering why she was so distant.

The next morning Ethan again arose first. He stopped at the bathroom, as had become his routine, then went into the kitchen and poured himself a glass of orange juice. All the glasses were dirty but he found a stack of paper cups on the counter and took one. He loved the sensation as the cold juice went down his dry throat. After finishing he threw the paper cup in the nearby trashcan. As he did so a piece of paper protruding from the trash caught his eye. It was an envelope, but the thing that grabbed his attention was the return address. It was from Renee Cooper, Rachel's best friend. Although he knew he shouldn't, he took the envelope from the trash and removed the letter inside. What he read shocked him but also explained a lot of things. He read:

Hey Rach,

How's it going? Not much new here. I saw Terry and Barbara yesterday. They said Hi. I'll sure be glad when I have enough money to move out. My mother is driving me crazy. Maybe I'll move in with you when you become a big star.

Speaking of that, how's it coming? You make it with that band yet? Even more importantly, have you talked to Ethan about him getting you in to that record company that Senator Coleman owns? As you said, it's the least he can do after not even introducing you to him when you helped save his wife and daughter. Or does he even know that he owns a record company? If I had saved a Senator's family you better believe that I would take advantage of it. And it's not like you ain't got the talent girl. One break and you are on your way.

Did he ever say anything more about his colored girlfriend? Well, if nothing else happens, you put a stop to that...........

The letter went on to talk about other things, but he had read enough. He found a pen on the counter and, with trembling hands, began to write a note to her. Before he could do so, he looked up to see her in the doorway.

"What are you doing?" she demanded.

"Leaving you a message," he said bluntly, "but now it looks like I won't have to."

"Do you always go through people's mail?" she asked as she grabbed it from him.

"No, not often, but it's better than manipulating and lying to someone."

"I didn't lie to you," she snapped. "I just hadn't found the right time to ask you."

"Three weeks wasn't long enough? And it's nice to know what you really think of me."

"What do you mean?"

"Her comment about not introducing you to Senator Coleman before. You've always been angry at me for that."

"It wouldn't have hurt you to let him know I was involved."

"Damn it Rachel," he exploded, "you would have stood by and let those two people die. You didn't do anything."

"I was scared, Ethan. And I'm a woman. What could I do?"

"Fine," he returned, "but what did you expect me to tell the Senator? That you wanted to leave them there? That I pulled them from the wreck after you ran away? That you stood by and watched the car burn? Exactly what did you want me to say to him?"

She took the letter and threw it back in the trash. She stood with her arms folded glaring at him. Finally, after a few seconds, Ethan continued.

"This would have turned out pretty good for you—you get even with me for not introducing you to the Senator, you get a shot at recording a record, and you end whatever relationship I had with that, as you say, 'colored girl.'

"You know what, Ethan," she shot back, "you're probably right about a lot of things. I know I'm not as sensitive as you—as a lot of people. And I look out for myself because no one else will. But do you ever really look at yourself?"

"Why don't you do it for me?"

"You're such a goody-two-shoes. You always want to see the best in people. You see a nigger shoot down a policemen in front of you but you make sure it doesn't affect how you look at them—even start dating a colored girl. You are a Boy Scout—a Polly Anna. Someday you're going to wake up and see the world for what it is. I just hope it's not too late."

"Well, I came a long way today—for seeing people for what they are."

He walked to the living room and got his jacket.

"There's only one thing I want to know, Rachel. Have you ever really cared for me?"

She thought for a moment before responding.

"Ethan, I've always cared for you. But I am not like you. I cannot make another person my entire existence. I have to think of myself also. And I'm sorry for hurting you but that's the truth."

"Well, at least you answered my question," he said, trying to hold back the tears. "Goodbye Rachel."

He turned to walk out the door.

"How will you get home?"

"It's O.K.," he said calmly, "there's always someone going back to campus. I'll get a ride."

"Let me know if you have a problem," she said.

He walked out closing the door quietly behind him. As he walked to the road another thought came to him. Was it really a coincidence that she had shown up at his room at the same time as Sally? He didn't think so. She had been watching him. He started to go back and asked her but stopped. It really didn't matter.

It didn't take long before he got a ride. A nice elderly couple in a gray Chevy sedan pulled over. From their dress he surmised they were on their way to church. They introduced themselves as the Reverend and Mrs. Holmes. They informed him he was a retired minister and that they were on their way to Shelbyville to do the service for a friend who was on vacation. The woman soon turned to him.

"And what's your name young man?"

"Ethan. Ethan Ward."

"It's kind of cold to be out here hitchhiking, young man," she said. "Especially with that flimsy little coat on."

"I know," he said "I really didn't have it planned that way but sometimes things happen."

It was obvious to them that he was troubled.

"It looks like you're having a bad day, son," the man commented.

"It's just one of those days. I'll be fine."

"Well, if you don't mind I can tell you what I do when I'm having one of those days."

"What's that?" Ethan asked more from respect than a real need to talk.

"I think what kind of days Jesus had. I mean, he was God in the flesh—the only perfect person to ever live—and yet He had to suffer and die on a cross. When I think of that it reminds me that I have no right to feel sorry for myself."

Ethan did not respond but stared out the window.

"Anyway, I hope you will think about what I said, son," the man continued.

"I will, sir. And I appreciate your concern."

They continued the ride mostly in silence. The couple was kind enough to take him to his dorm room. He thanked them and went inside.

TEN

It was the last week of February and an unusually warm day at the MTSU campus. By mid afternoon the temperature hit sixty degrees. The spring-like weather brought the students from their rooms. Some tossed a baseball, others threw Frisbees, and some just sat on benches enjoying the weather.

Sally Robertson enjoyed the sun on her face as she walked to her dorm after Chemistry class. She was lost in thought about her upcoming exam and did not notice the man coming up behind her until he was at her elbow. When he touched her arm she turned with a jolt.

"Ethan!" she squealed, "you startled me."

"Sorry," he said. "How are things going?"

"O.K. I guess. Nothing much new. Just been really busy."

"I'm sure," he said, then, after a second's hesitation added, "Sally, can I talk to you for a minute?"

"Sure, go ahead," she said.

"Well, maybe we can go somewhere and sit down."

"Oh, well, all right."

They walked until they found an unoccupied bench. He turned to face her but before he began she surprised him with a question.

"So, how is your cheerleader girlfriend?"

"Cheerleader? How did you know she used to be a cheerleader?"

"Well, if she wasn't, then no other girl ever could be."

He laughed at her response. She was a very perceptive person.

"I guess she's alright," he said. "But she's not my girlfriend."

"Oh, that's too bad," she said flatly.

"No, it is not. Look, that is what I want to talk to you about. I already told you that I was sorry for what happened."

"You don't have to apologize again, Ethan. It really wasn't a big deal. I think I can survive one little comment."

"That's not what I am getting at. I just want to explain. Rachel and I dated during high school and, to be honest, she is not the nicest person in the world. When she showed up I thought maybe she had changed, and, to tell you the truth, I still had some attraction for her. Well I quickly found out that things had not changed. She is still the same old insensitive manipulative person she always was. So we're not together any more."

"That's too bad."

"No, not really. It's for the best," he said. He struggled for the next words. "Look, Sally, we had just met each other when this happened and....well, I don't know if you had any interest or not, or if you were just looking for a friend or....whatever....would you like to go out with me?"

While trying to keep a straight face, she enjoyed seeing him grasping for the right words.

"You mean like on a date?"

"Well, like of course on a date. Maybe Friday we could go to a movie or to a restaurant."

"Sorry. I have plans Friday," she said politely. "A girl can't wait forever."

"Oh, I understand," he replied.

Then, with a smile she said, "How about Saturday? Would you like to go to a party with me?"

"A party? Well, yeah sure. Where—what time?"

"Some students who live off campus are having it. It starts at nine."

"Well, that's great. Yeah, I would love to go."

They talked for a minute about the details of the party. Sally told him she could get her father's car and pick him up. They decided to stop for a pizza again at Lenny's before the party.

"It sounds like a plan," she said as she turned to walk away. "See you Saturday at eight."

"Great," he said, then after thinking for a minute added, "you were enjoying that, weren't you?"

"Enjoying what?"

"How I was struggling for what to say."

"Well of course," she said with a smile. "Why shouldn't I have?"

He just laughed and turned down the sidewalk. She called after him.

"Oh Ethan, just so that you know....my plans Friday...."

"Yeah?"

"They're with my dad."

She winked, turned and walked away.

Ethan met Sally early Saturday evening at her dorm room. She had straightened her hair and had it styled so the ends curled underneath her chin giving her a 'pixie' look. She was wearing tight fitting white jeans and a burgundy blouse.

"You look great," he commented.

"Thank you," she said. "You like my new hair style?"

"Sure, it's really nice. And I didn't think you could be more beautiful."

"Wow," she said, "you're getting awfully bold. I like it."

They walked to the parking lot where she had left her father's car. She directed him to an almost new Chrysler New Yorker.

"This is some car," he commented.

"Here," she said as she handed him the keys. "You can drive."

"You want me to drive? What would your father say?"

"He wouldn't care. Besides, it's only ten minutes from here. You're not going to wreck, are you?"

"I hope not," he said as he opened her door and walked around to the driver's side.

They arrived at the restaurant and parked across the street. This time he did not notice, nor did he care, if people were staring at them. The place was much more crowded than on their first trip, so the only table available was in the corner. This suited Ethan well since it gave them more privacy. After ordering they began to get to know each other better.

"So, you sure your father won't be upset if he finds out I drove his car?"

"Heck no. He doesn't worry about things like that."

"He sounds like a pretty nice guy."

"Yeah, I think so. Maybe some time you'll meet him."

"I hope so. So, if I'm not getting too personal, it sounds like you had a pretty happy childhood—that your parents had a real good marriage?"

"Well, yes and no. For the last few years they did, but not when my sister and I were young."

"Really? That surprises me—I mean as well balanced as you seem."

"Thanks," she said with a slight laugh. "But things are never that simple. My parents got married very young—were childhood sweethearts you know. Got married—actually had to get married— at sixteen. My sister, Merita, was born a short time later."

"Merita," he repeated, "that's an unusual name."

"It's Spanish. One of my ancestors was Hispanic—about four generations back—so I guess that makes me about one sixteenth Hispanic."

"I can see that."

"Anyway, when we were young it seemed our parents were always fighting over something—money, working too much—us kids. I think at least once a month my father would take off and be gone for two or three days at a time. I didn't know where—I imagined it was somewhere exotic or exciting. I didn't know until later that it was just over at my grandparents."

"They lived around here?"

"No, we didn't grow up around here. My parents were from over around Harriman—you know where that is?"

"Oh yeah, it's just this side of Knoxville. I drive by there when I go home."

"Well, that's where I grew up."

"In town or out in the country?"

"We lived in town. My grandparents had a farm about five miles from town."

"So what caused your parents to stop fighting?"

"Well, a big part of the problem was they both wanted something better for us which meant all they did was work and go to school. They both had full time jobs and also took classes over at UT which was about an hour away. So besides being young and poor and having two kids they were also tired most of the time. Then, about seven or eight years ago, they both got their degrees and things began to change."

"What did your mother do?"

"She was a nurse, and my father taught at the local high school. He continued to go to school even after he got his teaching degree. He got his Doctorate just a few years ago. My father was the first black Professor ever at MTSU, you know? My mother continued to work until she was killed, but she spent as much time with us girls as possible. For me that was fine, but my sister never forgave her— forgave them—for all the time lost when we were younger."

"That's pretty impressive about your father."

"Well, actually he's an Associate Professor. I guess they figured he could handle the title but not the money. Hopefully he will get a full appointment in a few years. You can still call him Professor, though."

"That's still impressive. I guess I can understand how your sister felt, though. Who stayed with you two when they were working all the time?"

"If they were not home one of our grandparents or our aunt would come by."

"Your grandparents still live there?"

"No. My Dad's mother died of cancer about seven years ago and our grandfather the following year. I guess he had no strength to go on living after he lost her. Our mother's parents died when I was very young. I can hardly remember them."

"That's too bad. Death is just part of living, I guess. You just have to learn to accept it."

The waiter soon brought their food. They clinked their glasses and began eating.

"So you say your father has still not recovered from your mother's death, huh?"

"No, not really, and it's been almost four years. He had just gotten his Doctorate and had taken the position here at the college, and Mom was able to work part time. For the first time in their lives they had a decent income and had the time to enjoy each other and then—just like that—she was gone."

"What happened?"

"A drunk driver. She belonged to a women's organization and was coming home from a meeting. A good ole boy had spent the last three hours at a bar and went through a red light. She never had a chance. My father still blames himself."

"Why?"

"He was going to take her that night but decided to stay home and watch a basketball game instead. He believes if he had picked her up it never would have happened."

"Or they both could be gone."

"Right. That's what I told him, but it doesn't make any difference. You would think after all this time he would get over it but that's not the case. I can't believe the change in him in the past few years."

"How?"

"My father is only thirty-nine years old. A few years ago he could pass for thirty or even twenty-five. He always took care of himself—exercised—ate right—everything. Now, he looks forty five or older. He has put on a lot of weight—I mean he is still not fat but he used to be slender. His hair is turning gray. He is just a different person. And it's a shame. He is still a young man—he has a good income and he got quite a bit of money when my mother died—but he has no interest in doing anything. He just goes through the steps of living."

"I'm sorry," said Ethan.

They continued eating as they talked. Sally turned the conversation towards Ethan. She asked him about his family, his childhood, and his hometown. Then she asked an unusual question.

"So what's the most exciting thing that has happened in your life so far? I mean other than tonight."

"That's a very interesting question," he said with a laugh. He thought of the irony of such a question, especially since she knew nothing of the two big events in his life. He did not want to discuss Deputy Pratt, however, he felt comfortable enough to relate the accident involving Senator Coleman's wife and daughter.

"That was you!" she almost yelled. "Are you kidding me Ethan," she demanded. "You wouldn't joke about something like that would you?"

"It's no joke, Sally," he said. "And yes, it really was me."

"That's unbelievable. I'm sitting next to a real hero. I can't believe I didn't put this together."

"Why would you?"

"It was in the paper and on the news. A high school boy from Greenville saving a Senator's wife and daughter. I bet they even had your name in the paper, although I guess I never paid much attention to that. But I should have thought of that when you told me where you were from but it just didn't register. How does it feel to have saved someone's life?"

"Actually, pretty good," he said. "At first I was kind of embarrassed to talk about it, but now, when I think about it, it is pretty amazing. I feel privileged that I had such an opportunity."

"Do you still talk to them?"

"Every once and a while. The Senator sends me a note from time to time to see how I am doing. And I talk to his wife and daughter a couple of times a year. Tina—that's the daughter—says I am her guardian angel."

"That is wonderful," she said. "Isn't it amazing how sometimes the smallest decisions you make turn out to change your whole life?"

"What do you mean?"

"Like that night. I don't know what happened, but if you had been a few minutes later you wouldn't have been there and they wouldn't be alive today. And who knows how many other lives they will touch because of that."

"Sort of like that movie, "It's A Wonderful Life", huh?"

"That's just what I was thinking!" she exclaimed.

They finished their meal and left the restaurant. On the way to the party Sally turned to him and said, "You know that the people who are having this party are seniors."

"And that's important because?"

"There will be people drinking there. Maybe even smoking pot."

"Oh, does that include you?"

"I never have. It's my sister who's the black sheep, remember? But what if I try a beer—are you going to be upset?"

"No, not really. I never have drank either, but I can't stay a Boy Scout forever. So let's just promise if we do drink anything we quit long before we have to drive home."

"A deal," she said as she held out her hand.

The party was just getting started when they arrived. One of the first people to greet them was Sally's friend Kim. Ethan felt she might be angry with him for never calling, but she simply looked at the two of them together and smiled. She said hello and, as she walked by, whispered to him, "You two make a nice couple."

There were only a few people there that Ethan recognized. Sally introduced him to friends of hers, both black and white. That was the thing that he noticed the most—the variety of people at the party. It seemed that almost every race and nationality were represented. He didn't know there were so many cultures represented on campus.

Creedence Clearwater Revival's Proud Mary was blasting on the stereo. People were scattered in groups throughout the apartment which, although it was about three times the size of the dorm rooms, was still crowded. Ethan estimated there were probably forty to fifty people there. He took Sally's jacket and put it along with his on the pile in the corner. Soon one of the hosts came by and told them that there was plenty to drink in the kitchen.

"Well," Sally said to Ethan, "should we have a beer?"

"I guess one won't hurt. It looks like everybody else here is drinking anyway."

As Ethan drank his first beer he realized it was probably the only time in his life he had done anything illegal. He again reminded himself that kids his age could be drafted and die in Vietnam—and many of his old classmates had—but they still could not vote or drink. He still felt guilty, and the beer didn't taste particularly good, but after a few minutes he began to see why people enjoyed it. Things became much simpler—much clearer to him. Like why he liked Sally. What was not to like? She was, first of all, gorgeous. She was also funny, thoughtful, smart, and caring. Who cared if they were not the same color? That was society's problem—not theirs. As he watched her standing and talking to Kim, he decided he would tell her how wonderful she was. But first, he had to go to the bathroom.

He passed Kim in the hall as he came back from the bathroom. She smiled and said, "It looks like you are having a good time."

"Pretty much. Ain't that why we're here?" he said, as he walked back into the living room. When he came back into the room he saw Sally talking to an attractive young black man. He had a number of gold chains around his neck and was wearing a tank top shirt to accentuate his muscles. From his build he appeared to be an athlete. Ethan felt a pang of jealousy as he watched them talk. He watched for a minute trying to decide what to do. Sally saw him, came over and took his hand and led him back to the stranger.

"Ethan, this is Roberto," she said.

"Ola," said Roberto as he smiled and put out his hand. "Good to meet you." The accent was one he had not heard before.

Ethan put out his hand slowly. "Good to meet you," he said cautiously.

"Roberto is from Puerto Rico," explained Sally. "We take Chemistry together."

"Oh, that's nice."

"This is a sweet lady here," stated Roberto. "I hope you appreciate her."

"Of course," said Ethan.

While he did not want to, because of his smile and charming personality, Ethan found he liked Roberto. They continued talking for a few minutes until a song Sally liked, Unchained Melody by The Righteous Brothers began to play. She took Ethan's hand and asked him if he wanted dance. While he had only danced a few times before, he eagerly agreed.

It felt good and natural to hold her close to him.

"Ethan," she said softly, "if I didn't know better I would almost think you were a little jealous of Roberto."

"Well I....I don't know about that," he stammered. "O,K., maybe just a little."

"That's nice. But I think I would have more reason to be jealous."

"What do you mean?" he asked as he pulled back.

"Don't you know? He's homosexual. He doesn't make it a secret."

"What? That's not right. I mean, look at him. He looks like a body builder."

"What does that have to do with it? Trust me on this. But anyway, it was sweet that you were jealous."

"So you noticed, huh?"

"A woman has a way to pick up on these things. Unlike men who are usually oblivious to little signs."

"What do ya mean?" he asked as he took his arm from around her back and took another drink.

"You're getting drunk aren't you?"

"Maybe a little. What da ya mean?"

She took the bottle from his hand and took a drink.

"Well, let me ask you a question. When did you figure out that I was interested in you? More than just a study partner, I mean."

"To tell you the truth, Sally, I guess I never have. Are ya tellin' me that now?"

"See, that's what I'm at talking about. Men are so blind," she continued as she drew closer, "I have been attracted to you since I first saw you. I mean, I couldn't be so blunt like Kim, but when I saw you in the snack room that night I thought, 'this is providence', and I have to take advantage of it."

"So you came in the snack room to see me?"

"Well of course, silly."

"Wow," he said, as he sipped more of his beer.

They finished drinking his beer and danced silently. Another slow song began. They picked up Sally's beer from the table and returned to the dance floor.

"Then I have to tell you somethin'," said Ethan.

"If you can get the words out," she said laughing. "What's that?"

"I really like you a lot."

"You are really getting drunk."

"That may be so. I think just from breathing the air in here you could get pretty high. But I liked you even when I was sober."

"Well, either way, it's nice to hear. And why do you like me?"

"Well, first of all, you're gorgeous. And you're smart, funny, and sensitive. And did I mention you're gorgeous?"

"That's sweet," she said. "I like you a lot too, Ethan."

"And why do ya like me?"

"You mean besides you bein tall, white and handsome?"

"I think yur gettin drunk too?"

"Maybe, but let me finish. You are sensitive. You are thoughtful. And ya really care about people. And did I tell ya you're really, really handsome?"

The two laughed and took another sip of beer.

"O.K.," said Ethan, "let me ask ya a serious question."

"O.K."

"Does this black, white thing bother ya?"

"Nope. Does it bother ya?"

"Well, I guess I think about it. I mean, I think prejudice or bigotry is thinkin' one group is better n another. I never think that, but I guess I think 'bout what other people might say 'bout us. Ya never worry 'bout that?"

"Nope, but I think it's different for a woman."

"Why?"

"Do ya know how difficult it is for a woman today to find a good man? It's even worse for a black woman. So many young black men are in jail or on drugs or come from broken homes an' never learned how to treat a woman. I think I deserve someone who'll treat me good."

"I think so too, Sally."

"Good, so maybe we'll jus see where this takes us—O.K."

"O.K."

They finished the dance and went back into the kitchen for one more beer. For the next hour they talked to friends, danced, and drank beer. At midnight Sally said it was time to leave. They said goodnight to their friends and walked to the car, which was parked a block away. Ethan opened the door for Sally then got in the driver's side. After doing so he leaned forward and put his arm around her and kissed her. She returned his kiss eagerly. After a few minutes she pulled away.

"Wow, this is getting serious," she said.

"An' what's wrong with that?"

"I like you jus' as much as you like me Ethan, but I need to take it a little slower."

"Why?"

"Maybe jus cause I'm a woman. This is still our first date, ya know."

"Yeah, but yur so sexy."

"So are you, Ethan, but I'm also kin' of drunk and I don't wanna do anything I'll regret tomorrow. Besides, the front seat of a car is not the most romantic or comfortable place for somethin like this."

"Well, we could get in the back," he said seriously, "There's enough' room back there for three or four people."

She burst out laughing. "You sure know how to sweet talk a girl, Ethan Ward."

When he realized how desperate he had sounded he began to laugh too. After they stopped, Sally turned to him more seriously.

"Are you safe enough ta drive?"

"Yes. It is only ten minutes and I will go very slowly."

"Then can we go home now? I have to get up early tomorrow to see my dad."

He agreed and kissed her gently before driving home.

ELEVEN

SPRING 1969

The Ebenezer Baptist Church building in Greenville always seemed to be in need of repair. Sometimes it was a window that needed replacing. Sometimes the doors needed oil. And something always needed painting. And for the past few months the roof had been leaking. And now, since winter was gone, the job of repairing it fell to Reverend Bell's son, Tommy. Tommy told his father that it would be better to wait until summer when there was less likelihood of rain, but he did not agree. Summer brought hot temperatures, especially on the roof of a building. And the wait could cause damage to the trusses. Tommy also thought it would have been wise to hire a professional to do the job, but his father said the church could not afford it. He did agree, however, to accept the assistance from two church members who had experience in such work. Together, after checking the weather report, the three of them began working on the project in early April. Since it was dangerous work, Mr. Bell insisted that anytime the men were working on the roof they be tethered to the building.

The work had one advantage for Tommy—it gave him plenty of time to think about his future. Unfortunately, he didn't know how long his life would be in his control. He expected every day to receive his 'greeting' from Uncle Sam welcoming him into the army. He did not know how he had made it so long. Many of his classmates had been drafted in the past year. Some had already been sent to Vietnam, and two had died in battle. He figured the only reason he had not been drafted was that he was a few months younger than the others. Either that or God had other plans for him. He wished he could have gotten a college scholarship, but that had not been the case. His grades were not perfect but they had been good—a solid B+ average. Others had gotten scholarships with no better grades than his. He didn't like to think about it, but he wondered if things would be different if he were white. Anyway, he decided, if he were still in town in the fall, he would enroll at the new community college, Walters State, that was to open in Morristown.

He was especially tired when he came home that afternoon. His mother had not gotten home yet, but he knew she would be arriving soon. She was always home in time to fix dinner for him and his father. The only thing he wanted to do was take a hot bath to soothe his aching muscles, have dinner, and listen to the baseball game on the radio. Before going in the house he stopped and picked up the mail. He quickly realized his wait was over. There, addressed to him, was a letter from the United States Selective Service. He knew before opening it what it said. Perhaps, at least, they would give him an extension to finish the roof. Such things had been done before. Instead of taking his bath, he went to his room and began writing a letter to his friend Ethan. He had a lot to tell him.

As much as Buster Ward hated to do it, he knew he had to make the call. His wife was in too much pain, and there was nothing he could do.

"What is your emergency?" the woman's voice asked.

"My wife can't walk and she has a lot of pain down her leg. Can you send an ambulance as soon as possible?"

"We will have someone there in just a few minutes."

The lady kept him on the line to get additional information, but there was not much more he could tell her. The ambulance came and took his wife to the hospital. He followed in his truck.

Sally Robertson had been dating Ethan Ward for over a month. They saw each other three to four times a week, sometimes more. They studied together when possible, played volleyball once a week, and almost always got together on Saturday night. However, she always kept her Fridays open for dinner with her father. She still had not told him about Ethan. The more she got to know him, the more she cared about and respected him, but she was still not certain their relationship would be permanent. And, unlike her sister, she worried considerably about making the right choices in her life. Perhaps that was the reason she had not told her father about Ethan. She didn't think it had anything to do with him being white. He had always told her to treat everyone the same, so she didn't believe he would have a problem with his color. Since they were having dinner together tonight she would soon find out if she were right.

It didn't take long before she had the opportunity to bring up Ethan with her father. They were sharing a meal at his favorite local diner when he asked, "So Sally, did you remember the Building Bridges Buffet that we are having next Saturday night?"

The buffet was a program that he and other members of the faculty had hosted the past few years. Each spring, on a Saturday evening, they held a buffet dinner at the school cafeteria. People from various races, religions, and ethnic groups were invited to attend. After dinner the guests were given real life scenarios that had happened in the community to discuss. Some of the situations dealt with racial prejudice, others dealt with gender issues, and some dealt with religious issues. The purpose was to see how individuals from various backgrounds perceived the same situation. Each person at the table was encouraged to give their opinion on the event. At evening's end each table summarized what they had discussed. The project had won numerous civic awards in the past, and was usually attended by forty to forty-five people.

"Sure, Daddy," she answered. "Matter of fact that's what I wanted to talk to you about. Is it O.K. if I bring a friend?"

"Well, of course. You know that. I take it this is a male friend?"

"Yes."

"And how long have you been seeing him?"

"For a few weeks."

"You haven't mentioned him. Is he nice?"

"Yes, very. But there's one thing you should know," she added hesitantly.

"Uh oh. What's that?"

"He's white."

"Oh, so that's why. And what did you think I would say?"

"Well I didn't think it would bother you, but....well, I wasn't sure."

"And you say he is nice?"

"Yes, Daddy."

"He treats you good?"

"Yes, Daddy."

"Not an alcoholic or druggy?"

"No, Daddy," she said getting impatient. "He is a student. He's about the straightest and nicest person in the world."

"What's his name?"

"Ethan Ward. He's from Greenville."

Sally saw a surprised look on his face.

"What's wrong, Daddy? You look like there's a problem."

"What....oh no. It's just the name sounds familiar. Like I should know it from somewhere."

"Probably, he's also a bit of a celebrity."

She told him about Ethan's saving the Senator's wife and daughter.

"Oh yeah, that's where I heard it. It was in all the papers."

"Yes, a real live hero. And you will get to meet him soon."

"I'm looking forward to it," he responded as he took a sip of coffee.

———————

Ethan stopped at his mailbox as he returned from class. He didn't get many letters—mostly from his mother and occasionally from his brother. Today was a pleasant surprise—he had one from his friend Tommy. As good a friend as he was, they had not been communicating much since he had gone away to college. He hoped nothing was wrong. He opened the letter and read as he walked to his room. It read:

Hi Ace,

Hope everything is going well there. I haven't heard from you in a while. I did hear about what happened with Rachel though. You know what I think so I won't go into it. A lot of hot girls on campus though, so you're better off. Well, I knew it would happen but it was still a shock. I got my letter from Uncle Sam today. I'm supposed to report to Knoxville for a physical in two weeks. If I pass (like that ain't gonna happen) then I guess I got about a month left. I'm gonna try to get an extension for a few weeks to finish some things at the church. I don't know if it will work but it's worth a try. I don't know if I should mention this but I will anyway. You're mother's back has been bothering her a lot. I saw her a week or so ago and she told me she was getting pain in her leg from it. I know it's not anything serious like a heart attack or cancer, but you might want to call her. I know she doesn't want you to worry so she won't say anything unless she's dying, but I just thought you should know. Please don't tell her I said anything. Maybe just tell her you haven't talked to her for a while and wanted to make sure everything is O.K. Anyway, better run. I hope you can come in so I get to see you before I go see "Charlie".

Your GI Pal, Tommy

Ethan felt his pulse quicken as he read the letter. He needed to call his mother to find out what was happening. Unfortunately, the students could not make direct dial long distance calls from the dorm rooms. A calling card was needed, which he did not have. Rudy had a card but he had gone to the library and would not be back until after eight o'clock. He found a student in the dorm who had a card. He offered him $5.00 for the use of the card for a ten-minute call. He agreed but required that he stay in his room while he used it.

His father answered the call, which was unusual since he disliked talking on the phone. Ethan made small talk to him, pretending that he knew nothing about his mother's problem. As Tommy suggested, he told him that he hadn't got a letter from them for a while—which was true—and wondered if every thing was O.K.

"Well, we do have a little problem," said his father. "We had to put your mother in the hospital a couple days ago. Now it's nothing serious, son," he cautioned. "Just a problem with her back."

"What is it?"

"Well, they got her in traction right now, but they believe it's a slipped disk. If it don't get better in a couple of days I reckon they'll do some more tests."

"And then what?"

"Well, if worse comes to worse, they'll have ta operate. But son, this ain't like open heart surgery or brain surgery. They would just remove the part of the disk that is pressing on her nerve. Then—a few days'n she'll be fine."

"And she has pain in her leg?"

"Yep, I reckon that is the real problem—her left leg. The back pain was a nuisance, but she couldn't deal with the pain down her leg—sciatica I reckon they call it."

"O.K., can I call her?"

"Sure, she would be glad ta talk ta you, son. Ethan, I'm sorry we didn't call but it's only been two days and she thought she would be out in a hurry and didn't want ta trouble you."

"I understand."

"And, son, when you talk ta her, remember they got her pretty doped up so she ain't feeling no pain, but she might talk a little strange too."

"O.K."

He got the number for the hospital. Since the first call didn't take long the student didn't charge him for the call to his mother. When she answered he hardly recognized her voice. She informed him that she was on a painkiller called Demerol. While it helped with the pain in her leg, it made her mellow and groggy. She was alert enough to tell him that they had scheduled a myelogram for her the next day. She explained that it was a test in which a contrasting agent would be injected into her spinal canal. An x-ray would then be taken to get an outline of the area. After they got the results of the test they would know if they needed to operate.

They talked until the student began giving him evil looks. He told her he would call back the following day to get the results. Before hanging up—mellowed by the drugs, she told him how much she loved him, what a good boy he was, and how proud she was of him.

The next afternoon his father called to inform him that the test showed they would need to operate to remove the part of the disk that was pressing on her sciatic nerve. The surgery was scheduled for the following day, Friday. Ethan said he would come home to be with her but his father insisted that it was not necessary. She would be in the hospital for three to four days, and his brother had made plans to spend a few days when she came home. Ethan could come the following weekend if he wanted, thereby not missing any classes. Ethan agreed to wait until after the surgery and see how she was doing.

The next afternoon his father called to inform him the surgery went fine. His mother was in some discomfort from the incision, but the good news was that the pain in her leg was gone. He suggested Ethan wait until evening to call her. When he called that evening she said that she was doing great and that he should wait a week or so to come see her. He reluctantly agreed.

While Ethan was still worried about his mother, the one good thing about not going home that weekend was that he would be able to attend the dinner with Sally. He was looking forward to meeting her father, although he was also more than a little nervous. He would find out if he was as nice as she had been telling him.

———————

Professor Warren Robertson was also nervous—not only about meeting his daughter's new boyfriend, but about the dinner he and other faculty members were hosting. He was good at organizing some things; how much food to buy; how to arrange the seating; the agenda for the evening. But other things he was not so good at, so he left them to the other faculty members who had volunteered for the project; sending out the invitations; follow up calls and publicity. But with everyone's help it should be another successful dinner.

At five-thirty the head janitor came up to see if there was anything else he needed.

"No, I think everything is fine, James," he said. "You've done a great job as always. It's too bad you don't like these type of things or you could join us."

"Well not everyone is as outgoin' as you, Professor, but call me if ya need anything else. I'll be down ta my office."

"We'll be fine."

"And ya don't need ta put things back like ya did last year. I'll take care of everything in the mornin'."

"We'll just do the dishes. I promise we'll leave the tables and chairs for you."

The two shook hands and the janitor left for his room in the basement. Professor Robertson thought of what a good employee he had been since the college had hired him three years earlier. He felt it sad that he kept to himself so much.

At five forty-five the first guests began to arrive. A few minutes later Sally and her new boyfriend arrived. They immediately came and greeted her father.

"Daddy, I would like you to meet Ethan Ward. Ethan, this is my father, Professor Robertson."

"Good to meet you, sir," said Ethan as he put out his hand.

"Good to meet you," said the Professor. "We're glad you could make it tonight. I think you'll enjoy the evening."

"I'm sure I will," he said then, after looking at the Professor more closely he added, "you look familiar. Did we meet before?"

"I don't think so, but, I am around the campus all the time so we might have run in to each other. Maybe it's just that I look so much like my daughter—or rather she got her good looks from me."

"I'm sure that's it," said Ethan with a laugh.

They talked for a couple of minutes before Sally turned to Ethan and asked, "Would you please get me a cup of punch?"

"Sure," he said as he left.

"Daddy," she said to her father, you seem awful nervous. Is everything alright?"

"Oh, sure, honey," he said "It's just that this is the biggest dinner we have had, and I found out that a reporter from the Tennessean will be here in a few minutes. And, it's not every day that a man meets his future son-in-law."

"Oh, Daddy, don't be silly. You know it's not that serious," she said with a giggle. "But how did you like him?"

"He seems like a fine young man. Now I have to get back to work."

Ethan returned with her punch and the two began mingling with the other dinner guests. Soon the ice-breakers began. There were almost fifty people in attendance. For the first exercise everyone had to find a person they did not know with whom they had the most in common. Ethan thought he was doing well when he found an elderly black lady who not only shared his birthday but was also born in Greene County and who was a retired teacher. The contest was won by a couple who had six major things in common. Next the guests were divided into groups of three and told to tell three things about themselves—two true and one false. The others were to determine which was the lie. A prize was given for the most creative lie. One heavyset woman, who was from Louisville, tried to convince the others that she once got in a fight with Muhammad Ali over a parking space and blackened his eye. Sally won the contest when she tried to convince the others that, as a child, because of her dimples, she won a Shirley Temple look alike contest.

After the ice-breakers the guests were seated for dinner. Sally complained to her father that she and Ethan were not seated together. He explained that couples were not to sit together so that the table would have diversity.

"Well, duh," she said, "he's male and I'm female. He's white and I'm black. He's Methodist and I'm Baptist. And despite what you think, Daddy, we're not married yet."

"O.K.," he agreed, "see if you can find somebody to change with you."

Ethan and Sally found the discussion interesting and enlightening. They discussed many different scenarios—equality in hiring and promoting; prejudice in the housing market; women's equality; and religious and homosexual issues. While some issues were divided along racial or ethnic lines, Ethan discovered that many people of the same race or background often did not agree. In fact, he found that on many issues he had more in common with the minorities at the table than they had with each other. At the end of the event a representative from each table stood and summarized their group's discussion and what they learned. Each table said they found the event to be stimulating and enlightening.

Sally found the evening to be extremely enjoyable. There was good food, good conversation, and she was with a handsome young man who seemed to really care about her. And the music playing in the background and the rain that had just begun to fall made it almost magical.

The dinner ended at nine-thirty. Sally kissed her father good night, then walked with Ethan back to her room. She wondered if he knew how close she felt to him. Their romance had gone no further than on that first date in the car, but tonight she knew she would not stop him. And her roommate was out for the evening, unfortunately, the women's dorm was off limits to males after nine o'clock and on Saturday night it was closely monitored. Still, there would be other times.

They stopped at the entrance to the dorm. It was still raining but they both had hooded wind-breakers. They stood in the doorway kissing good night.

"This has been a wonderful evening," she said.

"I agree," he said "One of my best ever."

"Well, I hope I can make it better."

"How?" he asked as he pulled back.

"Because there is something I need to tell you, and I hope it is the right thing. Simply, I love you Ethan."

He smiled and pulled her close to him and kissed her firmly but gently.

"I love you too, Sally."

"Wow, really?"

"Well, of course. Who wouldn't?"

The two kissed for a few minutes more before Ethan spoke.

"The night is still young. We could go somewhere for a while."

"There is no where close to walk to, and I don't want to go too far in this rain. Too bad we didn't get my father's car with that big back seat?"

"You're kidding me?" he said.

"No, but I guess we'll have to wait."

"Then that's not fair to say that."

"I know. I'm sorry. I just wanted you to know how I felt."

"Well....maybe we could...."

"I'm sorry, Ethan. You know we can't go anywhere on campus. And we can't get my father's car since he already left. And I have to get up early anyway. Did you remember I am going to Harriman to see my aunt?"

"Yes."

"And you still don't want to go?"

"I really can't Sally. I have two tests and a paper due. And next weekend I am probably going to see my mother. I'm sorry."

"There will be other times."

The two kissed again and reluctantly said good night. Sally went into her room, not remembering when she had been so happy. Ethan was also excited to learn how she felt about him, but he had other things on his mind; his mother's health; his friend Tommy being drafted; and worrying about how he would find the money for next year's tuition.

The next morning Rudy was awake and gone to church by ten o'clock. Ethan also arose early and began his studies. He wanted to have everything complete by the time Sally returned. He was studying at his desk when there came a knock at the door. He wondered if it might be Sally trying to convince him once more to accompany him to her aunt's house. He opened the door not to see Sally but her father. By the look on his face he knew something was wrong.

"Professor Robertson?" he said. "Is everything O.K.? Is Sally O.K.?"

"She's fine," he said seriously, "but I need to talk to you. Can I come in for a minute?"

"Sure," he said as he walked aside.

The Professor came inside closing the door behind him. He reached into his pocket and removed something to hand to Ethan. It was a bottle of orange soda."

"I thought this might mean something to you," he stated dryly.

It suddenly all came back to him—why the Professor looked familiar. He remembered that hot summer day six years ago clearly now—the truck, the two men, the bottle of orange soda, the Deputy, the gunfire. It was his worst nightmare come true.

PART TWO

TWELVE

Ethan backed into the room looking around for a weapon with which to defend himself. He found a pair of scissors on the table, grabbed them and pointed them toward the Professor.

"Keep away from me!" he yelled.

The Professor slid against the wall away from the door. "Son, I am not here to hurt you," he explained as calmly as possible.

"Just move away from the door!" demanded Ethan. "I'm leaving."

"Son, just give me a second to explain."

"I don't want to hear anything you have to say. Just keep away from me."

The Professor moved a few feet from the door then stopped. Ethan stood staring at him, his hand with the scissors in it shaking.

"If you don't move and let me out I will start yelling. The other students will be here in seconds."

"I know that, son. Please just give me thirty seconds—if not for me, then for Sally."

It was the only thing that he could have said that would have made him stop and think. Of course, the Professor knew that— that's why he said it.

"What do you want? Why are you here?" Ethan demanded.

"Son," he began, "things are not always what they seem. You were never in any danger from us—and you're not in any danger now."

"What do you want?"

"Listen to me carefully, Ethan. If it wasn't for my friend and me you would not be alive today."

"What!"

"I will tell you again. It wasn't about us. It was you the Deputy was after. If we hadn't come along you wouldn't be alive."

Ethan could not believe what he heard. It took a minute for him to even comprehend it.

"You are crazy. What are you talking about?"

"Son, I can prove what I am saying, but you are going to have to give me a few minutes. Again, you are not in any danger here. If we wanted to hurt you we could have six years ago or any time since. I am the only one in danger here, so can you please let me have a few minutes to explain?"

Ethan thought for a minute about what to do. He was still in shock at what the Professor had said, but his last statement made sense. If he wanted to hurt him why was he coming to his room in broad daylight? Still, he had to be cautious.

"O.K. you can talk for one minute, but just keep over there."

"Fine, son. I'm going to take a chair and move it back. Why don't you sit down?"

"I'm fine."

"Well, at least you could put those scissors away for a minute. What if your roommate came in and saw us like this?"

"He won't be back for a while."

As soon as Ethan made that statement he regretted it, but the Professor made no comment. He simply pulled out the chair and sat down.

"Son," he began, "I'm going to tell you a remarkable story, but every word is true. You can verify it. But it may take a few minutes to explain."

"Go ahead."

"In January 1963 I was a high school teacher in Harriman. One morning, before class, the principal came to see me. He said one of my students had been identified as breaking into a home in Greene County a few days earlier. Our local sheriff contacted the principal and told him that the Greene County sheriff had a warrant for his arrest, and that a deputy would be picking him up that afternoon.

They didn't want to do it at home since the boy's father had been known to be violent. I had the kid the last period of the day, so the principal told me to keep him after class until the other kids had left, then one of his deputies along with the Greene County Deputy would be waiting outside the classroom. I did as instructed and the deputies arrested him. As you might have guessed, the Deputy from Greene County was Andrew Pratt."

"That night when I got home I heard on the radio that a thirteen year old boy had not shown up for school that morning, and was still missing. A day later they found his body in an abandoned barn. He had been sexually assaulted and strangled. I didn't tie the two incidences together until a few days later when I happened to talk to a friend—the other man in the truck. I just happened to mention about the Deputy coming to our school. He told me that he thought Deputy Pratt had killed the boy."

He waited for a response from Ethan, but getting none, continued. "I thought he was crazy at first, and asked him why he would think of such a thing. He told me he had known the Deputy when they were younger. He said he had always been evil and he had always expected him to hurt somebody some day."

"That doesn't prove anything," said Ethan impatiently.

"I know it doesn't by itself, son, but I am just getting started. A couple of months later another boy about the same age disappeared around Knoxville and was found a few days later at a construction site. It was the same situation—sexually assaulted and strangled. My friend came to me again and told me he knew Deputy Pratt was in Knoxville that same day. Then there was a third boy that was killed a few weeks later over near Jefferson City—you may have heard about that one. For the third time my friend told me that the Deputy was involved."

"Yeah, I heard about it—it was less than an hour from our home." Ethan did not tell him that his mother had been so worried about the incident that she had not let him go anywhere by himself for over a month. He continued, "But those are all just coincidences. If your friend knew something he could have called the police."

"You are right, Ethan. It is one thing to know something and

something else to prove it. And I can't tell you everything I know—
or my friend knew—but he was certain that the Deputy was
responsible. And each time it happened it got closer to home—
closer to Greene County."

Ethan was now listening intently. He wasn't convinced of what
he was hearing, but he was at least curious.

"Is that all you have to say?"

"No, not at all. You may not be convinced from what I have told
you so far, but let's talk about what happened that day."

"O.K.," agreed Ethan with hesitation. He did not like the idea
of reliving that horrible day, but at least now he might get his
questions answered.

"Was it safe to say that you had walked that road before?"

"Yes, of course."

"And the Deputy would have known that?"

"I guess. I saw him on the road from time to time."

"And did you see his car that day?"

"No—you know the answer to that. None of us saw him."

"That's because he was hiding in the woods waiting for someone. Right?"

"I guess his car was in the woods. I don't know why."

"And, from what I remember from the newspaper, in his last call
to his dispatch he said he was on the other side of the county. The
Sheriff couldn't understand why he wanted them to think that—
right?"

"That sounds right."

"So he was hiding in the bushes waiting for someone who might
come by and he covered it up by telling his dispatch he was on the
other side of the county."

"Well, I guess you could look at it like that. But that doesn't
mean he was waiting for me."

"Do you also remember that he told us he had radioed for help?"

"Yes."

"But it never showed up, did it? He lied about that also."

"Or he just might have said that to scare you."

"The point is not that he lied. The point is that he didn't radio for help because he did not want anybody else to know where he was? You really think that he had two young black men he thought were dangerous but didn't call for backup?"

"These things are all interesting, but they still don't prove anything."

"Well, let's go on. Did you feel any threat from us?"

"No—I guess not, but that doesn't have anything to do with it. Even if you didn't plan on hurting me doesn't have anything to do with why the Deputy was killed."

"I guess that is true. But do you remember the Deputy pulling his gun on us?"

"Oh, yes," said Ethan.

"There was no need for that. The only reason was because he knew what he was going to do. He planned on killing all of us."

"You can't prove that just because he pulled his gun. He didn't know what he was getting himself in to. He was just protecting himself."

"Son, listen to me. He planned on abducting you and doing whatever he wanted, then leaving you like he did the other boys. When we came along it made it even better. He could take us all into the woods, shoot us, then strangle you, and say we abducted you and he got there too late. That way he got to satisfy his evil desires, and could pin it on two black boys. Who would have questioned him?"

Ethan stood silently, trying to decide what to do. Could this be possible? All these years could he have had it all wrong? There were still too many questions to be answered.

"There's one other thing," said the Professor.

"What is that?"

"The soda bottle you dropped—they got our finger prints off it."

"Yeah—so?"

"Why do you think they never found us?"

"I don't know?"

"Because neither one of us ever did anything to be printed for, before or after."

"So?"

"Listen to me, son. Does that make sense? Two young men that have never been in trouble decide to gun down a deputy in broad daylight for no reason but let the only witness go. Think about it, son. If you look at this objectively, you'll know I am telling you the truth."

Ethan's head was spinning. He had never considered such a possibility—never even dreamed he was more than a witness to the incident—and certainly not that he could have been the cause of it. He still was not convinced, but had to admit that a lot of things he said made sense.

"Look Ethan," he continued, "like I said, we have never been a threat to you. If you want you can call the police and I will be arrested. But, before you do, there are a couple of other things I want to say."

"What?"

"Well, first of all—as I am sure you have guessed—Sally never, ever knew anything about this. Matter of fact, no one but my friend and I ever knew about it, and we haven't talked about it in years."

"O.K."

"And the other thing is that if I am arrested, I will never identify my friend."

"That's noble."

"It has nothing to do with noble. The fact is that I will probably go to prison for a while but my friend would get a life sentence. I can't live with knowing I sent an innocent man away for the rest of his life."

Ethan didn't know what to do. His mind was filled with too many thoughts and questions. As shocked as he was, many of the things the Professor had said made sense. One thing he didn't understand, though, was why he came to him.

"Why did you decide to come here? I didn't recognize you."

"Yes, I know, it has been six years, and I have put on some weight—my hair is getting gray—I have glasses and a beard now. But, sooner or later it would come back to you. Something would trigger it and then I would not have a chance to talk to you. This way at least you had to listen. And maybe it is because I knew you were such a fine young boy. I knew I could trust you to do the right thing."

"We just met—and Sally told me she hadn't even talked about me until a couple days ago. How can you know anything about me?"

"Ethan," he said with a laugh, "I know more about you than you can imagine. I know about your father's battle with cancer and how brave you have been. I know about saving those two people in the car—of course the whole state knows about that. I know what a good boy you have turned out to be—someone that treats everyone the same no matter what race they are. And, I really admire you. If I had seen what you had at your age I probably would not have been so understanding."

Ethan looked at him with anger. It sounded like he had been following him for the past few years.

"How do you know so much about me?"

"Relax, son. Most of it I got just from reading the Greenville Sun. And the rest of it—well, let's just say from time to time my friend and I made inquiries. But it proves what I said earlier—if we had ever wanted to hurt you, it would have happened long ago. For whatever it matters, I am really proud of how you turned out."

Ethan put the scissors back on the table and turned back to him. Something came to him—another revelation.

"It was you who sent the money—the check so I could go to college?"

The professor did not respond, but he saw the answer in his smile. He turned to leave.

"Son, there is nothing else I can say. You have to do what you need to do. The only thing I ask is that you take time to think about it—maybe even do a little investigating of your own."

"How can I do that?"

"Well there is really no one better. Think about it. You are thinking of being a journalist. You could go back to the Sheriff and tell him this thing has been bothering you for all these years, and maybe if you looked over the records that something would stand out—something might trigger something to help solve it. I think if you look into it you will see that what I am telling you is the truth."

Ethan would think about what he had said. But right now he had one more question.

"One thing I have always been curious about—how did you all get away?"

"You know that God delivered Moses by having him put in a basket and in the river, right? Well, I truly believe that God's hand has been in this since the beginning. Even though we had our suspicions about Deputy Pratt, we didn't go there looking for him. That was just chance. And, I won't tell you everything, but the fact that we had over an hours head start had a lot to do with it. And I never understood that. How come it took so long for you to tell anybody?"

"I was too scared to come out of the woods," Ethan said sheepishly. "I hid until I heard the sirens."

"Well, anyway," said the Professor, "I believe God had His hand in this. It would be a big enough coincidence just for you to come here to college, but to meet my daughter and start dating her—well I guess He can arrange anything He wants."

Ethan still stood a safe distance from him, but he felt little threat. The Professor reached the door then turned back to him.

"Son, I'm not going anywhere—my life is here. So, if you decide to call the police I would appreciate you letting me know."

Ethan nodded as Professor Robertson walked out the door. After he left he sat at the desk, still in shock. His head was filled with dozens of thoughts and questions. As much as he had to admit it, what he had said made a lot of sense. Why had the Deputy been out there? Why had he not seen him? Was his car really in the brush, or had they just not paid attention and not noticed him? Why had he called in and told dispatch that he was miles away? Why had he pulled his gun? Why did they let him get away? What about their fingerprints? He must have been telling the truth about that since neither one were ever identified.

And what about the three other boys? It would probably be easy enough to verify if Deputy Pratt really was in Harriman the day the first boy was killed, but what would that prove? And how could he ever know if he was nearby when the other boys were killed?

After a while he began to consider all sorts of possibilities. Was it just coincidence that he had come here to MTSU? And meeting and dating the Professor's daughter? That was almost too much to accept. And, the most frightening possibility of all—what if Sally really did know about what had happened? Had her father seen him on campus and—knowing that sooner or later he would identify him—convinced her to get to know him—to get him to fall in love with her so he would not turn him in?

That idea he quickly dismissed as being absurd. He would never believe she could be that deceitful. He soon thought of an even greater concern. Even if he believed Professor Robertson when he said he was not in any danger from him, what about the other man? He was the one who had the most to lose. Of course, for six years he had been safe, but now he could identify the men—or at least one of the men, who killed the Deputy. Should he just go ahead and call the police and let the authorities worry about it? If they were innocent, wouldn't the truth come out? But how could they ever be proven innocent unless their story could be verified, and the only man who could do that was dead.

He was becoming ill from thinking about it. His head pounded, his stomach ached and he felt exhausted. He lay down but could not rest. He tried to return to his studies but could not concentrate. He wanted to talk to somebody, but if anyone found out and told the authorities, an innocent man—his girlfriend's father—could go to prison. And the one person he wanted to talk to the most was the last person he could tell about it. What would he say to Sally when she called him that afternoon? He could not talk to her—not now. He needed time to think. He would tell her he was sick, which was true. At least that would give him a day or two to think about it. And tonight, he would get some sleeping pills to help him get a good night's rest. Maybe tomorrow things would be clearer.

THIRTEEN

With the help of two sleeping pills Ethan was able to get some rest that night. Sally called upon returning from her aunt's to see if he wanted to get together, but he told her he was not feeling well—perhaps he was getting the flu. He attempted to study for a while but finally gave up and went to bed early. The next day, although still exhausted, he made it through his classes.

Once class was over he went to the library to begin research. If he could verify the information the Professor had given him, it might help decide his next course of action.

The library had no newspapers from the towns of Harriman or Jefferson City, however, they did have the last ten years of the Knoxville Journal and Knoxville News Sentinel on microfiche. The most complete information was found in the News Sentinel. The first article was from Wednesday, January 23, 1963, but provided very little information. It simply stated that a young boy, Anthony Thomas, a thirteen-year old student at Harriman Middle School, had not shown up for class that day. A search was underway for the young boy. He was described as being white, five-foot six inches, and weighing 135 pounds. The following article, two days later, was much more informative and very disturbing. It read:

BODY OF MISSING BOY FOUND
Special to the News Sentinel
Friday, January 25th

Harriman—The body of young Anthony Thomas was found today, one day after he was reported missing by his mother. The body was found in a barn at an abandoned farm outside of Harriman. While police would not give details, the case is being investigated as a homicide. The location of the body was less than two miles from where he was to meet the school bus. Authorities expect his abduction occurred along the half- mile stretch of road from his house to the bus stop, a rural section of the county infrequently traveled. Anyone who observed anything or anyone suspicious please call the Sheriff's office at 615-555-3388, or the Tennessee Bureau of Criminal Identification at 615-555-4433. Anthony, a white thirteen year old was five-feet six inches and weighed 135 pounds, and was last seen wearing blue jeans and a burgundy coat.

Ethan felt a lump in his throat as he read the article. He found it difficult to continue but knew it was necessary. He located a number of follow up articles written during the next few weeks, but with little new information. A later article stated that the cause of death had been strangulation and that there had been signs of abuse. It also said that the authorities were following a number of leads but no arrests had been made. The only other thing of interest was a statement by the boy's mother who explained that her son was a strong willed and cautious boy and she could not imagine him willingly getting into a car with a stranger.

Ethan continued his search now concentrating on information related to the second young boy. He found the information he was looking for. It was dated Thursday, March 14th. This time there was no first article announcing the boy's disappearance—only one discussing the body being found. As he read the article he understood why the boy had not been reported missing.

BODY OF MISSING BOY FOUND NEAR
CONSTRUCTION SITE
Special to the News Sentinel
Thursday, March 14th

Knoxville—The body of twelve-year-old Lawrence Fegan was found by a bulldozer operator at an abandoned construction site early yesterday morning. Work at the site had been temporarily halted because of permit issues. The worker stated he had come to the site to check on his equipment when he noticed a lock broken on a storage shed. Upon investigating he found the boy's body inside. While authorities would not comment on the cause of death, it is being investigated as a homicide. The boy had last been seen alive Monday evening. His parents had reported him missing Tuesday evening, although he had not been seen since the day before. They would not comment on why there was a delay in reporting him missing, however, an un-named source at the school said it was not unusual for the boy to have un-excused absences at school. When asked if his murder is related to the one in Harriman in January police stated it is too early to tell. Police are seeking help from anyone who might have seen or heard anything suspicious. Lawrence was white, five foot two inches, and weighed 125 pounds. He was last seen wearing blue jeans and a gray hooded sweatshirt. Anyone having information please call the Knoxville police department at 615-555-2525 or the Tennessee Bureau of Criminal Identification at 615-555-4433.

Ethan again found a number of follow up articles but, as in the other case, no arrest was ever mentioned. He found the article about the third boy.

THIRD BOY IN PAST THREE MONTHS
FOUND NEAR JEFFERSON CITY

By Terry Lawton, Staff Writer
May 8th, 1963

The body of a young boy—the third found strangled in east
Tennessee in the past few months—was found near Jefferson
City yesterday evening. William Brophy, thirteen, was found
in a field in a remote part of the county at approximately six
P.M. He was first reported missing when he did not report
to school. His parents stated that he had remained home
awaiting the school bus when they left for work that morning. When he did not arrive at school, a staff member placed
a call to the father's work. The parents, however, could not
be reached until eleven A.M. Once notified the father left
work and returned home. Not able to locate his son he immediately contacted the Sheriff's department and a search
was begun a little after noon. The area where the boy was
found was approximately ten miles from his house and fifteen miles from the school. As in the other cases, no witnesses have come forward, and no suspects have been identified. Anyone having information about this case please call
the Jefferson County Sheriff's department at 615-555-1234,
or the Tennessee Bureau of Criminal Identification at 615-
555-4433. William was five feet five inches and weighed
145 pounds. He was last seen wearing black jeans and a red
checked shirt.

While Ethan had only vaguely remembered the case, he now
recalled the boy's name. He remembered his parents talking about
it and how they would not let him go anywhere by himself for the
next few weeks. He now wondered where he would be today if they
continued protecting him a little longer. If everything the Professor
had said was true, it would have only meant that some other boy
would have been the next victim.

He looked back over the articles and realized the Tennessee
Bureau of Criminal Identification (TBCI) had been involved in all
the cases. He thought of the story his father had told him about

how the unit had its origin in Greene County. The organization began as the result of a highly publicized murder case in the County in 1949. A man, James Lutz, had been murdered in his bed when a shotgun blast ripped through the window. The case was never solved and in 1951 the Manager of the Greenville Sun, John M. Jones, in an address to the Tennessee Press Association stated that a separate state investigative agency was needed to help local authorities solve serious crimes. A short time later, mainly through the work of Mr. Jones, a bill was signed establishing the Tennessee Bureau of Criminal Identification. The first agent to be appointed was Brad Hobson, a retired FBI agent.

Once he had determined he could gather no further information from the library, he returned the microfiche and left for his dorm room. He knew Sally would be expecting his call. He missed talking to her, but he still did not know how to handle their next conversation. Surely she would detect something was wrong. He figured he could use the "sick" excuse one more day. He called her and said he had made it through his classes but still did not feel well. She offered to come by and check on him—even bring him food from the cafeteria—but he stated he had no appetite and only wanted to sleep.

That night he slept better—even without a sleeping pill. While there were still many questions to be answered—and he realized some may never be answered—he was feeling more and more certain that what the Professor had told him was true. The pieces just all fit together. He knew he still had to have more information before making a decision on what action to take. And the information could only come from one place—his hometown. And with his mother still recovering from surgery, he had a ready-made reason to go home for a couple of days. The following day he would inform his teachers that he had to take Friday off. He could get a ride home—there was always someone headed for East Tennessee—and return Sunday. That would give him a couple of days to spend with his mother and to see what he might uncover. The next afternoon he met Sally in the library to study.

"You look worn out. I guess this bug has really knocked you out, huh?"

"It has been pretty bad, but I think I am getting over it. I should be able to play volleyball tomorrow night."

"Right," she said. "Got to be macho, huh? Anyway, have you talked to your mother in the past couple of days?"

"Yes, I just talked to her today. She's home now."

"How's she doing?"

"She said she is fine but I'm not so sure. Her back is very sore from the surgery and she still has a little pain down her leg, but she said the doctor told her that is to be expected for a while. He said it should go away soon."

"So are you planning on going to see her soon?"

"It's funny you should ask. I was just going to tell you that I am going home this weekend."

"That's nice, Ethan. She'll appreciate that," she stated, then, after hesitating for a moment, added, "and are you going to tell your parents about us?"

Her question would have been so much easier a few days ago. But, at least for how, he had to pretend that nothing had changed.

"Well of course—at least if that is alright with you."

"You're a silly boy," she said with a smile.

The two studied until after five then went to get something to eat. Afterward they went to her dorm room. The school's policy was anytime a male visited a girl's room he had to sign in with the dorm mother and the door had to be left ajar. It still left a small degree of privacy. After talking for a while, Sally turned to Ethan with a serious look.

"Is there something wrong, Ethan?"

"Why do you ask that?"

"You just seem awful distant—like something is bothering you but you don't want to tell me."

"Actually I guess it is a lot of things. My mother having surgery; Tommy getting drafted; me getting sick and getting behind in my studies. And now I feel I have to go see my mother which will only put me further behind. I guess I just have a lot of things on my mind."

"And you are sure that's all it is?"

"Of course. Why do you ask?"

"And nothing to do with us?"

"That's the only thing that isn't a problem," he stated, hoping it sounded convincing.

He got a ride home with a student from Johnson City who was also going home to visit a recuperating mother. Ethan did not find that unusual since making the trip home this time of year was usually because of a family emergency or problem. Ethan soon learned that the boy's mother had just had a mastectomy. Although the surgery had gone well, and they thought they had caught the cancer early enough to stop its spread, he could hear the concern in the boy's voice. While he shared his experience with his father's battle with cancer, he could not answer the young man's questions about why such things happened.

The student dropped him off at his parents' house a little after noon on Friday. He was glad to see his brother's car in front of the house. His mother was lying on the couch watching TV while his brother washed the dishes. They immediately stopped to greet him.

"How you doing little brother?" asked Horace as he gave him a hug. "How was the trip?"

"It was fine. Where is Emily? I thought Mom said she was coming with you."

"She couldn't get off work, so it has just been me to entertain Mom."

Ethan walked to his mother who was just getting up from the couch.

"Mom, you don't have to get up. Just relax."

"Oh don't be silly. I am fine. Besides, the doctor said I shouldn't be laying around too much anyway," she said as she slowly walked over and gave her son a hug. Ethan noticed how gently she was moving.

"Are you sure you are O.K., Mom? You are sure moving slowly."

"It's a good thing you didn't see me a couple of weeks ago," she said laughing. "Trust me—I am ten times better. The doctor says it will just take a little time to get back to one hundred percent."

"So everything is O.K.?"

"Well, as you can see I am pretty sore from the operation, and I still have a bit of ache in my leg, but that's because the nerve was compressed for so long. It will get better."

"It sounds like you've had a pretty rough time."

"Yeah, it was pretty bad, son. Sort of like having someone cutting the back of your leg open with a rusty knife."

"Wow, Mom, I didn't know it was that bad."

"It's fine, Ethan. That's why I didn't tell you until I knew what was going on. Everything will be fine now."

Ethan sat down and talked to his mother while Horace returned to the kitchen. She spent the next few minutes telling him about her medical tests and surgery. He noticed his father was not around.

"Is Dad at work?"

"Yes. He wanted to be here when you got in and to say good bye to Horace, but he has missed so much time with me being sick he couldn't take off."

After a few minutes Horace joined them. They talked about the surgery and about old friends and classmates. He told them about Tommy's draft notice. While his mother usually knew everything going on in town, she had been out of the loop lately. While the news was not a surprise, it was still upsetting. They also talked about Horace's upcoming wedding which was only a few months away. Since they were talking about marriage and relationships, Ethan felt it was the right time to bring up his relationship with Sally. As much as his mother had always preached to him about treating everyone the same, he was still uncertain of her reaction. He decided the best approach was the most direct.

"Mom, speaking of dating and such," he began, "I have met someone I think is pretty special."

"That's great news, son," she said as she patted him on the leg.

"It's about time," chimed in Horace.

"I'm not even twenty yet," said Ethan before turning back to his mother.

"Tell me about her, son. Is she nice? What's her name? I take it she's a student. What's her major? I bet she is cute."

"Yes, she's a student and her name is Sally. She is very nice. She plans on being a teacher. And....well....I have a picture of her. That will show you how cute she is."

Ethan pulled the picture from his wallet and handed it to his mother as his brother looked on. He hoped they would not notice how nervous he was. He examined his mother's eyes for a look of shock but could not judge her reaction.

"Well," she said eventually, "she certainly has a good tan."

Ethan and Horace both laughed.

"So you are not shocked?" he asked.

"No, not shocked. A little surprised perhaps."

"But not disappointed?"

"Honey, if you like her that is the important thing. Is this serious?"

"I really don't know yet, Mom, but she is a wonderful person. She is smart, thoughtful, witty, and, as you can see, beautiful."

"Yes she is, son. But the only advice I can give you is that....well, if this becomes more serious, it will not be easy. Society is not ready for racial mixing yet....at least not in East Tennessee."

"Well, marriage is always difficult."

"Yes it is, and that is why you need to know what you're getting yourself into. This will make it more difficult, but that is all I am saying about it."

Ethan turned to his brother who had made no comment.

"Well?" he asked.

"Well what?"

"You know what. What do you think?"

"I think she is beautiful, and if she is all those other things you mentioned she should be worth it."

Ethan loved how things were always so simple for his brother. It was either yes or no—no in between. He wished he were more like him. He thought for a second before voicing his biggest concern. Turning to his mother he asked,

"So, what do you think Dad will say?"

"That I don't know, son, but you better let me talk to him first."

They talked for a while longer before Ethan offered his second surprise of the day.

"Mom, while I am here there is something I need to do."

"That sounds so serious. Should I ask what?"

"Well, it's just that ever since the incident....you know....with Deputy Pratt....I feel like it's been hanging over my head."

"I can understand, Ethan, but it's been almost six years now. I think everyone agrees that you're not in any danger anymore."

"Oh, it's not that. I just wonder if there is something I missed that might have helped catch them. I feel that if I could go through the records I might pick up something. Do you think Sheriff Benlow would let me do that?"

"I don't see why not. He's a very reasonable and honest man— and no one wants to solve it more than him. But I don't think there is much of a chance of you picking up something that he and all the other officials missed. But if it is bothering you go ahead and ask."

"Well if you don't mind, I think I will go by and talk to him. Can I take your car?"

"Sure, son, take your time. I will be here when you get back."

He gave his mother a kiss and turned to leave. As he got to the door his brother called to him, "Hey, Ethan."

"Yes?"

"You sure have a much more interesting life than I do."

He just smiled, took his mother's car keys off the wall, and walked out.

FOURTEEN

The drive to the Sheriff's' office was less than ten minutes. That was the good thing about being in a small town—everything was within a short drive of where you happened to be at the time. The Sheriff's' headquarters was in a red, one story, brick building on the edge of town. Ethan walked in to find the receptionist, Holly Moore, on the phone. She motioned for him to wait until she finished her conversation. Although he knew her well enough to speak to her, he found her unpleasant and serious. After hanging up the phone she turned to him. "May I help you?" she asked flatly.

"Hi, Holly," he said. "Is the Sheriff in?"

"He is. May I tell him what this is regarding?"

"I would just like to talk to him for a minute. Tell him it's Ethan Ward."

"I know who you are," she said as she turned and walked down the hall.

Within a couple of minutes the Sheriff appeared. He walked up to Ethan and shook his hand.

"Good to see you, son. How is school?"

"It's fine, sir. Uh....the reason I am here is....well, could we talk in your office?"

"Sure, Ethan," he said as he turned and led him down the hall.

Once there they talked for a few minutes about school, about what was going on in town, and about Ethan's mother's surgery. The Sheriff knew his was not a social call. He soon asked Ethan why he was there. Ethan told him the same thing he had told his mother—that Deputy Pratt's killing had been bothering him for years—and that since he was the only witness to the event, maybe, if he were allowed to go through the records, he might pick up something that could be helpful.

"Let me ask you something, son. To be blunt, why do you think you could notice something that a whole string of professional law enforcement people could not?"

"Well I don't mean it to sound like I am smarter than anyone else, but, at the same time, I was the only one who saw what happened. I doubt that there would be anything worthwhile, but maybe I would see something that might trigger a memory. Don't you think it would be worthwhile even if there was a one percent chance of it helping?"

"It's just not something we normally do, son. But I guess, after all these years and getting nowhere, it's not going to hurt anything. But let's just keep this between you and me."

"Sure," he said, making a mental note to tell his family not to mention this to anyone.

The Sheriff led him down the hall and unlocked the door to a large storage room. He turned on the light and walked over to a row of storage shelves which ran the length of the wall. He removed a box and brought it back to Ethan. He directed Ethan to a desk and turned on a lamp.

"Here is everything we have. Just let me know when you are finished."

Before he could leave, Ethan had one more question.

"Oh, Sheriff," he began, "would all of Deputy Pratt's records be in here?"

"No," he returned with a confused look, "just those related to this case. Why?"

"Well, I thought the shooting might be related to something that happened earlier, and if I could look through his records I might see a description of somebody or something that might be related to this case."

"I guess that is conceivable. The problem is that information would be filed related to the individual case and I can't let you go through those."

"Oh, sure. Then what about his individual personnel records?"

"I don't see how that would help you, son. It's not going to tell you much about any cases he was working on."

"You are probably right, Sheriff, but again even if there is a small chance of picking up something don't you think it is worth it?"

"You would make a good lawyer. I guess the Deputy's not going to object. O.K., his personnel records are in this filing cabinet."

He took out his key and opened the file cabinet, then removed a hanging folder and handed it to Ethan, then closed and locked the cabinet.

"You've sure grown up in the past year, Ethan. Any more requests before I go?"

"Actually I do have one more question. Can I ask how come this case wasn't compared to the other three cases of boys being abducted?"

"Well, well. You certainly have been spending some time studying this haven't you? To tell you the truth, son, we did examine that but dismissed it."

"Can I ask why?"

"That is still an open case too, you know."

"So there is nothing you can tell me about it?"

The Sheriff thought for a minute. He knew that Ethan had a legitimate right to know some of the information. He was, as he had said, the only witness to a horrible crime. And, if he now thought the two men had been after him, he could see his need to know as much as he could. But at the same time he had to protect the ongoing investigation.

"Ethan, let me tell you this. You are not aware of this....and there was no reason you should have been. As a young boy we had to do our best to protect you physically as well as emotionally. We looked very hard at any tie in with those other boys being abducted and there was almost zero chance of that being the case."

"And, you can't tell me any more than that?"

"Boy, you are stubborn. All right....what can I tell you? First, and this is just general knowledge from people who have worked on such cases, there has never been a known case like those where there were two perpetrators. Child molesters do not work together—it is as simple as that. Also, the chance of the abductors being colored—or black as they now like to be called—is almost non existent. They generally do not commit those types of crimes. And there was also the high likelihood of the individual being noticed if he had been black. There is also other information that I cannot share with you which ruled out those two boys having anything to do with the other abductions. No, I think it's just what I said in the beginning. The Deputy just happened to stumble upon two boys that weren't gonna let themselves be taken in. And you just happened to be at the wrong place at the wrong time."

Ethan agreed with everything the Sheriff had said. It also fit in with everything the Professor had told him. However, the Sheriff had never thought of his Deputy being the one guilty of the abductions. And now was certainly not the time to offer his theory. Maybe at a later date, when he had more information, he would discuss it with him.

The Sheriff left him alone with the records. He began by opening the box with the documents regarding the case. The first thing he came to was the write-up of the event. While it provided a few details he had not thought of, it offered very little new information. There was one note that the Sheriff probably would not like him seeing, and that was the reference to the tire tracks left by the pickup. It stated that they had compared them to those found at the sites of the other boys' abductions and there was no match. The tires from the other scenes were from a full sized car. He wondered what would have been the results if they had compared the prints to the Deputy's personal or patrol cars.

After that he examined the information regarding the fingerprints. There was no useful information here. It simply stated that the fingerprints had been run through the FBI's national database with no match. Next he came to the pictures of the crime scene. Even though he had been there when it happened, the pictures were still shocking. He realized that he had never actually seen the Deputy's fallen body before. He had seen the gun and had seen him fall, but after that he had headed for the fence and had never looked back. He spent little time looking at the pictures.

The only other pictures of the crime scene were of the tire tracks and footprints as well as the bottle of orange soda the man had given him. He put the material back in the box and closed the lid, then opened the folder which contained Deputy Pratt's records—the real reason that he came.

Despite what he had told the Sheriff, there was very little information he was looking for here—just enough to determine the whereabouts of the Deputy on the days the boys were killed. He quickly found an entry in the personnel log showing the Deputy was sent to Harriman to pick up a suspect on the day of the first killing. Unfortunately it did not show if he had left that morning or the day before or what car he drove. He imagined he had driven the squad car if he had to bring back a prisoner. While it took some searching, he was also able to determine that he was scheduled off the day the second boy was killed. Unfortunately, he could find no information regarding his actions or whereabouts the day of the third killing.

Satisfied that he had obtained all the information available he left the box and folder on the desk and walked back to the Sheriff's office.

"Did you find anything worthwhile?" asked the Sheriff.

"No, sir," he answered, "unfortunately I didn't. I guess it was a waste of time. Sorry."

"Oh well, at least you tried. As I said before, let's keep this between you and me."

"Of course. Thanks for letting me try, Sheriff."

He left the building and returned to his mother's car. He had one more stop to make. The other good thing about living in a small town was that you knew where most everyone lived. It only took him a few minutes to drive to the house where Deputy Pratt had lived. Although it was a long shot, considering what was at stake, it was worth it.

The house was a modest rambler, probably about thirty years old, located in an isolated part of the county. A blue Dodge Dart was parked in the dirt driveway beside the house. He parked the car and walked to the door and knocked. An attractive young woman, about thirty, came to the door carrying a baby. He did not remember ever seeing her before.

"Can I help you?" she asked.

Ethan thought about making up a story about why he was there but quickly decided against it. He knew he could never be creative enough or a good enough liar to make her believe it, so he told her the truth. He explained who he was and why he wanted to look around.

"So you are really the little boy who was there when the Deputy was murdered?" she asked.

"Unfortunately I am," he answered. "Do you remember it?"

"No, we didn't live here then. My husband and I just moved here a couple of years ago, but we've heard enough about it. We're just renting this house. Why would you want to look around? What are you looking for?"

"I don't really know," he said honestly. He went on to explain how the murder had haunted him for years and he was searching for anything that might help solve the case.

"Well, I really don't care if you look around, but I can tell you, you won't find anything. A couple of other families have lived here before us and the place was totally vacant when we moved in."

"So, no old boxes or anything like that around?"

"No, there sure wasn't. And my husband and I stored some stuff in the attic and the only thing left up there was an old chair."

"And no storage shed out back?"

"No—sorry. Trust me, there ain't nothing of any use to you here."

He apologized for bothering her, then turned to leave.

"Oh, Ethan," she called after him, "you might have better luck at his parents' house. It's only down the road a mile or so. Maybe they will have some of his things."

Why had he not thought of that? If there were any of the Deputy's possessions left that is probably where they would be. He decided he had a long way to go before becoming a journalist. He wasn't sure of the Pratt's reaction if he showed up, but if they thought he was trying to solve their son's murder, they should not object to him looking around.

Their house was similar to their son's except more run down. An older Ford Galaxy sat in the driveway along with a newer Ford Falcon. He knocked on the door and waited. Soon an elderly gentleman appeared. Even though he and the Deputy would forever be associated with each other in many people's eyes, this was the first time he had ever met his father. Ethan realized he was probably only around sixty, but looked much older. He was about five feet six inches and skinny and frail. He wondered if he had always looked as he did today or if the past few years had destroyed him.

"Can I help ya?" he asked.

Ethan explained who he was and what he was doing there. The old man just looked at him with sad eyes. Finally, after thinking of what Ethan had said, he spoke. "Boy, ya really think ya can find somethin' after all this time what the police didn't think of?"

"Sir, I have no idea. I know it's a really long shot, but I'm the only one that saw what happened, and if there is something in his belongings that might lead to who did this don't you think it is worth a try?"

"I reckon, but I can't imagine they'd be anything here that might have to do with our boy gettin' killed."

"Well, maybe if he had a note about a case he was working on, or a lead or a letter from somebody it might trigger something for me. Do you even have any of his stuff?"

"Yep, I reckon. We got a pile in the garage yonder. Come on in."

He pushed the door back and moved aside to let Ethan enter. As he walked into the room he saw a woman, presumably Mrs. Pratt, coming from the kitchen. She was wiping her hands on an apron. Ethan introduced himself and reached out to shake her hand. It was cold and lifeless.

"He's gonna look through Andy's things. Gonna try ta find somethin' ta help find out who shot him."

She just nodded and walked down the hall. The two men walked into the garage where piles of furniture laden with boxes stood. Ethan found it hard to believe that, after all these years, his belongings were still in the garage.

"Is this your son's stuff?"

"Purty much," he answered. "Might be some other things scattered around about, but it's purty much Andy's. Couldn't stand ta touch it first couple years. Now reckon we just got used ta it."

"And did the Sheriff or anybody else go through this after he was shot?"

"Don't rightly know. Maybe over ta his house. We hauled it over a few weeks later when his landlord had a new renter."

"So it's O.K. if I go through the boxes?"

"Go ahead at it, boy," he replied as he turned to leave. "Let me know if'n ya find somethin'."

While at first look the mess in the garage looked overwhelming, as he examined it more it did not look so bad. There were fifteen to twenty boxes piled on top what appeared to be bedroom furniture. There were also a few paper bags scattered around the floor, but he quickly determined that those contained only clothes. He began examining the boxes. It gave him a strange—almost perverse—feeling to be going through the boxes. It was as if he were spying on the Deputy.

A half hour later he had gone through the majority of the boxes and had found nothing worthwhile. With only a few boxes remaining, he found what he had been looking for. At the bottom of one of the boxes, covered with yearbooks and roadmaps, was a large brown envelope. He reached inside and removed the contents to find a large number of newspaper clippings. The clippings were in three groups, each clasped together with a large paper clip. As he examined them he quickly realized they were all related to the three boys that had been killed. Each set of clippings covered a different boy. The first group had stories from the Harriman, Rockwood, Oak Ridge and Knoxville newspapers. The second group had clippings from various Knoxville newspapers as well as stories from Oak Ridge and Maryville papers. The final group had stories from numerous papers including The Tennessean, the most popular newspaper in the state. On each group of clippings was a big red circle with a number inside. They were labeled *One*, *Two*, and *Three*. Ethan quickly understood what he was seeing. It was momentos of the boys that had been killed—a sort of scorecard. The evidence left little doubt in his mind as to whether the statements made by Professor Robertson were true.

Ethan put the clippings back in the envelope wondering what he should do with them. As he was deciding he heard footsteps drawing near. If he had had more time perhaps he would have uncovered even more information. Unfortunately he had to put the envelope back in the box and cover it with the yearbooks. He stood up just as Mr. Pratt entered the room.

"So, did ya find anything worthwhile?" he asked.

"No, I'm afraid not," replied Ethan as he walked toward the garage door. "I think I put most things back as I found them."

"That ain't no problem. Reckon we gonna have ta have somebody go through this mess someday. Getting too old ta do it myself."

"I understand," replied Ethan as they walked back down the hall. "I really appreciate your letting me go through these things. Sorry I couldn't find anything. And I'm sorry about your son."

"Me too, son. Reckon life just ain't fair. First it was my brother got killed a long time ago, then my boy. Sometimes it's more than a man can bear."

Ethan apologized again and left the house. As he got in his car and drove away he realized the car sitting in front of their house was a full sized American car—the same kind that matched the tire prints at the one crime scene.

The road where the Pratts lived was similar to the one where Ethan's family had lived previously. That was not unusual since there were dozens of sparsely populated dirt roads in Greene County. As he neared the main road back into Greenville, he had a flashback to the night eighteen months earlier. There, turned sideways in the road, was an older green Chevy Nova. Unlike the last time, this car did not seem to be damaged. Ethan expected it had just broken down. Since the passenger side was toward him, he could not make out the driver. He pulled his car to a halt and walked forward to see if he could assist. As he got closer, the driver got out of his car. As he did so Ethan's pulse began to race.

"Well, if it ain't my old buddy, Ethan," began Ted Russell. "Imagine running into you out here on this country road."

"What do you want, Ted," returned Ethan sharply.

"Where's your 'Oreo' friend Tommy?" asked Ted, ignoring his question.

"I'll ask you again, Ted. What do you want?"

Ted walked around his car and toward Ethan's. Ethan wondered why Ted had always disliked him so much. He could never think of anything he might have done to instill such hatred. At least now perhaps he would discover the source of his anger.

"So, you out here lookin' into why the Deputy was shot, huh?"

"How do you know that?" asked Ethan, then quickly remembered that he was related to the Sheriff's receptionist, Holly Moore. She must have overheard their conversation and called him. He quickly added,

"It's none of your business why I'm out here, Ted."

"Well I'm about to make it my business. The Deputy was a bully who liked to push people around and he got just what he deserved."

"A bully—you mean like you?"

Ted got closer—almost in Ethan's face as he stood with his back against his car.

"Well, I tell you what—I ain't no purty white boy like you who has everyone fooled."

"What do you mean, fooled?"

"Always a goody two shoes. Saw two black men shoot a poor Deputy so everybody feels sorry for you. Reckon you used that every chance you got. Then a big hero by pullin' two people from a car—Senator's family even. Reckon life just falls right into your hands."

"I don't have time for your silly games, Ted. Move your car."

He got closer, within inches of Ethan's face.

"Don't reckon I will. What'cha gonna do about it without your friend here to protect you?"

Ethan didn't plan what happened next, and later wouldn't remember much of it. Before he realized it, he grabbed Ted's head and banged it into the car window. He quickly followed up with an elbow to the back of his head. Ted turned and swung wildly at

Ethan who ducked the blow and countered with a jab to his ribs. As Ted tried to protect himself Ethan put his leg behind his and threw him to the ground. As Ted grabbed for his legs, Ethan kicked him in the ribs. He tried to fight back but once more Ethan kicked him, this time with all his strength. As he rolled onto his side Ethan bent down and put his knee on his throat.

"You son-of–a bitch," yelled Ethan, "you ever bother me again and I will put you in the hospital. You understand!"

He got no response.

"I said you understand?" he repeated. Ted only nodded.

Ethan got up and turned to walk away, then quickly turned and walked back.

"I want to know what you know about the Deputy getting killed."

"I think you cracked my rib," replied Ted.

"I don't care. I want to know what you know about the Deputy getting killed."

"I don't know anything," he moaned as he rolled on to his back and tried to sit up. "I just know he was a bully and was always picking on people—black people—so he got what he deserved. That's all."

Ethan went to Ted's car and, noticing the keys were still in the ignition, started it and moved it to the side of the road. He left it running and came back to his car. Ted had managed to stand although still holding his side. Ethan stopped and looked at him.

"I've never wanted any trouble with you, Ted, but if you ever bother me again, you'll be sorry."

Ted could only shake his head as he staggered to his car. Ethan started his car and pulled around him. He was both proud and embarrassed at his actions. While it had been some time since he had played sports, it looked like all those years as an athlete had paid off. He couldn't believe how he had lost his temper, but that was probably the only thing that had saved him from a beating. *Ain't adrenalin wonderful,* he thought. He decided he would not mention their encounter to anyone.

FIFTEEN

Hilda Ward did not consider herself to be overly liberal—just a realist. She had always taught her sons to treat everyone the same no matter what their background, their religion, or their race. While she did believe in God, it was more than that. She had seen what prejudice and hatred had done to her country, her family, and to her father. She knew once people began judging others based on their differences, it never ended, and eventually all of society would pay. She had seen it in her country and, for the past twenty-five years, in her husband's country. It would be nice to live in a society where people treated everyone else the same, although she knew that would never happen.

Now, her beliefs were getting the ultimate test. Although she had tried to instill her beliefs in her sons, she had never considered the possibility that one of them might actually fall in love with someone of another race. And what if Ethan married Sally? She was still trying to sort out her feelings about that. While she did not believe that one race or nationality was better than another, she wondered if it was wrong to want her grandchildren to look like her? And even though she believed that all people were the same in God's eyes, was it wrong to want her children to marry someone like her? They were tough questions and ones she had never had to consider before. Whatever happened, she knew she would be able to adjust. She was not so certain about her husband. He had come a long way since they had married. It had been a long journey breaking the prejudices instilled in him by his parents, but he had made great strides. She was not sure he had come far enough.

She had not yet had a chance to talk to her husband when Ethan returned that afternoon. She quickly took her son aside and told him to wait until the following day to talk to his father about Sally. That would give her time to discuss the matter with him.

Hilda suggested to her son that he get together with his friends that evening but he told her he came to spend time with her. Horace left for home after dinner leaving his brother alone to entertain their parents. They spent the evening watching TV and talking.

The next morning Ethan slept until after nine, which was rare for him considering his normal hectic schedule. Upon arising he walked to the kitchen to see his father sitting solemnly at the table. He knew his mother had already talked to him.

"Morning, Dad," he said.

"Son," his father acknowledged with a nod of his head.

Ethan walked to the refrigerator and poured himself a glass of juice then stood by the sink drinking it. The wait for the discussion to begin was not long.

"So, your mother tells me you got a new girlfriend," he stated.

"Yes, sir."

"What's wrong, son, don't they have no decent lookin' white girls over there?"

"I guess they do," he answered defensively, "but you always taught me I should have the best."

"And exactly how serious are you about this colored girl?"

"They are not colored, Dad," he said sternly.

"O.K., black. You gonna answer my question?"

"I don't really know. I just know she's one of the smartest and nicest people I have met. I just have to see what happens."

His father took a sip of his coffee and stared at the table a second before continuing.

"Ethan, you're a good boy, and I'm proud of the way you turned out. I reckon your mother and I did somethin' right. And I'm glad the way you treat people—all people. But I don't think you have any idea what you're getting yourself in for here, son."

"Well I think you are wrong, Dad," he shot back. "First, I don't even know if anything will become of this, but if it does, you really think I haven't thought about all the possibilities?"

"Thinking about somethin' is one thing—experiencing it is somethin' else. If somethin' does become of this are you ready for people ta stare at you when you go out in public? Are you ready ta be discriminated against when ya try ta buy a car or house? And have you thought about what it will be like if ya have kids?"

"You really think I haven't thought of any of these things, Dad? What do you think—that we have spent the last couple of months not going out in public so no one could see us? Well I got news for you—we've been out a lot and it really wasn't that big a deal. Times are changing. And discrimination is illegal now you know. And, if it ever does come to that and we do have kids—if they look anything like her they will be beautiful."

"Well, all I can say, son, is that I hope ya take your time. You are still awfully young and ya might look at things a lot different in a year or two."

"Did you look at things different with Mom after a year or two?"

By the look in his father's eyes he thought maybe he had gone too far.

"What exactly does that mean?" he asked sternly.

"Well, when you and Mom got married everyone hated the Germans. It had to have been hard for you."

"It ain't nowhere near the same. If you ain't noticed your Ma and me are the same color and I think we can say the same as you boys. When we walked down the street no one stared at us or made comments. And we were also a mite older and experienced. Not just a couple of young kids in lust."

"So, that's what you think this is huh, Dad—just a case of young lust?"

"Well, let's face it, son, you are still pretty young, and ya ain't had a lot of experience with girls."

"I'm not exactly naive, Dad. I have been out with quite a few

girls, most recently Rachel. And there is no comparison between her and Sally, no matter how much you and Mom like her."

The two sat silently for a while, each trying to think of what to say to get the other to see things from their point of view. Finally, his father spoke, more calmly. "Look, Ethan, I'll admit this is kin' of hard for me ta understand, but I have always wanted what is best for ya....."

"I know that, Dad."

"So I reckon I'll just wait and see what happens, but I don't want this ta drive a wedge between us."

"It'll be fine, Dad," said his son softly, "there's a good chance that after she gets to know me better she won't want to have anything to do with me anyway."

"I doubt that, son," he said laughing, then added, "so ya got a picture of her?"

Ethan took out the picture from his wallet and showed it to his dad. He was pleased with his father's reaction.

"Well, I can see why ya were attracted to her."

Neither wanted to continue the argument so they let the conversation die—they both knew to be revisited another day.

––––

Ethan spent most of the morning around the house, visiting with his mother and watching TV. By afternoon she insisted that he spend some time getting together with friends. He called Tommy and suggested they go to a movie. They selected "Beneath the Planet of the Apes." Ethan borrowed his mother's car and picked his friend up at six-thirty. After the movie they stopped at the drive-in for a hamburger.

"That was an awesome movie," said Tommy.

"That was a horrible movie," returned Ethan.

"Oh no, man. It's nice to escape reality sometimes and just forget about all the problems of this world."

"I guess that's true. There was no resemblance of reality there," he conceded. They ordered their food and watched the parade of people come and go. Ethan brought up the subject they had both been avoiding.

"So, any luck about getting an extension from Uncle Sam?"

"No, man, but it's O.K. It looks like it will be over a month anyway before they can get me processed. I didn't know how slow Uncle Sam works. I thought they would'a snapped up a prime specimen like me a long time ago."

"Man, take every day you can."

"Only problem with that, Ace, is it will be that much longer until I get to come home."

"I hear you," said Ethan, then, more seriously asked, "Are you worried?"

"I guess—a little. Who wouldn't be?"

"Well, maybe you'll be lucky and won't be sent to Nam."

"Right."

"Well, it's possible. They got to have a few troops here."

"Check with me in six months. Guess where I'll be?"

Ethan knew it was true. He didn't know what to say to comfort his friend.

"You know, I feel really guilty about all you guys being sent over there while I am still in school."

"Sure you do."

"I'm serious, Tommy. It bothers me a lot."

"I know it does Ethan," he said, "but it shouldn't. You saved two people's lives—you got $5,000 and you got to go to school. And no—I haven't told anybody else about the money. But you shouldn't let it bother you. I wouldn't."

"Are you serious? You are the one who is always preaching to me about the battle between good and evil. You always said it is the right thing to do to be over there protecting those people."

"Yeah, I guess you're right," he conceded, "but it's a lot easier to talk about the right thing to do when your life is not on the line."

They continued talking about the war and the friends that were already there or who had been lost in battle. They were distracted by the car-hop bringing their food. Shortly Ethan had a surprise for his friend. He removed his wallet from his pocket.

"So, you been dating anybody lately?" Ethan asked.

"Nothing serious," he said, "ain't a whole lot of sisters in town here you know. Besides, I figured I better wait until I knew what was happening to me before I got into anything too heavy. What about you?"

"Well yeah, there's one girl I haven't told you about," he began as he opened the wallet and showed him the picture.

"Wow!" he said with a whistle, "Are you serious?"

"Afraid so. What do you think?"

"I think she is fine."

"That's not what I meant."

"That's between you two," he said. "I'm sure you already got the lectures about how tough it will be, so you don't need me saying nothing else."

"Yeah, my father is still trying to cope with it."

"Is this serious?"

"I don't know. It's too early to tell, but she sure is nice."

"And, you know what they say."

"No, what?"

"Once you have black—you can never go back."

"Or, once you have white….."

"Yeah?"

"I don't know…I thought I could make up something clever but it didn't work."

There was another subject on which Ethan wanted his friend's advice.

"Can I ask your opinion on something?"

"Sure—I'm great at giving advice."

"So," he began hesitantly, "do you think pre-marital sex is still a sin?"

"What do you mean still—like since last week?"

"No—like compared to the old days in the bible. You always told me that God gave laws for a reason—not just to make life difficult for us, right?"

"Yeah, so?"

"Well if he gave rules about sex because it leads to unwanted pregnancies and disease and stuff like that and today you don't have those problems, why is it still a sin? I mean unless you are using it to hurt somebody."

"So you really think we don't have unwanted pregnancies and disease because of sex today?"

"Well, you do, but you can protect yourself against it."

"O.K," returned Tommy, "we both know that is not always the case but aside from that, yes, it is still a sin."

"Why?"

"Because sex is a gift from God to be used by a man and woman in marriage. It's as simple as that."

"Oh," returned Ethan with a touch of disappointment in his voice. Tommy knew that was not the answer he was looking for.

"Look, buddy, I don't mean it to sound like I am 'holier than thou', but you asked me what I thought so I had to tell you. But remember, we all commit sins everyday. Sometimes I can't even get through an hour without doing something wrong. So I don't know if that type of sin is worse than any other."

Ethan said nothing further and Tommy felt that he wanted to discuss the matter no more so let it drop. They finished their meal as they talked about other things. Ethan badly wanted to tell Tommy about his meeting with Sally's father and what he had learned since then, but he decided against it. He still did not know for sure what course of action to take and, if there was any personal danger from what he had learned, he did not want to involve his friend. He soon devised a way to get his friend's view on the subject without having to share what he knew.

"There is something else that has been bothering me, Tommy," he said.

"You got a lot of things on your mind today, Ace. What is it?"

He told him that the incident with Deputy Pratt had been following him around like a dark cloud for six years. He also told him that his classes in Journalism had renewed his interest in finding out what had happened.

"So, you planning on doing what the Sheriff, the police, and the TBCI couldn't do, huh? Glad we sent you to college. You gonna work on Kennedy or my main man Martin Luther next?"

"Despite what you think, they've already been solved. But seriously, I was just looking at it from a different angle. Maybe the two guys had planned in advance to kill him. You ever hear any word on the street about him?"

"Any word on the street?" he repeated. "What do you think I am—a drug dealer?"

"You know what I mean. You ever hear anybody talk about Pratt—what kind of person he was? Was anybody out to get him?"

"Only thing I ever heard," he said, "was that he was a real S.O.B—and that was towards everybody—black and white."

"But no details?"

"No, not really. Black people just learned to keep out of his way. But as far as what happened on the road, I don't know any more than you do. If I did I would turn them in myself," he added strongly.

"Why do you say it like that?"

"Cause, Ace, what they did was wrong. Even if he was a bully, they gunned him down in cold blood—and with a young boy watching. And it just promotes the good-ole-boys view of the black man. We're all animals you know."

"I never knew you felt so strongly about it."

"Well, racism works both ways. The Deputy probably picked on them because they were black, but they killed him because he wasn't."

Although it was interesting to hear his friend's opinion on the shooting, it provided little new information and did little to help him decide his next course of action. He needed to make a decision soon though, for he would be heading back to campus the next day—and back to Sally and her father.

SIXTEEN

Professor Warren Robertson carried the stack of papers into the dining room and placed them on the table. He turned the TV toward him so he could watch the Cardinals/Dodgers baseball game as he graded the tests. It should be a quiet and restful day. He had just dropped his daughter off at her dorm after lunch. They had gone to church then stopped at a Chinese restaurant for the Sunday buffet. Now she would be joining her friends for an afternoon softball game while he would spend the day working. He just started to the kitchen for a glass of tea when the phone rang.

"Robertson here," he answered.

"Professor Robertson," came the familiar but unrecognizable voice.

"Yes."

"Hi, Professor. It's Ethan Ward."

"Oh, hi, Ethan. How is your mother?"

"She is doing better. Still kind of sore," he said. "Professor, can I come by and talk to you in a little while?"

"Well, of course. I thought you weren't getting back until later this evening."

"We left a little early. We're only a few minutes away but had to stop for gas. If it is O.K. the guy I am riding with can drop me by there."

"That will be fine. Do you know how to get here?"

"Yes, Sally and I drove by your house once. I should be there in about twenty minutes."

"See you then."

The Professor looked at the stack of papers. 'Guess this will have to wait', he said to himself. 'Some things are more important'.

Twenty minutes later Ethan arrived at the Professor's door.

"Good to see you, son," he said as he let him in. "Would you like some tea or lemonade?"

"Lemonade would be good," said Ethan.

The two took their drinks and went into the living room. The Professor turned the sound down on the TV.

"Are you a Cardinal fan?" asked Ethan.

"Oh yeah, and you?"

"There's only one team—the Reds."

"I guess we'll have to agree to disagree," he said.

Ethan sat on the couch—the Professor in a nearby chair.

"Well," said the Professor, "I guess it's good news that you're here. Hopefully you have discovered that everything I told you was true."

"It certainly appears so," he said. "but there are still a lot of unanswered questions. That's why I'm here."

"As I said earlier, son, there are some things I won't answer—and other things I just don't know myself. But I will tell you what I can. But first, I'm dying to know what you found out on your own."

Ethan told him that he had followed his advice and got permission to look through the crime records. He confirmed that the records did show that it was Deputy Pratt that had been sent to pick up the boy in Harriman that winter day in 1963.

"Just as I described," said the Professor.

"Yes, and I also was able to determine that the Deputy was not on duty the day the boy in Knoxville was killed, but that does not place him at the scene or even in the city. And I could find nothing that placed him anywhere near the third kid's murder."

"He was there," said the Professor forcefully.

"You keep saying that—and I do believe you now—but how did you all know that?"

"Why don't you keep going and tell me what else you found out and then I will share everything I can."

Ethan went on to tell him about the fingerprints on the soda bottle, which he already knew, and about the tire tracks which was new information to him.

"So they compared the tracks from our tires to those found around the boys' crime scenes?"

"Well I only saw the records that referenced those at the Knoxville murder, and, as you already know, there was no match with your truck. And obviously they never did make a match but—and here's the interesting part—they were able to determine that the prints came from a full size American car."

"It's too bad they didn't have any prints from the first murder since he was driving the patrol car that day. And it would be interesting to know Pratt's personal vehicle back then."

"I think it was a Ford Galaxy," said Ethan.

"How do you know that?" the Professor quickly asked.

"Because I went to his parents' house and they had an old Ford Galaxy sitting in front along with a newer car. I bet it was his."

"You're kidding," he said in amazement. "You actually went to their house? It sounds like you are well on your way to being a journalist. But, even if it was his, it wouldn't do any good now. The tires would have been long gone—and the same with the patrol car."

"Yeah, I thought of that. But there is one other thing."

"What?"

He told him about the newspaper articles he found with the Deputy's other belongings. He described how they were bundled together—each group being numbered and circled.

"It sounds like a trophy."

"That's what I thought," said Ethan. "So maybe I'm too trusting, but it appears like everything you told me and everything I uncovered points to the same conclusion."

"That's because it's the truth, son."

"But, as I said, there are still things I don't understand."

"Go ahead, Ethan. I will answer what I can."

"Well, first of all, There is no way your friend could have known the Deputy was guilty of the first boy's murder just because he was in the same town. Even if they had known each other and he knew how evil the Deputy was, there had to be more."

"You are a smart boy," he said with what appeared to be a proud smile. "How can I respond to that? Shall we say that it would not have been a surprise to my friend had the Deputy killed someone even earlier. And the fact that it took place in Harriman—well he felt like it was not a coincidence that he lived there—but because he lived there that he chose that spot to begin."

"Are you actually saying," said Ethan in amazement, "that the Deputy killed the first boy to show your friend that he could do it?"

"Not exactly. As I said earlier, it was a perversion—a sickness—that was the reason he did it. But I think it gave him a little added pleasure knowing that my friend knew and could do nothing about it."

"Well, if he knew, why could he do nothing about it? I don't understand that. Especially when two other boys died."

"Remember, we are looking back at what happened. That is always easier. And, in the beginning, all he had was a suspicion. And...well, there are still other things I can't tell you."

"O.K.," Ethan said with a shake of his head. "The other thing I can't figure out is how you could have gotten away. I know you had a head start, but everybody in the state was looking for you. That's impossible."

"Really," the Professor said laughing, "then I guess I'm not here. Anyway, I guess it won't hurt to tell you about that. It was really quite simple. Some call it luck—I call it divine intervention. We drove the back roads until we found a suitable place on Cherokee Lake to submerge the truck. We hid out in the woods until nightfall then hiked down to Jefferson City and waited for the first freight train to come by. We were back in Harriman the next morning."

"But the Sheriff searched all the lakes and rivers," said Ethan.

"There's probably a few hundred miles of shoreline in east Tennessee," he said. "Like I said—Divine intervention."

"But didn't anybody see you on the road?"

"We took all the back roads—some of them were almost impassable. We probably only saw one or two other vehicles on the road. And even at twenty miles an hour, we were probably thirty or forty miles away before they started looking for us."

"But the whole state was looking for that truck. Somebody must have known that it belonged to you."

"It was actually my dad's truck, and he had died a couple of years earlier. I don't know if Sally told you, but they had a small farm out in the country. After my parents died I used to go up there to check on things from time to time. I always left the truck in the barn when I wasn't using it. And how many dark blue trucks are there in Tennessee? Probably a few thousand at least. Nobody even asked about the truck for months, and I told them the transmission was going out so I took it to the junk yard."

"And your wife or kids didn't miss you when you were gone for two days?"

"My wife and I had a fight—I don't even remember over what— so I told her I was going up to check on the farm. So, no it was not unusual for me to be gone for a day or two."

"But how did you end up in Greenville in the first place? You said you weren't going there looking for the Deputy."

"No, I wasn't, and my friend swears he wasn't either, but sometimes I wonder. Anyway, he came by the farm and wanted to know if I wanted to take a trip over there. There was a man there that raised hunting dogs and he wanted to go buy one. The old man was sort of a recluse and didn't even have a phone, so we just took off for the day. When we got there, he wasn't even home. We waited for a while but he never showed up so we started back. My friend said he knew a shortcut back to highway 11. That's when we got lost and— as they say—the rest is history."

"And when you saw me on the road how come you offered to give me a ride? You had to know that could have been trouble for you?"

"Well, part of it was simply what we said—you seemed like a good boy and could use a lift. And I guess in both our minds we figured if you were with us you wouldn't be in any danger from anyone else. Of course, no one knew he was watching."

Ethan thought about everything he had told him. It explained a lot of things. The one question remaining though, was what did he do now, if anything. That was the main question on the Professor's mind as well.

"So," he asked, "where do we go from here?"

"That is what I have been trying to decide," said Ethan. "I'm still in the dark on some things because I don't know the other person, and I don't know how he knew all these things about the Deputy."

"And I told you that in the beginning."

"So my options are the same as before. Do nothing and try to just forget about what happened, or go to the authorities with the belief that justice will be done."

"What justice would be done, Ethan?" he asked. "By now you have to be almost as certain as I that the Deputy killed those boys and would have killed all of us. What could possibly be gained by having me or him arrested?"

"Well, one of the things that concerns me the most is that those three boys' parents still don't know what happened to them."

"Yes, I have thought of that a hundred times. But—and I hope this doesn't sound calloused—they do know what happened to them—they just don't know who did it. It's not the same as if someone had a child disappear and never found. Then I could understand because you go your whole life wondering and praying. As horrible as this is, they don't have that situation."

"But they would still want to know that the person that did this got what he deserved."

"I agree, Ethan, but I don't want to go to prison in letting them know."

"But there has to be another way. We can do it anonymously."

"Would it surprise you to know that we already tried that?"

"Really?" he quickly asked. What happened?"

"Nothing. We sent letters to both the State Police and the TBCI. We never heard anything about it. I guess they thought we were quacks. They get hundreds of leads in cases like this. Or maybe they thought it was someone who had it in for the Deputy. And remember, we still don't have any proof to tie him to the murders. We finally just gave up and for the past few years, tried to put the whole thing out of our minds. At least until you showed up."

Ethan thought for a minute about everything they had discussed.

He was quickly coming to the same conclusion as the professor.

"So," asked the Professor, "What do you do now?"

"Well, I would love to have this all come out in the open—for you and your friend to be cleared—and for everyone to know what really happened, but I don't see how that can ever happen. I know I'm much more inclined than you to think people would believe you, but I also know there is a good chance you would go to jail, and I'm not going to risk that. So I guess I'll do just as you have done—nothing. I keep wishing that none of this had ever happened. It's like a bad dream. I guess the good thing is that I started praying that God just make this whole thing go away."

"Father, if it is Your will, take this cup from Me."

"What are you talking about?"

"Jesus—in the garden before his arrest. He prayed that the cup of death be taken away. But He knew that the only way He could save mankind was through His own death and resurrection, so He said, 'nevertheless not My will, but Yours be done.'"

"I seem to recall reading that in Sunday School. And, speaking of the bible, isn't one of the Ten Commandments 'Thou Shall Not Bear False Witness Against Thy Neighbor?'"

"Yes it is. Why?"

"Because I think that one was written just for me."

"Son," he said laughing, "bearing false witness against someone means lying. You never lied about anything, and I doubt if anyone in the world who experienced what you did would have seen it any different."

SEVENTEEN

JUNE, 1969

Sally Robertson wished her father had bought a smaller car. At over 5,000 pounds, the Chrysler New Yorker she was driving was a monster. However, one of the main reasons he had bought it was because of its size. Knowing his daughter would be driving it frequently, he felt if she were ever in a crash, the sheer size of the vehicle would help protect her. As she made her first trip to Greenville she would have preferred a small sports car, but she did appreciate her father's concern.

As she neared their old hometown of Harriman she noticed the temperature gauge light flashing. While she knew little about cars, she realized how dangerous it was to drive with an overheated engine. Luckily she was near their old neighborhood so quickly pulled off the road and into a Shell station where her father used to take their car. The owner, Carl, was happy to see her. He pulled the car into the garage and soon informed her she needed a new thermostat. Within thirty minutes she was back on the road. While she offered to pay, he told her he would send the bill to her father.

Once the car was repaired she had a greater concern as she drove to Ethan's brother's wedding—how would his family react to her being there. Or, more accurately, how would his father react to her being there. From what Ethan had told her, both his mother and brother were excited about meeting her, however he had been rather evasive when asked about what his father had said. "He is getting used to the idea," he had said. What did that mean? How would he treat her? Would this trip be a mistake? And, almost as big a concern—would there be other black people there? She knew that his brother had black friends that had been invited, but would they show up? She certainly hoped so. No matter what happened, it could be a defining moment in their relationship. And the fact that she had not seen Ethan since he came to spend the weekend three weeks ago made her even more nervous. After school ended he returned to his job at Western Auto and she was working five days a week at a hair salon. Their schedules made it very difficult for them to spend time together.

The trip took a little over five hours. She arrived at the Days Inn a little after three on Friday afternoon. Ethan's mother had offered for her to stay with them, but she declined, saying she knew how crowded and hectic it would be with both the boys there. The thing that made her feel good was the fact that Horace's fiancé, Emily, had sent her a nice letter thanking her for coming to the wedding. She said she hoped they would have time to get to know each other.

She had just begun to unpack when the phone rang.

"Hey, cutie," came the welcome greeting.

"Hi, sweetie," she said. "How are you?"

"Fine. Did you just get in?"

"About fifteen minutes ago. Did you finish with the rehearsal already?"

"We just did. Not much for an usher to do. And right now I'm just trying to think of something clever to say to toast the lucky couple. What time do you want me to come by for you?"

"I know the dinner starts at seven but I can be ready around four, so you can come by anytime after that."

"That sounds good. I'm looking forward to seeing you."

"Mmm—me too. See you soon."

She lay on the bed and stretched her muscles which were tight from the long trip. She took a hot shower, letting the spray massage her neck and back. She had just gotten dressed when there was a knock on the door. She opened the door to find Ethan holding a rose and smiling gently.

"Why, thank you, sir." She said.

"A rose for a peach," he said as he closed the door and pulled her close. "It sure is good to see you,"

"I've really missed you," she responded.

"Good, then we have a little time to kill," he said as he led her toward the bed.

"But what if somebody comes by?"

"The only person that might come by would be Emily and I know that she and her maid of honor had to go into Johnson City to get something and won't be back until almost seven."

"What did they have to get?"

"I don't know and don't care," he said as he pulled her down on top of him.

The rehearsal dinner was held at the General Morgan Inn in downtown Greenville. It was a stately, four story hotel and restaurant which dated back to the 1890's. It was where, last December, Horace had proposed to her. The wedding itself would be held at her church in Johnson City, less than an hour away.

Guests started arriving as early as six-thirty. Emily and her maid of honor arrived at the restaurant a little before seven. They met Ethan and Sally in the parking lot as they were getting out of her car. Without waiting for an introduction, Emily walked up to Sally and welcomed her with a hug.

"It's so nice to finally meet you," she said "Ethan has talked so much about you."

"Well, I hope it was all nice," she said.

"But of course, except that you are more beautiful than he said."

"Thank you," she said shyly.

Emily turned and introduced her friend, Barbara, to the couple. The foursome then turned and walked to the hotel. The dining room was almost full when they entered. Sally estimated there were about forty people in attendance. Even though they had never met, she recognized Horace immediately as he walked toward her. He was a slightly larger and older version of Ethan, with the same wavy brown hair, and the same innocent smile.

"So good to finally meet you, Sally," he said as he hugged her.

"Good to meet you, Horace," she returned, "I would have recognized you anywhere. You look just like your brother."

"Except I am the one with the brains."

"And I'm curious—Ethan would be the one with the...?"

"Well, we still haven't figured that out yet, Sally," he said laughing. "But he is still young."

A middle-aged couple came walking toward them, the woman with a slight limp. She knew it must be Ethan's parents.

"This is my Mother and Father," said Ethan, "Hilda and Buster Ward."

"Hi Sally," said Mrs. Ward as she greeted her with a hug. "Welcome to Greenville. We're glad you could make it."

"Thank you Mrs. Ward," she said attempting to conceal her nervousness. "It was certainly nice of you all to invite me."

"How was the trip?" asked Mr. Ward politely, as he shook her hand.

"It was fine except for a little overheating problem with the car. But luckily my father knows a man in Harriman who owns a garage who took care of it for me."

"That's good," he replied.

An announcement was made that the dinner was about to begin. The head table included the bride and groom to be, their parents, along with the maid of honor and the best man. Horace's best man was Ralph, his best friend since childhood, and the person who had introduced him to Emily two years earlier. Sally was glad that they were not sitting at the head table. At their table were two of Horace's friends from college, Tom and Louisa, as well as Horace's favorite teacher from high school and her husband, Betty and Wilber Farrell. Ethan had never had Mrs. Farrell for a teacher but had heard only positive things about her. After they had been seated Sally looked around and noticed she was the only black person at the dinner. For many reasons she wished that Ethan's friend Tommy had not left for the Army.

After a few minutes Mrs. Farrell turned to Ethan and asked, "Ethan, you were friends with Rachel Mills, right?"

"Yes, why?" he replied as Sally pinched his leg.

"I just had her brother this year and he told me that she is over at Nashville singing in a band."

"Yeah, I heard that," he said.

"He says they are doing well. That they are becoming quite popular. Isn't that something."

"Well, she's a talented girl," he replied more for Sally's benefit than Mrs. Farrell. The pinch was harder this time.

"And did you all just hear the news on the radio?" added Mr. Farrell.

"No, what is that?" asked Sally

"I just heard that Senator Coleman has announced that he is running for Governor."

"That's nice," said Sally, then, turning to Ethan, added, "it's always nice to have friends in high places."

Ethan ignored her remark.

The meal was enjoyable and the conversation light and pleasant. As Ethan's mother got up to go to the ladies room, Sally again noticed her limp.

"Is your mother doing O.K.?" she asked.

"She says she is, but I don't know. I know her leg still bothers her some but she says it's nothing like it was before. I know it's hard for her to work."

"And what do the doctors say?"

"They say she is doing fine—that there was just a little nerve damage and it will just take time to heal. I worry about her though. I don't think she should be working."

"Does she have to?"

"I don't think so, but we still have bills from my father's cancer and her surgery. That's why I am working so much this summer."

"You're a good boy, Ethan Ward," Sally whispered in his ear as she rubbed his thigh. "At least that's what Rachel Mills would say."

The dinner was over a little after nine. Ethan gave Sally a tour of the town in her father's Chrysler. Of particular interest was President

Andrew Johnson's home and burial place. By ten o'clock they were
back at her motel room, continuing to enjoy each other's company.

While the next day would be a hectic one for everyone else, Sally
had little to do until the wedding. She was very pleased that Emily
and her friend asked her to breakfast. She found Emily to be warm
and caring—someone she would love to have as a sister-in-law if
things ever came to that. Her friend, Barbara, however, was quiet
and reserved. It did not matter, since this may be the only time she
had to interact with her. Once back in her room she removed her
dress from the hanger and began ironing out the wrinkles. Soon the
phone rang. It was her father calling to check on her. She told him
everything was O.K. and she was having a great time. It was only
minutes after she hung up from him that the phone rang again. It
was Ethan asking if she wanted to come to their house for lunch.
She accepted. He said he would pick her up around eleven.

Their house was as she had imagined except perhaps a little
smaller. Horace greeted them as they walked into the living room.

"Hey Sally, welcome to our humble abode."

"Good morning, Horace. Thank you."

"I heard you had breakfast with my bride this morning."

"Yes, I think you are a lucky man."

"Thanks, but whatever she told you about me is a lie."

"Oh darn—I've never known anyone who won the Nobel Peace
Prize and the Heisman in the same year."

"Oh, yeah, yeah, that part is true."

A laugh came from Ethan's father who was sitting on the couch.

"Good morning, Mr. Ward," she said.

"Morning," he replied simply. She still could not read him or
what he thought of her being there. All she could do was be herself.

Mrs. Ward came into the room, went directly to Sally and greeted
her with a hug.

"So how do you like our little town?"

"It's very nice. Ethan showed me around last night. I got to see
Andrew Johnson's home—at least as much as you can in the dark."

"Well, maybe you will have time to visit it while you are here.
Would you like something to drink? Maybe a Coke?"

"That would be nice, thank you," she replied as the two women walked into the kitchen.

As she was getting her guest a drink Ethan rushed into the kitchen.

"Look at this, Mom," he complained, carrying his shoes. "The sole is coming off of these shoes I got with the tuxedo. Can you believe that?"

"Well, just go exchange them. You've got plenty of time."

"I guess," he said with exasperation, then turning to Sally asked, "you want to go with me?"

"You can go by yourself," said his mother as she took Sally by the hand, "She just got here and we haven't had a chance to talk. She'll be here when you get back."

"Oh—well O.K. I'll only be a little while," he replied as he turned to leave the room.

"Reckon I will go with you,' added his father. "I ain't had a chance to read the paper today. I'll see what's going on in the world."

The two men left the ladies alone. Horace was busy in his room preparing for the wedding, leaving them to get to know each other.

"You like hamburgers?" asked Mrs. Ward.

"Sure—I live on hamburgers. They're my favorite food."

"Well, sorry we don't have anything more fancy, but it's easy and fast."

"That's great. My mother used to make hamburgers every Saturday for lunch, so it will be like going back in time. Can I help you?"

"Absolutely," she replied as she began removing the food from the refrigerator.

"Ethan told me about your mother. I guess that has been pretty rough."

"Yes, I still miss her every day."

"So you were very close?"

"Not so much when I was young. She was so busy—her and my dad trying to build a better life for my sister and me. But the last couple of years we became very close. Maybe it was me getting older or her having more time for us, but—just when I really started to appreciate her, she was gone."

Mrs. Ward saw a tear in her eye and put her hand on her

shoulder to comfort her.

"I'm sorry," said Sally, "I just met you and I act like this."

"Honey, it's fine. Shows you got a good heart," she returned as she put the hamburgers in the skillet.

The two continued talking and getting to know each other. Mrs. Ward turned to her with a more serious look.

"Look, Sally, I know it was not easy for you to come here today, so I just want to let you know that you are welcome here any time."

"Thank you."

"And what ever you and Ethan decide with your lives—well, you have to do what is right for you—not what society thinks."

"I really appreciate that, Mrs. Ward, but—well, I don't get the feeling that your husband shares the same sentiment."

"Buster?" she returned. "Yeah, he is—as they say—from the old school. It is a little hard for him to accept, but Sally, he has a good heart so just give him a little time. And the truth is honey, that, no matter who you are, it would take a while for him to warm up to you."

"So, he was the same with Emily?"

"Oh yeah—well, I mean we both know we have different issues here, but yes—it did take a while for him to accept her. I think that's funny since it is usually the mother who usually is more protective of her sons."

"I know. I think, from what Ethan has told me, that you are a very open-minded and unusual woman."

"Thank you. I guess I am—at least for East Tennessee. But we are all a victim of our circumstances, you know. If I hadn't grown up in Germany and saw the things I saw, I probably would be a different person."

"The war, you mean?"

"Yeah—well, actually, after the war. Everybody in our town had to go view the bodies you know."

"No, I wasn't aware of that. That must have been awful."

"Yes, it was," she replied with a distant look in her eyes. "You can't even imagine—men, women, children—even little babies by the hundreds. And why? Because they were different—Jews, you know. And you couldn't even tell who was a Jew and who was German from looking at people. It was just an excuse. And I see a lot of the same thing here—only difference it is usually black and white."

She shook her head to bring herself back to the present.

"Well, I see where Ethan got his values. I appreciate you teaching him every thing you have."

"Thanks Sally," she said with a laugh. "He's certainly had an eventful life hasn't he? I keep telling him I don't know what God has in store for him next, but I think it will be something great."

"You mean about him saving the Senator's wife and daughter?"

"Yes, and him being there when the Deputy was shot."

"When the Deputy was shot?" she repeated with a look of confusion.

"You mean…," began his mother. "Uh, oh, I just assumed he had told you about that."

"No, he didn't," she replied slowly.

"Well, I know he doesn't like to talk about it. It is very unpleasant for him. He was only thirteen. Sorry, I shouldn't have said anything. You should ask him about it."

"Yeah," she replied still trying to recover from the news, "I guess I will."

Horace and Emily's wedding was scheduled for five at the Presbyterian Church in Johnson City. Ethan and Sally left his parents' house for the motel a little after two. Ethan watched the baseball game while she readied herself for the wedding. They left for the church at half past three. As soon as they were out of town Sally turned to him with a question.

"So how come you never told me about what happened with the Deputy?"

"Uh oh," he began, "I see you and my mom had a nice long talk."

"Yes, we did. So how come you never mentioned it?"

"It's not something I like to talk about, Sally," he replied defensively. "It is an incident I would really like to forget. Why—are you mad at me for not telling you about it?"

"No, I wouldn't say I'm mad, but I guess a little hurt you didn't think you could talk to me about it."

"I haven't told anybody about it since I have been at school, Sally."

"But I would hope I am not just anybody."

"Of course not—and maybe I should have told you, but, again, I really have been trying to forget it."

"O.K.," she replied "I guess I can understand that."

Ethan now felt guilty. The last thing he wanted to do was discuss the matter with her, but neither did he want her to feel shut out. He thought it best to discuss it briefly and hopefully that would be the end of it.

"What exactly did my mother tell you?"

"Really nothing. She thought you had already told me, so she just said that you saw a Deputy get killed when you were thirteen years old. She said I should talk to you to get the details."

"O.K., let me tell you what happened."

He quickly recapped what he had seen that hot summer's day six years earlier. Since he did not want her to hear it from someone else later, he told her that the two men were black. She listened patiently until he had finished.

"So they have no idea who did it?"

"As far as I know they don't even have any suspects," he answered truthfully.

"That's terrible, Ethan. I had no idea you had gone through something like that. I'm sorry."

"Thank you. It was an ordeal but I know a lot of people have gone through worse."

She hesitated before asking the next question. She was afraid what his response might be, but she had to know.

"You promise you won't get mad if I ask you something?"

"Have I ever got mad at you?"

"No, but….O.K. do you think what you saw has anything to do with your dating me?"

"What could one possibly have to do with the other?" he returned quickly, his voice rising.

"I don't really know—and you said you wouldn't get mad at me."

"I'm not mad, but I just can't understand the question. What could it possibly have to do with us?"

"I don't know, but the fact is that you saw two black men kill a white man and you are also probably the only white person from your town to ever date a black girl. Maybe you just needed to prove to yourself that black people are the same as everyone else."

"Well, do you want to know something?"

"Yes, I really do."

"The truth is—and I don't know if this will make it better or worse for you—but the reason I wanted to get to know you was that I thought you were the most beautiful girl I had ever seen. Maybe I am just a male chauvinist, but if you had just been average looking I wouldn't have been interested. I don't think there is anything hidden or subversive about that."

"Are you sure?"

"I'm sure."

"Then," she returned smugly, "I can live with that."

After the wedding the guests began leaving the church for the reception. Sally watched happily as the photographer took pictures of the wedding party. When he was free to go, she and Ethan left for the restaurant. They joined the other guests awaiting the new bride and groom's arrival. She and Ethan were joined at the punchbowl by Mr. and Mrs. Farrell.

"So," began Mr. Farrell, "Where are the happy couple spending their honeymoon?"

"At Daytona Beach," returned Ethan. "Both of them have always dreamed of going to Florida so they are pretty excited."

"Too bad they'll be spending all their time indoors,' he quickly quipped, for which he got a slap on his arm from his wife.

"Are they flying?" he asked.

"No, driving. They would like to fly but, well, Horace paid for last night's dinner you know."

"Yes, I know," returned Mrs. Farrell. "Ethan, if I am not being too personal, are your parents doing O.K.? I know they have had a string of bad luck in the past couple of years."

Ethan was not offended by her remark because he knew it was out of sincere concern.

"It's been rough for them, but I think they're doing O.K. now. My mom still has some pain in her leg, but she thinks it will get better. I wish she didn't have to work, but they're determined to get all their bills paid off."

"Well, tell her if there is anything we can do to help please let us know."

"Thanks. I will."

Dinner and dessert were followed by the cutting of the cake. Despite the guests prodding, neither the bride nor groom smeared cake in the other's face. Soon the band began playing. Horace and Emily enjoyed their first dance together as husband and wife. Ethan commented to Sally what a great looking couple they made.

"Almost as cute as us," she replied.

"But not near as smart," he joked.

"Not as smart as one of us anyway," she quickly returned. Not about to let himself fall into another one of her traps, he let the remark go.

Others quickly joined them on the dance floor. Ethan took Sally's hand and led her to the floor. A couple of months earlier he might have been concerned what others thought. Tonight he did not care. He knew he had the most beautiful and sweetest girl there.

"Too bad they don't have any liquor here," she whispered in his ear.

"Why is that?"

"You might get lucky—just like at the party."

"We had liquor at the party and I didn't get lucky."

"Oh—right. Never mind."

"You're an evil woman, Sally Robertson."

"Well, we'll see about that later."

The next morning Ethan came to the motel to take Sally to breakfast. Having made plans to stop and see her aunt and uncle in Harriman on the way home, she needed to leave by eleven. After breakfast they returned to her room. While Ethan had seemed preoccupied at breakfast she said nothing. She figured it was due to his brother's marriage, or concern over his mother's health problem. If there were something else he would tell her.

They sat on the bed watching a news report on the past twenty-four hours in Vietnam. Sally shook her head as she watched.

"Every day it's the same thing. When will it ever end?"

She looked at Ethan who sat solemnly.

"Is there something going on, Ethan?"

"Well, actually," he began as he nodded toward the TV, "there is something I need to talk to you about."

"Oh no," she began. "I have the feeling I'm not going to like this. What is it?"

"I don't know of any easy way to tell you this. I joined the Army last week."

"What! No, you can't be serious. Ethan tell me you are joking."

"No, it's no joke. I have a month before I report."

She got up from the bed and walked around the room, wringing her hands.

"I don't know which bothers me more—the fact that you would do this, or that you wouldn't talk to me about it."

"I didn't talk to you because I knew you would talk me out of it. But you're the first one to know."

"So you haven't told your parents?"

"No one."

"But why Ethan? This is insane. Please tell me why you would do something like that."

"It's not just one reason, Sally. There are a lot of reasons."

"I have time."

"O.K. It was going to happen sooner or later. I don't know if I even have enough money for one more year of college. So about this time next year I would probably be drafted."

"You don't know that. The war could be over by then."

"They have been talking about it being over for years. The French were over there for what—fifteen or twenty years? This could go on forever. And at least this way I can have some say about what happens to me"

"You could find a way to stay in school."

"That's possible, but that's not the only reason. You know my parents' financial situation. They still haven't paid off all the bills from my dad's cancer, and now there's bills from my mother's surgery. She shouldn't even be working. This way I can give them the rest of the money I have saved for college and they can pay off their bills and Mom won't have to work. I can also send home money. And, when I get back I will have the G.I bill to pay for school."

"And which do you think your mother would rather have—a couple thousand dollars or her son alive?"

"That's why I didn't tell her. But there's still other reasons."

"Like what?"

"Like it is the right thing to do. Tommy is over there as well as a dozen other classmates. They are all fighting for what is right. Why should I be different? I'm no better than them."

"I understand that you want to do what is right, Ethan, but this could cost you your life. I am just so upset I think I will be sick."

He walked toward her but she turned away. He came up behind her and put his arms around her.

"Honey, I know how upset you are and I am sorry. I have been thinking about this for a couple of months now, and I really believe it is the right thing to do. It will work out fine. You'll see."

She began to sob as he held her tighter. When she was able to talk she asked,

"So, does this decision have anything to do with you and me?"

"Well of course. It has everything to do with us, but I'm not sure what you are asking."

"I just find out yesterday that you had a major secret you didn't tell me, and now, without talking to me, I find out you will be going to Vietnam. It seems like you are sending me a message."

"Look, Sally," he said as he turned her to face him, "we both know I had a little problem adjusting to this relationship, but right now you are the only thing in my life I am sure of. There is nothing hidden going on here. I didn't tell you about the Deputy because it is too painful to talk about. And I didn't tell you about this because I knew it was something I had to do and I knew you would probably talk me out of it. I feel closer to you than I ever have and—well, this is bad timing I know, but someday, when I get back, maybe you would consider being my wife."

She began sobbing harder. She turned toward him and hit his chest.

"I hate you, I hate you," she repeated. Then, after a moment stopped and drew closer to him saying, "if only I didn't love you so much."

EIGHTEEN

FALL, 1969

For a young man who had never traveled more than a few hours from home Ethan's life changed quickly. In July he reported to the Army recruiter in Knoxville to be transported to Ft. Benning, Georgia. After six weeks basic training he was given a week's leave to return home to visit his family. The first few days of his leave were spent in Murfreesboro visiting Sally. From there he went to Greenville to visit his parents, then, back to Ft. Benning for eight weeks of advanced training. Another week's leave and he said goodbye to his friends and family for a year. November found him on his way to Vietnam, via San Francisco and Honolulu. As he sat on the C-130 Transport plane for the last leg of his trip, he wondered if perhaps his mother and Sally were right—he was insane for enlisting. He had searched his mind and soul trying to determine if there were subconscious reasons why he had volunteered. Was he desperate to get away from Professor Robertson and that situation? Was he uncertain about his relationship with Sally but would not admit it to himself? Or was it simply as he had told himself—it was the right thing to do? Whatever the reason, it was too late to worry about it now, for in a short time he would be landing in the most dangerous country on earth.

The seat on the plane was even more uncomfortable than those in his father's old truck. His heart began to race as the pilot announced they were coming into Vietnam airspace. He loosened his strap long enough to stand and peer out the port in front of him. He could see the shoreline coming into view. Just for a moment he closed his eyes and pretended he was landing on a beach in Florida. Unfortunately he was jolted back to reality by the sound of the landing gear being lowered. The plane came in high to avoid 'Charlie's' 50 caliber machine guns, then made a sudden dive toward the airfield. After the plane came to a halt he gathered his gear and took his place in line with the other troops waiting to debark. The hot muggy air engulfed him as he exited the plane. The new reality set in as they were directed into an armored personnel carrier for the short, five-minute journey. Upon exiting the carrier they were greeted by a burly Sergeant. He barked,

"Well, well, what do we have here?" he began sarcastically. "Welcome to Xuan Loc. Did you enjoy the plane ride? Your bunks will be in the second building on your right. Be back here at 14:30 for a briefing."

'That was short and sweet,' thought Ethan. He only had time to store his belongings and hit the latrine before it was time for roll call. The recruits stood nervously at attention waiting for their new sergeant to address them.

"Good afternoon gentlemen," he began. "I am Sergeant Rodriguez, and for the next year I will be your mother, your father, your priest, your psychiatrist, and your boss. I am a man of few words and simple rules. I have two major objectives here in Nam—which we like to call the armpit of the universe. First—to keep you newbies alive—and second—to kill Charlie. As long as we understand each other we will get along fine."

He walked up and down in front of the men. Ethan made sure he kept his eyes straight ahead. He wanted to do nothing to draw attention to himself.

"Rule number one," he continued, "don't ever question anything I tell you. This is my second tour here—some people think I am crazy—but I have a little experience so I usually know what I am talking about, and I don't have a need or the time to explain things."

"Rule number two—don't salute any of the officers here. Charlie is everywhere and they want the same chance as everyone else."

"Rule number three—your weapon is your best friend. If I ever see it more than an arm's length from you—well, shall we say your ass is grass and I'm the lawn mower."

"Rule number four—Charlie is everywhere, even on base—so make sure you watch what you say at all times."

"Rule number five—when we are on maneuvers make sure we take plenty of dry socks. I don't need to lose someone from toe rot."

Ethan had to stifle a smile. Along with the seriousness of the place, his comment seemed out of place. He had little time to think about it.

He pointed to a young man standing behind him.

"This is Private Stanley. It would be a good idea to introduce yourself to him. His job is not only to introduce you to camp life here but to also make sure you have the proper supplies."

"Now gentlemen," he continued, "the good news is that until we get orders for our next maneuver—which should be in the next day or two, you can relax and enjoy yourselves. We've got volleyball, horseshoes, maybe a friendly card game. Mail call will be in a couple of hours, and mess is at 18:00. Company dismissed."

Ethan, like all the other soldiers, walked slowly back to the barracks. Once there he continued unpacking and talking to the other soldiers. While he had gotten to know some of them quite well, he had been cautioned not to become too close to anyone. He realized one never knew when it might be the last time you spoke to a friend.

Soon mail call was announced. Since he had only arrived he paid little attention to the endless roll of names. His pulse quickened when he heard his name being called. He quickly ran to get his mail. A smile came to his face as he saw the letter from Sally. He realized she must have mailed it as soon as he left. It gave him a warm feeling to know she had planned it for his arrival. He read the letter three times and put it under his pillow.

The next couple of days were calm and routine. At times he would close his eyes and forget where he was—pretend he was back in college getting ready to go to a football game or meeting Sally in the library. Then the roar of personnel carrier or a jeep backfiring would jolt him back to reality. The most unusual thing was the weather. It was November and still over eighty degrees. He was told the weather would not change until spring when the rainy season would begin. While the temperature would only increase slightly, the rains would create widespread flooding.

Two days after his arrival Ethan was laying on his bunk reading a letter he had just received from his mother when his thoughts were interrupted by a voice over the loud speaker.

"Listen up soldiers," began Private Stanley. "The Sergeant just received a Warning Order. Be at the briefing tent in fifteen minutes."

In fifteen minutes the entire unit was at the briefing tent. He expected to see the Lieutenant or perhaps the Captain there but it was only the Sergeant. As always, his briefing was short and to the point. He informed them that an entire battalion was being transferred to a base deeper inside Vietnam. They would be moving out in two days. Then he told them that twelve members of his unit were to report to duty at 06:30 hours the next morning for a special one-day assignment. He passed around a piece of paper with the names for the assignment. Ethan noticed that six of the names, including himself, were newbies, while the other six were veterans. He wondered what the assignment would be.

He did not have to wait long. He was awake by 05:30, had breakfast in the mess, and joined the other members of the unit in the briefing tent at 06:30. At exactly the appointed time Sergeant Rodriguez and Captain Tanner arrived. Behind them walked a Vietnamese man he had not seen before. The soldiers jumped to attention.

"At ease soldiers," said Captain Tanner. "We have a simple mission for you men this morning. Sergeant Rodriguez will explain it to you."

"Good morning," began the Sergeant as he moved closer to the men. "Today's mission is very simple. There is a small Vil just an hour west of here that is harboring a high level Viet Cong informant. Not only has he been causing us a lot of problems, but the information he has about Charlie could be very helpful. Our mission is simple—go into the Vil and bring him back. Accompanying us will be Major Tran of the Vietnamese army. Major Tran will be identifying the informant. Here is a picture of our target."

The Sergeant passed around a picture of a middle aged Vietnamese man. The rest of the briefing was regarding logistics of the plan. When he heard the village was an hour west of their base Ethan assumed it was an hour's drive. He discovered it was an hour's walk. The men were dismissed at 07:00 and told to report back at 09:00.

Promptly at 09:00 the soldiers began their march toward the village. Leaving the base they walked down a gravel road which soon turned into a narrow dirt road. It was little more than a footpath winding through rice patties. The Sergeant spread the men out along the trail walking two abreast, with one man at point. Every fifteen minutes he rotated the soldier at point. As they walked deeper into the heartland Ethan became more and more nervous. He kept repeating the Captain's words—'it was a simple mission.'

They had walked for about thirty minutes when the Sergeant turned to the soldier next to Ethan and motioned for him to take point. As he watched the soldier move forward, the summer of 1963 came back to Ethan in a flash. Suddenly the soldier was knocked backwards as a bullet ripped through his chest. While Ethan stood frozen at what he had seen, his Sergeant pushed him to the side of the road.

"Scatter, scatter!" he yelled as he dove for the cover of the rice patties. Immediately his men followed suit—some to his side of the road—others to the opposite side. Ethan found himself lying next to the Sergeant, wondering what to do next.

"Anybody see where the shot came from?" he yelled.

"I saw a flash, Sergeant," answered Ethan.

"Where?"

Ethan pointed out where he had seen the flash. The area was about 100 meters ahead of them and up a slight incline.

"Anybody else see anything?"

There came no response.

"Corporal Allen," called the Sergeant. A young soldier only a few years older than Ethan scurried through the brush towards them, carrying a Bazooka.

"Private Ward, point out to the Corporal where you saw the flash."

Ethan pointed to the area.

"Now Corporal, I want you to put one round about twenty meters to the right of there."

The Corporal did as ordered. The explosion cleared an area just to the right of the sniper.

"Now put one twenty meters on the other side," ordered Sergeant Rodriguez.

The Corporal quickly re-loaded and fired as instructed.

"Major Tran!" yelled the Sergeant to the other side of the road.

"Yes Sergeant," came the reply.

"Will you please tell the soldier up there that he has ten seconds to come out or his days are over. Tell him he will be treated as a prisoner of war.

The Major called out in Vietnamese. The soldier's answer came in the form of another bullet cutting through the grass.

"I guess that gives us his answer," said the Sergeant. Then, turning to the Corporal he simply nodded.

A few seconds later a third shot exploded in the area where the shots had originated.

"Private Reynolds," yelled the Sergeant across the pathway.

"Yes, sir," came the reply.

"I want you and Private Ward to go up there and confirm the elimination of the sniper."

"Yes, sir," came the reply from both soldiers.

"Private Reynolds you go up through the brush from your side and Private Ward from this side. When you two get within twenty meters you spread out and come in from each side at a ninety degree angle. I don't want you two shooting each other. You understand?"

"Yes, sir," they returned again.

Ethan start to move through the brush then hesitated and turned back to the Sergeant.

"Is there a problem Private?"

"No, sir. I was just wondering, sir—could there be another sniper up there, sir?"

"Anything's possible in war son, but snipers hardly ever travel in pairs. Now, do you understand your orders?"

"Yes, sir," he returned as he moved forward.

His hands were frozen to his gun as he crept forward. The brush began to thin as they got closer to the target. It made it easier to see Private Reynolds, but it also made it easier for the enemy to see them—if there were anyone left. They soon came to a clearing. They looked at each other for a second, nodded, and ran the last short distance to the area that had been leveled. To their relief they found the sniper—or at least what was left of him—lying next to his weapon. As badly damaged as his body was, it did not appear he had been hit directly by the rocket. It looked as if it had hit a few feet from him and he had been killed by the explosion. As they drew nearer Private Reynolds spoke.

"Are we supposed to bring his body back?"

"I don't think so. Maybe just his gun and any ID to prove we got him."

"O.K.," he returned as he picked up the weapon, "I got the gun. You can get his ID."

Ethan gave him a nasty look and bent down to go through the sniper's pockets. The only thing he could find was a picture of a woman and young boy. He shook his head as he put the picture in his pocket.

They got back to the unit and gave their report. Ethan showed the picture to the Sergeant. He instructed him to hold on to it until they got to the village and turn it over to someone there. The Sergeant ordered the men back to the road. He instructed them that they would pick up their fallen comrade on the way back from the village. As they started to move out Ethan walked along side the Sergeant.

"Sergeant Rodriquez," he began.

"Yes, Private."

"I hope it did not appear I was questioning your judgment when I asked about another sniper, sir."

"You had a valid concern, son. None of us want to die. However, I had already thought of that possibility."

"Thank you, sir."

As they marched toward the village Ethan wondered if the gunfire could have been heard by the residents there, and, if so, what impact it might have on their mission. He wondered if the sniper was sent because the informant knew they were coming for him, or was it just coincidence? That was the problem with a war in a country like this—nothing was certain. No matter—they still had their orders so nothing had changed.

A short time later they arrived at the village. From their cover they could see a dozen or so huts and the villagers as they went about their daily activities, seemingly unconcerned of the war in their country.

Sergeant Rodriquez reminded his men that their mission was to take the informant alive and that they were to fire only if they were in danger. The men spread into a semi-circle around the village, making sure they were not in each other's line of fire. Upon the signal they moved quickly into the village. Even with Major Tran's repeated yelling that they would not be harmed, the villagers screamed and scattered—some into the huts and some into the fields. One concern on which the soldiers had been briefed was the possibility the informant might reach a rat hole hidden in one of the huts and escape. That was any soldier's worse nightmare—being sent into a tunnel after Charlie.

As quickly as possible the soldiers took up positions on all sides of the village closing those escape routes. Sergeant Rodriquez and Major Tran immediately began their search for the informant, inspecting each house. It was only moments before they returned with a villager, hands cuffed behind him. Major Tran seemed to be giving him instructions although the man gave no response. The Sergeant turned the prisoner over to two soldiers to guard and gave the order to move out. Ethan took the picture from his pocket and gave it to Major Tran explaining that he had taken it from the sniper. The Major turned to a woman holding a small child and gave her the picture. He spoke a few words in Vietnamese. She nodded, took the picture, and turned and walked away. It was unclear to Ethan if the woman had ever seen the man in the picture before, but he expected that eventually the message would get to his family.

On the way back to their base they stopped and picked up the body of the fallen soldier. As they marched toward base Ethan turned to see the Sergeant walking beside him. He turned to Ethan and asked,

"So, Private, was your first mission what you expected?"

"I didn't really know what to expect, sir." he responded.

"Neither do I, son. Neither do I."

"Permission to ask the Sergeant a question, sir," said Ethan.

"What is that, son?"

"I was just wondering, sir, why we did not take jeeps or armored vehicles on this mission. Not that I am complaining about the walk, sir."

"Oh really," the Sergeant said, laughing. "Well first of all, in case you haven't noticed, we are kind of short on vehicles right now and we would have needed at least three for this mission. Jeeps also make a lot of noise so there is a good likelihood of us being heard by someone who could signal the village ahead. And, finally, if a gas tank gets hit by a sniper you lose half a dozen soldiers, not just one. Did that answer your question, son?"

"Yes, sir. Thank you, sir."

"But if our next mission is going to be longer I'll make sure you have some transportation," he said with a smile.

"Thank you, Sergeant," Ethan returned.

"And, Private," he added as he walked away, "I appreciate you treating me with respect, but I'm a Sergeant—not a General. Loosen up."

"Yes, sir."

The rest of the trip back to base was uneventful. He watched as they took the prisoner into base headquarters. He never saw nor heard about him again.

During the next few months Ethan saw more combat than he could have ever imagined. By springtime he had become what he considered to be a "seasoned veteran". And while he had seen many battles and skirmishes, it was an event in late April he found most upsetting. His unit was returning from an unsuccessful mission to locate a new enemy camp when they came under enemy fire. They quickly scattered, taking cover behind their vehicles as well as the surrounding rice patties. In the confusion Ethan became separated from the other soldiers. He moved slowly through the field as he listened to the gunfire. He saw a young Viet Cong soldier only thirty meters in front of him. The soldier—unaware of him—quietly raised his weapon and aimed toward another GI. Ethan pointed his gun at the young boy and called, "Stop! Drop your gun!" To his dismay, the soldier—who he estimated to be only about sixteen—turned the gun toward him. In an instant it was over, with the young boy lying in the rice field. It was only when the battle was over and the enemy had been repelled, that the impact of what he had done hit him. He had been in many battles before—and had probably killed many of the enemy—but never had it been this certain—this personal. Up until now the fighting had been at a distance—at least enough so that he could comfort himself in the fact that he had not actually seen his fire kill someone. Now that all changed. And, to make matters worse, it had been a young boy. While he knew he had no other recourse, he could not get the young boy's look out of his mind. He said nothing as he rode back into base.

That evening he walked to the edge of camp and sat under a tree. He threw pebbles at a nearby tin can, his vision blurred by the moisture in his eyes. Hearing a shuffle he turned to see his Sergeant walking toward him. Saying nothing he seated himself next to him and leaned against the tree. The two sat silently for some time before the Sergeant spoke.

"It's not easy, is it?"

"No, Sergeant, it isn't."

"The only thing I can tell you is that the pain will lessen in time."

"He was so young," returned Ethan as he tried to hold back the tears. "No more than sixteen."

"It probably won't help much but you know you had no choice."

"That's the only thing that lets me live with myself."

The two sat for a while saying nothing. Finally Ethan spoke again.

"So do you think this is worth it Sergeant—us being here?"

Sergeant Rodriquez thought for a moment before answering.

"Let me ask you a question, Private Ward. Your time here will be up in about six months, right?"

"Yes, sir."

"What do you plan on doing when you get home?"

"What?"

"What do you intend on doing with your life when you get out of the Army?"

"Well, I have a girlfriend. Maybe someday we'll get married. I plan on going back to college—hopefully someday becoming a teacher. Why?"

"You like to buy a little house? Save up some money and buy a nice car? Maybe take a vacation? Raise children and provide for them?"

"Yes, why?"

"These people have none of those things. The government tells them what to do, what to think, where to live. They work like slaves all their lives and have nothing to show for it. And if they ever complain then they disappear. Communism is evil and corrupt. It destroys humanity; it destroys the individual; and it destroys the soul. It lets the strong—those in power—prey on the weak."

"Then why do they hate us? I thought when I came over here that the people would be grateful—thankful that we came to help them—but they often hate us as much as Charlie."

"They are scared and don't know who to trust. They have also been brainwashed into believing that there is no existence other than what they have known. And those who do want us here are afraid of what will happen to them if they even show us a little kindness."

"So what's the answer, Sergeant? Do we have a chance of making a difference here? Can we win the war?"

"That I don't know, son. All I can do is what my superiors tell me to do. Hopefully they have a lot more insight into what we're doing here than I do."

NINETEEN

SPRING, 1970

By May the rainy season had begun. It seemed the rain was continual, yet the temperature was still near eighty every day. At least the weather had brought a lull in the fighting. It was either that or the fact that the war was winding down—even though the U.S. Government would not say as much. Ethan didn't care what the reason—he was just happy that there were fewer battles lately. It gave him more time to write letters and think about what he would do after returning home. He would go back to school and get his teaching degree. After graduation, he would ask Sally to marry him. They could move to Knoxville or perhaps Oak Ridge. Oak Ridge was probably the better choice. Having been the birthplace of the atomic bomb and now the nuclear energy center of the country, it was a modern town with an international flair, drawing engineers and scientists from all over the world. People there would be more accepting of a racially mixed couple, and if they weren't, tough. After what he had seen here he understood what his mother had told him years earlier. People had to learn to be more accepting of others no matter their race or color.

He still got letters from Sally almost every day. While she always told him how much she missed him and loved him, he felt as if there was something wrong. He couldn't identify it but there was a vagueness about her letters. The words were there but somehow the emotion was missing. He had written her a few weeks earlier and asked if there was a problem, but she had assured him that nothing had changed. She cared as much as ever and was excited that he would be coming home in less than six months. But yet he wondered—could she have found out about the situation with him and her father? He felt that that was highly unlikely and, if so, would she be able to not mention it to him? Whatever the situation there was nothing he could do about it at the time.

He had also gotten letters frequently from Tommy who was stationed only a hundred miles west of him. While they had tried to get together on a number of occasions, the war always intervened. But today he had just received a letter from him saying he had three day's leave and would be in Saigon for the weekend. He asked Ethan to meet him. Since he had been given almost no leave since his tour began, Ethan thought it appropriate to ask his Sergeant for a couple of days off.

"We should be able to arrange that," said Sergeant Rodriquez. "Let me clear it through the Captain and I will get back to you this afternoon."

"Thank you, Sergeant," he replied.

While he was unsure of Sergeant Rodriquez in the beginning, he had learned to both like and respect him. He was a tough soldier, but that was what was required. And while he was intimidating, even frightening at first, he found him to be caring and compassionate. And even though they were from different backgrounds—he a Hispanic from Los Angeles, and Ethan a Tennessee hillbilly, he found they had a lot in common—their sense of duty, their respect for all people, and their love for baseball. And while his passion for the Los Angeles Dodgers was misdirected, it did allow them to have numerous conversations on the subject.

The Sergeant notified him that afternoon that he had been given a two-day pass for the weekend. He had to be back on base by 18:00 Sunday. Ethan thanked him and turned to leave.

"Son, just remember," he called after him. "It's just as dangerous in the city as it is here. Don't trust anyone—except your friend, that is."

"Thank you, Sergeant."

Getting the pass was only the first part of getting to Saigon. He still had to get a ride, which he had to do on his own. That should be no problem though, since personnel were frequently going back and forth to the city. Saigon was only about eighty kilometers miles from the base, however, on Vietnamese roads that could take two to three hours.

Ethan had little trouble in finding a ride into Saigon. Since his leave did not start until 18:00 Friday, he waited until Saturday morning to depart. He did not wish to get into Saigon at dark. Tommy had given him the name of the hotel where he would be staying so he would call his room the next morning.

The supply convoy left for Saigon the next morning at 07:30. The trip was uneventful and quicker than he thought. He arrived in Saigon a little after 09:00. The city was unlike anything he had ever experienced. Even at that hour of the morning there was activity everywhere. The streets and sidewalks were crowded with people. Except for the American and South Vietnamese soldiers on every corner, there was no evidence of war. At least not when he first entered the city. As they went further into town, he saw the bombed out buildings. It reminded him of pictures he had seen of tornados with some buildings destroyed with others adjacent to them left untouched. The driver found the hotel Tommy had given him and dropped him off. While there were two MP's stationed in front of the hotel, he still felt nervous as he watched the truck pull away.

He went into the hotel and showed the clerk the envelope with Tommy's name on it. He was surprised when the young man answered him in English.

"Oh yes, Mr. Bell. He very nice man. He say you might come."

"Do you know if he is awake yet?"

"Oh he awake. Already go for walk. Want to see our beautiful city. He say if you come he be at bar right down street at eleven. Name is G.I. Moe. Good name for bar, huh?"

"Yes, that is a very good name," Ethan said with a laugh. "I don't guess you have a room this early, do you?"

"Sure, we have room. Have lots of rooms. Best value in Saigon. For you only seven American dollar. You like?"

"Sure," said Ethan as he gave the young man seven dollars. As the clerk gave him his key he realized he was not much older than the soldier he had shot in the field.

Ethan found the room much as he had expected it. It was small and modest but at least clean. The bathroom was shared with an adjoining room, but the doors could be locked from the inside. He used the bathroom, then removed the few items he had brought from his knapsack and placed them in the dresser. He sat on the bed trying to decide what to do until he met Tommy. Since he had almost ninety minutes to kill, he decided he too would take a walk. Perhaps he could find a nice gift for Sally and his parents.

He found a gift shop where he bought a native doll for Sally, a throw rug for his mother, and a picture book on Viet Nam for his father. He made a leisurely trip around the block then returned to his room and placed his purchases in the dresser drawer. At ten-forty he left his room for the G.I. Moe bar.

The bar was not a place where Ethan felt comfortable and wondered if Tommy had seen the place or only took the clerk's recommendation. Except for the obvious difference in the patrons, it could have been mistaken for any run down bar in the States. At least there were MP's stationed outside the entrance, and, because of the hour, there were only a dozen or so customers inside, half of which were U.S. soldiers. Ethan looked for Tommy but, not seeing him, chose a table near the wall and waited. A young scantily clad waitress came and took his order. While he rarely drank alcohol, and it was still early in the day, he felt it out of place to order a soft drink in such a place, so asked the girl to bring him a beer. He had only taken a few sips when his friend came in. He watched as Tommy searched the bar, his eyes trying to adjust to the darkness. Ethan stood and called to his friend. He walked quickly to his table. Tommy leaned his weapon against the wall next to Ethan's before embracing his friend.

"Private Ward," stated Tommy.

"Corporal Bell," returned Ethan.

The two men laughed and sat down.

"Boy it's good to see you," began Tommy.

"You too brother. How have you been?"

"Can't complain for being in the middle of a war. And you?"

"I'd rather be back in the great state of Tennessee," returned Ethan, "but I guess I'm doing alright since I made it through half my tour and still have all my body parts. You had any injuries?"

"Yeah, I sprained my ankle playing volleyball."

"You're kidding?"

"No, I'm afraid not. My Captain was not too happy, but not much he could do since I was on his team."

"That's wild. I can always count on you for the unexpected."

The two went on to talk about the action they had seen. Ethan quickly learned that his friend too had seen more than his share of fighting and killing. He also learned that he had pulled his injured Sergeant back to cover during one battle."

"So now I can ask you, how does it feel to be a hero?"

"Well, I don't really feel like a hero," answered Tommy. "It was really pretty simple. I just ran out and pulled him back to cover."

"Did he survive?"

"Sure, it was not a bad wound. He just couldn't walk. Matter of fact he probably would have been fine even if I hadn't gone after him."

"Anyway, as you told me a couple of years ago, I am sure proud of you."

The waitress came to take Tommy's order. He also ordered a beer.

"So, what news have you heard from back home lately," asked Tommy.

"Well, I'm sure you heard that Senator Coleman was elected Governor a few months ago."

"Yes—your buddy. It's good to have friends in high places."

"Right."

"And, at the risk of upsetting you, have you heard the latest on Rachel?"

"What now?"

"My dad wrote me she has a hit on the radio. It's really big. I think it's called, "And Your Love Too.""

"That's nice. I guess we both knew she would either make it big someday or die trying. But how come you always bring up her instead of Sally?"

"Well," began Tommy indignantly, "I thought this was big news and, besides, I still haven't met Sally. Are things going O.K. with you two?"

"I'm not sure."

"How's that?"

"Well, in her letters she says everything is O.K. and she still loves me and can't wait until I get back but—well I just don't know. I can't put my finger on it. Her letters just seem vague. I ask her about school and our friends and she says everything is fine but she never gives any details. And in her last letter she told me that she just moved out of the dorm and back home with her Dad. Said she worried about him being home alone all the time."

"Maybe that's all there is to it. Or maybe she is worried about the money."

"I don't think so. They're not rich, but they are not hurting for money either."

"Well, look at it this way—if she had another boy friend she probably wouldn't be moving back in with daddy."

"No, I don't think that's it, but I don't know what it is. Maybe I'm just worrying too much."

Ethan had many things he wanted to discuss with his friend. He wanted to know more about his tour of duty and what he thought about the war. He wanted to know about his plans when they got back home. He wanted to hear about his family and friends from school. Unfortunately their conversation would have to wait. For, just after the waitress had brought his beer, they heard a terrible commotion out in the street. People were yelling and running. There was the sound of gunfire and then the sound of the MP's outside the door yelling, "stop, stop." They looked out the window to see the MP's running down the street with weapons drawn. Ethan and Tommy looked at each other, trying to determine what to do. Their course of action was quickly decided for them. A young woman ran in the door carrying a satchel. They both knew what it meant. Ethan reached for his weapon but Tommy was quicker, drawing his side-arm from its holster. The woman threw the satchel into the room as Tommy took aim and fired. The woman fell to the floor. Quickly Tommy grabbed the table and turned it on its side then grabbed his

friend and pulled him to the floor with him. The explosion occurred only a split second later. Ethan felt the pain in his back and
thigh. The last thing he remembered was the smell of gunpowder.

Ethan was forty years old and a Professor at the University of Tennes-
see. His wife, Sally was also a Professor there. Their son had just made the
football team as the starting quarterback. Their daughter was the vale-
dictorian of her high school class. Ethan was at an awards dinner held by
the University to honor him for his nomination for the Nobel peace prize.
Just as he started to the podium to accept his award he felt a stabbing
pain in his back and thigh. He fell to the floor in agony. As he looked up
he saw a nurse standing over him. He wondered where she could have
come from.

"Well, Private Ward," said the nurse, "It looks like you are back
with us."

"Where am I?" he asked.

"You are a guest of the Army Hospital in Saigon."

"Great—I liked my dream much better."

"I'm sure you did. Unfortunately this is reality."

"So, what happened to me?" he asked groggily.

"Well, you'll have to talk to your doctor for all the details, but
you took quite a bit of shrapnel in your back and leg."

"Will I be alright?"

"Oh, I think so. Again, you'll have to talk to the doctor, but I
think everything will be just fine."

As he became more alert he realized how painful his injury was.
The right side of his lower back throbbed, and his thigh ached almost as bad.

"You can't tell me any more than that?"

"You really need to talk to the doctor," she returned again then,
leaning in closer whispered, "you will be fine—probably as good as
new in a few weeks."

"What about my friend, Corporal Bell?"

"Is he the young black soldier that was in the restaurant with you?"

"Yes. Is he O.K.?

"He's in another section, but I understand he will be O.K. too.

How bad is your pain?"

"Pretty bad."

"Well, we can do something about that. The doctor gave me an order for Demerol. That should make you feel pretty good."

She left and returned soon with a needle, injecting the medication into his buttock. Within minutes not only was the pain virtually gone, but he felt a warmth and peace he had never experienced before. When the nurse came back by to check on him he told her how wonderful she was. She smiled and patted him on the leg and told him his doctor would be by soon.

Dr. Leonard was a middle aged balding man with a charming smile. Ethan wondered how he could be so happy in such a place.

"So you are awake," he stated.

"Yes, sir. How long have I been here?"

"Just since yesterday. You lost a lot of blood from your wounds so we had to get you stabilized before we operated."

"So I'm going to be alright—no permanent injury?"

"As the saying goes—you want the good news or the bad news first?"

"Uh oh. I guess the bad news."

"The bad news is that your injuries will probably not keep you from returning to duty. I don't make those decisions but—the good news is that I can think of no limitations you will have after your recovery. Other than some stiffness and occasional pain around the injury you should make a complete recovery. You are a very lucky young man."

"How so doctor?"

"Well, if the shrapnel had been two more inches to the left of your spinal cord could have been severed. Also, if your friend had not found a medic as quick as he did you would not be alive. You lost a lot of blood you know."

"You mean Tommy—I mean Corporal Bell?"

"Of course. He saved your life you know."

"Yes, I remember. If he hadn't pushed me behind the table I would have been a goner."

"Yes, but that's not what I was talking about. It was madness out there—six suicide attackers I think. They blew up three buildings and killed a number of our guys before we got them. People were running everywhere. Corporal Bell found a medic and pretty much forced him to attend to you."

"That's great. Thank you for telling me."

The doctor took his pulse and temperature then notated his chart before leaving. As he walked away Ethan called to him.

"So can you tell me how Tommy—Corporal Bell—is doing?"

"Sorry, he is not my patient, but I think he is fine. I'm sure now that he knows you are awake he will be along. Take care young man."

After the doctor left, Ethan took the time to look around the room. He was in a large rectangular room which held about twenty beds divided along each wall. Most of the beds were filled. Some of the injuries were evident—lost arms or legs. Others were not so evident, like the soldier in the bed next to him. His head was bandaged but Ethan could not determine the seriousness of his injury. Nor could he tell if he were unconscious or just sleeping. He would ask the nurse about him when she came back.

Since the shot had made him so mellow, he decided he would go back to sleep. He had just closed his eyes when he heard a familiar voice calling his name.

"Ethan Ward."

He opened his eyes to see his friend nearing his bed. Ethan smiled and greeted his friend.

"My hero."

"Now you're not going to start that are you?"

"For the rest of your life," Ethan shot back with a laugh. "You saved my life."

"It was nothing."

"I'll tell my mother that. Man, it's great to see you. Are you doing O.K.?"

He noticed his friend was wearing a hospital gown but did not appear to have any injuries. Then, as he turned, he noticed a bandage on his left ear.

"I'm fine," returned Tommy as he walked around the bed and pulled up a chair. "Just talk in my right ear."

"What are you saying?"

"The explosion busted my ear drum."

"Damn. I'm sorry to hear that Tommy. What can they do?"

"Nothing here. They are sending me to Tokyo tomorrow to see if it can be repaired. What the heck—I still got one good ear. My dad always said I only listen to half of what he said anyway."

"Does it hurt?"

"Oh yeah, but they got me on some good medication."

"Me too, and it makes me pretty mellow. So If I start telling you how much I love you I hope you understand."

The two laughed, then Ethan became more serious.

"Well I sure am sorry—and you got your injury saving me."

"No, I got it saving myself. You just happened to be along for the ride."

"And if you hadn't taken time to pull me down you would'a been fine."

"Lets not talk about it. It's over and done. So you doing O.K.?"

"Yeah, unfortunately. They say I will be fine. Probably be back on duty within a few weeks."

"Oh well, in less than six months you will be back in the great State of Tennessee."

"And you too—actually in a lot less time."

"Yeah, that's the other thing about this injury. Even if they can do surgery I will be going home."

"Really?"

"Yeah. They say the best case scenario is that I will have some hearing in this ear. And they can't have someone on the battlefield with a hearing problem. It's too dangerous for everyone."

"Well that's great news. You don't sound too excited."

"Well, I am, it's just—well, I just feel a little guilty about it."

"Man are you crazy. You did your time. Go ahead and go visit your family. Go to college. Find a girl. Start a family."

The two soldiers continued the conversation they started the day before. They talked of happier times—of dreams—of future plans and of someday living in a world where there would be no more war. The pain medication helped them see things so much more clearly.

TWENTY

Ethan realized that the medication was making him mellow, which made the time he was spending talking to his friend even more enjoyable. With the exception of Sally, there was no one else with whom he would rather spend time. As they continued talking, an idea began to formulate. They had almost died yesterday. What if he had died? As tragic as his death would be, the only thing he could think about was the situation with Professor Robertson. If he died no one would ever know what really happened. And what about the parents of the boys killed by Deputy Pratt? They would never know what happened to their sons. While he hated to burden his friend, someone else had to know the story. Someone he could trust to do the right thing. There was no better person.

"Tommy," he began, "I have something I need to tell you."

"That sounds serious."

"Well, actually it is. It's a long story though. You got time?"

"Where am I going to go?" he laughed. "I can hold out as long as my good ear or the pain medicine does. Go ahead, Ace."

Ethan noticed he had not called him that in some time. He guessed it was because they were getting too old—too mature. Funny he should revert to it at this time.

He told him the whole story—everything. He told him about his first meeting with the Professor, the investigation he had done on his own, and his follow up meeting with the Professor. He didn't recap the actual shooting of the Deputy. They had discussed that many times in the past years. Tommy listened intently, only briefly interrupting him to ask a question. When he finished the two sat silently, each waiting for the other to speak. Finally Tommy broke the silence.

"You know, Ethan, if I didn't know you better I would say you made this whole thing up."

"Yeah, I wish."

"Here we are in the middle of the Vietnam war—we both almost got killed—and you tell me a story that is the most unbelievable thing that I have heard in my life. How do you get yourself into such things?"

"I wish I knew. Right now I only want to know how to get myself out of it. You got any advice about what I should do?"

He thought for a minute before answering.

"You know I am always free with advice but first I have a couple of questions."

"Whatever you want."

"First, do you feel certain the two men let you escape?"

"I don't think there is any doubt. They could have easily killed me."

"And you are certain that the Professor has never been in any trouble before or since, right?"

"I'm virtually certain of that."

"And do you know that Sally knew—or knows—nothing about this?"

"Absolutely not. That is unless she found out in the past few weeks."

"Right, but my point is that there was no way she could have known about this and met you on purpose so you would fall in love with her?"

"I would never, ever believe that. As unbelievable as it is, it was just a coincidence. As the Professor said, "God can do about any-thing he wants.""

"So he's a Christian?" asked Tommy.

"He says he is."

"O.K. We have no way to know that. Only God knows what's in

a person's heart, so let's move on. We also know that three young boys were killed by someone in the months before this happened."

"Yes, and we know the killings stopped after Deputy Pratt died."

"You don't know that. You only know they stopped in our region."

"If they continued in any other part of the country we would have heard about it. It was just beginning to get nationwide attention," returned Ethan.

"O.K., but let's keep going. You know for sure that the Deputy was in Harriman when the first boy was killed?"

"Yeah, I saw his personnel records that showed he was sent to pick up the other boy."

"Anything else we know for sure?"

"Well, yeah, a lot of things."

"Like what?" Asked Tommy.

"Like the fact that the other person in the truck knew Deputy Pratt; Like the fact that the Deputy was in the area when at least one of the other boys were killed; Like the fact that the Deputy was keeping souvenirs of the boy's murders; Like the fact that...."

"Hold on, Ethan. You don't know those things for a fact. You don't know that the man who did the shooting really knew the Deputy. And you don't know that the Deputy was in the area where the boys were killed. And as far as the newspaper clippings go, he could have been investigating the cases himself."

"O.K., fine," returned Ethan with frustration, "but there are very few things about this case that I can ever be one hundred percent certain of."

"That's my point."

"What is your point?"

"That the only way that you will ever know what really happened is in a court of law."

"What? Are you really saying I should turn in the Professor?"

"Yes. That is the only way the truth will be uncovered and justice will be done."

Ethan was shocked at what his friend was saying. He thought, more than anyone else, Tommy would understand why the

Professor could never go to trial.

"Tommy, do you know what would probably happen to the Professor if I turned him in?"

"I think he would get a fair trail and that justice would be served and the truth would come out."

"Tommy," he said as he shook his head, "haven't you noticed what happened to black people in this country in the last—oh shall we say—four hundred years? The chance of him getting a fair trail for killing a white man is practically zero."

"I don't agree. Times have changed a lot and this would be a very visible trial. It would probably attract national attention. And, besides that, I don't think he would go to trial. The one who should be on trial here is his friend—whoever that is."

"And he will never turn him in."

"Why?"

"Because he knows that, as an accomplice, the worse could happen to him is that he would be put away for a few years. His friend could spend the rest of his life in prison. So he will never give him up."

"That's what he says now. I guarantee you after he spends some time in jail thinking about it—away from his daughters—he will change his mind."

Ethan tried to understand his friend's point of view. As hard as he tried, he could not. As a young black man growing up in the sixties he figured he would be the last person to want to see the two men go to trial.

"What's wrong?" asked Tommy.

"It's just that—well, to be blunt—I'm really surprised at what you are saying. I thought you would be the last person who would want to see two black men—two probably innocent black men—go on trial for killing a white Deputy."

"Well, let me ask you something."

"What?"

"If you were sitting here talking to Martin Luther King Jr., would you be shocked at him saying that justice has to be served for whites and blacks alike?"

His words were like cold water on his face. He felt guilty for the comments he had made.

"You know what—you are right. I apologize. I judged you by the society we live in and what you have seen rather than your character. I know you try to live your life according to God's standards so I should have known better. I apologize."

"Yes, you are right. I do try to live the way Jesus taught us, but there is another reason you should apologize."

"What do you mean?"

"Because I also got a lot of my character from you. You were the one who saw two black men gun down a white Deputy, yet it never turned you into a narrow minded, bigoted person like it would most people. You have always treated everyone the same. And now you want to protect two black men because they may be innocent. Yes, you should apologize for not seeing how you have impacted the people around you."

Ethan was shocked and deeply touched by his words. He had never thought that his actions could have affected anyone so much. And to hear those words from his best friend was overwhelming. Perhaps it was the time and place, or perhaps it was the drugs—but for whatever reason he tried to fight back the tears.

"Well," he returned, "Since we can later blame all of this on the drugs, there's something I want to say to you."

"What?"

"Remember when I had my little confrontation with Ted and Ed and you came in and helped me?"

"Oh yeah."

"I don't think you will ever know how much that meant to me."

"Why—they were jerks."

"I know. But if you remember, that was just after I saw the Deputy killed, and here were two black kids picking on me for no reason. I thought you and I were friends, but I didn't know how much our friendship meant until then. That really meant a lot."

The two set silently for a moment, then, both realizing the conversation had gotten too emotional, Tommy said,

"Now that didn't mean I liked you—just that I felt sorry for you."

The two broke out laughing. When they had stopped Ethan continued the conversation.

"O.K., Back to the point. Tommy, I do understand what you are saying, but I still don't think I can turn the Professor in."

"Then you shouldn't do it. You asked me my opinion and I gave it to you. You have to do what you feel is right. I hate to lay it on you but no one else can make that decision."

"Yeah, I know. I still have a little time to think about it before I go home. Lets talk about something else."

The two continued to talk for a few minutes longer before both of their pain medications began to wear off. Before leaving Ethan learned something new about his friend—something he had never told anyone either. Unlike himself who only longed for a happy but quiet life, Tommy hoped to advance himself as far as possible, perhaps becoming Governor or Senator.

"Wow, Tommy, I never knew that. I think you would make a great politician. And I could have a friend that not only saved my life but who is rich and powerful as well."

"You already have one rich and powerful friend. That's more than you deserve."

———————

A few days later Tommy was transferred to the U.S. Army hospital in Tokyo for surgery on his ear. Ethan could only pray that things went well. That was something new to him—praying—and something that he found himself doing more and more of lately. It was a strange thing that war did to people.

A week later Ethan was transferred to the rehabilitation center, and ten days after that he was released. While neither his Sergeant nor Captain visited him during his confinement—he never expected them to considering the circumstances—a jeep was sent to bring him back to the base. The doctor had been accurate regarding his injuries and recovery. While he was technically not incapacitated, it was still an effort to move around. His thigh had healed more quickly than his back, which was still very stiff and sore. For the next few weeks the Captain had put him on light duty, which meant mostly

K.P. Ethan didn't mind, except that he felt guilty at seeing all the other soldiers going into and returning from battle—and sometimes not returning from battle. The good news was that the war seemed to be winding down. The government had quietly been reducing the number of personnel in the country in the past few months. Ethan wondered what the coming next few months would bring. Would they actually pull out of the country? And if so, what was to happen to all of the Vietnamese soldiers and civilians who had helped them? Would everything be in vain? As Sergeant Rodriquez had said, 'such decisions were hopefully made by people a lot smarter and more informed than me'.

His own future was not in question for long. It was an afternoon in June and he had just finished K.P. duty. He was on the floor in the barracks doing his stretching exercises when Sergeant Rodriquez approached him. He began to get up when he saw the Sergeant draw near.

"Don't get up on my account, Private," he commented.

"It's no problem," returned Ethan as he continued to rise, not wishing to address the Sergeant as he lay on the floor.

"How's it going, Private Ward?"

"It's O.K., Sergeant. Kind of slow, I guess, but I should be able to return to full duty in the next couple of weeks."

"Well, maybe that won't be necessary."

"What do you mean?" asked Ethan.

"We just got new orders and—well soldier, you're going home."

"What? When?" stammered Ethan. "Why me—I mean, not that I'm objecting."

The Sergeant sat on Ethan's bunk. Ethan pulled up a nearby stool.

"The Army has just announced a further reduction in troop strength so a number of soldiers are getting an early trip back to the States. They're taking soldiers who have been wounded first so you are one of the lucky ones."

"Wow," said Ethan, still in shock. "When?"

"Probably as soon as you feel up to traveling and we can get you on a transport plane—two or three days I guess."

Many things flashed through Ethan's mind; his parents, Sally, college, Professor Robertson, Tommy. This was such a surprise that he was almost speechless.

"So just don't do anything stupid and injure yourself before you leave," continued Sergeant Rodriquez. "I'd hate to see you spend another couple weeks here because of a broken leg."

The Sergeant rose to leave. To show his respect Ethan rose and saluted him. He saluted back and held out his hand to shake. Ethan grasped it firmly. With a pat on the shoulder he turned and walked away.

The next couple of days passed faster than Ethan expected. There were many things to do. He had to coordinate his own travel plans. There were telegrams to send to both his parents and to Sally. He wanted to get a message to Tommy but was uncertain if he was home yet or was still at Walter Reed Army Hospital in Washington. Either way he was certain his mother would notify Tommy's parents. He wanted to have other gifts to take home so the following morning he visited a gift shop near the base. By the time he had finished everything it was the night before his departure.

The next morning he was outside the barracks at 0:800 awaiting transportation to the airfield when Sergeant Rodriquez came by for the final farewell.

"So, soldier, before you go, what have you learned from your experience in Nam?" he asked.

"Well," thought Ethan, "I guess it is the best example of what my friend Corporal Bell told me another lifetime ago."

"And what is that?"

"You see the best and worst of everything here. You see unbelievable cruelty and hatred. Yet at the same time every day you see people sacrificing themselves for others—even giving up their lives for people they don't know. Corporal Bell told me that God gave us all the freedom to choose good or evil and too often we choose the evil. That is why we are here—because there is so much evil in men."

"It sounds like your friend is a smart man. Tell him I said hello."

The jeep arrived to take him to the airfield. The two men said their goodbyes. With a tear in his eye Ethan looked down on the villages and countryside as the plane climbed into the sky.

From Vietnam he went to Tokyo then on to Honolulu. After an overnight layover he took another transport into San Francisco. As soon as he landed he called his parents who were ecstatic to hear his voice. His mother recommended—as excited as they were to see him—that he should spend a few days in San Francisco. He may never get the chance to see it again. Ethan told her the only thing he wanted to see were the hills of Tennessee. She informed him that Tommy had been home almost a week and that the surgery had been successful, although his hearing would never be normal in that ear. He decided to call Sally to let her know he was back in the States. Noticing he had no coins left he started to leave to get change, then decided she would not mind him calling collect. He dialed the operator and gave her the number. The phone rang a dozen times before he told the operator he would try again later. He thought it strange that this time of year neither she nor her father were home, especially since he had telegrammed her that he would be returning soon.

He checked with the airlines and discovered the next flight he could get on standby would not be leaving until almost four P.M. With the time difference that meant he would not get into Knoxville until one o'clock in the morning. He decided that was too late to ask his parents to pick him up so decided to take their advice and spend the night in San Francisco and leave in the morning. United Airlines had a nine A.M. flight he could get on which meant he would be at Knoxville by six P.M. He took a taxi to a nearby hotel and checked in. He tried Sally two more times before giving up for the day. He hoped there was not a problem.

The next morning he called Sally once more before his plane left. There was still no answer. He finally decided that she and her father must have gone to Harriman for a few days to visit relatives. He would wait until he got home to try her again.

He felt as if the flight home would never end. He glanced at his watch at eleven-thirty and realized it had been exactly six weeks since he and Tommy had been in the bar when the bomb exploded. Of course, with the time change, he realized his timing was off by twenty hours, but it still let him relive those horrible few seconds. If God was just, then hopefully his experiences with violence would be over.

His plane arrived at McGhee Tyson airport at five forty-five. He was so excited to see his home state that he could hardly remain in his seat. He waited eagerly in line for the plane to debark. He walked down the steps and under the covered walkway to the airport. As he drew closer he could see his parents waiting eagerly near the door. His mother gave him a big hug and smile. He was glad to see that his mother was walking without a limp. Hopefully her back problems were over. To his surprise his normally stoic father also hugged him.

"Welcome home, son," said his father as his mother wiped her eyes.

"It's so good to see you, son," cried his mother. "How was your trip?"

"It was long but good. It sure is good to get home. How was traffic getting here?"

"It's always a might rough through Knoxville. Why couldn't you get a flight into Greenville?" his father joked.

"Yeah, directly from San Francisco into downtown Greenville. Why didn't I think of that?"

"So how long is your leave, son?" asked his mother.

"I got thirty days, Mom," he replied, "then I have to report to Ft. Benning."

With a quick stop at the luggage area to pick up his duffle bags they were on their way. With his father complaining about the traffic and his mother asking about his trip, they were through Knoxville in no time. Even with a stop for hamburgers they were home by eight thirty. Once they had gotten into the house Ethan took his belongings to his room and returned to the living room. As he came into the room he noticed that his parents were seated together at the dining room table. He became concerned at the serious look on their faces.

"What is wrong?" he asked. "You two look like you have some bad news."

"There is something we need to talk to you about, son."

"What is it?" he asked. "Is there something wrong with Horace or his wife."

"No, it's nothing like that," replied his mother. "Nobody is sick or dead. But....well, you tell him, Buster."

Ethan sat at the table with his parents, wondering what could be the reason for such concern.

"We figured we ought to wait till ya got home before we told you about this, son. We just heard on the news as we was coming to pick you up that Professor Robertson was arrested for killing Deputy Pratt."

PART
THREE

TWENTY-ONE

JUNE 1970

Ethan felt as if all the life had gone out of him. Just when he had gotten back home and was looking forward to a quiet, simple, life, his world was shattered. His mind raced to understand all the possibilities of what he had just heard. It was too much to comprehend. But now he understood why there was no answer at Sally's house.

"He has been arrested? When? How? How do you know?"

"Well, son, like I said, it was on the radio. We just heard about it a little while ago so I reckon it was in the last two or three days."

"Were there any more details? How did they identify him?"

"I reckon they got a tip from someone which led them ta the truck. It was buried under about thirty feet of water up ta Cherokee Lake. They said the truck had been registered to one of the Professor's relatives—I don't remember which."

"It was his father's," interjected Ethan before thinking.

"What?" asked his mother and father in unison as they started at each other. "You knew about this, Ethan?" asked his mother wide-eyed.

Ethan realized there was no need to keep anything a secret any longer. Soon it would all come out. As he had done with Tommy a few weeks earlier, he relayed the whole story to them. They sat in shocked silence. Finally, his father spoke.

"Well, I reckon as long as I live I ain't likely ta hear anything as crazy as this. So how long you known about this, son?"

"For about a year, I guess."

"So that is why you wanted to talk to the Sheriff?" asked his mother.

"Yes, ma'am. And I know that everything the Professor told me is true. If it hadn't been for him and his friend I would not be alive today."

The three set silently, each trying to deal with what they had just heard. Finally, Ethan's mother spoke.

"Well, son, at least now you don't have to carry this burden around with you anymore."

"No, now I have a different burden."

"What do you mean?"

"Now an innocent man may go to prison, and I am the reason."

"Whatever are you talkin about—you're the reason?" asked his father.

"I can't explain right now, but there is something I have to do. Can I borrow your car?"

"I guess so," continued his father, "but what are you talkin about, son? You ain't makin' no sense."

"I know Dad, but trust me. I know what I am doing. I will explain to you all tomorrow."

With that he got up from the table and took the keys from the hook on the wall. His parents looked on as he went to the car and drove away.

There was only one possibility—Tommy had either called the authorities himself or had told someone who had called them. It couldn't be any other way. It couldn't be a coincidence that after all this time he was arrested just a few weeks after he had told his friend the story—and immediately upon him returning home. As hard as it was to accept, his best friend had betrayed him.

He drove quickly to Tommy's house and parked his car on the street. He rang the doorbell and nervously wrung his hands as he waited. Soon Mrs. Bell came to the door. Upon seeing Ethan she flung open the screen door and wrapped her arms around him.

"Ethan it is so good to see you. Welcome home, son."

"Thank you Mrs. Bell," he returned, trying to be nonchalant. "How is Tommy doing?"

"Better than he probably has a right to after what you boys went through. How are you doing?"

"I'm fine—just fine. Still a little sore but other than that I'm doing well. Is Tommy here? There is something I need to talk to him about."

"Sure, come on in," she replied as she moved aside. "You know the way to his room."

Ethan walked quickly down the hallway to Tommy's room. The door was open so he walked in. Tommy was on the bed reading a book. He got up quickly as he saw his friend.

"Hey, I didn't expect you for another couple of days," he began. He started toward his friend, then, seeing the look in his eyes, stopped short.

"What's wrong?"

"I think you know what's wrong."

"What are you talking about?"

"I guess you don't listen to the news."

"Not today I haven't. What are you talking about?"

"I thought friends could trust each other."

Tommy came close to Ethan with anger in his eyes.

"Before I throw you out of my room I will ask you one more time. What are you talking about?"

"Sally's father was just arrested for the shooting of Deputy Pratt. It was on the news today."

"You're kidding. And you think that I was the one that turned him in?"

"It's been seven years since the shooting and now, just weeks after I told you what happened, someone gives a tip to the police and he's arrested."

"I will tell you one time Ethan," he said as he drew closer, "if someone notified the authorities about this it wasn't me."

"And you never mentioned this to anyone else?"

"I haven't said a word about what you told me until right now. Now if you want to talk about this we can. But if you accuse me of this again you can leave."

Ethan had been so upset—so distraught—that he had never considered any other possibility. Now he had to think.

"O.K., O.K.," he said as he held up his palm. "If you tell me you didn't say anything then I'll believe you."

"So you want to sit down and talk about this?" asked Tommy as he motioned to a chair.

Ethan sat in the chair as Tommy chose the bed.

"O.K., I am sorry for flying off the handle like that," he began, "but I hope you can see how this looks."

"I guess I can see how it looks, but that should not destroy all your faith and trust in me. I told you I wouldn't say anything and I haven't."

"Alright, do you want to help me figure out what happened?"

"There are all sort of possibilities, Ethan. You don't know who else might have known about this or may have overheard something. What did the news say?"

"Just that they got a tip that led them to the truck. They got the serial number off the truck which led them to the Professor."

"I think that makes it even more difficult."

"Why?"

"Because it could have been somebody who saw the truck years ago and never thought anything about it, then somebody says something about the case and it triggers their memory."

"That's a stretch."

"Well, there is one other possibility."

"What's that?"

"The guy in the bed next to you. We assumed he was unconscious. He could have just been asleep and woke up when he heard us talking."

"You think we were talking that loud?"

"I don't know—we were both drugged. All he would have had to hear were the few words about them getting away by dumping the truck in a lake and catching a train home. Anybody could probably narrow down the area from that. And there is still a reward out for the killers. That's plenty of incentive for anyone."

"Hmm, I never thought of the guy in the bed."

"But Ethan, I don't want to sound too heartless, but what matter does it make now who gave the tip?"

"It does matter," he responded quickly. "I don't want the Professor or Sally to think it came from me."

"Then I don't know what to tell you," Tommy returned, then, after thinking for a moment added, "there is one thing I might do, though."

"What's that?"

"As you know, my Uncle Joe is a policeman in Knoxville. Maybe he heard something. I'll call and ask him."

"That's nice of you after the way I treated you. So, are we still friends?"

"Sure, but next time ask me—don't accuse me."

Ethan got up and shook his friend's hand and apologized once more. Before leaving he asked about his surgery. He told him it went well and he had about sixty percent hearing in his injured ear. He informed him, because of his injury, he had gotten a full discharge from the Army. He also told him he had applied for a job in the City Manager's office and would be going to the local community college in the fall. They said goodbye and Ethan returned to what he knew would be further questions from his parents.

The next morning, after another lengthy discussion with his parents, Ethan started to call Sally again but then changed his mind. He decided to visit her in person instead. Then she would have no choice but to talk to him. Borrowing his mother's car, he headed for Murfreesboro. He imagined, as soon as the Sheriff heard he was back in town, he would be getting a phone call. He wondered what the legal possibilities were of him testifying for both the defense and prosecution. Those issues he could worry about later. Right now he had more important things to do. He was on the road less than a half-hour when he heard the first news report about the Professor's arrest. It provided little new information. The only thing significant was that the authorities stated they had ample evidence for a conviction. He laughed when he heard that the only eyewitness would be returning soon from Vietnam to testify.

As he got closer to Nashville he tuned into a local country and western station. It only added to the incredible events of the last twenty-four hours when he heard the announcer introduce the next song.

"And here's a hit that has been on the charts for a long time, folks. It peaked at number three but is still in the top twenty. A newcomer and local gal, Rachel Mills with, "And Your Love Too.""

Ethan turned up the radio and listened.

A gentle breeze on a summer's day,
Flowers dancing in the month of May,
A starry night on a tropic Isle,
The babbling of a newborn child.

A meadow kissed with morning dew,
All of this and your love too.

A mountain stretching to meet the sky,
A kaleidoscope of butterflies,
Freshly fallen snow in the moonlight,
Crickets calling through the night.

A sunbeam spreading its golden hue,
All of this and your love too.

Leaves fading from green to brown,
A carpet of moss upon the ground,
Ice cycles melting in the sunlight,
Fireflies playing tag at night.

A new ring sparkling crystal blue,
All of this and your love too.

Ethan wondered if Rachel really understood the meaning of the words she was singing. Perhaps he was too harsh on her. Perhaps she really did have some compassion in her heart after all.

A short while later Ethan pulled into Professor Robertson's driveway. He was comforted to see both his car and truck in the driveway. That meant Sally had to be home. Now, all he had to do was convince her to talk to him. As he walked to the door he wondered what her father had told her about their relationship. Did she know everything? If not, she soon would. He saw no need to try to keep anything a secret anymore. With the investigation, everything would come out anyway.

He rang the doorbell and nervously waited. The door opened and there stood Sally, as beautiful as ever, although looking as though she had not slept in days.

"Hi, Sally," he said simply. "Can I come in?"

She said nothing but stared at him blankly. She then put her hands over her face and began sobbing. Ethan moved closer and pulled her to him, wrapping his arms around her.

"Are you alright?" he asked.

She did not respond.

"Sally?" he repeated.

Finally she moved her hands away and looked at him.

"I'm sorry, Ethan. I don't think I've slept in days."

"Can we go inside?" he asked.

She said nothing but moved aside to let him in.

"Would you like a cup of coffee or a soda?" she asked as she tried to regain her composure.

"A Coke would be nice," he responded. He followed her into the kitchen. She poured him a glass of Coke.

"So, how is your dad doing?" he asked as they sat at the table.

"I guess as well as anybody who has just been charged with murder."

He didn't know how to begin. The first thing was to find out what he had told her.

"So I assume he told you about his discussions with me?"

"As far as I know, he told me everything."

"Sally," he said as he patted the table, "will you please sit down with me?"

She folded her arms and chose a chair across from him.

"The first thing I want to tell you is that I had nothing to do with turning him in. I don't know how or why it happened this way, but I believe everything your father told me and I swear to you I didn't do it. Do you believe me?"

"I believe you Ethan. You have never lied to me."

"Other than not telling you about your father and I."

"Well," she began with an attempt at a laugh, "I was really upset at first then, after I had time to think about it and talk to my father, I understood. I mean, what could you do—tell me that my father was involved in a murder years earlier and you witnessed it?"

"It's been an impossible situation Sally. As bad as I feel for your dad, maybe this will be for the best. Hopefully he will be cleared and won't have to worry about this any more. Has he told the authorities the whole story—about the Deputy killing those boys, I mean?"

"He's talked to his attorney about it, who I think is going to talk to the District Attorney in Greenville today."

"And has he said anything about turning in his friend who did the shooting?"

"He said he'll never do that. The worst they can do to him is send him away for a while. He thinks the other man could get life."

"You really should try to convince him to turn him in. Do you have any idea who it is?"

"No, but if I did I would turn him in myself. I wondered if it could be my uncle. They used to get along well but, about the time of the shooting, they had a falling out. I don't know why and never thought about it until now. There are also a few friends in Harriman he keeps in touch with. I really don't know what to think."

The two sat silently for a while. Ethan was afraid to ask the next question but knew he had to.

"So what about us, Sally. I felt like there was something going on with you before this happened. Do you still feel the same way?"

"Wait here, Ethan, There is something I have to show you before I answer that."

FALSE WITNESS   *211*

He wondered what she could be talking about? He watched as she walked toward the bedroom. He nervously sipped his drink awaiting her return. She came back carrying something in a small pink blanket.

"Ethan, I don't know any other way to do this. Meet your daughter Emily."

Ethan choked on his drink. Just when he thought there could be no more shocks, this topped them all. At least now it made sense—all the vagueness in her letters; the uncomfortable feeling he had that there was a problem.

"Oh my God," he exclaimed. "When....what?"

"Well, as far as the when, she was a little premature so she is almost two months old now. As far as how—I had never been on the pill before, Ethan, so I guess I missed a couple. I didn't think it would make any difference."

"Sally, I hate to ask you this, but...."

"She's your daughter Ethan. I have never been with another man. You're the only person I have ever loved."

"I'm sorry, but I had to ask."

"I understand."

"But why didn't you tell me. I don't understand that. This is not right. You had no right to keep this from me."

"You may be right, and I am sorry, but I thought I was doing the right thing."

"How can you say that?"

"Because that's what everyone told me to do."

"Everyone told you that you should not tell me I had a daughter?"

"Yes. I have a girl in one of my classes who went through the same thing. She found out she was pregnant just after her boyfriend left for Vietnam. She wrote him a letter telling him about it and, a few weeks later, he was killed. She always felt like it was because he was so upset—or so distracted—about the news. She said that is not a place to have a lot of other problems on your mind. I was afraid to tell you, Ethan, because I didn't want to worry you while you were over there."

"And your father agreed to this?"

"No, not really. He thought you had a right to know, but a lot of my friends agreed with the other girl. I'm sorry, Ethan. I don't know if I did the right thing or not, but I was only trying to do what was best for you. I hope you will forgive me"

Ethan got up from the table and walked to her. He pulled the blanket back to look at his daughter.

"So this is Emily?"

"Yes."

"The same name as Horace's wife."

"Yes, but actually I named her after my grandmother. My mother always said if either my sister or I had a daughter she would like her to have her mother's name."

"Can I hold her?"

"Sure. She should be waking up soon so you can give her her bottle if you want."

"She sure is cute," he said as he took her to the couch and sat down.

Sally joined him on the couch, watching their daughter as she lie sleeping.

"Little does she know all the turmoil going on all around her," stated Ethan.

"Yes, and I hope we can keep it that way," returned Sally, then added, "so, where do we go from here?"

"I don't know Sally. Right now my mind is just as messed up as yours. Maybe the answers will be more clear in a day or two."

"Do you want to spend the night here, or do you have to go back?"

"I guess I can do that. I need to go talk to your father anyway."

TWENTY-TWO

The next morning Ethan and Sally found a friend to watch the baby and left for the jail. While Sally told him what to expect, it was still a very unsettling experience to be searched and have the iron doors close behind him. They were taken to a waiting room with a long table in the middle and rows of folding chairs on each side. They were seated at one end of the table. The only good news was that there was only one other visitor present in the room. After a short wait Sally's father was brought into the room. While this was her third visit to the jail, she still could not get used to seeing him in shackles. The jailer seated him in the chair across from them, locked his chains to a hook on the floor, then removed his handcuffs. Sally leaned forward to hug her father. While the guard gave her an angry look, he said nothing.

"So how you doing, Daddy?" she asked.

"I'm fine, baby. You O.K.?"

"Sure. I'll be better soon as we get you out of here."

"Good to see you, Professor," stated Ethan, "although this is not the best circumstances."

"No, not exactly. It was really good of you to come. So how does it feel being a father?"

"I'm still trying to adjust to the shock. She sure is cute, though."

"Yes, she is a little sweetheart," he returned as he gave Sally a look that said, 'you should have told him.'

They talked for a minute about how he was being treated—his food, his bed, and such. Ethan felt he had to explain that he had not given the police the lead.

"I hope you know, Professor Robertson, that I'm not responsible for this."

"I figured as much. At least if you were you probably wouldn't be here," he added as an afterthought.

"No, but there is one thing I have to tell you."

Sally looked at him, wondering what he had not told her the day before. He told them about his and Tommy's conversation. He made sure they knew they had almost been killed and that they were both on drugs at the time. He also assured them that Tommy had never repeated their conversation with anyone.

"I honestly don't know if the soldier in the bed next to us could have heard and turned you in. If that is the case, I am sorry."

"It really doesn't matter," returned the Professor. "I have lived with this for years. Maybe it is for the best."

Sally decided to change the subject.

"So, did you see your lawyer today?"

"Yes, as a matter of fact he just left a few minutes ago."

"What does he say?" asked Ethan.

"The D.A. in Greene County has begun extradition procedures. He says we can try and fight it but it will only delay it a little. That is where the crime took place so I will probably be transferred in a few days. He will be talking to the D.A. again today to inform him I will be pleading self-defense."

"So then it will be pretty much public knowledge about Deputy Pratt and the other boys?"

"I imagine so."

"Have you and he talked about your friend that was with you?" asked Sally.

"Oh yes, that has been the main focus. Of course, just like you, he thinks I should turn him in."

"And?" she asked.

"We've already had this conversation honey. They already know, based on Ethan's testimony and the evidence, that I was not the one that did the shooting. The worse I can get is seven to ten years and I would be out in three or four. He could be put away for life."

"I think you are being naive, Daddy."

"What do you mean?"

"If they wanted they could find a way to charge you with murder and not just an accessory. You could get a lot longer than seven to ten years."

The Professor looked at Ethan. "What do you think, son?"

"I don't know, sir. I haven't talked to them yet—I imagine I will have a call when I get back—but I will certainly tell them that you were not the one who did the shooting. But I don't know the law so I can't comment on what they might charge you with. But, since they haven't even talked to me yet, how do they know you were not the one who did the shooting?"

"From your testimony and the fingerprints."

"What do you mean?"

"Because you told them that I was the one that gave you the soda—remember? And only my fingerprints were found on the bottle so they knew I was the passenger and—from your testimony—the driver did the shooting."

"I'm surprised they would give you that much information already. They usually like to keep people in the dark as long as possible."

"Well, they really want the driver."

"You might re-consider giving them his name, Professor."

"It's not going to happen."

Sally knew how stubborn her father could be, so attempted to redirect the conversation again.

"Was there anything else your lawyer told you?"

"Yes, as a matter of fact. He said he is not the best person for the job."

"Really," she replied. "What does that mean?"

"Well you know I was referred to him by someone at the University. He is a good man and has some experience at criminal law, but he said I need the best I can get for my case."

"And who is that?" asked Ethan.

"Well, there are a number of them around, but the one he recommends is a young woman by the name of Ellen Cornblossom."

"Ellen Cornblossom," repeated Ethan. "That is quite an unusual name. Is she Native American?"

"Yes, she is. She is from over your way—the other side of the Smokies—somewhere around Maggie Valley I think. He says she is pretty impressive. Got a law degree from Vandy. Graduated near the top of her class, and practices at one of the top firms in Nashville. And she is only thirty years old. Ralph—my attorney—says she would be the best person for me not only because of her reputation but also because she's a woman and a minority. He thinks that would make a big difference."

"Well, can you get her?"

"There's only one problem—money. She does some pro-bono work but not for something this big—especially since the trial will probably be over at Greenville."

"Don't we have the money, Daddy? Nothing else is more important than this."

"I want this over as much as you, honey, but we may be talking about $15,000 to $20,000 including all her fees. She would have travel expenses and I'm sure there would be a lot of expense for research. And I still don't know if I can get bail or how much I would have to post for that."

"Well, Daddy, you need to get her no matter what it takes."

"We're still working on it little girl."

They spent the rest of the time talking about the baby and other more pleasant issues. Ethan told him he was being stationed at Ft. Benning. The Professor wanted to know about their plans for the future. They said they would wait until the trial was over before making any decisions. Soon the guard came and informed them their time was up. Sally kissed her father and they left the jail.

Upon returning to Sally's house Ethan called his mother at work. She informed him the Sheriff and the District Attorney had called a number of times to talk to him. She told them he would be out of town for a day or two and she could not get in touch with him. They asked her to have him call as soon as she spoke to him. He asked her to call the Sheriff and tell him he would be back in town the following afternoon and would see him then. He did not mention visiting the Professor nor did he tell them about the baby. Discovering they were grandparents was something they should hear in person.

Sally and he spent the afternoon trying to relax and forget about her father's arrest. Emily served as a nice distraction. Ethan found her fascinating. While Sally told him it was his imagination, he was certain she had smiled at him. He quickly decided she was probably the cutest and smartest little girl ever. She had her mother's looks while her complexion was closer to her dad's. They would have to wait to see whose hair hers matched.

They talked about everything that had happened to them since he had left for Vietnam. She was deeply saddened to hear about him having to shoot the young soldier—information which he had left out of his letters. He found out that she had remained in her dorm room until March and then returned home. Even with the pregnancy she was able to finish her second year of college. And, until the situation with her father had arisen, she had been determined to return in the fall. Her aunt had agreed to move in with them and watch the baby while she attended classes. She made sure that Ethan understood that her plans could change based upon his decision. He informed her that he needed time to think about the future.

The next morning Ethan arose early for the trip home. He left her house by eight-thirty, but instead of heading towards Greenville as he had told Sally, he had a stop to make first. He drove north towards Nashville. Forty-five minutes later he was in front of the Capitol building. He did not know if the Governor were in his office but it was worth a try. He had told him that if there was ever anything he could do to let him know. He could not think of a better time to take him up on that offer.

He parked the car and walked briskly to the entrance. He found that walking, while somewhat painful at first, loosened up his back and thigh muscles. He was directed to the Governor's office and was soon standing in front of his receptionist. He gave her his name and asked if the Governor was in.

"I'm sorry, Mr. Ward, I don't have you on the list," she stated. "Did you have an appointment?"

"No, not really, but if you tell him who I am I think he will see me. Is he in?"

"Well he has a number of meetings scheduled this morning so it will be impossible for him to see you."

"Ma'am, when I saved the Governor's wife and daughter from being killed in a car wreck he told me I could call on him anytime. Now I would appreciate it if you would call and ask if he has a couple of minutes."

"Oh, that was you?" she returned. "I didn't know. Please have a seat and I will see what I can do."

The receptionist called the Governor's secretary who said she would have to call her back. A few minutes later the phone rang. The receptionist informed Ethan he could go in to see the Governor.

He entered another large office with another woman sitting behind a desk. She got up to greet him.

"Mr. Ward, I am Sheila Phillips, Governor Coleman's secretary. The Governor has a meeting which should be ending in a few minutes. Won't you have a seat."

"Thank you."

"It's nice to finally meet you. The Governor has spoken about you many times."

"Thank you."

Shortly Ethan heard voices and looked up to see a number of people exiting the Governor's office. They seemed a jovial group as they walked past the secretary.

"Your boss is a tough man," one of them commented with a smile to Sheila.

"Yes, but a fair one," she returned as the group walked out the door.

After they had left she called the Governor and informed him of his guest. She hung up the phone and turned to Ethan.

"The Governor will see you now, Mr. Ward," she informed him.

While he knew it was the right thing to do, Ethan was quite nervous as he entered the Governor's office. Upon seeing him Governor Coleman jumped up from his desk and hurried toward him. Ethan held out his hand and was somewhat surprised when the Governor greeted him with a hug.

"It is so good to see you, Ethan. Thanks for coming by."

"I'm sorry about just barging in like this, Governor," he began, "but I had something I needed to talk to you about."

"That's fine, son. It gives me a nice break. I have about fifteen minutes until I have to leave for another meeting so my time is all yours. But first, tell me how you have been. I know you joined the Army, but what has happened since then."

Ethan was impressed that he knew he had joined the Army. It showed him that he really did care about people—that he had not just been talking when he said he would always be grateful for what he had done. Perhaps he really would help. He told him about his experiences in Vietnam and how he was wounded. They also talked about the Governor's wife and daughter. He told him they were doing fine and would be glad to talk to him.

"It's good to hear that you survived Vietnam, but I don't think that is what you came here to talk about," said the Governor.

"No, sir," returned Ethan.

"Then how can I help you, son?"

"Well, sir, I'm sure you heard the news that an arrest was made for the murder of the Deputy over in Greenville a few years back."

"Yes, I heard about that."

"Well, I don't know if you are aware of this, but I am the only witness to that shooting."

"Yes, I am aware of that also."

"You're kidding. You never mentioned that when we met before."

"I know, son. I'm sure that was a horrible experience for you, and you had just gone through another with my wife and daughter, so I didn't think that was the right time to bring it up. If you had wanted to talk about it I figured you would mention it."

"Thank you. I appreciate that."

"And now that an arrest has been made you have to live it all over again."

"Yes, sir, but it is a lot more than that."

"I figured as much. Go on."

"Well, sir, I think—no, I know—that the Professor is not guilty of this."

"You mean they have the wrong man?"

"No, sir, not exactly. It's a lot more complicated than that."

The Governor walked to his phone and pushed a button. When his secretary answered he told her to make a call and let the people know he would be a few minutes late for his next meeting. He then returned to Ethan and instructed him to go on.

Ethan told him the whole story. He told him about dating Sally and his discussions with her father. He told him about his trip to the Sheriff"s office as well as Deputy Pratt's parents' house. He told him about the newspaper clippings. He told him everything he could think of.

"So you really think this Deputy killed those boys?"

"Yes, sir, I do. And I think if the Professor and his friend had not come along, I would have been next."

The Governor walked around the room and looked out his window, then turned back to Ethan.

"Has the Professor and his attorney informed the D.A. in Greene County of this?"

"He and his attorney talked about it so I think the D.A. should know about it by now."

The Governor directed him to a nearby leather couch. He seated himself in a chair next to him.

"So what do you want me to do, Ethan?"

"Well, from what I know about you, sir, you would not want an innocent man sent to prison."

"That's true, son, but you and I both know it is not that simple. If I could look into everyone's heart and know the truth—well, then I would be God, wouldn't I?"

"Yes, sir."

"But, I'll tell you what I will do. I will inform the Attorney General and the D.A. in Greene County to look into these claims. And, if there is any evidence—well, we'll have to take it from there."

"I appreciate that, sir."

"But I also have to tell you, Ethan, my guess—as a lawyer

myself, that the best place for these things to come out is in court."

"Oh really," returned Ethan with disappointment in his voice.

"I know that is not what you want to hear, son, but it really may be the best thing here. Besides, if he goes to court and is cleared, then he can never be tried again. If they drop the charges now they can always come back and charge him later."

"So, there is nothing you can do to make this go away?"

"Look, Ethan," he said as he patted him on the leg, "I know I told you that you could always call on me if you needed something, and I meant it. Unfortunately, in this case I honestly don't know how much I can help. First, I don't know if you are aware of this, but there is not much I can do legally. I can call and use my persuasive powers, but I can't make the D.A. drop the charges. And, unless they uncover some absolute proof that, not only was the Deputy guilty of these crimes, but that these two men knew that their lives were in danger, would I even ask the charges to be dropped."

The disappointment showed on Ethan's face.

"Look, son," continued the governor, "as I said, I will have them look into it. Maybe they will uncover some new evidence and we can take the right action at that time. For now that is all I can promise."

"I appreciate that, sir," he responded.

"Look, I have to get ready for my next meeting. I will be in touch with you about this."

"That's the other thing, sir. If you don't mind I would rather you keep this between you and I."

"I understand. Then what I will do is wait until I hear that the Professor is pleading self-defense, then I will have them look into the charges. How is that?"

"That is great, sir. I really appreciate your listening."

The Governor walked him to the door. He shook his hand and returned to his desk. Ethan wondered why he had not hugged him as he did when he greeted him. He also wondered if he had done the right thing. Perhaps he had been naive. It had probably been too much to hope for to expect the Governor to get the charges dropped. At least he would look in to it. That was something.

He left the Capital and returned to his car. Soon he was on the road back to Greenville estimating he would arrive by early afternoon.

As he drove home he thought of everything that had happened in the past couple of days; his returning home; hearing the news about the professor; the fight with Tommy; and—the biggest shock of all—finding out he had a daughter. He was upset with Sally for keeping it a secret, but he believed she was doing it only to protect him. The question was, what did he do now? He knew the proper thing to do was to marry her. He loved Sally, and their daughter needed both a mother and father, but marriage was for a lifetime. And, right now he realized he was too emotional and had too many thoughts going through his head to make a rational decision. He would have to think about it for a while.

His afternoon would not be a pleasant one. He would first have to meet with the Sheriff and the D.A., then he must tell his parents the news about the baby. Was it Shakespeare or the Bible that said, "all things must pass?"

TWENTY-THREE

After arriving back in Greenville Ethan first went to his parents' house and made a sandwich. Upon finishing lunch he called the Sheriff's office. Sheriff Benlow had been waiting for his call. He told Ethan to meet him at the courthouse in forty-five minutes. While waiting, Ethan took the newspaper from the table and sat in the living room reading. The headlines were all about the professor's arrest. While he was mentioned in the article as the only witness, he had expected that he would have received a much bigger focus. He then realized that the public was not yet aware of his total involvement in the case. He couldn't wait to see the future editions.

Sheriff Benlow did not like Randy Richmond, the young D.A. who was elected the year before. He found him to be arrogant and insensitive. While his job required a person with thick skin, it did not need someone who took pleasure in the misfortunes of others. And that was how the Sheriff perceived Richmond. He felt that he viewed the job as nothing more than a steppingstone to a higher office—perhaps Senator or even Governor. He felt that to him a person's guilt or innocence was secondary to getting a conviction. He did not like coming to his office, and knew he would enjoy it even less today, especially after the conversation he had just had with him on the phone.

He met Ethan Ward outside the D.A.'s office and the two walked in together.

"Ethan, have you met our District Attorney, Randy Richmond

before?" began the Sheriff.

"I don't think so," replied Ethan, "but I have seen you around."

Ethan walked towards his desk to greet him, however, the D.A. stopped him by pointing to a nearby table.

"You two can sit here," he instructed.

As soon as they had seated themselves the D.A. took a seat directly across from Ethan. He wasted no time in beginning.

"I called you two here originally because I wanted to go over the details of the case, but, just a couple hours ago, I received new information."

He looked at Ethan as if he were expecting a response but, receiving none, continued.

"I just found out from Mr. Robertson's lawyer that he will be pleading self-defense. I guess you are aware of that though aren't you Mr. Ward?"

"Yes, I am aware of it."

"So, I assume it's safe to say you spoke to Mr. Robertson recently?"

"Yes, I spoke to Professor Robertson today," returned Ethan, emphasizing *Professor.* He did not mention that he had seen him in person. He hoped he would not ask that question.

"I also just found out that you have a relationship with Mr. Robertson's daughter. Is that correct?"

"Yes, that is correct."

"And exactly what is that relationship and how did it come about?"

Ethan told him how he and Sally met and that they had been dating since. He did not tell him about the baby.

"So how long have you known about the defendant's claim of the Deputy's intent to kill the three of you?"

"I don't remember exactly. It's been some time."

Ethan waited for the Sheriff to comment, but he made none. He wondered how much the Sheriff already knew and how upset he was with him.

"Since you admit, Mr. Ward, that you were aware that Mr. Robertson was wanted for these crimes and said nothing—even protected him, are you aware that I can have you arrested for a number of things including aiding and abetting a criminal—accessory after the fact?"

"You're kidding," Ethan said as he stiffened in his chair.

"Oh, no, I'm very serious. You didn't know that Mr. Robertson was wanted for the murder of Deputy Pratt?"

"That's enough!" Sheriff Benlow said bluntly to the D.A.

"Sheriff don't you...."

"No, don't you....," he yelled as he leaned in towards the D.A.. "This is a good young boy who saw a horrible crime take place and has lived with it for years. And whether he should have come forward with the information about the Professor or not, he thought he was doing what was right. Now, if you want to play hardball you go ahead and arrest him and just try to get a conviction. When the people of this county find out about it, you will probably get laughed out of office. And, even if you don't, you will never, ever get a conviction. And, to take it one step further, after arresting him, do you still expect him to testify against the defendant? I wouldn't. Don't play any more games, Richmond."

The D.A.'s face was red. Ethan was shocked at the Sheriff's outburst but was glad the he was on his side. Finally Richmond continued.

"Fine, lets forget about this for now. I want to review the testimony before I decide what charges to bring against the defendant."

The rest of the meeting was calm but uncomfortable. Ethan again recanted the story about what happened that day. He expected the D.A. to question him more about the Professor's claims of self-defense but he did not. He guessed it was because the Sheriff was present, or that he felt he already had the answers. Finally, as they were wrapping up, Richmond gave him one final warning.

"Mr. Ward, I don't want you having any more contact with the defendant before the trial. Is that clear?"

"Yes, it's clear, but I don't understand. He has never asked me to protect him or lie for him. It was my decision not to say anything. Besides, there is nothing new we can talk about."

"Well, whether you understand or not, that is the way it is going to be. Do I need to get a court order?"

"No, that won't be necessary."

"And that goes for his daughter too."

"Well, then there is something else you should know. His daughter—Sally—and I just became engaged. And if you don't want me talking to her then you will have to get a court order."

Ethan decided it was better to tell a small lie than to let them know that they had just had a baby together. He especially did not want anyone else to know before he had a chance to tell his parents. Richmond stared at him angrily.

"Fine, there is an easy way to handle this. I will have all the defendant's communications monitored—phone, mail, and personal. And I will make sure he knows it's you who brought it about. How's that?"

Ethan had nothing else to say to him. It appeared that the D.A. had nothing left to discuss with them for the time being.

"That's all I have now. We'll meet again when I have more information on these outrageous claims."

Ethan and Sheriff Benlow turned and walked away. After they were safely out of ear shot Ethan turned to him.

"Do you believe he would really bring charges against me?"

"Even he is not that stupid, Ethan. He was just trying to get to you. And if he did—trust me—there's no court in Greene County that would convict. Now that has nothing to do with how stupid it was for you to keep this to yourself. You should have come to me. I'm not very happy with you."

"I'm sorry, Sheriff. Maybe I should have come to you, but I felt certain that everything the Professor told me was true, and I could not take a chance on sending an innocent man to prison—especially one who saved my life."

"So you really think Pratt might have done it, huh?"

"Yes, sir, I do. You never thought of it?"

"No, never even imagined it. I know my men pretty good and I know he was a bully and a pain in the butt sometimes, but I never thought of anything like that. I think we need to go sit down and talk so you can tell me everything you know."

"O.K."

Ethan and he found a bench in a secluded area where Ethan could tell him everything the Professor had told him, as well as what he had discovered on his own. After finishing he waited for the Sheriff to comment.

"So you are basing your beliefs on what the Professor told you plus the newspaper clippings you found, which could mean nothing, and the fact that Pratt had a full size American car whose tire tracks might have matched those found at one of the crime scenes?"

"Yes, and the fact that the whole thing just makes more sense. Can we get a search warrant to test the tires?"

"Too late, son. I know for a fact that Pratt's father had those tires changed a couple of years ago."

"How would you know that?"

"Cause I was in the garage the day he stopped by to have new tires put on."

"So I guess we will never really know what happened and just have to wait for the jury to decide."

"Well let me do a little investigating on my own—which is what I would have done if you had come to me."

"I'm sorry Sheriff, but I thought I was doing what was right."

Ethan started to walk away, then remembered an important question.

"I don't guess you know who the tip came from?"

"No, I only know that it went through the State Police. I think they said it came from someone in Pennsylvania."

"Pennsylvania?" he repeated, trying to remember anything about the soldier in the bed next too him. Unfortunately he never spoke to him and didn't even know his name.

He said goodbye to the Sheriff and left for home. The second part of his 'longest day' was about to begin—telling his father about the baby.

His parents were both home by five-thirty. He did not want to wait until after dinner. He knew that they would know something else was wrong, and he wanted to get it over with as soon as possible. He asked them if he could talk to them. They sat in the living room.

"So how did it go with the D.A. today," asked his father.

"About as well as expected. He's not a very nice person."

"No he ain't, but that ain't what he's paid for."

Ethan did not feel like getting into a discussion about the D.A.—especially now.

"How is Sally and her dad doing?" asked his mother.

"Not too well. She said it is like living a nightmare. She said her dad is actually doing better than her."

"So," said his dad slowly, "I reckon you actually believe his story?"

"It makes more sense than anything else, Dad. But I obviously will never know for sure. I don't think anyone living will ever know, maybe not even the Professor or his friend."

Ethan did not really want to go into the details of the case. When he had a chance he began to tell them his other news.

"There is something else I need to talk to you all about."

They exchanged a worried glance.

"What is that?" asked his mother.

"Well," taking a deep breath he began, "like you said the other day when you told me about the Professor, there is no easy way to do this. Sally just had a baby a couple of months ago."

His mother gasped while his father stared at him angrily.

"A baby?" she repeated.

"And I reckon she is saying it's yours?" asked his dad.

"She is mine, Dad. There is no doubt about it."

"It's a little girl?" asked his mother, trying to catch her breath.

"Yes, Emily. She is two months old."

His father got up from the sofa and walked to the kitchen and stared out the window.

"And when did you find out about it?" asked his mother.

"Just when I went to see her."

"Just now?" repeated his dad. "What does that tell you, son?"

"It tells me that she was afraid of telling me while I was in Nam because she was afraid I would be so upset and distracted that I might get myself shot."

"That's ridiculous," he shot back.

"Well, Dad, on that I will have to agree with you. But I know her and I know that that is the real reason. She has worried about me and what I would say."

"And what did you say?" asked his father.

"About the future? I didn't say anything yet. There are so many other things going on I just decided to take it day to day."

His father returned to the living room and sat staring blankly at the wall.

"Well?" asked Ethan

"Well, what?" returned his father.

"What do you want to say? How do you feel about it?"

"Well," began his mother, "She is here now and there is nothing we can do to make her go away. And you are certain she is yours?"

"If you see her, Mom, you will know. Besides, Sally is not like that. She really is a faithful and loving girl."

Ethan knew his problem would not be with his mother. As much as he hated to push it, he had to know where his father stood.

"So, Dad, are you going to accept this?"

"What do you mean accept it? If she is your daughter nothin' I can do or say will change it. But I don't reckon a man is a racist just cause he wants his children and grandchildren ta look like him."

"Well, actually she does look like me—well, like both of us."

"What—with black curly hair and dark skin?"

"Actually her complexion is closer to mine. And I imagine her hair will be somewhere between the two. So I take it that you are not going to be able to accept her as part of the family?"

He said nothing but walked out and closed the door.

Warren Robertson was transferred to the Greene County jail a few days after his meeting with his daughter and Ethan. It was the first time he had been in the county since the shooting. He imagined how the Christians felt as they were put in the lion's den. He remembered Jesus' words, 'I have overcome the world'. For now, all he had was his faith to comfort him.

His attorney, Ralph Sorenson met him in the holding cell at the courthouse. While he liked the guy immensely, he did not feel comfortable with his experience as a criminal attorney. Hiring an expensive criminal attorney would limit any funds he would need to post bond. And there was still Sally and the baby to think about. They still needed him, and for now Sally could not work. At least for the time being, he could only place himself in his attorney's— and God's hands.

The bailiff came and brought them into the courtroom. The D.A., Randolph Richmond, was waiting. He disliked him immensely. In their first meeting he had offered him a plea to manslaughter with an eight to twelve year sentence if he would identify his accomplice. He had declined. Since he had turned down the offer, he had not been informed what charges would be brought against him, although he knew it would not be good.

The clerk called the court to order as Judge Phillip Wallace entered the room.

"Good morning, ladies and gentlemen. What do we have this morning?"

"The first case is the people versus Warren Robertson, Your Honor, stated the clerk."

"Mr. Richmond," he said with a nod. "Please begin."

"Your Honor, this case is against Warren Robertson from Murfreesboro. He is charged with second degree murder in the death of Andrew Pratt, Deputy Sheriff of Greene County."

"And how do you plea, Mr. Robertson?"

"Not guilty by self-defense, Your Honor," returned Mr. Sorenson on his behalf. "And we have a motion this morning, Your Honor."

"Let's hear it."

"The motion, as was filed with your clerk, is for a change of venue."

"Your reason being?"

"Your Honor, this is an emotionally charged case. The Deputy was a local man. The defendant is an outsider. The victim was white, the defendant is black. In most cases in this county the jury is all white. It would be impossible for my client to get a fair trial in this county."

"Mr. Richmond?" replied the Judge.

"First of all, this is not an emotionally charged case as Mr. Sorenson would like us to believe. The crime was over seven years ago now so to make a statement like that is ridiculous. The victim has only elderly parents and a few distant relatives left in the area. And for Mr. Sorenson to begin by stating that the people of Greene County only make decisions based on race is an insult to everyone in this courtroom. And, if Mr. Robertson did not want to be tried here, maybe he should've stayed home to do his dirty work."

"Your Honor...." protested Sorenson.

"Let's keep it civil," admonished the Judge. "But I have to agree with the D.A. I see no grounds for a change of venue. Motion denied. What else do we have, Mr. Sorenson?"

"There is the matter of bail, Your Honor."

"Mr. Richmond?" he asked.

"We ask that bail be denied, Your Honor. As his attorney just stated, he is an outsider. And he is charged with a vicious crime. If you let him go there's a good chance we will never see him again."

"Your Honor," said Sorenson. "My client is an English Professor at Middle Tennessee State. He has lived in Tennessee his whole life. His roots are here. He has nowhere else to go. And he has no prior record."

"This crime was committed many years ago, Your Honor, and we are just now finding out about Mr. Robertson's involvement," returned Richmond. "Perhaps there are other crimes he has committed we do not know about. And, the fact that he refuses to provide us with the name of his accomplice shows his disdain for the law."

"Bail is set at $250,000," ordered the Judge.

"Your Honor," pleaded Sorenson, "That is the same as denying bond. He can never raise that kind of money."

"No, Mr. Sorenson, if I had wanted to deny bond I would have said so. And his ability to come up with the money is his problem, not mine. Are there any other issues?"

Neither attorney spoke.

"Fine, then lets put this on the docket for October 4th. See you all there."

The Professor and his attorney left the courtroom—he back to jail, and Sorenson back to planning his defense. Sorenson was very disappointed at the outcome of the arraignment. The Professor, while disappointed, was not surprised. It had gone about as he had expected.

TWENTY-FOUR

JULY, 1970

Sally Robertson could not believe how her life had come to this. She had always tried to do the right thing—always treated people fairly and with integrity, as had her father. She knew that they were both good people, and yet their lives were in shambles. Her father was in jail half way across the state. She was home alone with a new baby, unmarried, and no family nearby. Her aunt had come to stay with them when the baby was born, but was then forced to return home when her uncle had fallen and broken his leg. Ethan had been wonderful but he had to return to the base. Her sister had informed her that she would be coming home soon to help out, but she doubted it. She could not take the stress nor the shame of having her father arrested. So, for now, it was just her alone. She would like to return to college in the fall but felt it was now impossible. The only good thing in her life today was Emily. She was a beautiful and sweet baby. She rarely cried, and, in the past week, had began to smile. That smile, which reminded her of Ethan, helped her get through the day.

Emily was asleep, allowing Sally to continue a book she had been reading. The doorbell interrupted her thoughts. She hoped it was not another reporter. She opened the door to see the last person she ever would have expected.

"Hi, Sally. You remember me?" said the visitor.

"Of course. What do you want?"

"I would like to come in and talk to you for a minute. Could I please?"

At first she thought of slamming the door but decided against it. Perhaps it was out of curiosity, or perhaps it was because her visitor appeared so different. She stood aside and allowed Rachel to enter.

"I know you are shocked to see me here, and I know you wonder what I am up to, but I just wanted to talk to you for a minute. Could we sit down?"

She said nothing but led her into the living room. The two sat facing each other. Sally waited for her to speak.

"How is your dad holding up?" she asked.

"He's fine," she returned bluntly, "What do you want?"

Rachel took a deep breath and continued.

"Look, Sally, I have not been a good person my whole life—I know that. I could go into all the things that happened to me when I was young, but it is not worth it and that is not why I am here. But I will tell you this. All my life I have been told how beautiful and smart and talented I was. You would think that would make me feel good about myself, but it never has. I have never felt confident so always tried to put others down or use them to make myself feel better."

"Yes?" returned Sally, hoping she would get to the point.

"So, whether you believe it or not—and I can't blame you if you don't—I am here to help if I can."

"Help how?"

"I'll get to that in a minute, but first—I want to make sure you believe me. I guess you know I have been pretty successful lately?"

"Yes, an overnight sensation," she returned with a touch of sarcasm.

"I guess. Anyway, what people don't know is how I became successful. I tried everything else—using people—sex—whatever would work. I was so desperate to be famous and successful. Anyway, I was getting nowhere and I was depressed and felt so bad about myself, and one Sunday morning I heard the church bells ringing down the street and decided to go in. There, believe it or not, I met the man of my dreams."

Sally had always wondered if Ethan was still the man of her dreams. At least now the story was becoming more interesting.

"Anyway, he and I started dating and I noticed he was different from any man I had dated—nothing against Ethan, I hope."

"Go on," said Sally with a slight laugh.

"The thing that was different about him was that—while he was all man—he also loved the Lord. He is a Christian and lets everyone know it. And he told me that it was important that I be a Christian too."

"So, he talked you into becoming a Christian also?"

"I don't know if you can talk somebody into it—that has to be something that comes from the heart, but he helped lead me in that direction. But yes, I accepted the Lord. I know some people think that is just a saying, but I can tell you Jesus changes people's lives. For the first time in my life I feel good about myself and actually care about others. I really am a different person, Sally. Although I can't blame you if you don't trust me."

"I always keep an open mind."

"Well, anyway, I didn't even know this until we had been dating a few weeks, but his brother is a record producer. He introduced me to him and I had an audition. Well, you probably know the rest."

"Rachel, if you tell me that you have changed then I believe you. Besides that, you have really never done anything to me—other than being a little catty the time we met, that is. But right now— and I don't mean to sound heartless, I have a lot of other things on my mind. I am just trying to survive."

"I know, Sally, and that is why I came here. I want to help."

"How can you help?"

"Before I tell you that, I need to tell you one more story. I'm sorry but it is important."

"Go ahead."

"First I want to tell you that I believe what your father says. It just makes sense to me, and, besides, if Ethan believes it then it must be true. But there is another reason why I want to help. I sort of have a personal interest in this case."

"What do you mean?"

"You remember just a couple of months before the Deputy was shot one of the young boys was killed over in Jefferson City?"

"Yes."

"Well, I knew him—at least I had met him."

"Really?"

"Yes. My father was looking for a new car—actually a used car but it would be new to us. He saw an ad in the paper for a car he liked over in Jefferson City. I went over with him to look at it. While he was talking to the owner the boy and I went outside and shot basketball and talked. He was a real nice kid."

"Ethan never told me that."

"I probably never mentioned it. Remember, it was always about me. But, in the last few weeks I have been thinking about it more and more and it makes me very sad to think what that young boy went through. For that reason, and the fact that I think your father is telling the truth, I want to help."

Sally saw the sadness in her eyes as she spoke of the young boy. Perhaps she really had changed.

"And how can you help?"

"The good thing about being from a small town is that everyone tells their neighbors everything. I understand that your dad's attorney is not the best."

"Well, he is not that experienced at criminal law, but he is all that we could afford. Not too many top attorneys want to do pro bono work, especially when the client is a black man accused of murdering a policeman."

"Yeah, I know, but that is where I think we can help. My fiancé's brother is pretty well off and knows a lot of people. Wasn't there a mention of a hot young Native American attorney—Ellen Cornblossom—that would be ideal on this case?"

"Yes, Why?"

"Wow, what a name. Anyway, Bobby—my fiancé's brother— uses her law firm. I think there is a chance we could get her to do it—as you say—pro bono."

"Your kidding," she returned, then, still cautious about her intents, added, "but I don't know..."

"Sally, please let me do this. It would make me feel better about myself, and it would sure help your dad."

She thought for a second but, knowing there was only one answer, responded,

"O.K., I think that will be fine. But I don't want to say anything to my dad until I know for sure."

"Sounds great. I will work on it and call you in a day or two."

The two got up and Rachel started for the door, then stopped and turned back to Sally.

"There is one thing I expect in return, though."

Sally wondered if she had been taken in by her. What would be the cost?

"What is that?"

"You let me see the baby."

"O.K.," she said laughing.

The two walked into the bedroom and watched Emily sleeping.

"She is so beautiful," said Rachel. Sally saw a tear from her eye.

"I have a question for you," Sally said hesitantly.

"The answer is no."

"What?"

"You were going to ask me if I was still in love with Ethan, right?"

"Something like that."

"No, you don't have to worry about that. Like I said, up until the past few weeks I don't think I cared about anybody but myself. It's a good feeling to have a heart."

They walked to the door again. Sally turned to her new friend.

"Rachel, I really appreciate your doing this."

"Well let's just hope we can get her. I do have two final things, though."

"What?"

"First, Jesus really does change lives. And He said that the only way to heaven is through Him. As the saying goes, 'don't leave earth without Him'."

"I believe that. I just sort of keep my beliefs to myself, but I do try to live my life that way. What is your other thing?"

"Next time I want to see you I will actually call instead of just showing up at your doorstep."

"And I have one thing for you," returned Sally. "I love your new song, 'And Your Love Too'".

"Thanks. I have a good writer."

"Who's that?"

"My fiancé."

The two hugged and said goodbye. The day was looking up.

Once charges had been filed and Professor Robertson had responded with his claims of self-defense, Governor Coleman could then make a formal inquiry on the case without anyone becoming aware that he had talked to Ethan Ward. He made two phone calls—one official and one unofficial. The first to the Attorney General instructing him that he would like him personally to look into the Professor's claims to see if there was something in the investigation into the boys' deaths that had been overlooked. The second call was to an old friend who owed him a favor. The results of that call he would keep to himself until the right time to reveal it—if that time ever came.

Ellen Cornblossom was a driven woman—that, no one, even herself—could deny. Valedictorian of her high school, a scholarship to Vanderbilt University, third in her law school class, and now practicing at one of Nashville's most prestigious law firms by age thirty. But, contrary to some people's belief, she was not an insensitive or heartless individual. She was simply a woman on a mission. She had grown up near the Smoky Mountains where her ancestors had lived for centuries—well before the white man had moved in. She had heard the stories handed down from generation to generation about their proud people and how they had lived in harmony with nature. She loved the stories from her grandfather about his hunting and fishing expeditions as a youth. She learned cooking and crafting from her mother and the other women in her tribe.

She also saw the problems of her people. She saw the drop-out rate in school. She saw the problems with drugs and alcohol. She saw teen pregnancy. She saw many of the youth incarcerated before they were eighteen. And she saw the un-employment and the frustration men faced from trying to take care of their family—many of them forced to perform tribal dances at the nearby amusement areas for donations.

She wanted to help change that. One of the things that her people needed was strong role models—someone to show there was a better life. That was her goal. To accomplish as much as possible in as short a time as possible and then return to her people. She knew she could not change the whole world, but perhaps she could influence some of the youngsters growing up. And one thing that all people understood was success and power. And that was not a bad thing—if used in the right way.

At first she had been unhappy when the Senior Partner had requested she take the Robertson case. She had too many other cases that needed attending. But, as she studied it more, it became more interesting, almost an obsession. She had heard of the case, as had almost everyone in the state, but having little time for TV or newspapers, had not followed it closely. Now, as she examined the information given her by Ralph Sorenson, she too became convinced that Professor Robertson was being railroaded. After having turned over her other cases to another partner, she instructed her assistant to begin research for her in Nashville while she made plans to go to Greeneville. The fee and expenses were not her concern. The Senior Partner had already made arrangements with Robert Bank's Company to cover those. Her only concern was to get an acquittal for Professor Robertson.

Once in Greenville she checked into the General Morgan Inn. After she was settled she called the jail and informed them she was Professor Robertson's new attorney and would like to come by and talk to him. She met him for the first time that afternoon.

"Good afternoon, Professor," she began. "It's good to meet you."

"It's a pleasure to meet you also, Miss Cornblossom. Although I wish it were in different surroundings. That's an unusual name. Is it Cherokee?"

"Yes it is, thank you."

"So, your people from the other side of the mountain?" he asked, referring to the Smokies.

"They are now, but my name came from one of my ancestors, Princess Cornblossom who was born in the late 1700's near the Kentucky-Tennessee line. It means Blossom of the Corn."

"She must have been quite a woman to have her name passed on through so many generations."

"We think so. Legend has it that she was a very beautiful and strong woman. She married a white man—his last name was Troxel—and later became ruler of our tribe. They had eight kids."

"That's fascinating. Maybe when we have more time you can tell me more."

"I would love to, thank you. But right now the thing we have to work on is getting a change of venue."

"We already tried that."

"I know but let me see what I can do. Now, I know you have been through this before, but I need to know everything there is to know about your case."

The Professor went over his story for what seemed like the tenth time. His new attorney sat patiently, asking a few questions and taking notes. When they had finished she closed her notebook and said,

"I think that's all I need for now. I will be back to see you tomorrow."

The Professor was impressed by her but was surprised that their meeting was so brief.

"Aren't you going to ask me the question?" he said.

"The question?"

"Yes. If I did it."

"But Professor, I don't think there is any doubt what happened at the crime scene. You have told us—the witness, Mr. Ward has said the same thing, and the evidence supports it. The only real question will be what you knew beforehand. And that is my job—to convince the jury that you had no idea the other man was about to shoot the Deputy. That is the truth, isn't it?"

"Absolutely."

"Then that makes it simpler. I'll see you tomorrow afternoon."

The two parted company—the Professor back to his cell and Cornblossom back to preparing for his defense. She needed to do her own investigation of the claims made by the Professor, although after seven years and investigations by three different law enforcement agencies, she was skeptical she would uncover anything new.

———————————

Judge Phillip Wallace was not happy. Not only did the Professor have a new young attorney from Nashville, but now, less than a week after taking over his case, she had already made two motions that he had to hear. And they were motions on which he had already ruled. He wanted to refuse to see her but he knew he could not do that. That action would only give her more cause for an appeal. The meeting was scheduled for ten that morning in his chambers. She and the D.A. arrived a few minutes before the scheduled time.

"So, Mrs. Cornblossom, what is this about? Did I get the name right?" he began.

"It is Miss, but yes, the name is right. As I explained in my motion, Your Honor, I have new information regarding the request for change of venue as well as bail reduction."

"I have already ruled on those, Miss Cornblossom, but, to show that I am a reasonable man, I will hear your new information."

She opened her notebook and took out two documents handing one to the Judge and one to Richmond. While the Judge was looking at the papers the D.A. blurted out, "This is an insult. You have actually given the Judge a copy of the Constitution? She should be held in contempt, Your Honor."

"Not the whole Constitution Mr. Richmond. Just the sixth amendment. It says..."

"I know what the sixth amendment says, young lady—the right to a fair and speedy trial," stated the Judge.

"By an impartial jury is the part I am concerned with, Your Honor."

"Your Honor....!" began the D.A. again.

"I can handle this, Mr. Richmond. "You are treading on very thin ice, young lady. Are you really saying that the people of this county cannot render a fair verdict?"

"My name is Miss Cornblossom, Your Honor, and I mean no disrespect to the people of Greene County. I know that you do not have a history of racial problems here, but the fact is that approximately three percent of your population is black and, from everything I have been able to uncover, the representation of blacks on juries here is practically zero."

"And where did you get that information?" asked Richmond.

The Judge gave him a stern look then turned back to Cornblossom.

"I would like to know that also, Miss Cornblossom."

"From a variety of sources. From court records when I could find them. From old newspaper articles about jurors being interviewed after the fact. And my assistant and I have talked to as many blacks in the county as possible. We have yet to find one who has served on a jury."

"We have had blacks on juries here before," interjected the D.A. The Judge ignored his remark.

"Really?" she responded. "In a criminal trial? I would be glad to meet them." Then, turning back to the Judge, she continued, "Your Honor, if you or Mr. Richmond were traveling through another city and were charged with a serious crime and discovered that not only the Judge and the Prosecutor were black, but also all the members of the jury, I think you would look at things a lot different."

"Assuming everything you say is accurate, Miss Cornblossom, and your client would have an all white jury, are you saying the people of this country cannot give a fair verdict?" asked the Judge.

"Your Honor, again I wish to make no disparaging statement against the people of Greene County. I know you have not had racial problems here like in some of the major cities in this country. I also know you integrated the schools before most other jurisdictions in the state. But the fact is blacks make up approximately eleven percent of the population in the State yet account for over fifty percent of the prison population."

"That is because they commit more crimes," said Richmond.

"That may true, but not five times more. And they also get longer sentences for the same crimes."

"Where did you get that information?" asked the Judge.

"From the Justice Department's crime statistics. I can show you if you would like."

"That is not necessary," returned the Judge, now more subdued as he pondered his decision. He knew the statements Miss Cornblossom had made were accurate, although he was not aware of the extent of the problem. He also knew that by denying her motion, a guilty verdict could likely be thrown out on appeal. The racial turmoil of the sixties had had a major impact on the judicial process.

"Miss Cornblossom, I have to tell you I am impressed with your research. Being a Judge in this county I would be a fool not to realize that the law does not always favor the poor and minorities, but I will say that these figures are a surprise to me. Despite what you might believe, all of us small town hillbillies are not racists. Therefore I am going to grant you your motion. I am open to suggestions as to which district it should be transferred."

As upset as Richmond was, he knew he could not dwell on the ruling. He had to concentrate on the next issue.

"Nashville is beautiful this time of year, Your Honor," she replied. "However, I doubt that that would be suitable for Mr. Richmond. I would settle for Knoxville. It is close by and a big metropolitan area where jury selection should be equitable."

"And where one of the boys just happened to be killed," said the D.A. "That would be convenient since your client's only defense is the ridiculous story about the Deputy killing young boys."

"Fine, then. Why don't we let the Judge decide."

"That's awful nice of you since it is my decision anyway. I think I will transfer this to Judge Landry down in Chattanooga. He is a good and fair man, and he owes me a favor. Let him baby-sit you two for a while."

"Oh, there is one other thing, Your Honor," stated Miss Cornblossom, "about my motion for bail reduction. I have some information here I would like to share with you."

"I'm sure you do, however, I'm going to let Judge Landry deal with that. Now, as much fun as this has been, I do have other things on my agenda. You two have a wonderful day."

The two turned and walked away. Once out of the Judge's earshot Miss Cornblossom turned to the D.A. and said, "I can give you the name of a good hotel in Chattanooga if you would like. Since I already have my reservation perhaps you would like a room nearby."

TWENTY-FIVE

Ethan was happy with his new responsibilities at Ft. Benning. He was afraid after being sent home early he would be assigned to permanent kitchen duty or worse. That had not been the case. Along with three other soldiers he was in charge of maintaining the base's telecommunications equipment. While it was a job he had never considered, he learned to enjoy it. The technician's job was to maintain the equipment—performing scheduled testing as well as correcting any problems which might arise. While he found that he liked working with his hands and troubleshooting, the thing he enjoyed the most was that the job was simple and predictable. That was what he could use in his life right now.

His life had actually been much calmer and quieter in the past few weeks. There had been no war to fight—no explosions in a bar— and no more major surprises since he had found out about the baby. The only surprise he had had lately was Rachel's actions in helping secure a new attorney for the Professor. He kept waiting for the other shoe to fall, but Sally felt certain she had no motive other than to help. Perhaps she was right. Perhaps Jesus could change people's lives. He would have to give it more thought.

He had purchased a car the previous week. While he had been flying standby when he went to Greeneville or Murfreesboro, it was a hassle. He had to wait to see if a seat was available, and there was always the issue of transportation to and from the airport. So when a soldier who was being transferred posted an ad to sell his 1965

Mustang, he was the first one there. Because the soldier had to leave in a hurry, Ethan got it for $800—a real steal. No matter what happened between he and Sally he knew he would always be a part of his daughter's life. For that reason alone he needed a car. Being a fastback not only made it more attractive but practical for carrying things. Of course the bright, candy-apple red finish did not hurt.

———————

Sally was very pleased her father had been transferred to Chattanooga. Not only did she feel that he would get a fairer trial there, she was even more excited about his new attorney who made it happen. It seemed she was the real thing. She had sent Rachel a thank-you card for her help. Rachel called her back to see how things were going. They committed to getting together once the trial was over and Rachel's schedule slowed down. Sally didn't know if they would actually become friends, but she would be eternally grateful for what she had done.

Another reason for her to feel good was the fact that Ethan's family had come by to see the baby. At least most of his family had come by—his mother, brother, and sister-in-law. She broke into tears when Hilda had said, "I know that you and Ethan are not married, but in my eyes you are my daughter-in-law and I am proud to have you. You are a good person and I am glad to know you."

Big Emily, as Horace now called her, was convinced that Little Emily looked like her. Horace disagreed and said she had his nose. The get-together was overshadowed only by Mr. Ward's absence.

———————

Ellen Cornblossom loved Chattanooga. While it was only a few hours drive from her home, it was only the second time she had been there, and the first time she was only driving through. She loved the way the Tennessee River wound around the city. She loved visiting Ruby Falls and exploring Rock City. She loved standing atop Lookout Mountain and seeing the city below as well as the surrounding country. While the advertisements said you could see seven states, she was not certain that was true. At present she did not have time to investigate so she would have to take their word for it.

Unfortunately she didn't have a lot of time for sightseeing. She had a case to win. Her time, as well as her assistant's, was spent going back and forth between Chattanooga, Nashville, and Greenville. And while the Professor had been transferred less than a week ago, she had her first motion to present to the Judge. She needed to get the Professor's bail reduced, and had spent much time in planning the proper strategy.

Randy Richmond was very angry about his first encounter with Ellen Cornblossom. It was easy for her to come into town with all the resources of a Nashville law firm behind her. She had her own personal assistant to do her research, plus a team of other attorneys back in the main office. He had only himself and an assistant D.A. to represent all of the citizens of Greene County. But whatever it would take, he would make sure he was not caught off guard again. For the upcoming hearing on her latest motion he would be prepared.

Judge Landry had been briefed on the Robertson case by Judge Wallace. Not that he needed much briefing—most of the aspects of the case were well known to members of the court as well as most of the people of Tennessee. The press had made sure of that. While Judge Wallace had had little involvement with the case, he did relate to him Miss Cornblossom's use of the Bill of Rights to prove her point. Judge Landry wondered what tactics she had planned for today's meeting. He agreed to hear her motion during his lunch break. She and Mr. Richmond entered his chambers at eleven forty-five.

"Good morning, counselors," he began, "please be seated."

"Good morning, Your Honor," the two responded in unison as they sat in front of his desk.

"So, Miss Cornblossom," he continued, "we're here to revisit the bail that Judge Wallace established," he stated.

"Yes, Your Honor," she replied as she opened her briefcase. While she did so, Richmond took the opportunity to speak.

"Your Honor, if I may—I have information which I have put together for this hearing."

While there was no formal protocol, normally the counselor who presented the motion went first. The Judge looked to Miss Cornblossom.

"That's fine, Your Honor."

"Your Honor," he began, "it is the people's belief that the bail set by Judge Wallace was proper and in line with all other similar cases. I have here a report of all murder cases in our county in the past five years. I also have a listing of all murder cases in the state wherein the victim was a law enforcement officer. You can see that the average of all cases is just over $200,000."

He handed the report to the Judge who began to read it.

"May I see that when you are finished, Your Honor?" asked Miss Cornblossom.

Without speaking Richmond handed a copy of the report to her. She studied the report for a moment then said, "If I am not mistaken these defendants were all charged with first degree murder. At least the ones I am familiar with were."

"Is that correct, counselor?"

"Yes, Your Honor, however, there are also special circumstances surrounding Mr. Robertson's case."

"Yes," she interrupted, "he never fired the gun nor even knew his friend had a gun."

"Please don't interrupt," stated the Judge. "Go on, counselor."

"While it is true that the defendant is only charged with second degree murder, we will be able to prove that he not only knew about the gun but knew that the shooter might use it against the Deputy. He has also eluded capture for seven years. The people feel that every caution should be taken to keep this man off the street."

"O.K.," he replied, then turning to Miss Cornblossom added, "so what do you have to say? Did you bring the Constitution or Lincoln's Gettysburg Address for me to read?"

"No, Your Honor—sorry. I do have documentation to show you, however, I would first like to make a statement."

"I'm sure. Go ahead."

"There are really only two factors effecting bail—the defendant's risk to the community as well as his likelihood to not show up for a trial. Is that a fair statement, Your Honor?"

"Well, we here on the bench sometimes consider the seriousness of the crime," he said sarcastically, "but, yes, those are major considerations."

"Then I would like to show that not only is the defendant no risk to the community but also poses no flight risk."

"Go ahead."

She reached into her briefcase and removed a brown envelope.

"Here, Your Honor, are letters from fifteen members of the faculty at Professor Robertson's college stating they believe he should be freed on bail and that they find him no risk to the community. I also have similar statements from the Dean of the school as well as the minister at his church. Here is a petition signed by over a dozen of his neighbors requesting he be released."

She handed the envelope to the Judge who read them and passed them on to Richmond.

"Any doubt to the authenticity of these documents counselor?"

"They are all notarized, Your Honor," stated Cornblossom.

"I'm sure they are authentic, Your Honor," said Richmond, "But I still feel that this man is a risk to society."

"Of course who would know him better?" she returned, "you or a couple dozen of his friends and coworkers who have known him for five to ten years?"

"Miss Cornblossom, please direct your comments to me."

"Yes, Your Honor."

"Do you have other information before I make my decision?"

"Yes, Your Honor, I do. Regarding a flight risk, I think that he is the most unlikely person in the world to run. His reason for being here - as Mr. Richmond will have to admit - is that he will not give the name of the shooter. He is a very loyal and stable person and a good family man. Since his wife was killed a few years ago he has devoted his life to raising his daughters. He also has very close ties to the community. I have some pictures, Your Honor, of Professor Robertson over the last year showing him at various school and community functions."

She handed the Judge another envelope with pictures.

"Those pictures there, Your Honor, were taken at a dinner which the Professor organized at his college. It is held to bring together people from all races and religions to discuss social issues."

"Finally, Your Honor—and I think most importantly, the Professor is a new grandfather. Here is a picture of his granddaughter. He worships this little girl and he would die before he had to leave her or his daughter alone."

The Judge examined the pictures.

"From reading some of the statements from the witnesses I understand that the chief witness, Mr. Ward, is also dating the defendant's daughter. I'm assuming this is their daughter?"

"Yes, Your Honor."

"Unbelievable," he commented.

"Which is another reason this man should not be out on bail, Your Honor," interjected Richmond. "So that the two of them can't get together and coordinate their stories."

"Yeah, because eighteen months was not enough time," returned Cornblossom.

"That's enough, you two," warned the Judge.

He examined the pictures and letters provided him by Miss Cornblossom as well as the report from Richmond. He dropped them on his desk and looked up.

"This is a serious crime and the defendant did elude justice for some period of time. However, Miss Cornblossom does have some valid points. One other issue, counselor—does he have a passport?"

"Your Honor, I don't think he has ever been out of the state of Tennessee."

"That's good. Can he go back to work?"

"I don't know, Your Honor. The problem is not MTSU taking him back—it is one of logistics. If released he still has to come back for trial in a few weeks so it's hard to teach when you can't be there much of the time."

"That's true. One other thing which neither of you have brought up is the amount of publicity this case has created. The Professor is probably known on sight by about two thirds of the people in the state, so even if he did decide to run he probably wouldn't get far. Therefore here's what I am going to do. I am lowering his bail to $125,000 with the condition that he cannot leave the city of Murfreesboro except to come to court. Is that clear?"

"Yes, Your Honor, very clear."

"Your Honor," pleaded Richmond, "what about conversations between him and Mr. Ward? I would like to have those blocked."

"I don't see any need for that Mr. Richmond. Like Miss Cornblossom said—what can they talk about now that they haven't already covered? And even if they couldn't talk you think they couldn't communicate through his daughter? Request denied."

The two took their documentation and left the Judge's chambers. Richmond waited until his adversary was through the door before he left. He disliked her more and more each time he met her.

TWENTY-SIX

OCTOBER, 1970

The change in venue from Greenville to Chattanooga delayed the start of the trial until October 25th. Ellen Cornblossom told her client she did not expect the trial to last more than a week, although the length of jury deliberations was impossible to forecast. She checked into a hotel near the courthouse on Friday, the 22nd. She planned to spend the last couple of days before the trial re-examining all aspects of their defense. She and her assistant, Terry Bailey, spent most of the weekend in the hotel planning their strategy and re-checking their facts.

On Sunday Professor Robertson and his daughter checked into a two-room suite at a nearby hotel. While he was very happy to be out of jail and was pleased with the job his attorney had been doing, he didn't like the idea of taking out a bond to be released. He had to put up his house as collateral, as well as most of the remaining insurance money from his wife's policy. In affect, almost everything he had worked for in his life—everything he had planned on leaving to his daughters—was now in the hands of the bondsman.

The subpoena had given Ethan a week's leave. If the trial ran longer he was instructed to call his C.O. While he had been told to be ready at any time to testify, he expected he would be called to the stand on Tuesday. Although he was listed as a witness for both the prosecution as well as the defense, he felt his testimony would help free the Professor. He did not like the fact that, as a witness, he was not allowed in the courtroom until after his testimony was complete.

Ethan's mother would arrive in Chattanooga on Monday afternoon. Having had some experience with jury duty, she expected most of the first day would be taken up with jury selection. Besides being there to support her son, she would also be available to watch the baby leaving Sally free to attend the trial and support her dad.

Randy Richmond had been hard at work the past few weeks. If he were to lose the trial it would not be from lack of preparedness. He had interviewed everyone who had been even remotely involved in the case. He traveled to Murfreesboro and talked to everyone who knew the Professor, hoping to pick up new information. The most he hoped for was to uncover the identity of his friend—the shooter. The trip had been fruitless. Still he felt certain he had enough evidence for a conviction.

Tommy Bell was also at the trial. His name was not on the witness list since any information he could provide would be hearsay, but he wanted to support his friend. Also, it gave him an opportunity to finally, after a year and a half, to meet Sally. She was just as beautiful and pleasant as Ethan had said. And little Emily was a cherub.

"You better marry that girl before someone steals her," he chided his friend.

Tommy, like most of the people in Greenville, had been interviewed by reporters. The press loved the story. It had all the makings of a soap opera; the murder of a deputy; the only witness a young boy who now was also a witness for the defense; the charges by the defendant that the Deputy had planned to kill them to cover up his crimes; and finally, the unbelievable coincidence that the main witness was now involved with the defendant's daughter.

Tommy found one reporter in particular quite interesting. His name was Eugene Mason, a reporter for the Nashville Tennessean. His angle on the story was different in that he wanted to see how the events had affected the people caught up in it. He talked to everyone in town who had anything to say. Tommy wasn't sure what it was, but he felt the man had another agenda. He would not know for some time since the reporter informed him that the story would not be released until after the trial was complete.

Jury selection began nine A.M. on Monday morning. The Judge made a very simple statement to the prospective jurors about the case. He admonished them to not bring any preconceived ideas into the courtroom and make their judgment only on the facts in evidence. By mid afternoon the pool of forty prospective members had been narrowed to twelve jurors and three alternates. The make-up was four white females, three white males, two black females, one black male, one Hispanic, and one Asian. The alternates were two white males and one black female. Richmond was not pleased with the make up of the jury but, considering the pool from which he had to select, it was the best he could do.

Since it was getting late in the day, Judge Landry informed both attorneys that they could either present their opening statements now or wait until morning. Both, eager to begin their case, chose to start immediately. The air was tense as Richmond took the floor.

"Good afternoon ladies and gentlemen. We appreciate your being here today. During jury selection it became clear that virtually all of you have heard something about this case. For good or bad, there has been a lot of publicity. There has been so much written or talked about this case, it makes it confusing. Well, I am here to tell you that this is a simple case. A law enforcement officer, Deputy Andrew Pratt, was gunned down on a hot, dusty, country road in Greene County over seven years ago. There was only one eyewitness whom you will hear from. That witness will tell you one of the men involved in the shooting is the defendant. The evidence confirms that the defendant was one of the two men involved in the shooting. The defendant himself has admitted to being there. He has also avoided prosecution for the past seven years. The prosecution and defense are in agreement on all these details. But this is where the differences begin. The defendant makes a claim—no, two ridiculous claims regarding the shooting. First, he said he had no prior knowledge of his partner's intent to shoot the Deputy, nor even that he had a gun—even though it was in his truck. He then claims that if his partner had not shot the Deputy he would have killed them to cover up crimes of his own. How utterly ridiculous. You can't have it both ways. Either he knew about the gun and what would happen if they were stopped, or he knew nothing about why his partner shot the Deputy. It is his feeble attempt to confuse the court—to confuse you, and it is nothing but lies."

"The defendant's ridiculous claim is that Deputy Pratt was responsible for the murders of three young boys in East Tennessee in the previous months, and that, somehow—we don't know how—the defendant's partner had knowledge of these events. The murders of these young boys has been investigated for over seven years and there is absolutely no evidence that the Deputy had any involvement."

"Finally, please remember, just because the defendant did not actually pull the trigger does not mean he is innocent. We will show, beyond a reasonable doubt, that he had prior knowledge of what was about to happen and did nothing to prevent it thereby leading to the death of Deputy Pratt. Then you will have no choice but to find him guilty. Thank you."

Richmond gave Cornblossom a smug look as he returned to his chair. The Judge instructed her to begin her opening statement.

"Good afternoon, ladies and gentlemen, Your Honor. Actually, the D.A. is correct on many of the things he told you. The defendant, Professor Robertson, has admitted to being at the scene of the crime. But do you know the only reason we are here today? Because the Professor would not provide the D.A. with the name of the man that was with him that day. He could have easily done so and have gotten off with a light sentence. But he chose not to do so. Do you know why? For two reasons. Because he knows what he said is true. The Deputy had committed horrible crimes and would have certainly killed not only he and his friend but the witness as well. We will show you overwhelming evidence to support this statement. The other reason is that he could not take a chance on sending his friend to prison for the rest of his life, and that is a possibility if he turned in his friend. That is the kind of man the Professor is. He is a good loyal family man who has never committed a crime. His mistake was being in the wrong place at the wrong time and trying to protect a friend."

"One thing the defense does not agree on—that this is a simple case. I wish it were. But I know that you all are capable of sorting through the information to find the truth. One thing I ask you to remember though—use your conscience—use your common sense. Look at the man Professor Robertson is and determine if he is capable of watching an innocent man be gunned down. I can tell you I have gotten to know him and he is not that type of person. And, after you hear his testimony I know that you will see that also. Thank you."

After finishing her opening statement Miss Cornblossom returned to her seat. As she sat down she patted the Professor on the arm, hoping the jury would see. The Judge instructed the jurors to not discuss the case with anyone and excused them for the day.

The trial resumed promptly Tuesday at nine A.M. The first witness called by the D.A. was Jean Thompson, the woman who found the Deputy's body. She was a little woman of sixty-three with gray hair and wire rimmed glasses After she was sworn in he began his questioning.

"Thank you for coming all the way down here, Mrs. Thompson," he began.

"I just wanted to do my duty."

"I'm sure. Now you live in Greene County just down the road from the Ward family right?"

"Yes, sir. Only a half mile or less."

"Now, is this an isolated area?"

"Yes, very much so. There are only—I believe four other houses on the road."

"And to the main road is about how far?"

"I guess a couple of miles."

"So you don't get much traffic back there?"

"No, sir. Other than the people that live there you might get one or two cars a day—visitors or people lost, you know."

"I see. Now, on the afternoon of June 26, 1963 you had to go in to town, right?"

"Yes, sir."

"What time was that?"

"A little after two o'clock."

"Please describe what you saw at that time."

"Well, I had only driven a couple of minutes when I saw the Deputy's car in the middle of the road. I knew something was wrong because the lights were on and the door was open. When I got closer I could see the Deputy laying in the middle of the road."

"And what did you do?"

"I stopped the car, of course, and ran to see if I could help. I had never seen someone shot before but I was pretty certain that was what had happened."

"Why is that?"

"Because he was laying face down with his gun beside him. And I could see what looked like blood coming from underneath him. I was pretty certain he was dead. I ran back to his car and pushed the little button for the radio and someone answered. I told them to get there as soon as possible because the Deputy had been shot."

Ellen Cornblossom wondered why he was spending so much time with her. The defense would have stipulated that the Deputy had been shot and that she had found him.

"And how long was it until someone arrived?"

"The Sheriff and another deputy got there within—oh I guess about five to ten minutes. An ambulance arrived at about the same time."

"Your Honor," said Cornblossom, "the defense stipulates that there was a shooting and that Mrs. Thompson found the body. Is there some other information this witness can offer?"

"Mr. Richmond?" asked the Judge.

"I only have one or two other questions for this witness, Your Honor."

"Go Ahead."

"Now, Mrs. Thompson," he continued, "was it common to see the Deputy on your road?"

"Yes, I guess so. I mean I didn't see him there every day, but he would patrol there from time to time."

"And you knew him?"

"In a small town you know just about everybody. I didn't know him well but good enough to talk to."

"Did you find him to be a person of good character? Did you think he was honest and fair? Did he have any problems or complaints with you or any of your neighbors'?"

"Your Honor," began Cornblossom, "she cannot possibly know about the relationships between the Deputy and the neighbors."

"Then she can comment on what she knows. I'll allow it."

"No, sir—well, I mean he was a rather serious type—didn't smile or laugh much and kept to himself—but, no I never had any problem with him and never had any complaint from any of my neighbors."

"Thank you, ma'am. Your witness."

The defense attorney walked to the center of the courtroom, looked at her and asked,

"Mrs. Thompson, you really don't know if Deputy Pratt molested or killed young boys, do you?"

"Your Honor!" shouted Richmond.

"Well, that was what he was trying to show—that he could never do any such thing."

"Counselor, please re-word your question."

"Yes, Your Honor. Mrs. Thompson, do you have any knowledge of what the Deputy did when he was out of your sight?"

"No, ma'am."

"Thank you for your time."

The D.A. next called the dispatcher for the Sheriff's office, Mrs. Rebecca Talley. Richmond's used her testimony only to confirm the testimony given by Mrs. Thompson. Miss Cornblossom had a different objective in her questioning.

"Mrs. Talley, I have questions about something that happened just before the shooting," began Cornblossom.

"Yes, ma'am."

"You brought your log book for that day, right?"

"Yes, ma'am."

"And in it you log all of the calls from the Sheriff, the deputies, as well as emergency calls, right?"

"Yes, it's all right here."

"Do you ever make a mistake and write down the wrong time?"

"Oh, no, ma'am, that is one of the most important parts of my job. I reckon the Sheriff would let me go if I screwed that up."

"And what was the last time Deputy Pratt called in?"

"Let's see," she said as she looked at her book, "that would have been at twelve-thirty-four P.M."

"And, from your notes, do you show where he was when he called?"

"Yes, ma'am. He said he was up to Baileytown."

"Did he say what he was doing up there?"

"No. Just patrolling."

"Is that his normal area to patrol?"

"Well, we only had six deputies total and only two or three on at any time, so they didn't really have a territory."

"And how far away was that from where the shooting occurred?"

"It's on the other side of the county—about thirty miles I reckon."

"And how long do you think it would take to get from where he said he was to where the shooting took place, under normal driving conditions?"

"Well, some of the roads ain't too good so I would say about forty-five minutes."

"And, if he had his lights and siren on?"

"About thirty minutes."

"But, as far as you know, he was not answering any calls, right?"

"No, ma'am."

"And since the shooting occurred at between twelve-thirty and twelve-forty-five how could he have been where he said he was at twelve-thirty-four?"

"Objection, Your Honor," said Richmond, "evidence not yet in question. The time of the shooting has not been established yet."

"Sustained."

"Well, let me ask you this," continued Cornblossom, "if the shooting took place before twelve-forty-five could the Deputy have been where he said he was at twelve-thirty-four?"

"No, ma'am. He would have had to leave there at least twenty to twenty-five minutes earlier if he had his lights on, and probably forty-five minutes earlier if he hadn't."

"That's all I needed to know. Thank you for your help."

Before leaving the stand the D.A. stated he had a couple of additional questions for the witness.

"Mrs. Talley, is it possible that the Deputy said he had just left Baileytown and, in reality, had already driven ten or fifteen minutes?

"No, sir. I am sure he said he was at Baileytown when he called."

"Then is it possible that he said that but really meant that he had just left Baileytown?"

"Well I don't know what he meant—only what he said."

"No further questions."

The County Coroner was called next. He gave the cause of death as two shots from a 38 revolver fired from approximately fifteen to twenty feet. He estimated the death as between twelve-thirty and twelve-fifty P.M. Richmond made sure the jury knew that the estimated time of death could be off as much as fifteen minutes. Cornblossom was not concerned since Ethan Ward would be able to place the shooting time closer to twelve-forty-five.

Defense counsel had no questions for the Coroner. The jury was dismissed for lunch just before twelve. The only two prosecution witnesses left to testify were the Sheriff and Ethan Ward. While the D.A. was not required to give the exact order of their testimony, Cornblossom was certain that he would save Ethan's testimony until last. That meant he would probably not testify until the following day.

TWENTY-SEVEN

Sheriff Carl Benlow took the stand a little after one o'clock Tuesday afternoon. After giving his name and being sworn in, the D.A. began the questioning.

"Sheriff Benlow, how long have you been in the law enforcement business?"

"About twenty-five years."

"And how long have you been the Sheriff of Greene County?"

"For a little over twelve years now."

"Then you were Sheriff when Deputy Pratt was shot?"

"Yes I was."

"Can you tell us the version of what happened that day from the time you received the call from Mrs. Thompson?"

"Yes, sir. Mrs. Thompson called dispatch on the car phone around two-fifteen P.M. Mrs. Talley took the call and immediately informed me that Deputy Pratt had been shot. I told Mrs. Talley to call the ambulance and I left for the crime scene. I got there about two minutes before my other deputies and the rescue squad."

"So you were first on the scene?"

"Yes—well, after Mrs. Thompson. When I got there it was obvious to me that the Deputy was dead. There was nothing I could do for him so I made sure the paramedics did not disturb the crime scene."

"And you had no idea what had happened?"

"Absolutely none. There was really no evidence other than tire tracks which we preserved best we could. I put out an APB to the Greenville police as well as the State Police to stop anyone with out of county license plates or who looked suspicious."

"But soon you discovered you had a witness, right?"

"Yes. A few minutes later young Ethan Ward appeared. He had been hiding in the woods since the shooting. I guess he heard the sirens and came out. His mother had arrived just a few minutes earlier and was totally distraught. We quickly discovered that he had witnessed the whole thing."

"So he had been hiding some time?"

"Yes, we estimate over an hour."

"And what did he tell you?"

"He informed us that he had been walking to a friend's house when two black adult males came by in a pickup truck. They stopped to ask him directions—said they were lost—and he directed them back towards highway 11. They offered him a ride to his friend's house which he accepted. They had just started to drive away when the Deputy pulled up behind them with his lights on."

"And what did he tell you happened next?"

"Deputy Pratt ordered the men out of the truck. The passenger, Professor Robertson, and the boy got out but the driver did not. The witness told us that the Deputy then pulled his gun and again ordered the driver out of the truck. The driver came out of the truck but obviously had a gun. He fired two shots into the Deputy, probably killing him instantly."

"What did the witness do at that time?"

"When he saw the Deputy shot he crawled under the fence and headed for the woods."

"Now, one thing I want to make clear, Sheriff—was this a barbed wire fence or a mesh fence or what?"

"No, it was a slat fence."

"So therefore the youngster could just slide right under it, correct?"

"Yes."

"So, in reality, the men had no chance to stop him?"

"I would not necessarily say that. It's true that it didn't take him much time to get under the fence but they were in an isolated area. If they had wanted they could have run him down in a couple of minutes. Also, the driver probably could have shot him if he had wanted."

Cornblossom wondered why the D.A. had brought up the issue. It did him as much harm as good. However, he had to know that if he had not done so she would have. He probably wanted to deal with it himself rather than leave it to her.

"Hmm, a small moving target at forty to fifty feet as opposed to a full grown man at fifteen feet. So you don't think it's possible the real and only reason the boy escaped was because they couldn't catch him or kill him?"

"Of course it is possible, but that's not my opinion. I believe they let him go. And, even if everything the defendant says is a lie and they gunned down the Deputy just for the fun of it, it is still a lot more difficult to kill a young child."

Richmond decided he had gotten as much as he could out of that line of questioning so decided to move on. He walked back to his desk and glanced at his notes then continued.

"What evidence did you find at the scene, Sheriff?"

"Not very much. The tire tracks which I mentioned. They were not very clear because it was so dry and dusty, but we were able to get some prints. The most important piece of evidence was the soda bottle we found beside the road."

"Please explain."

"The passenger had given Ethan a bottle of orange soda when he got in the car. When he got out he dropped it beside the road. We got a couple of good prints off of it, unfortunately we were never able to match them up with a suspect."

"Until lately, you mean?"

"Yes, until we got a tip that the Professor was the man on the passenger's side."

"And his prints matched those on the bottle?"

"Yes, they did."

"Let's talk about the tip which led you to the defendant," he continued as he turned back to the jury. "This case went unsolved all these years until you recently got a call. Can you tell us about it?"

"O.K. The tip actually came in a few months ago to the State Police tip line. The caller explained he had overheard a conversation—or at least bits and pieces of a conversation. The main thing he could remember was that the perpetrators dumped their vehicle in the lake and caught a freight train back home."

"But you had already searched all the surrounding lakes years before, right?"

"Yes, but we thought it was worth a try. After all there is probably a hundred miles of shoreline within an hours drive of Greenville. Now we had more information and the detection equipment is more sensitive. We began searching at the closest location near a railroad track and moved out from there. I guess we got lucky."

"And what did you find?"

"We found a truck that matched the description of the one used by the suspects."

"How could you tell after all this time?"

"It was the right age, the right color, and had a license plate from 1963."

"What did you do then?"

"We got the serial number of the vehicle and were able to trace it back to the defendant—actually it had been registered to his father but we determined he had access to it. When they went to talk to him and ask if they could take his fingerprints, he confessed."

"Just like that?"

"Yes. I guess he knew, with the truck and his fingerprints, there was no need in denying it."

The D.A. walked back to his desk and looked at his notes once more. He said something to his assistant then turned back to the Sheriff.

"Sheriff, you are aware of the defendant's plea of self defense, correct?"

"Yes I am."

"So you are aware of his preposterous claims that the Deputy had killed three young boys and that the driver of the vehicle had evidence as such?"

"I am aware of those claims, yes."

"So, have you looked into those claims?

"Yes. I had to—it's my job."

"And did you find any evidence that any of it was true?"

"It raised some interesting questions and possibilities. For example…."

"I'm not asking you for your speculations, Sheriff. Please just answer the question. Did you uncover any real evidence that what the defendant said was true?"

"No, I did not."

"Thank you. We have no more questions for this witness at this time, although we would like to reserve the right to recall him later, Your Honor."

"So noted," replied the Judge. "Miss Cornblossom?"

"Thank you. I do have a number of questions for the Sheriff," she began.

"Sheriff, you were not there when the Professor was arrested, right?"

"No, but I did go and bring him back to Greene County."

"And you said when they questioned him he confessed. What did he confess to?"

"What do you mean?"

"Well, did he confess to killing the Deputy? Did he confess to planning it? Did he confess to giving the other man the gun?"

"No. He confessed that he was the passenger in the truck."

"So basically he confessed to being there?"

"Yes, I guess so."

"And did you and he talk in the car on the way back?"

"Very little. I didn't like him and he didn't like me."

"So when did you find out about his claim of self-defense?"

"When his attorney—his original attorney—entered his plea."

"And did you find any credence to his statements?"

"Your Honor—does she understand the law?" interjected the D.A. "The question has already been asked and answered. He already stated that he uncovered no evidence."

"That's fine," she shot back. "I withdraw the question. We can go about this another way. Sheriff, let's go back to the shooting itself. Given the time line that has been established, how could the Deputy have been in Baileytown at twelve-thirty-four and been shot by twelve-forty-five?"

"Your Honor," began Richmond again, "the coroner agreed that the shooting cold have taken place as late as twelve fifty, possibly even a few minutes later."

"And the only witness's testimony will show that it was much closer to twelve-forty-five."

"Again, evidence not yet given."

"We have the witness's statement from the time of the shooting as well as his mother's statement that he left the house at twelve-thirty. If the D.A. would like we can recall the Sheriff and go through this again later."

"Miss Cornblossom, please just re-word your question. I'm sure you can figure out how," admonished the Judge.

"Yes, Your Honor. Now, Sheriff, if the shooting, as we believe, took place around twelve-forty-five, how could the Deputy have been at Baileytown at twelve-thirty-four?"

"He could not have."

"Even if he had his lights and siren on—as Miss Talley stated—it would have taken at least twenty minutes, correct?"

"That sounds right."

"But no one saw him headed in that direction with his lights on, right?"

"Not that I know of."

"Was there a reason for him being in Baileytown?"

"That I don't know. He could have been anywhere in the county. That is up to my deputies."

"Were you curious about this discrepancy at the time?"

"Yes."

"Did you ask if anyone had seen him in Baileytown?"

"Yes. I didn't spend a lot of time on it but I did ask around."

"And the result?"

"No one had."

"What did you surmise from this?"

"That he probably had a lead on something and he wanted to be the hero. That's why he didn't want us to know where he was"

"And now, do you see another possibility?"

"I really don't know, Miss Cornblossom. I would only be speculating."

"O.K., lets move on. When your deputies stop someone, what is the first thing you instruct them to do?"

"They are supposed to call in and let us know what is going on."

"And give the license number of the vehicle?"

"Yes."

"Did the Deputy do that?"

"No, he did not."

"But yet Mr. Ward said he told them he had called for backup?"

"Your Honor," began the D.A. "Not in evidence."

"Withdrawn. Do your deputies normally draw their weapons when they make a stop?"

"That is a judgment call and is entirely up to them."

"But does that happen most of the time?"

"No, but then most of their stops are not two strange men picking up a young boy."

"After the shooting did you examine the Deputy's vehicle for any scratches that might have been caused by shrubs or trees?"

"No, I had no reason to."

"But the witness told you he came out of nowhere, right? He thought he might have been hiding in the brush."

"He told us he didn't see him when he got in the truck, then, a short time later, the driver noticed his car pulling up behind them."

"Didn't the witness also tell you that he had not seen the Deputy's car as he walked down the road?"

"Yes, he did."

"And don't they live on a dead end road?"

"Yes, but there is a side road down to another house just a quarter mile or less from where the shooting occurred."

"Do you think that if these two men saw a Deputy's car nearby they would have still stopped to pick up a young boy?"

"Objection, Your Honor," yelled Richmond with exasperation.

"Speculation."

"Withdrawn. What do you think the odds are that one of the three people there would have seen the Deputy's car if he had not been in hiding?"

"Your Honor...."

"Both of you approach," instructed the Judge. Once there he looked at the defense attorney sternly.

"You think I don't know what you are doing? You're not looking for an answer—you just want to give the jury enough things to think about to create doubt."

"Your Honor, there are valid points."

"And ones that no one can answer—not even the Sheriff. Now stop it or you will be looking at some heavy fines lady."

"Yes, Your Honor."

She returned to her questioning, knowing she had accomplished what she wanted.

"Sheriff, when you talked to Mr. Ward after the Professor's arrest, didn't you find out he had been doing a little investigating of his own?"

"Yes he had."

"Did he uncover anything of significance?"

"No, not really."

"He didn't tell you that he got access to the Deputy's personal belongings and in them found newspaper clippings—souvenirs—of the three boys murders?"

"Yes, but I don't know if there was any significance to him having newspaper stories about the boys."

"Sheriff, did you or your deputies have any involvement in the murder investigation of these young boys?"

"The one in Jefferson City was not too far from us so I told them to keep an open eye for anything or anyone suspicious. I would not say we were actually involved."

"So would you be surprised if one of your deputies was doing an investigation on his own?"

"I don't know how to answer that."

"Well, can you think of a reason that a deputy would be

investigating it and not tell you?"

"No, I cannot."

"And did Deputy Pratt tell you he was doing his own investigation?"

"No, he did not."

"And if one of your deputies were doing an investigation on a case, can you think of a reason they would keep their records at home rather than in the office?"

"Again, I would only be speculating."

"Well, do you know of any deputy that has done that?"

"No, I do not."

She thought about bringing up the issue with the tires but thought that was too much a stretch. Half the people in the county had a full size American car.

"Just one final question, Sheriff. Have the murders of young boys stopped since the Deputy was killed?"

"As far as I know."

"Thank you, Sheriff. I have no further questions for this witness."

TWENTY-EIGHT

Ethan was eager to testify. At first he had been nervous but now he was eager—even a little excited. He had been re-living that day in his mind for over seven years now. Perhaps, after today, he would be able to finally put it to rest. And even though he was being called by the prosecution, he thought his testimony would be of more benefit to the defense. He wore his Army dress uniform as he sat in the witness room patiently waiting to be called. Sally and his mother took turns waiting in the hallway with the baby so they could each hear part of his testimony. He was called into the courtroom a little after nine A.M.

After being sworn in the D.A. began the questioning.

"Private Ward, where do you live currently?"

"I am stationed at Ft. Benning Army Base in Georgia."

"But your home is Greenville, Tennessee, right?"

"Yes, sir."

"And you also lived in Greenville in the summer of 1963?"

"Yes, sir—oh, actually we didn't live in the town of Greenville at that time. We lived just a few miles south of Greenville."

"Yes, of course. Now we have heard from Sheriff Benlow as well as Mrs. Thompson and Mrs. Talley about the events of June 26th of that year but you are the only witness to what really happened on that day, correct?"

"Yes, sir."

"Please tell us what happened that day to lead up to these events."

"O.K. My mother told me I could go down to visit my friend Billy Caldwell if I finished my chores. We had lunch and I left for his house at twelve-thirty."

"Now you mean around twelve-thirty don't you?"

"No, I mean twelve-thirty. I looked at the clock as I was leaving."

"Fine. And how far was it to your friend's house?"

"About a mile and a half—maybe two miles."

"And on the way did you encounter two strangers in a truck?"

"Yes."

"Please tell us about that."

"O.K. I had only been gone about ten or fifteen minutes—I guess I was about half way to my friend's house—when I saw a pick-up truck coming down the road towards me. It was pretty old and dirty but it looked blue."

"And were there two black adult males in the truck?"

"Yes, sir."

"Fine—Please continue."

"The truck drove past me. The driver nodded and I kept walking, not thinking much about it. Then, a minute or so later, I heard them coming back."

"But you did not see them turn around?"

"No, sir."

"But, from the time frame you just gave, they could not have gone to the end of the road—down to your house?"

"No, I'm sure they couldn't have. They must have turned at the little side road I had just passed."

"And how far back was that."

"Maybe five hundred to a thousand feet."

"Then what happened?"

"The truck pulled up along side of me and the passenger asked me how to get back to highway 11."

"And do you see that man in the courtroom?"

"Yes I do. It was Professor Robertson."

"Let the record show that the witness identified the defendant," he said.

"So noted," replied the Judge.

"What happened next?"

"I gave them directions and they asked me if I wanted a ride."

"Did you accept?"

"I hesitated a little but I remembered what my mother taught me—you should always treat everyone the same. Besides, he offered me an orange soda, and who could turn that down?"

His comment received muffled laughter.

"O.K.," returned Richmond, ignoring his remark, "then what happened?"

"I got in the truck and sat between the two men."

"You sat between them? Didn't that make you a little uncomfortable?"

"Maybe a little, but the passenger—Professor Robertson—explained that you had to slam the door hard or it wouldn't close. That was why he put me in the middle. Anyway, we talked for a few seconds and then we started to pull away."

"And what happened next?"

"The driver said, 'we got a problem'. We looked behind us to see the Deputy's car pulling up. He turned on his lights so the driver pulled the truck over."

"Did the men seem worried?"

"Yes, especially the driver."

"Go ahead."

"The Deputy got out of his car and yelled for us to do the same. The Professor and I got out of the car but the driver waited. I guess we weren't moving fast enough for the Deputy because he waved the gun in our direction and said for the Professor and I to move back away from the truck."

As he made his last statement Ethan realized something for the first time. As many times as he had gone over those few moments in his mind he couldn't believe that it had never occurred to him. He knew it was significant. He wondered if the D.A. had picked it up. He seemed oblivious to it. He looked at Cornblossom. She nodded her understanding. She knew. He would wait for her cross-examination.

"So then what?"

"Well, it happened so fast—the driver got out of the truck and, the next thing I knew, he shot the Deputy. I don't even remember seeing the gun—just the Deputy fall."

"What did you do then?"

"I ran. I stood there in shock for a few seconds and then, without even thinking about it, I was under the fence."

"Before the men could do anything?"

"I guess. I really don't remember them saying or doing anything or trying to catch me. I just ran and ran until I made it into the woods."

"How long were you in the woods before the Sheriff arrived?"

"I'm not sure. They tell me about an hour. I was too scared to come out until I heard the sirens."

"Good, Private Ward. Now I want to go back over a few things. The defense attorney made a statement that the Deputy had to be hiding in the brush somewhere since you did not see his car along the road. Is that correct?

"Correct."

"But you weren't looking for it were you?"

"No, but there weren't many places he could have been."

"So you looked around all three of the houses along the way?"

"I didn't search for his car—no—but I didn't have much to do along the road so I always look up at the neighbor's house."

"But none of the neighbors were home so isn't it possible that the Deputy could have pulled around back?"

"Your Honor, now who's speculating?" objected Cornblossom.

"Move along, counselor."

"Yes, Your Honor."

"Couldn't he have been down the side road?"

"Your Honor," objected Cornblossom again.

"Your Honor," countered Richmond, "this is important. The defense has charged that the Deputy had to be in the woods hiding—up to no good. I need to show there were other possibilities."

"Very well. Just keep it brief."

"The point is this, Private Ward. You do not know beyond any doubt that the Deputy was not just sitting behind somebody's house or along the side road and just happened to pull out when the men picked you up, do you?"

"No, I don't know that, but that is not my opinion."

"Let's move on. Let's go up to the time when you had your next encounter with the defendant. Where and when did that happen?"

"It was spring before last—mid April. I was attending MTSU."

"And where did you meet him?"

"At a dinner he was hosting at the University."

"How did you come about being there?"

"As unbelievable as it was I had met the Professor's daughter at school. We had just started seeing each other."

"You mean dating?"

"Yes, sir."

"That's quite a coincidence."

"Yes, the Professor later said that God arranged it—that he could do anything he wanted."

"That's nice that an accused murderer believes in God."

"Your Honor, that kind of remark is uncalled for," said Cornblossom.

"Let's keep it above board, counselor."

"Yes, Your Honor. So did you recognize the defendant as soon as you saw him?"

"Oh no. It had been six years and he had changed quite a bit. And besides, I had only seen him for a minute or two and had never really studied his face."

"So how did you know he was the man in the truck?"

"He came to my room and told me."

"And why did he say that he did that?"

"He said he figured I would recognize him sooner or later—would remember where I had seem him and then go to the police. He wanted to talk to me and tell me his side of the story before that happened."

"That's interesting. He never told you how sorry he was it had happened?"

"No…I'm sure…"

"He never told you it had been bothering him all these years and he just couldn't live with himself?"

"No, not in those words but...."

"Please just answer the questions. So he didn't say it was guilt or remorse that brought him to you—only that he figured you would someday recognize him and go to the police?"

"I guess so."

"And what was your reaction when you first recognized him?"

"I was terrified."

"I'm sure. Go on."

"I grabbed a pair of scissors and threatened to stab him if he came near me. But he pleaded with me to just listen to him and then he would leave and I could do whatever I needed to."

"And then he told you this preposterous story about the Deputy?"

"Your Honor," objected Cornblossom, "do we have to listen to these continual remarks?"

"I'm getting tired of both of your games. The next one who tries it gets a five hundred dollar fine."

"Yes, Your Honor," returned the D.A. "So what did you think of his story?"

"I didn't believe it at first but after I spent the next couple of days thinking about it and researching it, it made more sense."

"Research? How?"

"I went to the library and verified the things he said about the three boys were true—about them being killed, that is."

"So the fact that there actually were three boys killed was enough evidence for you? And the fact that you were in love with his daughter in no way tainted your judgment?"

"No."

"Come on, Private Ward. You mean that you had a relationship with his daughter—that was how you met him—and you weren't hoping that what he said was true?"

"Maybe I was but I don't think that tainted my judgment. I also did other research."

"How?"

"I went to the Sheriff and asked him if I could go through the records on the case. Since I was the only witness and they didn't have a suspect after all those years he didn't see any harm."

"And did you find any evidence—and I mean real evidence—linking him to any of the boy's murders?"

"I guess not conclusive, but I did find information that led me to believe the Deputy was involved."

"Information such as?"

"I discovered that the Deputy was in Harriman the day the first boy was killed. And I discovered he was not working the day the second boy was killed so his whereabouts were not known."

"That's it?"

"I also went to the Deputy's parents' house. They let me look through his personal belongings. I found newspaper clippings of the three boys that had been murdered. They were bundled together and labeled, One, Two, and Three."

"And was there any other writing on them—like 'I killed these boys'?"

"Of course not."

"So when you told the Sheriff about these clippings he dismissed them as meaningless, right?"

"Objection, Your Honor. He would be speculating on what the Sheriff thought," said Cornblossom.

"Private Ward knows how the Sheriff perceived this information and what action he took, if any," countered Richmond.

"I think, under the circumstances, he can answer," ruled the Judge.

"Again, Private Ward, did the Sheriff dismiss your claims as meaningless?"

"I don't know if he dismissed them."

"Well, did anything ever come of this information which you thought was so important?"

"I guess not."

"So did the defendant ever say why he thought the Deputy had anything to do with these young boy's deaths?"

"He said his friend—the other man in the truck—had some knowledge of their deaths."

"But he never said exactly what knowledge he had?"

"No. He said the man would not tell him how he knew."

"Oh, really. This nice man knew the Deputy was going around killing young boys but wouldn't say how he knew or do anything to stop it?"

"He said they sent an anonymous letter asking the authorities to look into it."

"Was there any proof of a letter being sent?"

"Your Honor," objected Cornblossom, "The D.A. is asking for hearsay evidence. Private Ward obviously cannot prove the defendant sent a letter."

"I gave you some freedom here, Miss Cornblossom so I plan on doing the same thing for the prosecution as long as it supports statements already on file. You may answer."

"Again, was there any proof of them sending a letter?"

"I don't know."

"Well since the Deputy was never investigated and the Sheriff nor State Police nor TBCI knew about it then I would think that was probably a fabrication, wouldn't you?"

"I don't know."

Richmond moved away from the witness stand and turned toward the jury, though still addressing Ethan.

"So what we have here then, Private Ward, is a defendant who came to you, not out of guilt or goodness of his heart but because he was afraid you would turn him in. He told you some story about the Deputy killing young boys although neither you nor he knows where his partner got that information. You have no evidence to back up what he said, and neither have the authorities shown any tie in between him and any of the crimes. And, your judgment was skewed because you were in love with the defendant's daughter. Is that correct?"

"Objection, Your Honor. I didn't know we were in summation."

"I withdraw my comment. No further questions for this witness."

Ellen Cornblossom walked toward the witness stand.

"Good morning, Private Ward."

"Good morning."

"I know you have already covered a lot of territory so I will try to keep this brief. The day that you went to see your friend Billy—was that unusual for you?"

"No. At the time we were best friends. I guess we sort of grew apart, but back then, in the summer we would get together two or three times a week."

"Did you always go to his house or did he come to yours?"

"Mostly I would go to his. He had a bigger, nicer house and a lot more things to do."

"So you often walked to his house?"

"Yes, usually. We only had one vehicle and my mom made me do my chores in the morning so I would usually go after lunch."

"And on any of these other occasions did you ever see the Deputy?"

"Yes, I think probably a couple—maybe three—times since school got out."

"Which was?"

"About three weeks."

"So it would be safe to say he knew you might be walking along there at that time?"

"Again, speculation Your Honor," complained Richmond.

"I think that is a reasonable question," said the Judge. "You may answer."

"Yes I guess he could figure out I might be walking along the road."

"And when you saw him before on the road did he ever offer you a ride?"

"No."

"Why do you think that was?"

"Objection, Your Honor. I doubt if either the defendant or Miss Cornblossom know the Green County Sheriff's policies on having civilians in a patrol car."

"Agreed. Move on."

"Yes, Your Honor. Did the Deputy know your name?"

"I'm sure he did. My mother or father spoke to him often when we would run into him around town. They would often mention something about me. He must have known my name."

"O.K., now let's move forward to what happened when he stopped the truck. You said he ordered you all out of the truck and you and the Professor complied but the driver did not. Is that correct?"

"Yes."

"So you and the Professor moved to the back of the truck but that wasn't where the Deputy wanted you, correct?"

"That's correct."

"Your Honor," she said turning to the Judge, "I would like to recreate what happened next if that is O.K."

"You think that is really necessary, counselor?"

"Yes I do."

"Do you have any objections Mr. Richmond?"

"Well, I think it's a waste of the court's time."

"I'll take that as a 'no' as far as a legal objection. Make it quick, Miss Cornblossom."

"Yes, Your Honor."

She instructed Ethan to use her table as the edge of the truck bed. She had him and the Professor stand near the table as they had at the scene of the shooting. The Professor stood about two feet from the edge of the table with Ethan by his side.

"Now is that about how the two of you were positioned at the time?"

"I think this is very close. Don't you Professor?"

He nodded his agreement.

"Now, I am the Deputy. Tell me what to do."

"Well," said Ethan, "he had the gun in his right hand."

A woman on the jury handed her a brush, which brought some laughter from the room.

"What caliber is this?" she said to the woman, then, turning back to the two men asked, "Now what?"

"He pointed it toward us," said Ethan.

"You mean he aimed the gun directly at you?"

"No, I wouldn't say aimed, but he did wave the gun towards us and instructed us to move farther away from the truck."

"What did the two of you do then?"

"We sort of shuffled back from the truck about five more feet."

"Show me."

The two men moved together.

"I just noticed that as you moved, you sort of got behind the Professor, Private Ward. Is that how it really happened?"

"Yes, I guess it was," he responded.

"Like he was protecting you."

"I think that is accurate."

"And did you realize that?"

"Not until a few minutes earlier during my testimony."

"Really—you never thought of it?"

"No I didn't. As many times as I have gone over this in my mind I didn't think of it until a few minutes ago."

"And, one other thing. Did the Deputy call you by your name?"

"No he didn't."

"Did he say, 'son move over here by me'?"

"No he didn't."

"Did he say to the Professor, 'you—get away from the boy'?"

"No, ma'am."

"He did not instruct you to get away from the Professor or get in the car?"

"No he did not."

"And now, what do you surmise from that?"

"Objection, Your Honor."

"I will allow it. Answer the question."

"That he was not concerned with my well being—that I was the same as the Professor and the driver."

"And if they had not come along that day where would you be now?"

"I wouldn't be here. I would be dead."

She had other questions planned but she quickly changed her mind. She could not think of a more dramatic place to stop.

TWENTY-NINE

Ethan was glad his testimony was over. He felt it had helped the Professor, but would only be certain when the trial was over. Now that his testimony was complete he could sit with the other spectators and listen to the rest of the trial. As he left the witness stand and looked towards Sally, he noticed his mother had joined her. He sat next to her and whispered, "who's watching the baby?"

With a nod toward the hallway she replied, "a friend." Confused, Ethan walked toward the hall.

As he left the courtroom he realized what his mother had meant. He watched for a moment as their friend held the baby and sang to her as she looked out into the courtyard. He walked over to her.

"Hi, Rachel," he said.

"Hi, Ethan," she replied as she turned to face him. "You have a beautiful daughter."

"Thanks."

"I think she likes me."

"I'm sure, but probably not as much as her grandfather."

"Maybe," she replied with a laugh.

"That was awful nice what you did. Thank you."

"Sure. I got your card. "You weren't sure I was sincere, huh?" she added with a smile.

"Well, uh, I…"

"It's O.K., Ethan. I didn't have too good a track record. So how's it going in there?"

"O.K. I think. I guess we'll know soon."

"So, any doubt he's telling the truth?"

"Not for me. We just have to convince the jury. So what are you doing here?"

"Oh, my fiancé and I are on our way to Jacksonville to do a concert."

"Where is he?"

"He had to go by a radio station. He thought it was best I come in to say hello by myself."

"You're quite the shooting star."

"I guess. It's mostly luck—or I should say God's will—and a little talent."

"I heard you sing, remember. It's a lot of talent."

The two stood silently for a moment as she rocked the baby. She soon stopped and handed her back to her father.

"Well, I guess I better be going."

As she handed the baby to him she hesitated, trying to think of the right words to say.

"So....Ethan, are we alright?"

"Sure, Rachel. I really appreciate everything."

"Sally is a great girl—and I know you love her, and I love my fiancé, but...well, do you ever think of what might have been?'

"Of course, everybody does that."

"I know. I guess it just makes me a little sad," she said, then, with a shake of her head, she continued. "Oh well, that's life. Take care, Ethan."

She reached forward and kissed him on the cheek. As she did so he could see a tear in her eye. She turned and walked away.

"Hey, Rachel," he called.

"Yes?"

"You're O.K."

He looked up to see the courtroom breaking for lunch. His mother and Sally and Tommy walked toward him.

"Did I miss anything?"

"Not really," said his mother. "The prosecution rested and they will start after lunch with the Professor's character witnesses. He will probably testify later today."

"And Sally and I were talking," said Tommy, "Since you two are not married we figured she and I..."

She hit him in the chest.

"You're terrible. How was Rachel?"

"She's fine—on her way to Florida."

"Well," interrupted his mother as she took Emily, "you two should be in the room this afternoon when the Professor testifies. I will take her back to the hotel."

She took the baby and headed back while the three of them went to the cafeteria for lunch. Ethan suggested they wait for her father but Sally informed him he had to talk to his attorney.

Professor Robertson and Ellen Cornblossom waited until the courtroom had cleared to begin reviewing the morning's events and planning their strategy for the rest of the trial.

The defense began its case with a number of character witnesses. Two neighbors, the Professor's minister, as well as his Dean were scheduled to testify. Ellen Cornblossom knew that there was little information any of the witnesses could provide, however she wanted the jury to get to know the man they were judging. The D.A. had few questions for any of the witnesses. In each case he asked each witness the same. First, 'did the defendant ever tell you that he had been involved in a homicide?' In each case the answer was no. He then followed up with one other question - 'therefore, is it possible that there may be other incriminating things the defendant may have not told you?' Each witness was forced to answer 'yes'.

The last character witness was Tony Caley, the Professor's minister at Bethlehem Baptist Church. He testified that he had known the defendant for over five years and held him in the highest regard. He also stated that, on various occasions he had served as usher at the church. When the defense attorney had finished the D.A. began his questioning.

"Now, Mr. Caley, you are aware that in the State of Tennessee any conversation between an individual and his minister is privileged, correct?"

"Correct."

"Then, if the defendant did have a conversation relevant to this trial, you are not required to share it, correct?"

"Your Honor," interrupted Miss Cornblossom, the defendant would like the court to know that he formally waives any right to privacy regarding this witness."

"Is that correct, Professor?" asked the Judge.

"Yes, Your Honor," answered the Professor.

"Then the witness may answer any question posed to him."

"Good," stated Richmond. "Then let me ask you the same question I asked all others. Did the defendant ever tell you that he was involved in a murder in 1963?"

"No, he did not."

"Then it is conceivable there are other things—incriminating things—you may not know about the defendant—correct?"

"Yes, I suppose."

"I have no other questions for this witness."

The highlight of almost all criminal trials is the defendant's testimony. It is something every jury wants to hear, and every defense attorney's worst nightmare. Ellen Cornblossom had decided that it would be to their advantage to allow the Professor to testify. Not only did she believe everything he had told her to be true, he was also a likeable and convincing witness. His demeanor and intelligence would make a positive impression for the jury. After he was sworn in and had given his name and address, she began her questioning.

"Now, Professor, before we begin our questioning regarding the events in question, I want to discuss an offer made to you before the trial began."

"Yes, ma'am."

"Is it true that the D.A. offered you a reduced sentence if you would turn in the man that was with you in the truck the day in question?"

"Yes, it is."

"And you could have received a sentence of eight to twelve years, and possibly have gotten off in three to four years with good behavior?"

"Yes, ma'am."

"Why did you not take it?"

"Because—just as you said—I would have to turn in the man that was with me that day."

"The man that shot the Deputy?"

"Yes, ma'am."

"But why would you not do that?"

"Because he not only saved my life and the life of young Ethan Ward, but most certainly other young boy's lives as well."

"So you really believe the Deputy was guilty of killing those young boys?"

"Absolutely."

"But, if so, wouldn't your friend receive a fair trial?"

"Well, I was only a witness, and I'm here aren't I?"

"And you realize by testifying that you will be asked to identify this man again?"

"Yes."

"And if you refuse, you could be in more trouble?"

"Yes, ma'am, but I am already on trial for a crime of which I had no participation nor knowledge. I don't know what worse they can do to me, but I will not provide his name."

She believed she had made her point.

She asked him general questions about himself and his background. She questioned him about his family, his education, and his career. She soon asked about his current position at the University.

"When were you appointed professor at the University?"

"Actually I am an Associate Professor. It has been a little over two years since I received the appointment."

"And at that time how many other black professors were there at MTSU?"

"I was the first."

"That's impressive. And today how many black Professors are there?"

"There are still no full Professors but we do have three Associate Professors—including myself."

"Thank you. Now let's go back to 1963. First I would like to talk about what happened that lead up to you being in Greene County in June."

"Fine."

"Do you remember the day it all began?"

"Absolutely, Thursday, January 24th."

"January? That's months before the shooting."

"Correct."

"Please tell us about it."

"I was a high school English teacher in Harriman—that was where I was born—just a little west of Knoxville. That day, before school, the Principal came to me and told me he had just been informed by the authorities that one of my students—a fifteen year old boy—had been identified as the individual who had broken into a home in Greene County. A deputy would be coming to pick him up and take him back to Greenville that afternoon. The Principal wanted me to keep him after class so the Deputy could take him into custody."

"And did you do that?"

"Yes, I did."

"And, did you meet the Deputy at that time?"

"No, I really didn't meet him. His focus was on the boy, but I did see him and saw his name tag."

"And what did it say?"

"Andrew Pratt."

"But you never spoke to him?"

"I did not. Like I said, his focus was the boy. I don't think he ever looked at me."

Cornblossom went to her desk and received a document from her assistant.

"Your Honor, here is the arrest warrant for the young man in question that day as well as a statement from the Principal which shows he was in Professor—well, then it was just Mr. Robertson's—classroom. I would like to enter these into evidence."

"Very good. Please continue."

She turned back to the Professor.

"But that was not the only significant event that happened that day was it?"

"No it wasn't. I found out later that day that another young boy—he was about twelve or thirteen—did not report to school that morning and his body was later found in a barn."

"And did you later have a conversation with a friend about these two events?"

"Yes, I did."

"Please tell us about it."

"It was a day or two later. I said something like, 'what a day. We had one boy murdered and a deputy came to school and took another one back to Greene County to stand trial.'"

"What was his reaction?"

"He immediately asked if I knew the name of the Deputy. I told him it was Pratt."

"What did he say then?"

"Something that really shocked me. He said he would not be surprised if the Deputy had killed the boy."

"I'm sure that was a shock. Did you ask him why he would say such a thing?"

"Yes. He would only tell me that he had some knowledge or association with the Deputy many years earlier and knew what type of person he was."

"And what type was that?"

"Evil. He said he was pure evil."

"Your Honor," Cornblossom said as she turned to the Judge, "here are two additional items we would like to place into evidence. One is a newspaper article detailing the young boy's murder. The other is documentation from the Sheriff's department showing that not only was Deputy Pratt sent to pick up the boy in the Professor's classroom, but that he did not report to work that morning so his whereabouts from the previous evening were unknown."

"So noted."

"Now, moving forward, was there another young boy found murdered a few weeks later?"

"Objection, Your Honor," stated the D.A. "This is all pure speculation."

"Overruled. Please continue."

"Yes, about six or eight weeks later, I think. It was over near Knoxville."

"And did you have a conversation regarding this murder with your friend?"

"Yes I did."

"And what was the gist of that?"

"He was more convinced than ever that the Deputy was responsible."

"But he still wouldn't give you any details about why he believed that?"

"No."

"And did he have any evidence?"

"I asked him that. He either didn't have any proof or he wouldn't tell me."

"Didn't you think his comments were ridiculous?"

"When he told me about the first boy I thought he was crazy. Then, after the second boy, I began to wonder if he really knew what he was talking about. But when I tried to get more information from him he would clam-up. I felt as if the Deputy had some leverage over him and that was why he wouldn't—or couldn't—tell me any more."

"But if he believed that young boys were being stalked—and if you believed him—shouldn't you have done something about it?"

"We tried to. But first, remember, from what he told me he didn't have any proof. But I convinced him—I believe it was after the second murder—that we had to do something. We sent an anonymous letter to the authorities."

"And did anything become of it?"

"We never heard of anything. I guess in those cases they get so many leads they can't follow up on them all. I don't know if they ever looked at it or not."

"Then let's move on to the third boy's murder. Did you talk to your friend about that?"

"Yes, he still didn't have any real evidence, but he was more convinced than ever, that the Deputy was responsible."

"O.K., lets move on to the day of the shooting. What can you tell us about that day?"

"It was a hot summer day. My wife and I had a fight early that morning. I don't even remember what it was about. It was a stressful time for us. My father had died just a few months earlier and my mother a year before that. Anyway, we had a fight and I walked out—told her I was going over to my parents' farm. It was really just a house in the country at that time. They didn't have any livestock any more. After my father died I would go by every once and a while to check on it. Anyway, it became sort of a refuge for me when things were going bad. I told my wife I would see her in a day or two."

"Then what happened?"

"I had only been at my parents' place a short while when my friend came by. He asked me if I wanted to ride over to Greene County with him."

"Did he say why?"

He and Cornblossom had already discussed his answer. She believed the reason they went there would not help the authorities in identifying his friend.

"He heard of a man who had a hunting dog for sale."

"Did he know the man?"

"No, at least he told me he did not. He was not from Greene County, but, obviously, he had some contacts there. Anyway, we went to see the man about buying the dog but when we got there he was not home."

"You didn't call?"

"He did not have a phone."

"So what did you do then?"

"We just left."

"You didn't leave a note?"

"We didn't have a pencil or paper. Besides, I wasn't planning on coming back over there again and he needed my truck to take the dog back."

"I see. Let's go back to that. You took your truck. Which one of you drove over?"

"I did."

"Did you know he had a gun?"

"Absolutely not or I would not have gone."

"So the logical question, Professor, is this—if you thought that

Deputy Pratt was responsible for the deaths of those young boys, and you were going to his home county, didn't you think that might be the reason your friend wanted to go there? Maybe to have it out with him?"

"No, not really. He had been talking about getting a hunting dog for a long time and I knew he either had friends or acquaintances in Greene County, so it didn't surprise me."

"And the issue of the Deputy never came up?"

"Yeah, I said something like, 'aren't you worried about running into the Deputy?'"

"And what did he say?"

"He said that was really unlikely to happen. It was a big county and we would only be there for a few minutes. He did say he would not let him—Deputy Pratt—control his life."

"Then is it fair to say that the two of you went there in spite of the Deputy and not looking for him?"

"Correct."

"So once you left the man's house you started home?"

"Yes we did. I was tired of driving so he took over. I guess he didn't know the area as well as he thought. He said there was a shortcut back to the highway but we got lost. I guess you know the rest."

"So that takes us up to the time when you ran into Ethan Ward on the road."

"Yes, ma'am."

"Why did you stop to pick him up?"

"It was like he said. He seemed to be a nice young boy. He gave us directions. It was hot and dusty. We thought he would like a ride."

"Was that the only thing you were thinking of?"

"Well, we never discussed it but I guess both of us were thinking of what happened to the other boys. I guess that was a factor. In my mind I figured that if he was with us he would be safe."

"Of course you must have known how dangerous it was for two grown black men in a strange county to pick up a young white boy?"

"I guess. I don't know—we really didn't think about it or discuss it. He was such a nice young kid and didn't seem leery of us like most white boys would be. It just seemed like the right thing to do."

"I see. Professor, I know that Private Ward has gone over what happened next but I would like your version. Do you agree with everything he said?"

"Absolutely."

"And you also believe the Deputy was hiding in the bushes?"

"Objection," said Richmond. "She's putting words in his mouth."

"Overruled. You may answer," returned the Judge.

"I don't know where else he could have been. We looked around when we stopped to pick up the boy. It was only a minute or less when we saw him behind us."

"What did you think then?"

"I was only slightly concerned at first, then, when he got out and we discovered who it was, I figured we were in trouble."

"How did you know it was Deputy Pratt?"

"Ethan—Private Ward—recognized him and said he would talk to him and everything would be O.K.

"But you didn't say anything to your friend?"

"No, not really. We may have said a couple of words like 'oh no' or something like that but we really didn't have time to talk."

"And he didn't say, 'don't worry—I'll take care of it', or something like that?"

"No, absolutely not. If he had, Ethan would have also heard it."

"So, when you got out of the truck, you still did not know your friend had a gun?"

"No, I did not."

"Did you think your life was in danger?"

"No. Even though my friend had been saying those things about him, I thought, even if they were true, he wouldn't do anything to all three of us in broad daylight. And since my friend had no proof of his suspicions I felt we were no threat to him."

"But, since that time you have changed your mind?"

"Well, yes. I thought about it and, once he saw who the driver was, I think he would not have had any choice but to get rid of all of us."

"But I want to make it clear—you had no knowledge that your friend had a gun or intended to use it?"

"I did not."

"And what about after the shooting. Did you two allow Ethan Ward to escape?"

"Yes, we did. I mean my friend started to go toward him—just a natural reaction I think. But when I said to let him go, he stopped. He would not have hurt the boy."

"But if he had wanted, he could have stopped him?"

"Absolutely."

"Fine. Can you tell us how you escaped?"

"It was simple. Some call it luck—I truly believe it was God's will. We simply drove slowly so as to not draw attention until we got to the lake. He knew the area so we found a good spot to sink the truck. We stayed in the woods until nightfall then caught a freight train at Jefferson City. We didn't know until we heard the news that it was about an hour and a half before they started looking for us. We made it back to Harriman the next morning."

THIRTY

As Ethan sat listening to the Professor's testimony, an idea began to formulate. He turned to Sally and whispered that he would be back shortly, then left the courtroom. In the hall he saw two people talking, one of whom had a notebook. He went to the woman and asked for a piece of paper. He found a bench and sat and listed everything he knew about what had happened that day in 1963 as well as everything he had learned about the Professor's partner since. Shortly he arose and walked back into the courtroom and whispered to Sally,

"I need to talk to you in the hallway."

He led her from the courtroom and back to the bench.

"What is it?" she asked, sounding irritated that he had taken her from her father's testimony.

"I think I may be able to uncover who your father's friend is," he answered.

"You're kidding. How?"

"I can't believe I didn't put this all together before. I was just listening to your father's testimony and I began thinking of everything I knew about him and everything that has happened."

"Yes?"

"Well, first of all, the reason this all began was because the two of them got lost and asked me for directions, right?"

"If you say so."

"Your father had never been to Greene County before but his

friend had obviously been there—probably many times."

"Yeah."

"But the fact that they got lost meant that he was not as familiar with the area as he thought. He probably had been there some years before and thought he remembered all the roads but did not. That means, more than likely he grew up nearby—probably in one of the adjoining counties. The fact that he knew the best place to dump the truck in the lake also points to that."

"But how does that help? The police probably investigated every black man in those counties."

"That means he had probably already moved away. And based on what your father has said he probably lived in Harriman or at least near there."

"I guess that would make sense."

"Yes, but there's a lot more. Your father said they drove all the back roads to get away. From the route they took they probably went through Hamblen County. That means the man probably was from Hamblen County but spent some time in Greene County when he was younger."

"Well, that is interesting, Ethan, but it is still not enough."

"I know, but there is something else your father told me that I just thought of. He also said the man knew the Deputy was not working the day of the second boy's murder, and he was right. How did he know that if he no longer lived around there?"

"Well, of course someone had to tell him, but that doesn't help much. He might have talked to any of hundreds of people there."

"Yes, but whoever he talked to has never come forward so that means it was a real close friend or probably a relative."

"That still doesn't help much."

"No, except I think I know who that relative is."

"You're kidding. Who?"

"The Sheriff's secretary, Holly Moore."

"Why do you think that?"

"Well obviously because she would know when the deputy was working and when he was not, but also because she has always been so cold towards me. But, the main reason is that she has two nephews, the Russell brothers, who have always made life miserable for me. Ted even threatened me to stop snooping around."

"I never knew that."

"It's not worth going into right now, but I think the person we are looking for is a relative of Holly Moore who grew up in Hamblen County but used to visit Greene County and is about thirty to thirty-five years old."

"And who had already moved away before the shooting occurred."

"Right."

"I hope you are right about all this, Ethan, but I still don't know how much it will help. Holly or her nephews will never say anything, and we only have another day or two to find him. After the trial it won't do my father a bit of good."

"I know, that's why I have to go back home and see what I can find. And I have to leave now."

"Are you sure about this? I want my father freed but it might be dangerous for you."

"I know what I'm doing. Don't worry, I'll be very careful. But I don't want anybody to know what I'm up to. What would be a good story? I know—tell them I got a call at the hotel from my C.O. and he said the telephone system on the base has died and they need every technician there. If I don't go back I will be considered AWOL. If I do find him, your father will probably be pretty angry with me."

"I don't care. Sometimes people need to be protected from themselves. If you're going to do this you need to take Tommy with you."

"I don't want to get him involved. Also, if he left, it would alert everybody that I am up to something. I'll take extra precautions so nothing happens to me."

Ethan said goodbye to her and then went by the hotel to see his mother and Emily. He told her about getting a message at the hotel from his C.O. After kissing her and Emily goodbye he got in his car and headed for Greene County.

Back in the courtroom Cornblossom continued her questioning

of Professor Robertson.

"So let's move forward until last year when Ethan Ward showed up. That's pretty unbelievable that he would start dating your daughter."

"Yes. That's a one in a million shot. Again, I believe God's hand is behind this."

"So God wanted you to be arrested? You can't be too happy about that."

"No, but we don't always understand His plan. Besides, the trial isn't over yet. Who knows what He has in mind."

"So let's talk about your meeting Private Ward. When you heard who your daughter was dating you could have just not gone to the dinner that time. Maybe they would have broken up."

"She seemed pretty serious about him, so I figured I would have to see him sooner or later. Besides, even if they had broken up I would have probably seen him around campus. I couldn't hide forever."

"But even after you met he said he didn't remember you."

"He said I looked familiar. It would have only been a matter of time."

"But, to be blunt, Professor, if you had told your friend he could have done away with Private Ward and all your troubles would have been over, right?"

"Well he, nor I, would have ever done that. I can't think of anything that would have been more wrong."

"I see. So instead you went to him and put your life in his hands?"

"I guess. I had tried to follow him over the years by reading their local paper so I knew what kind of fine young man he was. Besides, I felt I just couldn't keep this to myself any more. I thought I could trust him to do the right thing and I was right."

"I think we have covered about everything, Professor. One final question—do you have regrets over anything that has happened."

"I have regrets over everything. I regret that those young boys had to die. I regret that Ethan had to see what he did. I regret that my daughters have to go through this. And I even regret that the

Deputy had to die. But, under the circumstances, I don't know what we could have done different."

"Thank you, Professor. No further questions."

While Ethan had a vague idea of what he needed to do, as he drove the plan became clearer. He arrived at the Greene County courthouse at four-forty-five. He found the county's license and records department just before closing time. He was greeted by Rita Talbert, the clerk who ran the department, and an acquaintance of his mother's.

"Ethan," she began, "what are you doing here? I thought you were testifying at the trial."

"I just finished, Rita. And I am trying to get some information. Do you think you can help me?"

"Well, sure. Does this have anything to do with the trial?"

"I don't know if it does or not and I can't say anyway, but I would sure appreciate any help you can give me."

"O.K.," she agreed, "but if this has anything to do with the trial I want to be the first to know about it."

"Agreed."

"So, what are you looking for?"

He asked her if he could look through the county's marriage and birth certificates from the years 1930 through 1950.

"There's no problem with you looking at those, Ethan, they're public records. But that's a ton of work. If you can tell me what you are looking for, maybe I can narrow it down for you."

"I really can't, Rita. It's just a hunch and a really long shot, and if I am wrong I don't want to cause any problem for anyone. Are the certificates all filed alphabetically?"

"Yes, by year, but I think I can make it a little simpler. They are also entered in a record book each year. Come on back and I can let you go through them."

She led him into a room with shelves containing hundreds of books along the wall.

"These books here," she said, pointing to one wall, "list all the marriage certificates. Beginning further down are the ones containing birth certificates. You can see the labels on the books showing the years. They go back to 1890. You think that'll be far enough?"

"Yes," he said with a laugh. "You're getting ready to close, aren't you?"

"Yes, but I will stick around for a little while. Just let me know when you are through."

"Thanks."

She turned and left the room. He first turned his attention to the birth certificates. The most logical place to start was with the Russell brothers. Since he knew their ages the records were easy to find. Ted Russell was born in 1948, his brother, Ed, the same year as Ethan, 1950. Their parents were Marie Foster Russell and Leon Franklin Russell. Since he estimated their parents to be about twenty to thirty years older than the boys, he began searching for their birth certificates. He could find nothing.

He next turned his attention to Holly Moore. If his memory was accurate, she and Marie Russell were sisters. He could find no record of Holly Moore's birth, but he did find a record of her marriage to William Moore in 1952. Her name was listed as Holly Foster Moore. That virtually confirmed that Holly Foster Moore and Marie Foster Russell were sisters. While he searched further he could find no other helpful information. But, if his suspicions were correct, the critical information would only be available in Hamblen County.

He thanked Rita for her help but told her his search had been fruitless. He left the courthouse wishing it were earlier in the day. He would have to wait until the following morning before he could research the other records. Not wanting his father to know what he was doing, he drove into Hamblen County and took a room at a motel.

At five minutes after nine Professor Robertson was again back on the witness stand. With the D.A. asking the questions the day would be much rougher than the previous one.

"Good morning, Mr. Robertson," he began.

"Your Honor," began Cornblossom immediately, "his title is

Professor Robertson. He earned the title and should be addressed as such."

"I agree. Mr. Richmond, please address the defendant as Professor Robertson," instructed the Judge.

"Yes, Your Honor," he replied reluctantly. "Good morning Professor Robertson."

"Good morning."

"Why don't we go back over some of your testimony. When your friend told you that he believed the Deputy to be responsible for the boy's death in Harriman, is there another person who can verify that?"

"Not that I know of."

"Well if he had told other people about that don't you think someone would have mentioned it? I mean, that is pretty serious to go around accusing someone of murder."

"As far as I know he did not tell anyone else."

"Why did he only tell you then?"

"Objection, Your Honor," stated Cornblossom. "Speculation."

"I'd like to hear the answer. You may respond."

"Yes, Your Honor. I guess because we were friends. Or probably because I mentioned that I had seen the Deputy at our school."

"I guess you realize that since your arrest the authorities have examined everything in your life for the past ten years to try to identify your accomplice?"

"I would expect so."

"They have talked to everyone that you knew back then but yet have not identified him."

"Yes."

"So, that would lead one to believe that you and he were not that close—maybe even a casual acquaintance."

"I never said we were best friends."

"But, if you weren't best friends, why did he choose you to confide in and no one else?"

"I told you, because I told him about the Deputy coming to my school."

"Or maybe it's because you and he made up this whole story in case either of you were ever arrested."

"That's not true."

"And regarding your statement about you and he sending a letter to the authorities about the Deputy, is there someone else who can verify that?"

"Not that I know of."

"Do you have a copy of the letter?"

"No, I do not."

"So we really just have your word about that also?"

"I guess so."

"And, if you and he were really concerned about more young boys being killed why didn't you just call the State Police or TBCI?"

"I suggested that but he was afraid the call might be traced back to him."

"Traced back to him? You ever hear of a pay phone?"

"We also thought the letter would be taken more seriously."

"But when you didn't hear anything about it you just gave up. I guess young boy's lives weren't as important to you after all."

"We thought they might still be looking into it—actually investigating him."

"I'm sure. Now let's look at your statement about the gun. You say you had no idea that your friend had a gun that day?"

"That is true."

"Of course, again we only have your word that you didn't see it?"

"I didn't see the gun," he repeated strongly.

"But if he had had it on his person you would have certainly noticed it."

"Not necessarily. A handgun is not that big."

"And you drove with him all day, stopped and changed places, and still did not see it?"

"All I know is that I did not know he had a gun or I would not have gone with him."

"Yeah, I'm sure."

"Your Honor," objected Cornblossom, "must we be subjected to these continual sarcastic remarks?"

"Mr. Richmond," said the Judge sternly, "I'm tired of going

through this. Keep your comments to yourself."

"Yes, Your Honor. So the man you went to see about the dog was not home, right?"

"No, he was not."

"That makes it more convenient since then he could not identify you and tell the authorities, correct?"

"All I know is that we went to his house and he was not home."

"Then tell us who he is. We can then at least find out if he really does sell hunting dogs."

"I don't remember his name. He only mentioned it to me once and I don't think he ever said his last name."

"Then tell us where he lives. I'm sure we can find him from that."

The Professor thought briefly for a moment before answering.

"I will not do that."

"And why?"

"Because it might help you in identifying my friend."

"Your Honor, please instruct the defendant to answer my question. If not I would like him held in contempt."

"Please answer the question, Professor."

"I'm sorry, Your Honor. I mean no disrespect to you but I cannot do that."

Richmond was mad. "I would like this man held in contempt, Your Honor."

"I will take that under advisement counselor. I will make my decision once the trial is over. For now, please continue."

"Professor, since the shooting in 1963 are you aware of any evidence that has been uncovered to substantiate your claims against the Deputy?"

"No, I am not."

"Even though the police and TBCI have begun looking into this again since your arrest."

"The only evidence I have is that the murders have stopped since that day."

Richmond ignored his remark.

"Professor, you have gone to great lengths by bringing in character witnesses to show what an honorable person you are. You have also made reference to your belief in God. Is that accurate?"

"Yes, I believe in God."

"Then do you try to do what is right?'

"I attempt to, but I am a mere human and fail every day."

"Then why do you continue to protect this man? Isn't a court of law the best place to prove his guilt or innocence?"

"If I were certain he would receive a fair trial and all the evidence were known, then perhaps I would agree with you."

"And have you received a fair trial, so far, Professor? I mean, the trial was moved here so you would get a jury with a better racial mix. Your bail has been reduced by half. You have a lawyer from one of the state's top law firms representing you which I understand you are not paying for. And all of this just to make sure you are treated fairly—would you agree?"

"Objection, Your Honor," said Cornblossom. "This is pure speculation."

"I think the witness can share his own opinion, counselor. You may answer."

"I have no complaints about how I have been treated but I have been very fortunate. Whether you believe it or not, minorities are not always treated fairly in this country."

"But it should be up to you to determine who should be judged and who shouldn't, right?"

"No matter how you look at it Mr. Richmond, my belief is that if I gave you his name I could be sending an innocent man to prison for the rest of his life."

"Well, I have another theory why you don't want to give his name. If you did and he was arrested then, in retaliation, he might give us information that would be detrimental to you—maybe about other crimes you have committed."

"Objection, Your Honor," said Cornblossom.

"Sustained."

"O.K., Lets move on," continued Richmond. "You stated that the reason you went to Private Ward was that you believed he would eventually remember who you were and go to the authorities."

"I told him I wanted him to know what really happened before he went to the authorities, then he could do whatever he wanted."

"But the point is that you did not do it out of guilt or you would have done it years earlier. You only did it to protect yourself."

"There is a big difference between guilt and regret. I have always had regret over what happened. I don't have guilt because we didn't bring it about—the Deputy did. And yes, I will admit that I don't want to go to jail, but that has nothing to do with what happened. Everything I have told you is the truth."

"I have no further use for this witness, Your Honor," stated Richmond abruptly.

THIRTY-ONE

The next morning Ethan was at the Hamblen County court-house when the doors opened. While the clerk was not as accommo-dating as Rita had been, he soon gained access to the records for which he was looking.

Knowing Holly Moore's and Marie Russell's maiden names were Foster, and estimating their ages, he soon found records of their births. Marie was born in 1928 and Holly in 1932. Their parents were Henry Allen Foster and Deborah Ann Rutledge. Since he esti-mated the man in the truck to be a few years younger than the Professor, he began searching for any black male with the last name of either Foster or Rutledge born between 1930 and 1937. Soon he came up with three names which fit the profile—two with the name of Rutledge, and one with the name Foster—James Henry. He could find no common links between either of the Rutledge men and Deborah Rutledge, but, as he searched further he discovered that James Henry Foster's father—James Foster—and Henry Allen Fos-ter were brothers. That meant James Henry and Holly were first cousins. While he was excited, there was still additional information he needed. He went back to the clerk who he hoped could answer his questions.

"Excuse me ma'am," he began, "can I ask you a question?"

"What is that?" she answered.

"Do you know the James Foster family?"

"I know who they are. Why?"

"Do you know their son, James Henry?"

"I know who he is. Why?"

"Look, ma'am," continued Ethan, "I can't explain right now but it is really important if you can tell me anything you know about Mr. Foster."

She looked at him cautiously for a second before asking,

"You're not trying to cause trouble, are you?"

"No ma'am," replied Ethan. "It's just that I believe Mr. Foster worked for my father when he was younger and may have information that would be useful to me."

Ethan was surprised he had lied so well and convincingly.

"You're not from around here, are you?"

He wondered why such a simple question was so difficult. He thought that maybe he had a simple answer.

"Look, I am not trying to cause any trouble, but the information is important. It's worth ten dollars to me."

"How about twenty?" she responded quietly as she looked around.

"Fine," said Ethan as he took the money from his wallet and handed it to her.

"Now, do you know if James Foster is still around?"

"You mean James Henry Foster, the younger one, right?"

"Right."

"He moved away some years ago. I think to Harriman."

"Really," said Ethan, trying to contain his excitement. "Do you remember when?"

"Oh, it's been a long time ago—probably ten years or more."

"Would you have his address?"

"Like I said, I don't really know him or his family—I just know who they are. You can call his parents and ask."

"I don't really want to do that," returned Ethan.

"I see. O.K., I may know of a way to get his address."

"Really, How?"

He expected a request for more money, but she said nothing. She reached under the counter and removed a phone directory. She looked up a number and picked up the phone.

"Who are you calling?" asked Ethan.

"A cousin at Motor Vehicles. They know everything about you."

Soon Ethan could hear a faint voice at the other end—not enough to make out what was being said.

"Hi, Mary," said the clerk. "I'm trying to find an address for a nice young man. Can you help me?....Oh, you're always busy. It will only take a minute.... Thanks....His name is James Henry Foster. I think he lives in Harriman."

Ethan could hear a question being asked. She looked at Ethan as she said, "He would be in his mid-thirties."

The woman started to write something and then stopped.

"Oh, really, huh? He moved from Harriman about five years ago. Do you know where?"

Ethan's eyes widened as she wrote down the address. The clerk looked up to him for approval. He slowly shook his head.

"Thanks a lot, Mary," said the clerk and hung up the phone. Then, holding out the piece of paper said to Ethan, "How is that?"

"Uh...that is great. I really appreciate all your help," he responded as he took the paper and turned to walk away.

"If you need any more help just let me know. It's Susie. Susie Monroe, like the President."

Ethan thanked her and left the building. He got in his car and drove west. He passed Knoxville and then Harriman and headed for Murfreesboro. He could not believe the man was actually living in Murfreesboro. Not only that, but, from the familiar address, near the University.

It was still early in the day—a little after eleven o'clock—when the Professor finished his testimony. To accommodate the defense and the prosecution—who both requested a recess to finalize their closing arguments—the Judge called an early lunch. The trial would resume at two o'clock to hear summations.

Ellen Cornblossom had rehearsed her closing statement a dozen times so made only minor adjustments. Randy Richmond used the extra time to reexamine his remarks and make sure nothing had been overlooked. He began his comments a few minutes after two o'clock.

"Ladies and gentlemen of the jury, when we first began I told you that this was a simple case. And, despite the smokescreens and unfounded claims by the defense, that is still true. I wish to remind you that a trial is about truth and facts. It is not about suppositions. It is not about unfounded claims. It is not about gossip and publicity. This is a court of law and a court of evidence and proof. Now let's look again at the facts as they have been presented here."

"Two strangers picked up a young boy along a dusty country road in the summer of 1963. When a Deputy Sheriff stopped them they gunned him down. They escaped leaving the young boy to testify. And he has identified the defendant as one of the men involved in the shooting. The defendant has also been identified through fingerprints and through the truck he was driving. More importantly, he has confessed. He confessed not out of guilt or remorse, but because he knew the witness would sooner or later identify him. If he had remorse he would have come forward years earlier. There is absolute proof this was one of the individuals involved in the shooting."

"Now, what about the claims made by the defendant? Is there any substance to them? Absolutely not. In order to cover up their crime he claims that the victim had been murdering young boys. How did he know this? His friend and partner in crime told him. How did his friend know? We don't know because we don't know who he is. The Professor won't identify him. Is there any evidence to support this? Absolutely not. After seven years of investigating these young boys' deaths, there is not one ounce of evidence that points to the Deputy. The Professor claims they sent a letter to the authorities telling them the Deputy was responsible for the killings. Does he have a copy of the letter? No. Did the authorities look into it? No—because it was never sent. He claims he did not know his partner had a gun, yet they drove for three hours together in his truck and even changed sides. He claims they went to Greene County not looking for the Deputy, but to buy a dog from a man. Of course the man wasn't home so conveniently he could not identify them. Does he know who he was? No. Did the man have a phone so they could call him first and tell him they were coming? Of course not."

"The defendant also makes ridiculous claims about the behavior of the victim that day. They say he was hiding in wait and that is why they did not see him until the last minute. While this is highly unlikely, so what if he was hiding? Don't police do that all the time to catch criminals? Have you never seen a policeman behind a billboard or behind trees? Maybe he had a tip about a drug deal. Maybe there had been suspicious activity in the area. To take that another step and say the Deputy was waiting for young Ethan Ward is ridiculous and unfounded."

The D.A. turned and pointed to the defendant.

"Ladies and gentlemen, the law states that anyone who knowingly assists in the commission of a crime is also guilty of that crime. This man absolutely knowingly assisted in bringing about the death of Andrew Pratt while he was carrying about the duties of his job. You must find him guilty. Thank you."

Richmond looked smugly at Cornblossom as he took his seat. She ignored his stare and walked calmly to the center of the courtroom. She had two pieces of paper in her hand.

"Ladies and gentlemen, this is a copy of the definition of guilt in the Code of Tennessee. It says, 'the defendant must be found guilty beyond a reasonable doubt.' This was adopted from the Bill of Rights. Why in the world did our founding fathers—probably the smartest group of men ever assembled—say a person had to be found guilty beyond a reasonable doubt? Why did they not say a person had to be found guilty without any doubt? I will tell you why—because it would never happen. I have been involved in thirty-three criminal trials and I have never seen one where there was absolutely one-hundred percent proof that a person was guilty. And in the case of Professor Robertson there is more doubt than any trial I have ever seen. I have listed here eleven reasons why you should doubt the Professor's guilt in this case. Eleven things that just don't make sense. I wish to read them to you."

1. The Deputy said he was on the other side of the county when he really wasn't.

2. The Deputy knew when Ethan Ward would be walking down

the road and just happened to be there exactly at the same time.

3. The Deputy was hiding in the bushes.

4. The Deputy said he had called for backup when he had not.

5. The Deputy did not run their license plates as was normal procedure.

6. The Deputy pulled his gun without provocation.

7. The Deputy pointed his gun at the young boy he was supposedly rescuing.

8. The defendants let the only witness escape.

9. The Deputy was at the school the same day the first young boy was killed.

10. Fingerprints show the Professor has never been involved in any other crime.

11. The Professor went to the only witness and told him what happened.

"Eleven reasons to believe the Professor, ladies and gentlemen. And one more. Look at his life before and after this incident. Has there ever been a more unlikely person to let a man be gunned down? I don't think so."

"There is a story the Professor told me one day which I wish to share. It is an old, old story handed down from his ancestors. There was a village in Africa which had a honest and just Chief. Everyone knew they could trust him to do what was right. One day delegates from his tribe came to him and told him there had been a lot of thefts in the village. The Chief told them the thief must be caught and punished. He said when the thief was captured he would get twenty lashes with the whip. A few days later the thief was captured. It was the Chief's own elderly and frail mother. He was torn apart wondering what to do. If he let her go he would break his own word and would have to step down from the throne. Yet, if he carried out the punishment he knew his mother would die. The next day he had his mother brought into the center of the village and tied to the whipping post. He ordered the guard to apply the punishment. But then, just as he was about to begin, he went to his mother and covered her body with his, taking her punishment."

"Do you know why the Professor told me this story? No, it's not what you are thinking because it was not about him. He wanted me to know that Jesus had given His life for me, even though I am guilty of many sins. While he was on trial he was thinking of me. But I want you to think of that story, ladies, and gentlemen, when you are making your decision. Because this is also what the Professor has done. In order to spare his friend from a life of unfair imprisonment, he is here to take the punishment for him. What kind of man is that?"

"In closing I simply ask you to do what is in your heart. Do what is right. Thank you."

THIRTY-TWO

Ethan made one stop for gas and a hamburger, and was back near his old college a little after two. As he got nearer, another thought occurred to him. What if Foster actually worked at MTSU? With everything else that had happened it would only make the past eighteen months events even more incredible.

Once back in town he stopped at a local service station to use the pay phone. He called the main number at the University and asked if they had an employee by the name of James Henry Foster. The operator told him he worked in the maintenance department and she would connect him. Ethan hung up before anyone could answer. He thought of going to the maintenance building and finding him, but soon decided against it. He did not wish to expose the man yet, but give him the chance to come and testify for the Professor. He decided to wait until he got off work and confront him at his home. He had two other stops to make—at the drug store and the post office. After leaving the post office he found the address the clerk had given him. It was easy to find since the street was near the University and he had been on it many times before. It was a middle to lower class neighborhood with small rambler and cape cod style homes. Once he had found the address he drove to a nearby shopping center and walked around to pass time. He estimated he had a couple of hours to kill before Foster got off work. After a while he bought a newspaper and read it in the car. The story of the trial was on page six. He only glanced at it and turned the page. A short time later he started his car and drove back towards Foster's house and parked on the street a few doors down.

It was over an hour before he saw an older blue Ford Falcon pull in across the street. He watched as the man got out and walked toward the door. He was a large man—over 200 pounds, with a slight belly. He walked slowly with his head down. Even though it had been many years and he had only seen him briefly, he knew it was the man he was searching for. With sweaty palms he got out of his car and hurriedly followed him. He came up behind him as he neared his door.

"Mr. Foster," he called from a few feet away.

The man turned as he responded.

"Yes."

"We need to talk," began Ethan.

Ethan saw a quick flash of recognition in his eyes which he quickly tried to cover.

"I'm sorry, do I know ya?"

"You know who I am," stated Ethan bluntly.

"I don't think we ever met. You must'a got me confused with somebody else," he said as he turned to walk away.

"Mr. Foster, I only came to talk. If you don't want to, then I guess I can go back to Chattanooga and talk to the judge."

The man continued towards his house. Ethan stood for a second, then said, "I can't believe you would let the Professor go to prison for you."

The man stopped and turned slowly. With sadness in his eyes he said, "Why don't ya come inside, Ethan," he replied.

Ethan walked forward as Foster opened the door and stepped aside. Before going inside Ethan stopped and said to him,

"I don't think I have anything to fear, but I have sent a registered letter to myself explaining where I am. If I'm not there Monday to get it someone else will open it."

"You ain't never had nothin' ta fear from me or the Professor," he replied.

The two men went inside. Foster offered him a seat. Ethan sat in the front of the living room near a window. Foster removed his jacket and sat in a chair facing him.

"What do ya want'a me?" he asked.

"I had to know—to meet you," replied Ethan simply.

"And now ya met me. What now?"

"Are you going to help the Professor?"

"I told him I'd turn myself in," he answered with a look of defeat in his face. "He said he couldn't live with himself if I went ta prison after saving his life."

Ethan thought for a moment, trying to remember all the things he wanted to say—things he wanted to ask—if this moment ever came.

"Mr. Foster, while I believe him, I need to know that everything Professor Robertson said is true."

"Such as?"

"Such as the things about the Deputy, and whether you two went there looking for him. And did you let me escape on purpose?"

"Well, I don't know everything the Professor told ya, and I ain't heard his testimony, but I'm sure everything he said is true. We went there lookin' ta buy a dog. I only brought the gun for protection in case we did run into Pratt, though I never really thought it would happen. And Warren never knew 'bout the gun. If he had he wouldn't a gone. And of course we let ya go. We would'a never hurt a boy."

"And, of course, the main question—why did you think Pratt was responsible for those boys' deaths?"

Foster looked at him for a second, then took a deep breath as he closed his eyes and tilted his head back. He soon looked back at Ethan.

"Ain't never told nobody that story—even Warren. I reckon it don't matter any more. It's a long story."

"I got time."

"I grew up in Hamblen County—course ya already figured that out. In 1956 I was a young man. I had been working at a lot of different odd jobs since I graduated from high school. Then, in the fall, I went down and applied at the lumber mill. They said they would put me on but I had ta' wait a couple a' weeks. So, ta' pass the time I did some huntin' and fishin'. My daddy had bought me an old army jeep and he helped me fix it up so it was runnin' pretty good. One day while my Ma and Pa was at work I decided ta' go deer huntin'. It was a pretty remote area over near Greene County. I climbed a tree and waited for a deer. Sure enough, it weren't long before one came along. I saw him through the brush and fired. Only problem was it weren't a deer—it was a man. I had killed him. I was sick. It was an accident but nobody would ever believe me—a young black kid shootin' a white hunter. I would have been sent ta' prison or lynched, I reckon."

"So I did the only thing I knew—weren't nothing I could do for him—I ran. And I never told nobody about it—even my Ma or Pa. I heard about it on the news, of course, but nobody seen me so I figured nobody would ever know. The newspaper said he had been huntin' with his nephew but they had got separated so he didn't see nothin'. Then, a few days later I was home alone and this man shows up at my door. He weren't much older than me—three or four years I reckon. Said his name was Andrew Pratt. Said he had been with his uncle when I shot him. Said he had been a little ways down the trail but had seen what happened. I began crying and told him that he must'a seen it was an accident. He said it would be whatever he wanted it ta' be. If he wanted he could go ta' the Sheriff and tell them I killed him for fun. I didn't know what he wanted—why he was there. He told me as long as I did what he wanted he would keep quiet."

"And what did he want?" asked Ethan.

"Ya can't figure it out?" returned Foster.

Ethan returned a blank look.

"Let's put it this way," continued Foster, "he didn't start out with thirteen or fourteen-year-old boys. He had to work his way up ta' it."

"Oh," said Ethan slowly, "I see."

"Reckon ya can see now why I never told nobody 'bout this."

"Yes. I'm sorry, but it wasn't like you had any choice."

"Reckon that's what I kept tellin' myself. Anyway, this went on for 'bout six months. Finally I told him I wouldn't do it no more—

that I would go ta the Sheriff."

"What did he say?"

"He was mad, but reckon he liked the idea a people knowin' he liked men 'bout as much as I liked the idea a goin' to jail. Said he wouldn't bother me no more if I introduced him to a sixteen year old boy I knew."

"And you wouldn't do it?"

"No, but I told him I would. Then I told my parent's it was time I moved out—made it on my own. I had a friend I knew from school who lived in Harriman so I moved there."

"And you never heard from him again?"

"Nope. Least not till the Professor told me 'bout him comin' ta school. Reckon he found somebody else to blackmail."

"But when the Professor told you about meeting him at school you still didn't have proof he was the one that killed the boy."

"No, reckon I didn't have proof, but I knew. It was too much coincidence. Pratt bein' there, in Harriman, where I lived the same day the boy got killed. He wanted me to know it was him."

"Are you saying," began Ethan leaning forward, "that he killed that boy in Harriman to send you a message?"

"No. He killed him 'cause he was pure evil. But I reckon it gave him some added pleasure 'cause I lived there. Anyway, I told Warren—Professor Robertson—what I thought and I reckon he figured I was crazy. Then, a few weeks later the other boy was killed."

"That's when you called your cousin Holly?"

"You sure are a smart young man. Yeah—we talked from time to time anyway so I called her the evenin' I heard 'bout the boy. We was just talkin' and I asked her if Pratt was still as nasty as ever. She said he was, but at least the last couple days he had been off so it was a lot more peaceful."

"And you never told her anything about the shooting?"

"Oh, no. I ain't never told nobody 'bout this. Why? Is Holly what led ya ta me?"

"Well, actually not her as much as your Nephews, Ed and Ted. They always been mean to me. Ted even threatened me to stop looking into the shooting. Then, when I remembered that they were

Holly's nephews—and with a little help from the county records office—I just put the rest together."

"Those two boys," said Foster with a shake of his head. "They always been trouble. But I don't see how they could have known anything. Like I said, I ain't never told nobody. Maybe them or Holly just had a suspicion or somethin'—I don't know."

"Anyway," continued Ethan, "After the second boy was killed you still had no proof Pratt was involved, right?"

"I had proof, just nothin' that would stand up in court."

"What kind of proof?"

"He pretty much confessed ta me."

"You're kidding?"

"Nope. After the second boy I called him one night and said I knew it was him. He just laughed and said, 'knowin' is one thing—provin' is another'. Then he reminded me that there weren't no statute of limitation on murder—meanin' me shootin' his uncle."

"Wow," exclaimed Ethan. "That's when you sent the letter to the authorities?"

"Yep. I still didn't tell the Professor how I knew what I did. I was still afraid if Pratt was arrested it would get out it came from me, and I would go ta prison. So I just told Warren that I had strong suspicions. He recommended we send a letter. I really thought the letter would start an investigation but I reckon they just ignored it."

"So when the third boy was killed, you went looking for Pratt?"

"No, not exactly. If I'd a gone over there just to kill him I wouldn't a taken Warren with me. We really did go lookin' for a dog but I thought if I ran into him what might happen. I had relatives in that part of the country and I was tired of not bein' able to go home."

"That is some story," said Ethan as he tried to take it all in. "You know, with a story like that there is no doubt, if you went to testify, you would get off with self-defense."

"You're a pretty smart young man, Ethan, but I reckon ya are forgettin' a couple of things."

"Like what?"

"First, I still ain't got a bit of proof. It's just my word against the man I killed. And they done investigated these deaths for over seven years now and ain't found nothin that points to him. Besides, only way I can confess is to tell about shootin' the hunter, then reckon I'd go to prison for that too. Either way, my life would be over."

Ethan thought about what he said. As much as he hated to admit it, he was right. Even though he now knew the man's identity and the story behind what happened that hot day in 1963, nothing had changed.

"Mr. Foster, when I first figured out how to track you down my intent was to come over here and make you come and testify. Now, I honestly don't know what to tell you. I don't want the Professor going to jail, but I understand the charges would be a lot more severe for you. So, the decision has to be yours. I will also tell you that if you don't testify I will honor your and the Professor's wishes and not say anything about what I found out."

"Thank Ya, Ethan. What do ya think his chances are?"

"I don't really know. He's got a good attorney and she has put a lot of doubt in people's minds, but I really can't say. But, even if he is convicted, he will probably be out in three or four years and I know he would prefer that to you spending the rest of your life in prison."

"But the other problem is the people you talked to at the courthouses. They might be able to put things together."

"I don't think so. I was pretty vague, but even if somebody did figure out why I was looking for you, the Professor and I are the only ones who can ever testify against you. So I think you are safe."

He nodded his understanding.

"Thank you. I got one other problem, though."

"What's that?"

"I been in prison for the past seven—no, fourteen years. You can see what my life is like. I ain't got any friends, and I ain't never had a relationship with a woman. I'm afraid of meetin' anybody new. I'm afraid a goin' home 'cause somebody might figure it out like ya did. And, the worst part is livin' with the pain. As mean as Pratt was, it still is awful livin' with killin' somebody. And the guilt of shootin' his uncle is even worse. I reckon I'm gonna have to tell what happened. When are ya goin' back?"

"I was going to go back after I left here."

"O.K. I have a few things I got ta do. It's only a couple hours ta Chattanooga from here. Reckon I will leave in the mornin' and meet ya at the courthouse."

"Are you sure about this?"

"I'm sure. The Professor keeps talkin' 'bout trusting God. I don't even know if there is one, but if so he sure ain't been too kindly towards me. Reckon I'll see if he really does care 'bout a poor black man."

Ethan felt a sadness for the man. He wondered if he should have let the matter alone. It was too late now. He got up and shook the man's hand.

"I hope you are making the right decision," he stated.

"So do I, young man. So do I."

Foster walked Ethan to the door, making arrangements to meet at the courthouse the following morning.

———

Ethan arrived back in Chattanooga a little before eight o'clock and went straight to his hotel room. If he ran into his mother he would simply tell her the problem at Ft. Benning was resolved quickly so he was able to return so quickly. Luckily he ran into no one he recognized. Knowing that Professor Robertson usually went for a walk around eight-thirty, he waited to call Sally's room. She answered the phone on the first ring. She informed him her father was in the other room playing with Emily, so she may have to hang up at any time. He related to her the day's events. She became very excited when he told her about his meeting with Foster and his agreeing to come and testify.

"I don't think you should tell your father though," said Ethan.

"Why?" asked Sally. "If he has already agreed to testify why should he not know?"

"Because he might call and try to talk him out of it. And, besides, if Foster changes his mind it is better your father not know. Either way it is best not to tell him."

"I see. I guess you are right. If he does change his mind, though, then we need to give his name to the judge."

"It will be too late to help your father then, anyway, Sally. He only has bargaining power if he turns him in, which he won't do. Of course, if it comes to that, it may be grounds for an appeal. Anyway, that's too much to worry about now. I'm sure Foster will be there anyway."

"My Dad is coming this way. I have to go. I'll pray that Foster be there in the morning."

The next morning was the coolest of the fall in Chattanooga. The temperature dropped to 40 degrees overnight and was only slightly higher than that at eight-thirty. While Ethan was to meet James Foster at the parking lot near the courthouse at eight-forty-five, he was there fifteen minutes early. Wearing only a light sweater, he soon wished he had driven the short distance from his hotel. The longer he waited, the more concerned he became that Foster was not going to show. Then, at eight-fifty-five, he saw his Ford Falcon appear. He parked the car and walked slowly and deliberately toward Ethan.

"At least you were smart enough to wear a jacket," began Ethan. "Did you find the place O.K.?"

"Yes, no problem," he said solemnly. "There was just some heavy traffic comin' into town. I guess we need to get started."

The two walked quickly towards the courthouse.

THIRTY-THREE

Professor Robertson was relieved his testimony was over. He felt he had made the right decision about not turning in his friend, however, some of the questions raised by the D.A. made him rethink his relationship with the man. Such as why had he chosen him to relate his suspicions about the Deputy? At the time they were mere acquaintances. They had met at a basketball court at a school near his parents' farm. They would play one-on-one and talk about sports and cars and hunting—three things they had in common. While the man seemed like a loner, he enjoyed his company. He had a gentle nature and a quick smile, but yet there was something too serious—almost foreboding about him. He worked as a mechanic at a nearby garage. The Professor would often stop by for gas and chat. It was when he called him with a question on his car and had mentioned the incidents at his school, that the man first told him he thought the Deputy was responsible. Since his friend had no proof, he asked him to say nothing to anyone—a request which he had honored. He did not realize until many months later how important it was—for both their sakes—that he had not shared his concerns with anyone else.

At nine o'clock the jurors again took their seats in the jury box. Soon Judge Landry entered and called the court to order.

"Good morning, ladies and gentlemen," he began as he addressed the jurors. "It has been a long week and we appreciate your service to the court. Now the most important part of the trial begins—

your deliberation. Before you start I want to give you a few words of instructions. You are not being sequestered so first and foremost, I caution you not to discuss this case with anyone outside the jury room. This includes family and friends. Make your decision only on testimony and evidence presented in this courtroom. Remember that the defendant has been charged with second degree murder, however, you may find him guilty of a lesser offense, those being manslaughter or negligent homicide. If you have questions you may present them to the bailiff. Are there any questions?"

No questions were presented. The Judge had just started to dismiss the jury when the courtroom door opened and Ethan Ward and James Foster entered and walked down the aisle. Professor Robertson gasped as he recognized his friend. Ethan stopped while Foster opened the gate.

"I would like ta address the court, Your Honor," began Foster as he walked past the defense table. The bailiff moved toward the man but the Judge raised his arm to stop him.

"What is your name, sir?" demanded the Judge.

"James Foster, Your Honor. I reckon I'm the man ya bin lookin' for."

A stillness engulfed the courtroom. Ellen Cornblossom turned to her client who could only shake his head. Randy Richmond sat silently. The jurors looked to the Judge for direction.

"Mr. Foster," said the Judge calmly, "are you telling us that you are Professor Robertson's friend—the man that killed Deputy Pratt?"

"Didn't have no choice, Your Honor," he said. "It was either him or us."

The bailiff"s hand moved towards his gun. He was too slow. In an instant Foster reached into his jacket and pulled out a handgun. He aimed it at the bailiff who moved backwards holding his hands in the air.

"Ya can just loosen your gunbelt and let it drop to the floor," he instructed. The bailiff did as instructed. Foster then waved him backwards, away from the gun.

"Mr. Foster," yelled the Judge, "do you have any idea what you're doing?"

"I didn't come here ta hurt nobody, Judge," he returned.

"Then you got a fine way of showing it."

"I just want ever' body ta hear my story. You'all need ta know the truth."

"Then put the gun down and I promise you we will listen."

"Don't reckon I can do that yet, Your Honor. First, ya listen ta what I got ta say then I promise nobody'll get hurt."

The Judge looked angrily at Ethan.

"Private Ward, I will deal with you later," he stated.

"He didn't know nothin' 'bout the gun, Your Honor," said Foster. "He just wanted me ta testify—for people ta hear what I got to say."

"It doesn't look like we have much choice, does it Mr. Foster? What do you want to tell us?"

"First, I want ta be sworn in just like ever' body else."

"You're kidding!" said Richmond.

Foster only looked at him briefly and walked toward the witness stand.

"Your Honor," continued Foster, "I just want ta tell my story, and I want it ta be official like ever' body else."

"Fine," replied the Judge. "Please take the witness stand." Once he had done so the Judge asked,

"First, do you have any identification?"

Foster removed his wallet and slid it to the Judge who examined it and turned again to Ethan.

"Private Ward, do you attest to this man being James Henry Foster?"

"I do," answered Ethan.

"And you, Professor Robertson?"

"Yes, Your Honor, this is James Foster" he answered reluctantly.

"The man with you in the truck when Deputy Pratt was killed?"

"Yes, Your Honor."

The Judge instructed Foster to place his hand on the bible which he did.

"Do you swear the testimony you are about to provide is the truth, the whole truth, and nothing but the truth, so help you, God?"

"I do, Your Honor."

"Then go ahead and tell us your story."

He placed the gun in front of him where it could be easily reached. The bailiff looked to the Judge for direction. With a subtle shake of his head he let him know to try nothing. Foster looked in Ellen Cornblossom's direction.

"Miss Cornblossom, if ya don't mind, I could use your help in guiding me through this. I ain't never had ta testify afore."

"I'd be glad to help you, Mr. Foster," she said as she arose and walked towards the witness stand.

An eerie silence engulfed the courtroom as Cornblossom stood composing her thoughts.

"O.K., Mr. Foster, I am going to ask you questions just like I would do any other witness. Is that alright?"

"Yes, ma'am. That's why I'm here."

"First, please provide your full name."

"My name is James Henry Foster."

"And where do you live, Mr. Foster?"

"In Murfreesboro."

"And what do you do there?"

"I work at the University—Middle Tennessee, that is. I am a custodian."

"And are you acquainted with the defendant, Professor Robertson?"

"Yes ma'am—for 'bout ten years now I reckon."

"And how do you know him?"

"We met over ta Harriman. I used ta work on the Professors' car—well, he weren't a Professor then."

"So, in 1963 did you have a conversation with the Professor about Deputy Andrew Pratt?"

"Yes, ma'am, but afore we get into that, I need ta go back and tell ya how I knew the Deputy."

"Fine, Mr. Foster, when did you meet Andrew Pratt?"

"It's a long story," he said as he turned to the Judge.

"Why don't you just tell us in your own words," instructed the Judge.

Foster began the same story he had related to Ethan the day

before. The courtroom listened in stunned silence. When he got to the point of shooting the hunter the Judge interrupted him.

"Mr. Foster, are you telling us that you shot and killed a man in 1956?"

"It was an accident, Judge. I never meant to hurt nobody. He had on a brown coat and was carrying a bow and arrows. They was stickin' up just like antlers. Through the bush it looked just like a deer."

"Very well," said the Judge with a shake of his head. "Please continue."

Foster continued uninterrupted until he related his phone conversation with Andrew Pratt.

"And what did he say when you told him you knew he was responsible for the boys' deaths?" asked Judge Landry.

"Said, 'knowin' somethin' is one thing. Proving it is another'. Then he added, 'just remember—ain't no statute of limitations on murder'. He was referrin' ta the hunter. Said if anything happened ta him I would be goin' to prison."

"Continue," the Judge said to Cornblossom.

Foster continued relating the events leading up to the day they went to Greene County. He explained that they had gone to buy a dog and the man was not home. He also explained that the Professor knew nothing about the gun.

"How did you get it in the truck without the Professor seeing it?"

"That weren't no problem," he answered as he held up the gun. "I just put it in the pocket of my coveralls."

"So," she continued, "did you and the Professor have a conversation about going to Greene County and possibly running into Deputy Pratt?"

"Sort of. He said, 'ain't ya worried bout goin' over there and runnin' into him?' And I said that he weren't gonna keep me from goin' over there no more."

Cornblossom had no questions until he told about getting lost and stopping Ethan and asking for directions.

"You must have known it was dangerous to pick up a young white boy. Didn't you talk about it?"

"Nope. I guess we was both thinking the same thing. It would have only been for a couple a minutes and if he were with us then he would be alright."

"And when the Deputy showed up did you and the Professor talk about what was going to happen?"

"No, ma'am. I don't know what the Professor was thinkin', but I knew what I had ta do."

"And what was going through your mind?"

"Well, I sat in the truck for a minute tryin' to think of a way out of it. I finally realized once he recognized me he would know I was gonna turn him in. Course, it was still his word against mine, but I knew he weren't gonna let that happen. I knew he would'a killed both of us and then done whatever he wanted ta the boy and blamed it on us. It was him or us."

"So you and the Professor never talked about shooting the Deputy?"

"No, ma'am."

Cornblossom could think of no more questions to ask. She turned to the Judge for direction.

"Mr. Foster," asked the Judge, "why did you come here today."

The Judge saw a look of sadness and desperation in the man's eyes. It was a look he had seen hundreds of times before when there was no hope left. Foster bowed his head for a second then turned back to him.

"Reckon for a couple'a of reasons, Your Honor. I couldn't let my friend go to jail for protectin' me. And I couldn't live like I been livin' no more. I been a prisoner in my mind since 1956. "

"So, Counselor," said the Judge as he turned towards Richmond, "do you have any questions of this witness?"

"Oh...uh...no, Your Honor," he returned.

Cornblossom looked at him wondering if he could think of nothing to ask, or if he were simply afraid of approaching the man. She guessed it was probably the latter.

"Well, Mr. Foster," continued the Judge, "what now?"

Foster reached into his pocket and removed an envelope and tossed it to the Judge.

"What is this?" he asked.

"Everything I just told ya"

"And why are you giving me this?"

"Cause I ain't gonna be around to testify again."

"What are you saying, Mr. Foster? You promised me that after you testified you would give us the gun."

"Reckon what I said was I weren't here to hurt nobody, and I ain't. I didn't bring the gun for you."

The Judge did not understand what he was saying. The Professor did. His heart began to race as he tried to figure out what to do to save his friend.

"Mr. Foster, I'll ask you again, please turn your gun over to the bailiff."

"Can't do that, Your Honor. Now I'll just be goin' and ya won't have ta worry 'bout me again. Got one question, though—a person's dying statement is considered ta be fact, right? Consider my letter there my last statement."

Only then did the Judge understand what the man meant. He was unsure what to do. As he tried to calculate how to stop him, the Professor arose from his desk and walked forward.

"James, you need to give the gun to the Judge."

"Reckon I can't do that, Warren," he responded.

"James, listen to me. You will be alright. I will help you. Miss Cornblossom will help you. And now everyone knows your story."

"I ain't a smart man like you and the Judge here, Warren but I know some things. Everybody here is listenin' ta me cause I got a gun. I still ain't got no proof of what happened and I never will. And I just confessed ta killin' a hunter. Reckon I'll be in trouble for bringin' a gun into the courtroom too. I been in hidin' for the past seven years—no, since 1956, I reckon, and I can't do it no more. And I ain't goin' ta prison for the rest of my life. No, I reckon I'll just be goin and nobody else has ta get hurt."

The Professor moved closer to him, trying to reason with him. He knew it was his last chance to save his friend's life.

"You don't know all that, James. You might get off with a very light sentence—maybe even probation. You're still a young man."

Foster turned to the Judge.

"Judge, we both know I ain't gonna get off without goin' ta prison, don't we?"

As he turned to the Judge, the Professor saw his chance—his only chance to try and save his friend. He dove for the gun in front of him. He was too slow. Foster reached the gun just before him. The Professor grabbed his arm just as Foster raised the gun to his head. In a second the Professor was covered in his friend's blood.

THIRTY-FOUR

James Foster was taken to the hospital by ambulance, barely cling-ing to life. Judge Landry tried to restore order to the courtroom but soon realized that was impossible and dismissed the jury for the day. He needed time to sort out what had happened. He instructed everyone to be in the courtroom at nine the next morning. He read Foster's letter two more times. It only repeated the testimony he had provided earlier. His problem was what to do with it. He and his clerk searched the law library for precedent but could find none. He would have to make new law, and he would have to do so by the next day.

By nine o'clock the courtroom was filled to capacity. A few minutes later the Judge entered the room. He looked tired and disheveled.

"Ladies and gentlemen," he began addressing the court, "yester-day, to say the least, was a shocking and trying day for all of us. I think it is safe to say, in all my years as a lawyer and a Judge I have never seen anything like it. To be honest, I spent the remainder of the day yesterday trying to figure out how to rule on Mr. Foster's testimony. Then, late last night, I got a call that made it all mute."

Ellen Cornblossom gave a confused look to her client who could only shrug his shoulders. From his expression, she knew Richmond was as confused as they were. The Judge continued.

"Late last night I got a call from the Governor. It seems, unknown to me, or anyone else for that matter, he has had a special investigator looking into the charges Professor Robertson made against Deputy Pratt. I don't have all the details yet but they got enough evidence to get a search warrant for the house where the Deputy used to live. Late yesterday evening they uncovered the remains of what appears to be three young boys buried in his back yard. There was also evidence of torture found in the attic at the house. They also searched his personal belongings which had been stored at his parent's house and found a number of newspaper clippings—not only of the boys in Tennessee, but also of three other boys from other states who had disappeared in the previous year or so."

Everyone in the room stared in disbelief. The pain was especially evident on Richmond's face. While it was very upsetting to hear about the boys, his mind also flashed back to the past few months he had spent on the case.

"That's horrible, Your Honor but...."

"There's no buts counselor. Did you just hear what I said? He did it. Everything the Professor and his friend have been saying is true. He killed those boys—not only those but at least three more. It's over."

"But, Your Honor, that does not prove that Mr. Foster nor the Professor were not somehow involved. We don't know that every-thing Foster said is true."

"Use some common sense, man. What you are going to do is drop the charges on the Professor and—no I just changed my mind. Professor, will you please stand."

The Professor stood, wondering what was about to happen.

"Professor, based on new evidence uncovered in the past 24 hours, I find you innocent of all charges. You are free to go."

The courtroom erupted with cheers. The Judge turned to the jury.

"Ladies and gentlemen of the jury, I thank you for your time. You are dismissed."

"Your Honor," pleaded Richmond as he stood, "with all due respect you can't do this."

"You are wrong, sir. I can and I did. I have the right to override any jury verdict and take the trial out of their hands if I find it necessary. Of course, you can appeal my actions if you think you have a case."

Richmond threw himself in his seat.

"And," continued the Judge, "if his friend survives—well I guess that will be out of my jurisdiction but I will tell you that if you try to bring charges against him you will never get a conviction. Is all of this clear?"

"Yes, Your Honor," he returned sheepishly.

"Where did the shooting of Pratt's uncle take place? Was that in Greene County?" asked the Judge.

"I don't know," returned Richmond. "It was not in Greene County. It was a long time ago and I don't remember if it was in Hancock or Hamblen County but I know it wasn't in Greene County."

"Well, either way it won't be any of our problems. Still, if he survives, he's going to have to stand trial for that. He will also be facing charges for bringing a gun into my courtroom. Now the only other thing I have to say is let's all go home and get some rest."

That afternoon, after talking to the Judge, Cornblossom called the Professor and asked if she could come by. She had additional information she would like to share with him. The Professor waited in his hotel room with his family and friends for Cornblossom. Soon she arrived and began telling them everything that had transpired back in Greene County.

"The Governor had been true to his word when he told Ethan he would look into the case. He assigned a TBCI investigator, Eugene Mason, to go undercover as a reporter for the Nashville Tennessean, to look into the charges made by the Professor."

"I knew there was something strange about that man," interjected Tommy proudly.

"It sounds like Mason talked to virtually everyone in Greene County," continued Cornblossom. "While he became convinced that the Deputy was responsible for the boys' deaths he had no proof. Then, without a warrant, he convinced the owner of Dudley's garage to let him go through their old tires to try to find a match to the prints from the crime scene. I guess Pratt's father had the tires on his son's car replaced there some time back."

"You're kidding," said the Professor.

"Yeah, really," she returned. "Anyway, he and two State Troopers went through the old tires until they found a match."

"That's unbelievable," said Sally.

"Not really," injected Tommy. "It's a lot of work but remember, all tires have their size printed on the side. All they had to do was to eliminate those that would not fit his car."

"That's still a pretty big stretch," added Ethan. "You still have to prove those tires came from the Deputy's car."

"Not really," said Cornblossom, "remember, all he was looking for was enough evidence to get a search warrant—not a conviction. And with all the publicity this case has received—and with a special investigator appointed by the Governor—I guess it was kind of hard for the Judge to argue. He gave a search warrant for the Deputy's old house as well as any files or personal affects they found at his parents' house."

"His poor parents," stated Ethan. "They didn't come to the trial because they couldn't handle it and then this happens."

"Yeah, really," added Cornblossom. "Anyway, when they searched his parents' house they found the newspaper articles Ethan talked about, however, they also found the other ones relating to missing boys from North Carolina, Virginia, and Kentucky. Those went back a year or more."

"Isn't that unusual?" asked the Professor. "That means he originally abducted those boys and brought them back to his house long before he killed the other boys. It seems like it would be the other way around."

"I have never been involved in a case like that, thank God," she answered, "but from what I understand from talking to others it makes sense. He was originally more cautious by bringing them to a secure area—his house which was pretty isolated. As it continued he had a harder time controlling his impulses so he became more brazen—even desperate. Maybe he wanted to be caught—we will never know. Anyway, after seeing the newspaper articles they went to his old house. There they found a chair in the attic which they think he used to secure the boys—there were also signs of a rope being tied to the rafters. Finally, they began digging in the back yard and found the bodies. That's about it."

They all sat silently, thinking of everything she had said. Finally Cornblossom turned to the Professor.

"Any more on Foster?"

"No, not really. He is conscious so that is a good sign. The doctors said he may be able to talk in a day or two. I imagine the authorities are getting an arrest warrant related to the shooting of the hunter."

"Probably," she answered, "At least Richmond won't be handling that one."

"Any idea what might happen to him if he recovers?" asked Ethan.

"No, but I imagine he will have to serve some time. I think it will be minimal though based on what happened."

Soon the discussion broke up. The others said goodbye to Cornblossom who was returning to Nashville. Tommy also left for home while the others would remain behind a few days longer.

Two days later the Ward and Robertson families said their goodbyes. Hilda Ward gave her granddaughter a kiss and hugged the others goodbye. The Professor and his daughter thanked her for her support and for being such a good friend. Ethan kissed his mother and told her to drive carefully on the way home.

Sally clung to Ethan for as long as possible before allowing him to leave. He kissed her, then his daughter before turning to the Professor. He held out his hand to him but instead the Professor wrapped his arms around him.

"Son, I don't think you will ever know how grateful I am for all that you have done. I will never be able to repay you."

Ethan looked at Sally and the baby and turned to him with a smile.

"You already have," he said as he turned and left.

The Professor helped his daughter pack the car. She drove him to a rental car facility and dropped him off. He would be staying until he knew what would happen to his friend. After getting the rental car he walked back to his daughter and granddaughter. He kissed

Sally's cheek, locked her door and told her to drive safely. With a smile and a tear in his eye he got in the car and drove towards the hospital.

EPILOGUE

MAY, 1971

It was a beautiful spring day in Murfreesboro—the perfect day for a picnic. It was also unseasonably cool for Memorial Day weekend with the temperature only expected to hit seventy. Originally Sally planned only a small gathering—Ethan and Emily and her father—but the picnic seemed to take on a life of its own. While Ethan didn't think his family would make the trip they eagerly accepted his invitation, as did Tommy. They also invited Ellen Cornblossom who accepted and brought a guest—a male companion who she introduced as 'just a very good friend'. Sally had hoped her sister would come in from California for the occasion but she informed her she would be unable to make it. She had only been home once in the past year—for Christmas—a situation which was a continual irritation for their father. They also invited the Governor and his family to the picnic. He called Ethan and thanked him for the invitation but said they had already planned to spend the holiday at Clearwater Beach in Florida.

Ethan only had a few months left in the Army and would then be able to attend school full time on the G.I. Bill. Most weekends he made the trip north in his Mustang to see Sally and Emily. Sally still lived with her father but had just begun to look for an apartment.

Sally's father had become a local celebrity from his ordeal and had appeared on a number of radio and TV talk shows. At first he had been hesitant to do interviews but had finally agreed to do so at his daughter's urging. She insisted it was a story that people should hear. Not only did it show that minorities could get a fair trial, but it also discussed the many people of all races who had supported and cared for him. He had just signed a contract with a publisher to tell his story. Part of the proceeds from the book would go to a fund for abused and runaway children.

Tommy enrolled at night school at the local community college. He would transfer to either East Tennessee State or the University of Tennessee upon completion of his Associates degree. He also had taken a job with the city of Greenville in the finance department. He told Ethan that sometime in the near future—when he was old enough and experienced enough to be taken serious—he would run for a City Council seat. Ethan figured he would be State Senator by the time he was thirty.

Nothing had changed with Ellen Cornblossom. She hoped to be made a partner at her law firm but for the present she continued to work and visit her relatives when possible.

James Foster was sentenced to three to five years for the accidental shooting of Leonard Pratt in 1956. He pleaded guilty to criminal negligence and began serving his time in December. The Chattanooga D.A. also brought charges against him for brandishing a firearm in the courtroom, although he was allowed to serve the six month sentence concurrent with his other. He would be up for parole in a little over a year.

Ethan and the Professor sat on a bench tossing stones into a pond while the others were scurrying about preparing the food. When everything was ready they would do the important work—grilling the meat. Ethan watched as his dad tossed Emily into the air. For someone who had a difficult time accepting her, he now was convinced she looked more like him than any other family member. After the ordeal of the past year—no, seven years—things had turned out much better than either Ethan or the Professor had expected. While they didn't talk about the events of the past much, occasionally something would come up to jog one or the other's memory. The Professor had such an occasion earlier today.

"I had a conversation with the editor this morning," he began. "It made me think of something you said to me a year or so ago."

"Yeah," returned Ethan, "what was that?"

"Remember when you first realized that the Deputy was really waiting for you?"

"Yeah, I remember."

"And you said how you felt like a fool because all of these years when you spoke to anyone about what you had seen you had it all wrong—talked about bearing false witness I believe."

"Uh, huh. I remember."

"Well, of course you weren't bearing false witness—you were only telling what you saw. But I began thinking about James and when he accidentally shot Pratt's uncle. If Andrew Pratt had gone to the police and told them what really happened—that he knew it was an accident—none of this would have ever happened. He was the true false witness."

"Hmm, I guess you are right," he answered. "But then the same evil that made him blackmail James was what drove him to the other crimes."

Ethan turned to look up at the others. Sally motioned for them to come up.

"Oh, it looks like my wife is waving for us to come help. I guess we'll have to continue our conversation later."

Author's Note: This story is entirely fictional and resemblance to any actual person or event is coincidental. Certain background information, however, is accurate. The description of the event leading up to the founding of the Tennessee Bureau of Criminal Investigation (now the Tennessee Bureau of Investigation) is actual. The legend of Princess Cornblossom, an ancestor of mine, is believed to be true. Other background events may be actual or slightly altered to fit the storyline. The public school system in Greeneville, Tennessee was integrated in the early 60's, but a couple of years after the timeline given in the book. While I have tried to make sure the story was blended with accurate events as they were occurring at the time, please remember that this is a work of fiction and not a history book.

Larry Buttram